Praise for

The Huckleberry Murders

An Indie Next Notable pick for November 2010

"In McManus's amusing, folksy fourth Bo Tully mystery . . . Tully once again proves an unorthodox and effective lawman, while McManus's storytelling, be it about a haunted lake or a modern mountain man, never flags."

—*Publishers Weekly*

"Folksy humorist McManus' fourth Bo Tully mystery exudes lots of country charm and humor."

—Kat Cam, *Booklist*

"Genial, amusing and sweet, with quirky characters and just enough plot twists to engage."

—*Kirkus Reviews*

"McManus's folksy narrative keeps the reader's interest with plenty of humor, aw-shucks moments, and action. . . . Bo Tully is a treat for readers who like some Western flair and an old-fashioned approach to justice in their mysteries."

—*Library Journal*

This title is also avail

Praise for the Sheriff Bo Tully mysteries

"[McManus's] idiosyncratic characters and their lunatic ways are what make this folksy whodunit such fun to curl up with."

—Marilyn Stasio, *The New York Times Book Review*

"In Bo Tully, Patrick McManus gives us a man to watch."

—*The Oregonian* (Portland)

"A fine, funny tale."

—*Lansing State Journal*

"One of the most entertaining mystery debuts in years."

—*Kirkus Reviews* (starred review)

"Misdirection and understatement puts McManus in the Who's Who of humor writers. . . . A highly entertaining read, and longtime McManus fans will not be disappointed."

—*Wyoming Wildlife*

"Quirky characters and plenty of wit enliven this folksy mystery."

—*Booklist*

"An engaging romp that recalls the best work of Bill DeAndrea."

—*Publishers Weekly*

Also by Patrick F. McManus

The Double-Jack Murders

Kerplunk!

Avalanche: A Sheriff Bo Tully Mystery

The Blight Way: A Sheriff Bo Tully Mystery

The Deer on a Bicycle

The Bear in the Attic

Into the Twilight, Endlessly Grousing

Whatchagot Stew

Never Cry "Arp!"

How I Got This Way

The Good Samaritan Strikes Again

Real Ponies Don't Go Oink!

Kid Camping from Aaaaiii! to Zip

Never Sniff a Gift Fish

The Grasshopper Trap

The Night the Bear Ate Goombaw

Rubber Legs and White Tail-Hairs

They Shoot Canoes, Don't They?

A Fine and Pleasant Misery

The Huckleberry Murders

A Sheriff Bo Tully Mystery

PATRICK F. McMANUS

SIMON & SCHUSTER PAPERBACKS
New York London Toronto Sydney New Delhi

SIMON & SCHUSTER PAPERBACKS
A Division of Simon & Schuster, Inc.
1230 Avenue of the Americas
New York, NY 10020

This book is a work of fiction. Names, characters, places, and incidents either are products of the author's imagination or are used fictitiously. Any resemblance to actual events or locales or persons, living or dead, is entirely coincidental.

First Simon & Schuster trade paperback edition November 2011

SIMON & SCHUSTER PAPERBACKS and colophon are registered trademarks of Simon & Schuster, Inc.

For information about special discounts for bulk purchases, please contact Simon & Schuster Special Sales at 1-866-506-1949 or business@simonandschuster.com.

The Simon & Schuster Speakers Bureau can bring authors to your live event. For more information or to book an event, contact the Simon & Schuster Speakers Bureau at 1-866-248-3049 or visit our website at www.simonspeakers.com.

Manufactured in the United States of America

10 9 8 7 6 5 4 3

The Library of Congress has cataloged the hardcover edition as follows:

McManus, Patrick F.
The huckleberry murders : a sheriff Bo Tully mystery / Patrick F. McManus.
p. cm.
1. Tully, Bo (Fictitious character)—Fiction. 2. Sheriffs—Idaho—Fiction.
3. Ranchers—Crimes against—Fiction. 4. Idaho—Fiction. I. Title.
PS3563.C38625H83 2010
813'.54—dc22 2010008667

ISBN 978-1-4391-9084-5
ISBN 978-1-4391-9085-2 (pbk)
ISBN 978-1-4391-9086-9 (ebook)

To my excellent agent, Phyllis Westberg

1

BLIGHT COUNTY, IDAHO, sheriff Bo Tully drove slowly up the long gravel driveway leading to the ranch house. September had already begun, and still every day the temperature climbed into the nineties. The threat of forest fires remained. A trickle of sweat beaded up on the tip of his nose. He wiped it off. One of these days he would get the air-conditioning fixed on the Explorer. So far that summer, Blight County had managed to escape any major fires, but the mountains were powder dry. Any spark could set them off. He didn't want to think what would happen should a thunderstorm roll through. Or if his father, Pap Tully, went for a hike in the mountains smoking one of his hand-rolleds.

Tully was wearing his usual summer outfit of Levi's, long-sleeve tattersall shirt open at the collar, three-thousand-dollar alligator-hide cowboy boots, and a light khaki vest, which concealed the horizontal shoulder holster containing his 9 mm Colt Commander automatic. Today the gun seemed to weigh at least ten pounds. He preferred a lighter weapon, but criminals had become much more dangerous in recent years. He didn't believe in shooting a criminal more than twice in the body mass—the so-called double tap.

A roofed porch spread across the front of the sprawling ranch house. A man sat in a rocking chair on the porch. He had the brim of a battered cowboy hat pulled low over his eyes. Tully couldn't tell whether he was asleep or watching the vehicle approach. The man would know the red Ford Explorer belonged to law enforcement because of the light bar on the roof. He obviously was the alleged culprit the ranch owner's ex-wife had complained about.

Tully stopped the Explorer in front of the house. The man pushed the brim of his hat up with his thumb and sauntered down to greet him. He took off his hat as he approached. He appeared to be in his early thirties, slender, nice-looking, a tidy person, with short hair, a trim mustache, and under his lower lip, a tiny bush of brown hair. Tully got out of his vehicle and walked around to meet him. He stuck out his hand and said, "Howdy, pardner, I'm Blight County sheriff Bo Tully."

The man shook his hand. "Shucks, Sheriff, I know who you are. You're the most famous person in all Blight County."

"That tells you something about Blight County, doesn't it? I take it you're Ray Crockett."

"Yep, that's me, Sheriff. No doubt Marge Poulson told you how I done away with Orville."

"She has indeed. Numerous times. So what do you have to say for yourself, Ray?"

Crockett scratched his head. "Well, let's see. I have to admit I haven't seen or heard from Orville in several months. His Social Security check arrives every month, and I mail it to a P.O. box in Spokane. Somebody picks up the checks—Orville, I suppose—and probably cashes them. That post office box would be pretty full by now if nobody picked up the checks."

"Sounds like a reasonable guess. How long have you been mailing his checks to Spokane?"

Crockett squinted up, as if looking for the answer in the sky. "Quite a while. Going on a couple of years."

"You have an address or phone number for Orville?"

"Nope, I don't. He travels a lot and stays in hotels. He used to call me every couple weeks or so, but now months go by I don't hear from him."

"What do you do for a living, Ray?"

Crockett put his hat back on. "Not much, Sheriff. Orville lets me stay here free of charge to look after the ranch, but he sold off all the stock so there's not much to look after. I helped him sell the stock and he gave me five percent of the gross. I put my share in a CD. Then my dad died and I got a bit of insurance money. That's mostly what I've been living on." He gestured toward the ranch house. "This is a nice place to live and I guess I'll stay here till Orville tells me different or my money runs out. I'm not one of those people consumed by ambition but lately I been thinking about taking some courses at the community college. Do something with my life."

"You have a major in mind?"

"I've been thinking maybe law."

"Never can tell when that might come in handy. So, any other plans, Ray?"

"Haven't made up my mind yet. I guess I'll stick on here until Marge gets on my nerves so much I can't stand it. Small wonder Orville divorced her! Grab a seat up on the porch, Sheriff, and I'll go fetch us each a beer."

Tully pursed his lips, as if considering the offer. "Sounds mighty tempting, Ray, but I've got to get moving on. Give me the address of that Spokane mailbox, will you?"

"Sure thing. I have to go in the house to get it. My memory's like a sieve."

"Mine too. Write it down for me, would you, Ray?"

Tully looked around at the farm buildings. He made out a large boat in an open shed and behind it a barn that had probably once been cadmium red but now had faded with age into a weathered burnt sienna. No, that wasn't quite it. Tully felt the urge to give up on law enforcement once and for all and start painting full-time.

Crockett returned with the mailbox address written down on a piece of blue-lined paper apparently torn out of a small notebook. He handed it to Tully.

"Thanks, Ray. I'll check it out. Maybe that will satisfy

Marge and get her off my back. Maybe even off your back."

"That would be nice." Crockett's thumb stroked the bit of fuzz under his lip. "If I can be of any more help, Sheriff, let me know. The next time Orville calls, I'll have him get in touch. The last I heard from him, though, he said he was headed down to Mexico. I figure he must be having a pretty good time down there because I haven't heard from him since."

Tully nodded. "When was the last time you mailed his Social Security check to Spokane?"

"Just a couple days ago."

"How old is he now, late sixties?"

"Sounds about right. He was in great shape the last time I saw him."

"You a fisherman, Ray?"

"No, afraid not. Fishing is one of the few vices I've never tried. Why do you ask?"

Tully pointed at the boat.

"Oh, that. It belongs to Orville. He used to spend a lot of time out on Lake Blight. Said he knew the lake like the back of his hand. He was always bringing home messes of fish. Don't ask what kind because I don't know."

"That's about the biggest Boston Whaler I've ever seen. Looks like an outboard jet motor for power."

"I don't know one boat from another, Sheriff."

"Well, thanks for your help, Ray. If you hear from Poulson, let me know."

"You got it, Sheriff."

Tully got in his Explorer, drove around the circular drive, and headed back toward the highway, tugging thoughtfully on the corner of his mustache. In his rearview mirror he watched Crockett return to his chair and tilt the hat down over his eyes, apparently to resume his nap. He appeared to be a nice young man, polite, attentive, respectful. In other words, a classic sociopath. He lied as smoothly as if he were telling the truth. Marge was right. Ray killed the old man. The questions were, what did he do with the body, and how does he cash Orville's Social Security checks?

A fly walked across the inside of his windshield. He decided to let it live. It could suffer in the heat along with him.

2

IT WAS NOW almost noon. He decided to swing by his mother's house and see what she was making for lunch.

He rapped on her front door and then walked in. Katherine Rose McCarthy Tully O'Hare Tully Casey stuck her head out of the kitchen. "I've been expecting you, Bo. I made lunch for both of us. I'm still getting fresh tomatoes, so I made us BLTs and Campbell's chicken noodle soup."

"Sounds perfect." As he walked toward the kitchen he noticed a framed, sepia-tinted wedding photo on an end table next to the sofa, Rose and his father, Pap. Tully had a hard time remembering his mother's four marriages, two of them to his father, a former and much-feared sheriff of Blight County. Maybe Pap was back in her good graces.

Rose apparently had just got a new hairdo. He preferred

her white, but this short bob with a brown tint did make her look younger. "So what are you up to today, Bo?"

He kissed her on the cheek. "I'll tell you but I don't want it blabbed all over town." He slid into a chair at the kitchen table, pulled the Colt Commander from its shoulder holster, and laid it on the linoleum. Rose hated eating with him when he was armed.

She said, "Heaven forbid I would do such a thing."

"I mean it, Ma! I tell you about my cases only because you lead such a dull life. In this instance I'm pretty sure I'm dealing with a killer."

"He murdered someone!" Her eyes lit up. "You know I love murders best, Bo!"

"Yeah, that's why I'll tell you. But you better not utter a peep about this to anyone, you understand, or it will be the last murder you hear!"

"Cross my heart." Rose set a bowl of soup in front of him and a plate of BLT halves in the middle of the table. She had toasted the bread and cut the sandwiches into triangles. Bo sampled a BLT. For all of her hell-raising youth, Rose had somehow managed to become a good cook, at least as far as BLTs were concerned. She was pretty good with Campbell's chicken noodle soup, too.

"Okay then, here's the situation, Ma. An elderly rancher disappeared about two years ago. Nobody has heard from him in months except the young fellow running his ranch. The rancher's ex is sure he's been murdered."

Rose was about to bite into her BLT but stopped. "The wife did it!"

"That's certainly possible. But until I find the body, I can't be sure he's been murdered at all. His widow once removed, if she is one, thinks it's the fellow taking care of the ranch who did Orville in."

"Orville! You're talking about Orville Poulson! I know both the Poulsons, Orville and Marge! They're a wonderful couple! Marge certainly isn't the kind of person to kill her ex-husband, unless the husband was someone like Pap, and I can assure you he isn't, or wasn't, as the case may be. She's a very nice lady."

"Let's leave my father out of this. You're the one who said the wife did it." Tully helped himself to another BLT.

Rose sniffed. "That was before I knew we were talking about the Poulsons."

"Anyway, I don't have a body and I don't have a clue where to look for one. That ranch is huge. Orville could be buried anywhere on it."

Rose sipped her soup, slurped in a noodle, then dabbed her lips with a napkin. "Well, that's hardly a problem. You just go ask Mrs. Gorsich where the body is."

"Mrs. Gorsich! You think she did it? At the very least, I should arrest her for telling fortunes without a license."

"There's a license for fortune-telling?"

"I don't know. I guess not. I should put her in jail anyway. Maybe for taking money under false pretenses!" One of his main pleasures in life was to tease his mother.

"False pretenses, my eye! Bo, she's a real psychic! She taps into the spirit world and can tell both the past and the future! You go ask her and she'll tell you where poor Orville is buried."

"I find Mrs. Gorsich to be more of a physic than a psychic."

"That's all you know. Half the businessmen in town won't make a major decision without consulting Etta first."

"Why do I find that so easy to believe? Can you imagine what the commissioners would say if I turned in a bill for consulting a fortune-teller?"

"They would be pleased as punch, Bo, to find out the Sheriff's Department was finally using some common sense to solve crimes."

"Hmm. Knowing the commissioners as I do, I think you're probably right about that. Just to satisfy you, I tell you what. I'll go check out this Mrs. Gorsich." He pushed his chair away from the table with a sigh. "Anyway, the lunch is perfect. You make a great BLT, Ma."

"I have many talents, Bo, many talents."

He nodded at her hair. "Your new do looks terrific, by the way."

Rose beamed at the compliment. "Makes me look younger, doesn't it?"

"Oh yeah. Just to warn you, if I see any young bucks hanging around here, I'm going to throw them in jail. Maybe you, too!"

Tully got back to the department shortly after one o'clock. His staff was hard at work, probably because they had heard the *klock-klock* approach of his boot heels on the marble-chip floor. He wasn't surprised to see his undersheriff, Herb Eliot, still reading the day's *Blight Bugle,* with an intensity that suggested he was looking for clues to the day's crimes. How Herb could find so much to read in the paper Tully couldn't imagine.

The Crime Scene Investigations Unit—Byron "Lurch" Proctor—was bent over his computer in the corner. The corner space was exclusively his. Lurch thought of it as his lab. Tully had given him his nickname, Lurch. Even so, the sheriff was Lurch's hero. The CSI Unit was possibly the world's homeliest human being, with dull brown hair that stuck mostly straight up, a nose much too large for his face, rimless glasses half an inch thick perched atop the nose, floppy ears, and beady eyes. But he was brilliant. Besides that, his girlfriend, Sarah, was not only the most gorgeous young woman Tully had ever seen, she was also the smartest, a scientist who worked for a Boise hospital. Tully had begun to think maybe there was something to be said for homely. Oh, yeah, as long as you were brilliant, too.

Daisy Quinn, Bo's secretary and also a deputy, extremely compact and pretty, with close-cut curly black hair and brown eyes, was a woman who fairly exuded efficiency. Tully had recently made the mistake of having a brief fling with Daisy, a mistake that conceivably could have gotten both him and Daisy fired. Nevertheless, she had helped him over what Tully thought of as a rough patch and he now appreciated Daisy more than ever, even though he tried to make a point of not showing it. During his absences, he let his undersheriff, Herb, think he ran the department, but Daisy actually was the one in charge. All his deputies knew to take their orders from the secretary. Daisy brooked no nonsense from them.

Tully stuck his head into the radio room and said hi to Flo, his radio person. She gave him her usual big smile. Florence "Flo" Getts was his go-to person whenever Daisy wasn't available. Undersheriff Herb Eliot was so far down on the list, Tully often forgot about him, even if the department was extremely busy. He had long ago figured out that in any business, institution, or other kind of organization, there was always at least one totally useless person. Usually it was a person high up the organizational chart, if not at the top. He sometimes wondered if headhunters didn't advertise for totally useless people. This was the position for which Herb was totally qualified.

"Hey, Lurch!" Tully yelled across the briefing room.

Lurch looked up from his computer and gave him a big grin. "Hey, Bo!"

"I've got some work for you." He walked over to the Unit and handed him the piece of paper Crockett had given him. "See if you can find some prints on this—other than mine, that is. If you find any, run them through IAFIS and see if you can find a match."

"IAFIS" stood for "Integrated Automated Fingerprint Identification System."

"You got it, Bo. Shouldn't take long."

Tully walked over to his glassed-in office. "Daisy, bring your pad. I've got some work for you, too."

She got up from her desk and bustled in. "How did I ever guess?"

"Beats me. You must be psychic. Which reminds me, you know anything about this Etta Gorsich?"

"The fortune-teller? I've never met Gorsich but there are people in town who swear by her. I've heard all kinds of stories about how she's contacted dead relatives and come up with messages from them, that sort of thing. Weird stuff. You wouldn't get me within a thousand yards of that house of hers."

"Really? I was thinking of sending you over there for a reading, or whatever they call it."

"No way!"

Tully leaned back in his chair. "What does she look like, Daisy? Skip the part about a pointed black hat and a broom."

"I've never seen her. I don't think she leaves that creepy house of hers very often. She doesn't make house calls, as far as I know. You have to go to her if you want whatever she has to sell. I can feel the hair rising on the back of my neck just talking about her."

Tully smiled. He couldn't believe a person as sensible as Daisy could be affected by such nonsense. "Well, if you refuse to check her out, I guess maybe I'll drift over there after work. I had no idea you're such a chicken, Daisy."

She laughed. "I'll be waiting for your report first thing in the morning, Sheriff."

She got up from her desk and bristled. "How did I ever guess?"

"Beats me. You must be psychic. Which reminds me, you know anything about this Etta Gorsich?"

"The fortune-teller? I've never met Gorsich, but there are people in town who swear by her. I've heard all kinds of stories about how she's contacted dead relatives and come up with messages from them, that sort of thing. Weird stuff. You wouldn't get me within a thousand yards of that house of hers."

"Really. I was thinking of sending you over there for a reading or whatever they call it."

"No way!"

Tully leaned back in his chair. "What does she look like, Daisy? Skip the part about a pointed black hat and a broom."

"I've never seen her. I don't think she leaves that creepy house of hers very often. She doesn't make house calls, as far as I know. You have to go to her if you want whatever she has to sell. I can feel the hair rising on the back of my neck just talking about her."

Tully smiled. He couldn't believe a person as sensible as Daisy could be affected by such nonsense. "Well, if you refuse to check her out, I guess maybe I'll drift over there after work. I had no idea you're such a chicken, Daisy."

She laughed. "I'll be waiting for your report first thing in the morning, Sheriff."

3

ETTA GORSICH'S HOUSE sat by itself atop a steep but low hill. It was surrounded by overgrown trees, brush, dried grass, weeds, and dead wildflowers, mostly daisies, dandelions, and thistles. Apparently, the fortune-teller wasn't big on landscaping. He climbed the steep, rickety wooden stairs leading to the front porch. Tully ignored the two handrails on principle. He thought they were mostly for sissies. The front porch looked as if it had recently been worked on, here and there a new board showing fresh and clean. Tully, already nervous and regretting his decision to check out Mrs. Gorsich, started to knock on the door. It popped open before his knuckles made the first rap.

An attractive middle-aged woman stood there smiling at him. She was in fact one of the better-looking women Tully had seen in a long while. He instantly regretted jumping back and gasping "Whoa!" at the suddenness of the door springing open. She wore a cream-colored tailored suit on her slim, shapely figure and a necklace of pearls around her elegant neck. Her smile was large and gleamed with both amusement and sparkling white teeth. "Hello," she said in a husky voice.

"Uh, hello," Tully managed. "I'm Blight County sheriff Bo Tully and—"

"I know who you are, Sheriff. Everyone in Blight County knows Sheriff Bo Tully. Please come in. I hope you're not here to investigate the ridiculous rumors that I'm some kind of fortune-teller."

"Uh," Tully said.

"Please have a seat over on the sofa, Sheriff. I was just making a pot of tea. Would you like some?"

"Uh," Tully said again.

"A cup of tea?" the woman said. "Would you like one?"

"Why, thank you," Tully blurted as if coming out of a coma. "A cup of tea sounds great."

Mrs. Gorsich disappeared into what Tully assumed was the kitchen. He walked over to the sofa and sat down. The room appeared to be expensively and tastefully decorated. If the lady made her money from fortune-telling, she apparently did very well at it. Tully tapped his finger nervously on his knee and waited for her to return.

Mrs. Gorsich presently came out of the kitchen with a tray containing a silver teapot, two china cups on saucers, two silver teaspoons, a small pitcher of cream, and a crystal bowl of raw sugar, a tiny spoon sticking out of it. She placed the tray on the coffee table and sat down in a chair across from him. She had excellent posture, her back perfectly straight. He would have to tell his mother about Mrs. Gorsich's posture. Rose had a thing about posture.

"So, Sheriff, did you bring your handcuffs?"

"Uh, no. No, I didn't bring any handcuffs."

"Too bad. It might have been interesting."

Tully stared at her, his mind now a complete blank.

Mrs. Gorsich laughed. "Only joshing you, Sheriff. I'm sorry. Please tell me why you're here." She poured the tea.

Tully put two tiny spoonfuls of raw sugar in his tea, stirred in some cream, and took a long sip, all the time trying to think of why he was there.

"Basically," he finally said, "I guess I'm here because I try to know all the residents of Blight County, particularly those about whom I hear rumors."

"'Whom'!" Mrs. Gorsich exclaimed. "Sheriff, you are the first person in Blight County I've heard use the word 'whom'—at least, to do so correctly. You obviously are an educated person."

"I had a very mean English professor in college, Dr. Agatha Wrenn. We were terrified of her. Learning proper grammar seemed the safest thing to do. If you said 'snuck' for 'sneaked,' you were taken out behind the language arts building and shot."

"Maybe that's why you went into law enforcement after college."

"It was pretty much expected of me. Men in my family have been Blight County sheriffs for the last hundred years. But I'm here to find out about you, Mrs. Gorsich."

She refilled his cup. "Etta, please. You mean about my being a fortune-teller?" She laughed. "I admit that many Blight City businessmen come to me for advice about decisions they have to make. They are simple folk for the most part, and I'm sure they think of me as a fortune-teller, particularly when my advice works out for them. I'm actually a financial consultant. I have an MBA from an Ivy League university, the name of which would be too pretentious of me to mention. I worked on the Street for a dozen years and was quite successful at it."

Tully couldn't believe she had just confessed to having been a prostitute.

She apparently read the puzzlement on his face. "Wall Street," she said.

"Oh, right."

"So, you're wondering why I ended up here. Well, I didn't end up here. I may move on at any time, but I've become very fond of Idaho. It's a beautiful state, and the people are nice, and I just have a sense of peace here. Anytime I get bored I fly off to San Francisco or New York, but it's not long before I come zipping back to Idaho. I have quite a list of clients here I help with investments."

"I could never leave Idaho," Tully said. "So I'm not surprised you like it."

He set his empty teacup back on the tray. He couldn't remember having drunk any of the tea. Etta Gorsich picked up the teapot and refilled his cup. There was something about the woman that soaked up his total attention.

"I understand, Sheriff, that you are a very successful artist."

Tully laughed. "That all depends upon what you mean by 'very.' I've been painting most of my life and tend to view the world more as a painter than as a sheriff. Only in very recent years have my paintings started to sell. My hope is one day to give up sheriffing and become a poor but otherwise modestly successful full-time artist."

He set his cup back on the tray and pushed himself up from the couch. "I'd better not take up any more of your time, Mrs. Gorsich. Thank you very much for the tea."

"Please, call me Etta," she said, smiling, pouring him another cup of tea. "And is it all right if I call you Bo?"

"Sure," he said, settling back on the couch. "Everybody does, even my criminals."

"I hope you don't think of me as one of your criminals."

"Not at all." He sipped his tea.

Etta said, "I've traveled all over the world, Bo, and met hundreds of interesting people, but I have to say, you are the most interesting man I've come across in a long while."

Tully didn't know what to say. Finally, he managed to get out a modest "Well, uh, thank you. No one has ever said that to me before. I suppose maybe they didn't notice."

"Oh, I'm sure they noticed."

After a bit more conversation, he picked up his teacup, only to notice she had refilled it again. He set the cup back on the tray and stood up. "I really shouldn't take up any more of your time."

Etta stood and walked him to the door. "Please come again, Bo."

"You can count on that, Etta."

He turned to thank her again for her time. She came up close and put her hand on his chest. Tully thought she had stopped his heart.

"Next time, Bo," she said, "don't forget the handcuffs."

Tully fumbled with the doorknob, finally got it to turn in the right direction. He went out onto the porch and started down the steps. He knew Rose would be disappointed that he hadn't asked Mrs. Gorsich about Orville's body.

"Oh, Sheriff!" Etta called after him.

Tully stopped and turned.

"Look under the house!"

Tully gave her a brief smile and continued on down the steps. It was only at the bottom he realized he had been using both handrails.

For the first time in his life, he had met a woman he didn't think he could manage. She was like some kind of space alien, dropped into Blight City to spy on the populace. She would no doubt report back to her managers, some form of reptiles who would at some point descend on Blight and eat all the residents. To investigate her more thoroughly, he should invite Etta to lunch. He might even throw some really tough grammar at her. His tough grammar bounced undetected off local women, but Etta would be different.

He went back to the courthouse and down to the jail in the basement to check on his usual suspects. Sometimes the criminals got a little rowdy and had to be settled down. A riot or anything seriously dangerous he left to his jail matron, Lulu Cobb. Lulu's reputation was such that she had to do nothing more than open the cell-block door and yell, "All right, you idiots, knock it off—you don't want me down there with my stick!"

Tully had never seen her down there with her stick, and it was a sight he seriously wished to avoid. Tully himself took a much softer line toward the inmates. Most of them were young and stupid, and he thought maybe Lulu reminded them of their mothers.

He found her at her desk outside the cell-block door. A partially played hand of solitaire was spread out on the wood top of the battered desk. "How are our critters, Lulu?"

She shoved herself up. "Oh, they get a little restless along about feeding time, but they been quiet enough. You want to go in and visit with them, Bo?"

"I guess not, Lulu. My stomach is a little queasy today. Maybe tomorrow. Be careful."

"I'm always careful, Bo, always careful."

He tromped up the two sets of stairs and down the hall toward his office. The daytime shift had already left the briefing room, Herb and Daisy among them, but Lurch was still hard at work in his corner. Tully sometimes thought maybe Lurch had no other life, but then it would occur to him that the Unit had the beautiful Sarah. And Sarah was a major something.

"Hey, Lurch!" he yelled.

"Hey, Bo!"

"You get any prints off that paper?"

"Yeah, I got a match, too."

"So don't keep me in suspense."

Lurch thumbed through a notepad next to his computer.

"To begin with, his name isn't Ray Crockett."

"Big surprise."

"His name is Ray Porter. He did two years for possession with intent to sell. Got out in 2002. Since then he's been clean, at least as far as law enforcement knows."

"Right. As far as we know."

Lurch smiled. "I hear you checked on Mrs. Gorsich. How did that go?"

"Daisy has a big mouth. Yes, I went up and met Etta Gorsich. She's a very nice lady—attractive, too. And sophisticated. Not at all what I expected. Her so-called fortune-telling is nothing more than business advice. She's an investment consultant, not a fortune-teller."

"How good-looking is she?"

"I'm inviting her to lunch."

"That good, huh?"

"Almost up to Sarah's level, but a few years older."

Lurch feigned amazement. "Wow, that's dynamite, boss. I

was wondering what it might be like to date a fortune-teller. She would always know what you're thinking."

"Women always know what we're thinking, Lurch. But one last time, she's not a fortune-teller."

"Right, boss." The Unit gave him one of his snaggle-toothed grins and went back to his computer.

Tully stepped into his office to look at some papers Daisy had left for him. He flopped into his chair and began aimlessly tapping his fingers on the desk. Suddenly he stopped. *Look under the house!* What on earth had she meant by that? The hair stirred on the back of his neck.

4

TULLY TOOK THE next day off. It was getting late in the season for huckleberries but he wanted to get some digital photos of them for his files and maybe a gallon or so for huckleberry pie and pancakes. He had picked and eaten huckleberries all his life. Lately it had occurred to him that he actually didn't like huckleberries all that much. What motivated him to pick them every year? Maybe it was because they were free and all you had to do was go out in the woods and pick them.

He had been working on a painting of a chipmunk perched on a weathered log and had decided some huckleberries in the foreground would lend a nice touch. He had picked and eaten many thousands of huckleberries, but when it came to painting rather than eating, he couldn't seem to get them right. Besides, he felt like a long drive in the mountains. This late in the season, he knew if he were to find berries, it would have to be in the high country. With the economy scraping bottom, there were so many commercial pickers they cleaned out just about every berry, so there was hardly anything left for the ordinary picker. He hoped they hadn't found his secret patch, up on the back of Scotchman Peak. He didn't need many huckleberries for his photograph, but it would be nice if he could take Rose back enough for a couple of pies.

Having donned his lucky picking clothes, still stained with blotches of faded purple from many seasons and many washings, he added a khaki vest to conceal his Colt Commander. There had been a time when it never would have occurred to him to take a gun with him to pick huckleberries. But this was a different world, a different time.

He drove his battered 1985 blue pickup truck up along Scotchman Peak Road, his metal berry pickers and two gallon-size pails rattling in a cardboard box next to him. Finally he came to the steep grade that went up over Henrys Pass. Nearing the top of the grade, his rear tires began to spin on loose shale and gravel. When he reached the little road leading to his secret patch, he parked and turned the hubs on the front wheels, engaging the four-wheel drive. As he climbed back into the truck a faint chorus of screams reached him. The old logging road ran along the slope of the mountain off to his left. He walked over and peered in the direction of the screams. A green Chevy Suburban was parked a couple of hundred yards down the road. A dead tree lay in front of it. He got into his truck, drove down to the Suburban, and got out. The screams were moving toward him. He could tell they came from women, no doubt huckleberry pickers who had run into a bear. The bear was probably racing for his life over the top of the mountain. The ladies came around a curve in the road and were now huffing and puffing toward him, their huckleberry pails bouncing about from belts tied loosely around their waists. He leaned against the Suburban and waited.

There were five of them, three matronly types and two younger ones. They gathered around him, all too breathless to talk. They kept pointing back down the logging road. He scanned the woods on both sides of the road, hoping not to see an irritable grizzly charging in his direction.

"Oh, Sheriff Tully!" gasped a plump gray-haired lady with a red bandanna tied loosely around her neck. "Are we ever glad to see you!"

Tully smiled at her. "What seems to be the trouble, Blanche?"

"Bodies!" blurted out a younger blond woman, perspiration streaming down her reddened face.

"Bodies?" Tully said. "What kind of bodies?"

"Dead bodies!" blurted another one.

"Dead bodies all over the place!" cried another woman, who looked as if she were about to be sick. The women were now all leaning against the Suburban. He hoped none of them was going to faint.

He peered off down the road. "Exactly where are these bodies?"

One of the ladies pointed. "Down around that bend."

Tully studied the group. They looked relatively sane. "Okay, ladies, you all get in your vehicle and rest, but don't leave. I may need your names, addresses, and phone numbers." He took a pen and small notebook from his shirt pocket. "You can write them in here while you're waiting."

He walked down the road, watching for any movement ahead of him. Reaching under his vest as he moved around the bend, he unsnapped the strap retaining the Colt Commander. The dry grass along the edge of the road had grown up knee high and he had no trouble finding where the ladies had matted it down. He stepped off the road and began working his way down the slope toward a mass of huckleberry bushes. Three bodies lay on their bellies at the edge of the patch. They had ropes around their waists, maybe to hold berry buckets they were now lying on. He sat down on a stump and studied them. All had been shot in the back of the head. Each of them wore sneakers, now barely holding together, and pants and shirts in scarcely better condition. Clearly, they hadn't been killed for their money. He got up and lifted one of the hands. It was callused and darkened, probably from hard labor involving dirt. They appeared to be laborers of some kind, probably from a farm of some sort. None appeared older than twenty. He pulled one of the victims up slightly so he could see beneath him. As he expected, a two-pound coffee can had been outfitted with a wire bale. A length of rope ran around the picker's waist and through the bale.

Weird, Tully thought. All three had apparently intended to pick berries when someone shot them in the back of the head. There must have been three shooters. Otherwise at least one of the victims would have spun around at the first shot or reacted in some way. They were lying in a perfect line. He imagined himself as one of the young men headed down toward the berry patch. Why does someone haul you up in the woods to pick huckleberries? If he had been one of the intended victims, he would have sensed something funny from the start. The minute his feet hit the ground he would have run like a spooked deer down the side of the mountain. If there were three shooters, the three intended victims would have died instantly and simultaneously. On the other hand, if there was a fourth intended victim, it was possible he had managed to escape. Tully got up and walked down through an opening in the brush, examining leaves as he went. On the lower side of the berry patch he found what he was looking for. A tiny spot of dried blood glistened on a leaf. Maybe the fourth intended victim was lying dead somewhere down on the steep slope of the mountain. Or maybe, somehow, miraculously, he had gotten away. Tully worked his way back to the road. This was the worst case of cold-blooded murder he had encountered in his entire career in law enforcement. He noticed that his hands were shaking. He squeezed them into fists as he walked back to the Suburban.

Blanche, the apparent leader of the group, handed him the notebook. The ladies seemed exhausted. Tully suspected they had picked their last huckleberry. He checked the notebook to make sure they had included all the information he had asked for. They had. He walked back to his pickup and backed it out onto the main road so the Suburban could get by. After pulling back into the logging road, he stopped halfway to the dead tree, took out his cell phone, and called Lurch.

"Yeah, boss," the Unit answered. Tully suspected Lurch received phone calls only from him.

"Lurch, I'm up here on Scotchman Peak Road, about a mile from Henrys Pass. I've got three dead bodies in a huckleberry patch. They've each been shot in the back of the head. So bring your kit and a metal detector. We might be able to find some shell casings. Call Dave Perkins at the House of Fry and tell him I need him up here, too."

There was no reply.

"Lurch, you there?"

"Yeah. Give me a second. Three bodies. Dave? How come Dave?"

"He's probably the best tracker in the entire country."

"You think the killer might still be around?"

"No, but I need Dave up here."

"How about Pap?"

Tully thought for a moment. The old man relished any chance to relive his sheriff days and would never forgive him if he were left out of a triple murder. "Yeah, tell Dave to pick up Pap on his way." Then he remembered the medical examiner. "Call the M.E. and tell her we need her whole outfit up here. Tell Susan we've got three bodies, maybe a fourth."

"A fourth!" Lurch let a long breath sizzle through his teeth. "Right, boss."

5

TULLY HAD HEARD a logging truck go by earlier, so he walked out to the main road. He sat down on a large rock to wait for the next truck. Presently he could hear it growling down a steep slope up near the pass. It soon came swaying around the bend with a massive load of logs. He got up and waved his arms. The driver started working his way down through the gears and pulled up next to Tully with a hiss and squeal of brakes.

"Bo!" the driver said. "What the devil you doing out here?"

Tully climbed up on the running board. "Pete, I was trying to pick some huckleberries," he said, "but before I could get to it, I found three young guys out there in the brush, all of them shot in the back of the head."

Pete gasped out an obscenity. "What's the world coming to, Bo? Even way up here in the mountains you got folks getting themselves murdered!"

"As to what the world is coming to, I wish I knew, but I don't. Have you heard any shots the last few days?"

"Can't say I have. Oh, you know grouse season is open and occasionally we hear somebody popping off at one of them."

"Yeah, I suppose. I suspect revolvers were used. Otherwise, the casings would have been flying off into the brush and hard if not impossible for the killers to find. I figure there had to be three shooters. I've got Lurch headed up here with a metal detector, and maybe we can find some casings, if the shooters were using automatics."

Pete said, "We got trucks driving this road constantly, and I'll spread the word to the other drivers. Maybe one of them heard some shots. There's a driver either going up or down this road about every half hour. I'll pass the word, see if anybody's heard or seen anything."

"Thanks, Pete. They may know something useful." Tully dropped back to the ground. Pete gave him a little wave, and the truck went growling down the mountain.

Two hours later a caravan of cars came streaming up the road. Tully had built a small castle of rocks and was trying to think of something else to do when they finally arrived. He directed them into the logging road and walked up to the head of the line. They stopped behind his pickup, a hundred feet in front of the dead tree. It was possible Lurch might be able to find some tread imprints from the shooters' tires in that hundred feet, even though the women's Suburban had been driven all the way to the tree. A couple of state patrolmen had joined the group, as well as a U.S. forest ranger. Susan arrived in a coroner's van, trailed by another van. Stepping out the passenger door, she gave him one of her special smiles. They still hadn't gotten back together after their last breakup, a result of Tully's failure to be sufficiently attentive. Oh, yeah, and there had also been his brief affair with Daisy. That was before he made Daisy a deputy and issued her a department gun. It had later occurred to him that it wasn't such a good idea to issue a gun to a woman with whom you had broken up. He had so many women in his life he might have to hire a secretary to keep track of them. Then he would probably end up having an affair with the secretary. That's how his life went these days. Not bad, actually.

"Hey, Susan!" he said. "You get to go first." He pointed down the slope in the direction of the bodies. "If you need some help with your stuff, I'll haul it down for you."

She grinned at him. "I know, you're just trying to be attentive, Bo, but I've got some helpers along." She looked down the slope at the bodies and shook her head. "This is just so terrible!"

"Yeah." He remained on the road. Observing medical examiners at their work was not on his list of favorite activities.

Lurch hauled his metal detector over. Tully pointed out where he thought the shooters must have stood, and the Unit began sweeping the instrument back and forth. Nothing.

"Looks as if they picked up their casings, boss. Or maybe they were using revolvers."

"Give it another pass down the slope a ways."

Lurch walked a few steps down toward the bodies, swinging the detector back and forth. The instrument beeped.

"What is it?" Tully asked.

Lurch bent down and picked up the object. "A bottle cap." He cocked his arm as if to throw the cap off into the brush.

"Stop!" Tully yelled. "Let me see it."

Lurch climbed back up the slope and handed him the cap. "You think the killers took time out to share a beer?"

"Who knows?" Tully looked at the cap. "It's a twist-off, Lurch. Dos Equis. Mexican beer. Look around and see if you can find the bottle. We could get fingerprints off the bottle. If you can't find a Dos Equis bottle here, I want you to check the brush on each side of the road all the way back to that downed tree."

Lurch shook his head. "You want to arrest these killers for littering?"

"Just see if you can find me the bottle, Lurch!"

"Maybe I can get a print off the cap, Bo."

"Just find me the bottle! The guy twists the cap off the bottle here and starts drinking his beer on the way back to his car. When the bottle is empty, he tosses it out into the brush."

"Jeez, boss, I'd have to scour ten acres of brush!"

"What else do you have to do? You want to go help Susan?"

"Only kidding. I'll go look for the bottle." He sighed and started scanning the brush.

"If you find it, Lurch, don't mess up any possible prints."

"Thanks, boss. I'd never have thought of that."

Dave Perkins came walking up. He wore a buckskin shirt, jeans, and moccasins. His long gray hair hung in a thick braid down his back.

"I see you're wearing your tracking clothes," Tully said.

"Yeah, they help me concentrate." He glanced down at Susan and the three bodies. "Some really bad people running around nowadays. Maybe there always were. These guys look pretty young."

Tully nodded. "Yeah, I figure none of them is over twenty. No ID on any of them, at least that I could find. I did check their hands. Lots of calluses. I make them out to be farm laborers."

"Latinos?"

"Nope, all gringos, far as I can tell. They've been doing some hard labor, though, and I don't think they've been paid much, if anything. Their clothes are barely holding together."

Dave squinted down at Susan, then jerked his head around and gave an exaggerated shudder. "I can't believe you once dated her, Bo."

"Yeah, it was rough duty, particularly when she rehashed her day's activities while we were having supper."

"So what do you want from me, Sheriff?"

Tully told him about the possibility of an intended fourth victim who may have gotten away. "If I had been one of the intended vics, I'd have been very suspicious of anyone who took me up to pick huckleberries. At the first shot I would have taken off and run like a deer. So I walked down through the berry patch and found a tiny spot of blood on a branch down there. If one guy did get away, he may have been hit pretty hard, but I don't think so. Still, it's possible you'll find his body down the slope somewhere. On the other hand, if he was only nicked by the bullet, maybe he's alive and out there someplace. If we find him alive, we'll nail the killers."

"It's possible," Dave said. "Won't hurt for me to take a look in any case."

"You come up with Pap?"

"Yeah." He jerked his thumb in the direction of his truck.

Tully looked back down the road but couldn't see his father. "I'll have him drive your rig back to town. Once you've cut the track, if there is one, mark it and head out to the road. I'll pick you up on my way back into town."

Dave nodded. He circled far out around Susan and the victims and headed down the slope, zigzagging back and forth in order to cut the track, if there was one. Tully watched him until he was out of sight.

Pap came ambling up the road and stood beside him. He wore jeans, a denim work shirt open at the collar, cowboy boots, and a khaki vest similar to his son's. His thick white hair was cropped close to the scalp. The old man had been out of law enforcement for over ten years but he seemed as fit as ever. "A triple murder! You have all the luck, Bo."

"Yeah, don't I?"

Pap stared down at the bodies. "I see you got Susan up here already, along with most of the county. Everybody loves a murder, and here you land a triple. In all my years as sheriff, I didn't have but two triples."

"One that you committed?"

Pap blurted out an obscenity. "Those were three bank robbers and you know it! I killed them fair and square! Got plugged three times myself and even was awarded a commendation from the governor."

"I believe you've mentioned that to me a few hundred times. What was the other triple?"

"You made me mad, Bo, so I ain't going to tell you."

Tully glanced at his father. The old man was tall and lean, his skin deeply tanned from a lifetime of hunting and fishing and roaming the mountains. "Tell me," he said. He knew the old man couldn't resist.

"They was all gamblers. They cooked up a scheme to rip off one of the joints. Not a good idea. It was one of the few crimes I never solved."

"That because you had an interest in the joint?"

Pap laughed. "That's for me to know. I see you've notified just about everybody in the entire state, Bo. So I was wondering why the FBI hasn't showed up."

"The FBI? Why should I notify them?"

"This is a national forest. The last time I looked, national forests were on federal land. The FBI usually likes to investigate murders on federal land."

"Is that right? I didn't know. Well, as soon as I get back to town, I'll have to give them a call. If I don't forget. So why do you think these fellows might have been killed?"

"A killing like this, Bo, you got to figure it's about money."

"You think these fellows were done for money?"

"Somebody wanted to dispose of them, that's pretty obvious. The question is why. You usually dispose of a person because you don't want him blabbing something he knows about you. These fellers look pretty young, from what I can see of them. It's doubtful any of them knew enough of anything to get them killed. So what does that leave?"

"Beats the heck out of me."

"You're so dumb, Bo. The only other sensible reason to kill a person is money."

"I don't think these guys had any money at all."

"Maybe they was killed to keep them that way. And maybe to keep them quiet, too."

"You may be right."

6

BY LATE AFTERNOON, the bodies had been loaded into the coroner's vans to be hauled back to Susan's lab. She stood at the edge of the road, her face glistening with sweat, a wisp of hair stuck to her cheek. "I have to find another line of work," she told Tully.

"Can't blame you for that," he said. "So, can you tell me when they were killed?"

"Right now all I can tell you is, within the last couple of days, because—"

"Skip the details, please! Just give me your best estimate."

"That is my best estimate, Bo. I'll be able to narrow down the time once I get them back to the lab. If any of them has a record, you might be able to get an ID from his prints. My guess is that at least one of them has been arrested for something one time or another. You usually don't meet guys at a church social who wind up shooting you in the back."

Tully tugged on the corner of his mustache. "Yeah, I guess you're right about that. Print them for me, please, and I'll see if Lurch can find a match."

"I'll get them over to Byron tonight. Since you keep him working night and day, you might have at least one ID by tomorrow."

Tully laughed. "Sounds as if you've been listening to Lurch complain. Which reminds me, I've got him checking out a partial tire track as well as looking for a beer bottle."

Susan shook her head and climbed into the passenger side of the last van to back out. Other hangers-on had left the scene earlier. A few were standing around in groups out on the Scotchman Peak Road. The Unit came walking up carrying a plaster cast.

"You able to get anything we can use, Lurch?"

"Maybe. The lady pickers' car pretty much rolled over the top of the lower track, but I was able to cast several inches on the edge. The vehicle that made the lower track had very wide tires. Could even be dual tires. Probably made from the shooters' tires because the track looks just a bit older than the Suburban's. Has to be from a truck tire, or maybe a big van. I'm pretty sure if we find the vehicle, we can get a match."

"A big pickup maybe? Then the shooters would be in the cab, with at least some of our vics riding in the bed."

"Has to be, if this is a print from one of their vehicle's tires."

"Good work, Lurch. I'll see you back at the office. Did you ever find the Dos Equis bottle that goes with the cap?"

"As a matter of fact I did. I'm not sure if it goes with the cap, but it probably does. It smells pretty fresh."

"See if you can get a print off it. We don't have much else to go on."

"You bet."

Tully could see Pap out on the road talking to Harvey Grant, the forest ranger. He walked out and joined them. Most of the other vehicles were pulling out and heading down the road.

Tully said to the ranger, "Harvey, I wish you would patrol these woods a little better and cut down on the murders."

Harvey shook his head. "It's getting almost as bad as the cities. I personally wouldn't go out in the mountains anymore without a weapon. And that's pretty sad, if you ask me. When we were kids, we hiked and camped all over these mountains and never once carried a gun. By the way, I was just telling Pap the FBI is going to be in one hot fuss they weren't notified, this being federal land."

Tully smiled. "Must have slipped my mind. On the other hand, I was up here in the woods all by myself. What's a person to do?"

"You got everybody else alerted. A person can do only so much."

"That's right, Harvey. That'll be my story and I'm sticking to it. Well, I'm sure Pap has been keeping you entertained with accounts of his own murders, but I need him to drive

Dave Perkins's vehicle back into town. I'll pick up Dave on my way in."

"You got Dave out doing some tracking for you?" Harvey said.

"Yeah. I think maybe there was a fourth intended victim, and he might have got away. It's a long shot, but if anyone can turn up any sign of him, it'll be Dave."

Harvey smiled. "It's probably that Indian blood. He get his casino started yet?"

Tully rolled his eyes. "Yeah, right, Harvey. Over my dead body."

Pap got in Dave's pickup, whipped it around on the road, and sent rocks flying over the embankment. He headed down the mountain. Tully shook his head, then drove up to a turnout and made a similar maneuver with his own pickup, only much slower. Then he followed the trail of dust left by Dave's truck. A mile down the mountain he found Pap and Dave standing at the edge of the road. Pap was constructing one of his hand-rolleds. Tully parked on the edge of the road, got out, and walked over to them. "Find anything, Dave?"

"I think your hunch was right, Bo. I did find a few tracks. And a couple of these." He held out a leaf with a spot of dried blood on it.

"That all the blood you found?"

Dave nodded. "There might be more, but there's a lot of brush and I had a hard time staying on his track. He did cut over to the road right here. Stood back behind a tree over there, as if watching for someone." Dave pointed to the tree. "My guess is he was just nicked by the bullet. There's quite a few drops of blood at the base of the tree."

"You think he got a ride with someone?"

"I don't know. He was probably waiting for the shooters to go by. There were signs they had walked down the mountain a ways looking for him but then gave up. Maybe they figured he was hit hard enough he'd die out there in the brush."

Tully walked over and looked at the ground behind the tree. There were faint scuff marks in the pine needles and several tiny dark spots. "You call this 'sign,' Dave—this little disturbance?"

"Yeah, that's what I call it. You want something with his name and address on it? I'm not surprised you don't notice much, Bo, because you have to be Indian to know sign when you see it."

Pap had his cigarette going by now. Tully sighed and stepped upwind of him. "You going back with me, or Dave?"

"Depends on what you're planning to do."

"I'm walking back down that little road we were on until I find some fresh huckleberries. Then I'm going to take a picture of them, if there's still some light. I thought I'd pick enough berries so Ma could make us a couple of pies."

Pap took a drag on his cigarette and blew out a cloud of smoke. "Much as I prefer Dave's company to yours, Bo, the mention of huckleberry pies has caught my attention. I think I'll come along and help you pick."

Pap climbed into Tully's pickup and they drove back up to

the old logging road. Tully drove in as far as the downed tree and they got out. "How far we got to walk?" Pap said.

"Only about half a mile from here. You tell anybody about my secret patch, you're a dead man." He handed Pap his extra gallon bucket.

"You got to be kidding me, Bo! A secret patch! About ten thousand people roam about this mountain picking huckleberries every year, and you think you've got a secret patch!"

"Actually, Pap, they don't roam about the mountain. They roam about the roads. There isn't one huckleberry picker in a hundred goes off the road more than fifty feet. If they can't see the road, they think they're lost and start to panic. When you see my secret patch, you're not going to believe it."

"I don't believe it already."

They hiked along in silence for a few minutes. The road had deteriorated into scarcely more than a wide trail. The uphill side, thick with young fir trees, rose steeply up the mountain, and the downhill side dropped off sharply into a heavily logged area. Pap scuffed some dust into the air with his boot. "Dry as a bone out here."

"Yeah, the whole mountain could go up like a box of tinder if we get lightning. If it wasn't so dry, you'd see mushrooms along the road this time of year."

"What kind of mushrooms?"

"Shaggymanes. Giant puffballs."

"I could go for a batch of shaggymanes," Pap said. "I ain't going to touch another puffball, though. I ate one about five years ago and it nearly killed me."

"I bet it had some yellow in it. It was too old. It has to be pure white all the way through."

"It *was* pure white all the way through! You must think I'm stupid, Bo."

"Then you were drinking."

"A glass of Jack Daniel's before dinner, that's all."

"You should know better than to drink alcohol before eating wild mushrooms! What was that you said about stupid?"

Pap stopped and took a deep breath. "I always drink before dinner, and afterwards, too. I've eaten a ton of wild mushrooms in my life and I never even once before had an attack like that. Anyway, Bo, you picking with your fingers, or did you bring a picker?"

Tully paused and looked down into a drainage dropping sharply below. He had fished the tiny stream years ago. The fish had been small but hungry and plentiful. Back then the trout limit was all you could catch plus one fish. He said, "A picker. I got one for you, too, Pap."

"Good. You buy them from Pinto Jack?"

"Who else? Pinto makes the best huckleberry pickers in the world."

"I have to agree, Bo. I have a whole collection of pickers and not a one comes even close to Pinto's. You know those prongs on the front? He makes them out of bedsprings. They got just the right amount of flex to pop a berry off a bush and not crush it."

They walked along in silence for a ways.

Tully stopped. "This is it."

"What's it? I don't see nothing."

"If everyone could see my secret patch, it wouldn't be secret, would it?" He pointed. "We have to climb up to the ridge there and walk down it a ways."

"There's actually work involved? Now you tell me!"

Tully shook his head. "It's uphill no more than fifty yards. You're always bragging about what good shape you're in, I'm pretty sure you can make fifty yards!"

Pap uttered an expletive. "Of course I can make it! I just like to be warned, that's all. I don't like you sneaking actual work on me without no warning!"

When they reached the top of the ridge, Pap wasn't even breathing hard. Tully once again thought they should put him in ads promoting the use of tobacco and alcohol.

"So where's the secret patch?"

Tully said, "See that little bench going off to our right? We need to hike down it a ways and I'll show you."

Mumbling obscenities, Pap followed Tully down the bench for several dozen yards. "How much farther, Bo?"

"This is it," Tully said.

Pap looked at the huckleberry brush rising almost to his shoulders on both sides of them. He gasped. "I've got to tell you, Bo, I've never seen anything like this!"

Huckleberries the size of grapes hung in huge clusters from the bushes and in some cases dragged the bushes to the ground. The patch stretched all the way down the bench.

"You tell anyone about it, Pap, I'll have to kill you and him."

"Don't worry about me, Bo. I'm amazed the commercial pickers haven't found this and cleaned it out."

"I am too, actually."

Tully hated that there were so many commercial pickers out in the mountains now. They ruined it for everybody else, and some of them were pretty threatening, too, as if they thought you were depriving them of a livelihood by picking a gallon or two. It seemed as if there were more of them every year. He said, "Maybe there are more commercial pickers every year because there are more poor people every year."

"I hate poor people," Pap said. "Most of your criminals are poor. If we'd do away with poor people we'd do away with most of the crime."

"How about bankers and politicians, Pap? And how about you, speaking of corruption?"

"I may have engaged in a little innocent corruption, but I did it so I wouldn't be one of the poor people I hate."

Tully smiled and shook his head. "I see."

He took out his digital camera and shot close-ups of several clusters of huckleberries. Then he raced Pap to fill his bucket first. Within minutes Pap uttered the classic huckleberry boast: "I've got my bottom covered, Bo!"

"That's one thing I can be thankful for."

Driving down across the meadow to his log house that evening, Tully became aware for the first time how much shorter the days were. It wasn't eight o'clock yet and was already getting dark. He had dropped Pap off at his mansion on the hill and chatted for a while with his gorgeous housekeeper, Deedee, whom Pap had rustled from Dave's House of Fry the previous year. How Deedee put up with the old man, he couldn't fathom, but all signs indicated she was the one in charge. After dropping Pap off and flirting with Deedee, he had driven over to his mother's house and dropped off two gallons of huckleberries. Rose had been thrilled. She tried to talk him into eating something for supper, but Tully was too tired.

When he reached his house he turned the truck off and had a look around his front yard. The grass had all turned brown, probably because his well had dried up. As soon as he had time, he had to dig a new one. He walked in the front door, which he seldom bothered to lock. The large oil painting of his wife greeted him. Ginger had died over ten years before, but the sight of the painting never failed to lift his spirits. He heated a frozen Hungry-Man turkey dinner in the microwave, flipped on the TV, and sat down in his glider to eat and watch a crime show episode he'd seen only twice before. But he had barely begun to eat before he dozed off. The phone rang about twenty minutes later. Reluctantly, he answered. "Sheriff Bo Tully."

"Bo," a man's voice said. "I hope I didn't wake you."

"At this hour? Not a chance."

"This is Pete Reynolds. You told me about the murders up on Scotchman Road earlier today."

"Right, Pete." Tully rubbed his eyes and tried to wake up.

"I talked to some of the drivers about what you said, and George Henderson jumped like he had sat on a hot poker. He said he picked up a young fellow like you mentioned. He come out of the woods and waved George down. He had ripped a sleeve off his shirt and had it wrapped around his upper right arm. George asked him how he hurt it, and he said he'd fallen on a log and jabbed it with a broken limb. He was kind of pale and George said he would be glad to drive him by the hospital and drop him off at the emergency room, but the kid wouldn't have nothing to do with that. When they got down to Blight City, he said he would be fine, so George pulled over and stopped. The kid thanked him and got out, and that's the last George seen of him."

"Pete, this is wonderful! I find that kid, I've got the shooters. Did George say exactly where in Blight he dropped him off?"

"Yeah, right after you cross the railroad tracks when you come into town from the Scotchman Road."

"You did great, Pete! I owe you one!"

"I hope that means if logging don't pick up, you'll add me to the force."

"I've hired a lot worse, I can tell you that. You may have helped blow this case wide open, Pete. Many thanks."

He sat back down in his glider to finish eating. No way he would ever get back to sleep now.

7

TULLY WOKE UP at seven with *Good Morning America* on the TV and the Hungry-Man turkey dinner half-eaten and cold in his lap. One of these days he meant to get a life.

On his way into the office, Tully stopped at McDonald's for coffee and an Egg McMuffin, his third one for breakfast that week. By the time he walked into the briefing room, the day shift had already gone out. He stuck his head in the radio room and said, "Morning, Flo." She treated him to one of the smiles she seemed to reserve only for him.

Daisy was typing up something on her computer and Herb was reading the morning paper. As expected, Lurch was hard at work in his corner. Tully yelled at him, "Hey, Lurch!"

"Morning, boss!"

Tully walked over. "You get any prints off that beer bottle?"

"Yeah, got a match, too."

"No kidding. Anyone we know?"

"Lennie Frick."

Tully frowned. "Frick? He did a couple of months for multiple DUIs, and before that—what was it, Lurch?"

"Theft of a roll of telephone wire off a utility company truck. Sold it for the copper."

"Right. I can't imagine Lennie moving up to triple murder. So what's his current address?"

"You expect me to know everything, boss?"

"Yeah. What is it?"

"It's Four-oh-five East Sharp."

"I'll swing by and have a little visit with him. Thanks, Lurch."

"You bet." Lurch went back to his computer.

Tully walked across the briefing room. Daisy pretended she was too busy to notice his approach.

"Bring your pad, sweetheart."

Daisy sighed loudly but then got up and followed him into his office. Tully stood by the door and closed it behind her.

She sat down in a chair across from his desk, her back straight, her knees crossed below the short black skirt, and said, "I already have a ton of work to get done this morning, Bo. I hope you don't have a ton more."

"No, I don't, Daisy. I was just wondering how you're getting along these days."

"Where are we going with this?"

Tully smiled. "Nowhere. It's just been a while since I talked to you. All I want to know is if you're okay."

Daisy squinted at him. "Yeah, I'm okay."

"Good, because I've got some more work for you."

"I thought so."

"Get on the phone and your computer and find out everything you can about Lennie Frick. Known associates, possession of firearms, and things like that. I need it all about an hour ago."

Daisy shook her head and laughed. "You're something else, boss, you know that?"

"I suppose. You know, Daisy, you're not only the best deputy I've got, you're also the prettiest by far."

"I'm not up to that again."

"I suppose. Forget I mentioned it."

Daisy smiled. "But thanks anyway, Bo." She went out and closed the door behind her.

Tully picked up the phone and dialed. His mother answered. "I knew it would be you, Bo."

"Just wanted to say good morning, Ma."

"I'm sure. The answer is, yes, I already have four huckleberry pies in the oven. One each for you and Pap, and two for me. I carved a *B* in the crust of yours, and be sure you eat that one. I put arsenic in Pap's."

"I think that's a crime, Ma, but it's okay, as long as you marked the right one. I'll swing by later and pick them up."

He hung up and drummed his fingers on the desk while he thought about what to do next. Too bad he had given up smoking his pipe, because that would give him something to do while he thought. He got up and walked out to Daisy's desk. "Do you know where Pugh is?"

"He's on his way in. Brian worked until after midnight yesterday."

"I suppose he thinks that's an excuse for coming late to work."

"Yeah, he's such a slacker."

"Send him in as soon as he gets here."

"Yes, sir, boss."

He walked back to his office and stood for a moment staring out the window at Lake Blight. Only he could no longer see the lake because the window had been painted over. One of his criminals had taken a shot at him from a boat and missed him and Daisy by half an inch. Daisy had saved his life at the risk of her own. That had led to the brief affair. Hard to tell what other catastrophe might occur if another nut took a shot at him from the lake. So he'd had the window painted over.

Deputy Brian Pugh stuck his head in the door. "You want to see me, boss?" He was carrying a cup of coffee.

"Yeah, Pugh. Come in and grab a chair. What have you been up to?"

"Ernie and I were out last night trying to shake down some guys for info about that rumored marijuana stash." He grabbed a chair with one hand, spun it around, and sat down astraddle it across from Tully. Although Pugh was still in his thirties, Tully was pleased to see he was already picking up a bit of gray in his hair. The deputy shoved some papers aside and set his cup on Tully's desk. Pugh, Ernie Thorpe, and Daisy were his only plainclothes deputies.

"Get anything?"

"Not much. I've never seen so many bad guys tight-lipped about somebody else's deal, if it *is* somebody else's deal. They knew we could do them some favors, too, and maybe some hurt, but they wouldn't give us zip. I think they were scared."

"Really?"

"Yeah, really. You know our bad guys are pussycats compared with what's running around in the big cities."

Tully tugged on the corner of his mustache and thought about this. "What you're telling me, Brian, is that maybe some really heavy dudes have moved into town?"

"That's the feeling both Ernie and I get. Usually we don't have any trouble shaking loose a few tidbits of info, but now we're getting nothing. We even offered to drop some possession charges, but still nothing."

"You're right, our criminals usually don't refuse a deal."

Pugh took a sip of his coffee and made a face. "Where does Daisy get this stuff anyway?"

"Straight from China, at fifteen cents a pound. So don't be picky. You think the three dead guys I found up in the huckleberry patch yesterday might have something to do with it?"

"The coffee? Yeah, they were probably the importers. Serves them right."

"No, the fact you can't pry any info out of your snitches."

Pugh nodded. "That did occur to me. But why would they kill three huckleberry pickers?"

"Maybe the pickers had stumbled onto somebody's secret patch. Who knows? Actually, there were four intended victims. The fourth one got away. I think he was nicked in the arm by one of the shooters. Dave tracked him down the mountain for a mile and only found a few spots of blood. So he couldn't have been hit hard. Brian, I want you to drop everything else and find this guy. I'm pretty sure he will know who the shooters are."

Pugh stood up and retrieved his coffee cup. "You're probably right about that. You got any idea where I can find this picker?"

"George Henderson gave the kid a ride off the mountain in his logging truck and dropped him off just across the tracks where the Scotchman Peak Road comes into Blight. You know George?"

"The logger? Sure, I know who he is."

"Good. George should be able to give you a description of the guy. The kid probably isn't over twenty and hasn't had a shower in a few months. I checked the hands on the dead victims and they were all rough and callused, like they were farmworkers. So this guy probably resembles the other vics, but a little smarter."

Pugh smiled. "A dirty, young, smart farmworker. Shouldn't take me any time at all to find him."

"Don't be a wise guy, Pugh. The fact that the other vics hadn't come in contact with bathwater in a year probably applies to him, too. Even if he was only slightly nicked by a bullet, the wound would get infected. If it does, he'll probably show up at the hospital emergency room to get it treated. The kid isn't stupid. Otherwise, he'd be dead."

Pugh stood up to leave. "I know a nurse who works emergency. I'll check with her."

"The cute redhead?"

"How did you know, boss?"

"Maybe I'm psychic."

Pugh laughed. "Yeah, I bet. I've got my eye on her myself. Any other leads on the shooters?"

"Lennie Frick."

"Frick! You've got to be kidding me, Bo! If Frick went to swat a fly, the fly would take the swatter away and beat him with it!"

Tully shrugged. "But who knows what evil dwells in the heart of any man?"

"Hunh? I think you need to take a few days off, boss."

"You're probably right, Pugh. I need to relax a little. As a matter of fact, I'm thinking of phoning a beautiful fortune-teller and inviting her to lunch."

Pugh shook his head. "I'm not kidding, boss. You need some time off!"

8

TULLY DROVE OVER to 405 East Sharp. It was a tiny, ratty-looking house, scarcely big enough for the rats, let alone Frick. Parked out front was a battered red pickup truck with a blue door, the door no doubt salvaged at night from a wrecking yard. In the front of the house was a pile of empty beer cans taller than Tully. It appeared as if each can was the same brand of beer, Acme, the worst beer he had ever tasted but also the cheapest. He knocked on the front door. A voice inside called out, "Who is it?"

"The police, Frick. And don't try running out the back, because I've got men out there who will beat you senseless for the fun of it!"

The door opened a crack and Frick peeked out. "Oh, it's only you, Bo." He unhooked a chain and opened the door the rest of the way. "Come on in."

Tully preferred his criminals to have more fear of him. "No, Lennie, you come out."

Frick stepped out. He was wearing a dirty T-shirt, grungy jeans, and a pair of wire-rim glasses taped together over the nosepiece. His hair appeared to have been cut with a lawn mower. He nodded at the pile of beer cans. "What do you think of my collection, Bo?"

"Very nice, Lennie. All the same make of beer, I see."

"Yeah. I'm kind of a perfectionist. Me and my buddies emptied them all ourselves. I wouldn't let anybody toss on anything but an Acme can."

"I can see that. But occasionally you treat yourself to a Dos Equis, don't you, Lennie?"

"Jeez, how'd you know that?"

"Because we found a Dos Equis bottle at a crime scene and it had your prints on it."

Lennie looked as if he was about to faint. "I-I-I didn't do nothing to nobody, Bo!"

Tully smiled. "I know you didn't, Lennie. But if you tell me one itty-bitty lie, you're going to jail for it. Now, when you were up on that old logging road on the Scotchman, did you see anything unusual?"

Lennie was silent. Tully could almost hear the brain cells grinding together as he sorted through all the petty crimes he had committed in the last week. "No, nothing. There's a huckleberry patch in there a ways, pretty well picked over, and I got a gallon for my mom."

"Good for her. Did you notice anything unusual about the huckleberry patch?"

"Like what?"

"Three dead bodies."

Lennie's jaw dropped. "No! I didn't see no bodies!"

Tully tugged on the corner of his mustache as he stared coldly at the perfectionist. "Okay, I believe you, Lennie. Now tell me exactly when you were up there."

Lennie frowned. Tully could see his fingers down along his side, counting. "Three days ago."

"You're sure?"

"Yeah. I dropped the berries off at my mom's and she baked me a pie. I picked the pie up yesterday."

"So what time did you drive back down from Scotchman?"

"Jeez, it was pretty late. Maybe about four. Still mighty hot, though."

"Did you see anybody when you were driving back down the road? Any other pickers, for example?"

"Naw. Oh, there was one big white pickup parked at a turnout on the road when I was coming down. It had a bunch of young guys sitting in the bed. The pickup looked brand-new."

"Anything unusual about it?"

"Yeah, it was one of them dualies. That's the kind of pickup I'm going to buy next."

"You're saying it had dual tires on the rear, right?"

"Right."

"Anything else unusual about it?"

"Only the folks inside. A bunch of stuck-up rich guys. I waved when I drove by but not a one of them waved back. Then it occurred to me maybe they were having car trouble. So I stopped and backed up. The driver rolled down his window and I asked him if he needed any help. He said, 'Beat it!' and called me a nasty name. I would have said something back just as rude but he didn't seem like the kind of person you want to be rude to. So I just drove on."

"You think you could pick that guy out of a lineup?"

"Yeah, I'll never forget that face."

Tully gave Lennie his cold stare again. "Now, listen to me very closely. First, get in that red truck of yours with the blue door and park it in that little garage you've got out back. Don't drive it anywhere, until you hear from me."

"You're scaring me, Bo."

"I intend to. Now, do you remember how many people were in the cab?"

"Yeah, there was three of them, all in the front seat. The backseat was empty. It was still blistering hot out, and they had these other guys riding in the bed. All four of them could have fit into the backseat. You can bet the cab was air-conditioned."

Tully smiled. "You've done good. Just remember now, for once in your life, Lennie, you can't be dumb. Let me repeat, you can't be dumb! Don't drive that pickup anywhere until you get that blue door replaced and until you hear from me."

"How come, Bo?"

"Because somebody will kill you, Lennie, that's why."

9

BACK AT THE courthouse, Tully walked directly into his office. He thumbed through his phone book. No luck. He punched a button on his phone and got Daisy's extension.

"Yeah, boss."

"Daisy, work some of your magic and find Etta Gorsich's number for me."

"Why? You need your fortune told?"

"No! Just get me her number!"

A few minutes later Daisy came in and handed him the number on a piece of paper.

"That was fast. It's not in the book. Where did you find it?"

"I called your mom."

"Ma had it?"

"Of course. She keeps track of all the gossip, in this world and the next."

"I should have known." He hung up and dialed the number. Etta Gorsich answered.

"Etta, it's Bo Tully."

"Bo! So good to hear from you! I would love to!"

"Uh, how do you know what I have in mind?"

"Whatever it is, Bo, I would love to."

"Well, that's, uh, great. What I have in mind is lunch at Crabbs. Can I meet you there in an hour?"

"Perfect. See you there in an hour, Bo."

Scarcely had he hung up the phone when Daisy buzzed him. "Marge Poulson is headed your way. Are you in?"

"Daisy, how can I not be in? This office has glass on three sides."

"Last time you hid under your desk."

"I'll see her! Show her in."

He walked over and opened the door for Mrs. Poulson. She was in her early sixties, a few years younger than her ex-husband, Orville. She was one stern lady, a ranchwoman who had grown up in hard times, and all nonsense had long ago been washed out of her. She came directly to the point.

"Sheriff, when are you going to arrest Ray Crockett for the murder of Orville?"

"Would you like to sit down?" he asked, pointing to the chair in front of his desk.

"No, I simply want you to answer my question."

"As I've told you before, Mrs. Poulson, we have no evidence that Orville is even dead. We obviously can't arrest someone simply on your suspicions."

Her shoulders seemed to slump.

"Please sit down," he said, putting his arm around her and edging her toward the chair. She sat. Tully walked around his desk and sat down across from her.

The woman seemed tired and a little dazed, but something caught her attention. "Why is that window painted over, Sheriff?"

Tully turned and glanced at the window. Good question. "Well, one of our local criminals tried to shoot me through it a while back."

"Oh, yes, I read about that in the paper. I'm sorry, Sheriff, I know you have lots of problems, and I shouldn't be such a bother, but the murder of Orville weighs on me something awful. We have been divorced for five years but we were married for nearly forty. I don't know about other people, but just because Orville and I couldn't stand living with each other anymore doesn't mean we stopped caring. I know your wife died ten years ago, Sheriff, and you've never married again. You understand about attachment."

Her words caught Tully off guard. He felt a sudden constriction in his throat and hoped his eyes hadn't teared up. "Yes, I do, Marge." He cleared his throat. "I want you to know I haven't for a minute forgotten about Orville. What I'm about to tell you is between the two of us. If you breathe a word of it to anyone, it could get me in a lot of trouble and we might never find out what happened to your husband. So give me your word."

"You have it, Sheriff."

"I went out and met Ray Crockett the other day. He's a pretty smooth customer and seems like a pleasant enough fellow. Nevertheless, I suspect he did Orville in, just as you suspect. More likely, he had somebody else do it. But we have to find the body. And a body can be hard to find if the person isn't even dead."

Marge took out a hanky and dabbed at her eyes. "Oh, Orville could be buried anywhere out there. That ranch is over a thousand acres. Do you even have a clue where he might be?"

Tully didn't want to tell her he had a lead, because he didn't even know if he had one. "No, I don't," he said. "Crockett told me he mails Orville's Social Security checks to a post office box in Spokane each month. If, in fact, Orville has been murdered by him, Crockett must then go to Spokane, pick up the checks, and cash them. I'm not sure how difficult it is for someone to cash Social Security checks belonging to someone else. By the way, Marge, are you having any financial problems because of Orville's disappearance?"

She laughed. "You don't have to worry about me, Sheriff. I'm well off. Orville gave me half the money from his sale of the stock. Then I rented out the old farmhouse I inherited from my folks. The renters don't farm but say they like the isolation. There aren't any neighbors within miles."

"Where's the farmhouse?"

"It's a few miles down the road from my own little house, on the other side of Cow Creek. As for cashing Social Security checks belonging to someone else, I have no idea." Marge put her hanky back in her purse. "His Social Security checks didn't amount to that much."

"How much?"

"About fifteen hundred dollars. Not enough for somebody to murder a person for."

"Marge, people get murdered for a whole lot less than fifteen hundred dollars. Take my word for it."

"Really? It seems so little for a human life."

"Yes, it does. I guess the value goes down pretty fast if it's somebody else's life. In any case, Marge, I'll get in touch with you as soon as I know something."

"Thanks, Bo. Is it okay if I call you Bo?"

"You bet. You can call me anything you like, Marge. Oh, I understand Orville was quite the fisherman."

"Good heavens, no! Orville hated fishing. Said it was the most boring excuse for a hobby he could ever imagine. Why do you ask?"

"No reason. Just something I heard."

10

AFTER MARGE LEFT, Tully drove over to Crabbs. Etta was just getting out of her car when he arrived. She was dressed in what, to Tully, looked like sailcloth pants, the legs spreading into little flares slightly below her calves. She wore a little black jacket that also seemed to have an ancient naval look to it, although maybe it was just basic New Yorky, something she had picked up at Saks Fifth Avenue. Ever since Susan, he had made a point of being attentive to what women wore.

"Hey, Bo!" Etta cried. "We have perfect timing!"

As with almost everything Etta said, Tully wondered if there weren't something subliminal he was supposed to pick up on. He had never known a woman who made him quite as nervous as this one. Having enough trouble with his present world, he had little tolerance for people who claimed a knowledge of some other world. He hoped Etta wasn't one of those. She had impressed him as a person of few pretensions. The outside of her house displayed only cracked and peeling paint, a rickety porch, a yard that made Lennie Frick's beer-can pile look like a landscaper's display piece, and a set of stairs and handrails in serious need of warning signs. If she ran a business out of her house, she needed a visit from OSHA. Now he noticed that she drove a rather modest Buick LeSabre with several dents and dings, and in need of a wash. On the other hand, everything in the interior of her house had been strictly upscale. Something weird was going on with Etta Gorsich.

"Hey, Etta!" he called back.

She gave him one of her sexy but amused smiles. "I hope I'm not taking you away from your work."

"Actually, you are," he said. "And I'm profoundly grateful."

Etta responded with a throaty laugh. "I'm pleased, then. I've never dated a sheriff before. But maybe this isn't a date. Maybe it's only a business lunch."

"I prefer to think of it as a date," Tully said. "Crabbs, by the way, is the best restaurant in all of Blight City."

Etta smiled. "Sad, isn't it?"

"Yes, it is. Its strongest point is proximity. Crabbs's motto should be 'We're here.'"

"Perfect!" she said. "You should be in advertising, Bo."

"You really think so?"

"No, I think you're perfect as the sheriff. People love you, particularly the women."

Tully took her by the arm and turned her, so he could look her in the eye. "You've been talking to my mother, haven't you, Etta?"

"Your mother? Good heavens, no!"

"Come clean. I'm a sheriff, you know. I can spot a lie three blocks away."

She put on an exaggerated pout. "Well, if your mother is a fascinating woman named Rose, it's entirely possible I may have met her on some occasion."

Tully rolled his eyes. "Just as I thought! My mother is Gossip Central in Blight City and surrounding points. I happen to be the main topic of her gossip. You should never believe a single thing she says."

Etta pretended to be extremely serious. "But isn't it true, Bo, that all the women love you?"

"Well, that's true, of course. I mean all the other stuff."

"I'll say only this about my conversations with Rose: the other stuff is extremely interesting!"

Tully let his chin drop down onto his chest.

Lester Cline, the manager, showed them to a table. Tully watched as he spread a napkin on Etta's lap. She ran her eyes down the menu.

She looked up. "I'd love to go with the beef dip but I'm afraid I'd drip the *jus* all over me."

"You obviously have sophisticated tastes, Etta. I usually order the beef dip myself." He nodded at the manager.

"Yes, sir?" Lester said. "The usual?"

"One for each of us, please."

Lester hurried off. Etta leaned across the table toward Tully. "Didn't you just hear me say I was afraid I'd drip *jus* all over me?"

"I did, indeed. Ah, here comes Lester."

"Already?"

Lester came up behind Etta and tied a plastic bib around her neck. It went all the way down her front and covered her lap. For a moment, she seemed shocked. Then she burst out in a raucous laugh, much to Tully's relief. Lester then tied a bib around Tully's neck. Etta now laughed so hard she seemed in pain.

Lester took a pad from his pocket. "And what dressing would you like on your salads?"

Etta appeared incapable of speech. "Blue cheese on both, Lester," Tully said.

He tried to steer their conversation over lunch in a sensible direction. Etta was eating the beef dip with appropriate gusto and had an attentive expression on her face. Then suddenly she exploded with wild laughter, holding her napkin in front of her face, struggling to maintain a certain propriety.

"Am I correct to assume you don't usually wear bibs at your New York restaurants?" Tully asked.

Etta stretched the napkin like a curtain in front of her face. Her eyes peered over the top, full of tears and pain. She shook her head slowly back and forth—then broke out laughing again.

By the time the waiter took away their bibs and plates and returned with cups of coffee and a small plate of chocolates, Etta looked as if she were headed out for trick-or-treating. Streaks of mascara ran down both cheeks, but she had finally settled into an enduring calm.

"I hope you're sorry," she said.

"I can't believe you've never used a bib before."

"Not since I was about four years old. And don't you dare set me off again. The other customers in here probably think I'm crazed."

Tully held up his hands as if claiming total innocence. "I'm sorry. I had no idea a bib would have such an effect. In any case, I have an important question I need to ask you, in all seriousness."

"You're sure?"

"Yes. When I left your place the other day, you called after me from your porch, 'Look under the house.' What did you mean?"

Etta frowned. "I didn't call after you, 'Look under the house.' At least I certainly don't remember doing so. Why would I say something like that? I've never even seen your house."

"Not my house. Somebody else's house."

"Somebody else's house? I don't know what you're talking about, Bo."

Tully shook his head. "Here's the thing, Etta. It seemed to refer to a case I've been working on."

"Bo, I know nothing about your cases. If I were actually a

psychic, I probably could solve all your cases for you, but I'm not. My expertise is financial counseling. I can assure you I didn't call out anything to you."

"Forget I asked. Please! It was stupid of me."

Etta turned sober. "I will tell you something, Bo. I really don't have answers to anything. I'm not a psychic. Not a fortune-teller. I barely know what I'll be doing from one day to the next, let alone managing to predict the future for someone else. But occasionally an odd image will flash in my mind for no reason at all. Maybe I did blurt something out. If I did, it meant absolutely nothing."

Tully didn't know what to say or do. "Etta, it isn't important. I'm sorry I brought it up."

"I hope I haven't ruined our lunch, Bo. By the way, please tell me this really is a date. I'm badly in need of a date."

"Me too. It's definitely a date, Etta. I hope we can have another one soon."

"You don't think I'm weird, Bo?"

"Well, yeah."

It was a test. Etta passed. She laughed.

11

TULLY GOT BACK to the office in early afternoon. Lurch called to him as he came in. "Hey, boss, Susan says she's recovered three bullets from the vics. All three are .22-caliber shorts. I've got a theory about that."

"Let's hear it."

"I think the shooters used silencers."

"What makes you think that?"

"The fact the bullets were .22-caliber shorts. You want to kill somebody dead, you don't use .22 shorts. You're trying to hold the sound down. You want to really hold it down, you use silencers."

Tully scratched his head. "Interesting theory, Lurch. If the shooters used silencers, we're dealing with serious criminals. Our local boys wouldn't know a silencer from a bass drum. Susan sending the bullets over?"

"I told her I'd pick them up."

"Good. Too bad silencers don't leave marks. We may turn some up, though. Did you get the prints on the vics?"

"Yeah, but no matches, boss."

Tully headed back to his office. "Weird. I was hoping we might at least get a lead."

He stopped at Daisy's desk. Without looking up she said, "I know this can't be good. Besides, I smell a woman."

"You must be psychic."

"So, how was lunch with Etta Gorsich?"

"Not bad. Couldn't hold a candle to lunch with you, though."

Daisy checked her notepad. "I bet not. But to get back to business, Brian called. Said he wants you to meet him at three at Slade's Bar and Grill."

"Pugh say why?"

"He said it had to do with the killings up on Scotchman."

Tully frowned. "Slade's is in a rough part of town."

"Criminals seem fond of the place. Actually, he said to meet him across the street from Slade's."

"Probably wants me to watch his backside."

Daisy smiled. "I think the expression is 'watch his back.'"

"Is that it? I'm always getting my cop expressions mixed up."

Pugh was sitting in his blue Ford pickup across the street from Slade's. Tully drove up behind him in an unmarked department car. He walked up and climbed into the passenger seat of Pugh's truck. "What's the plan, Brian?"

"There's a hooker works out of here. Some guy beat her up pretty bad the other night. A small-time hood by the name of Jack Foley hangs out at Slade's. Deals some drugs and has a two-bit fencing operation. I could have busted him half a dozen times, but a year in jail would seem like a resort vacation to him. He tells me there are three very serious dudes in town. Been hanging out here all summer. The other night one of them cracked Bev—that's the hooker—up alongside the head with a pistol. Rang her bell pretty bad. The three guys have been sitting at her table about every evening they come in. I suspect Bev spouted out something she shouldn't have, probably something she heard from one of them."

Tully tugged thoughtfully on the corner of his mustache. "So, what do you need me for, Brian? This looks like a place I could get seriously hurt."

"Yeah, it is, boss. I thought you might like to come along to keep me from killing some of the patrons."

"I see. Well, I suppose I could do that."

They got out of the pickup and walked across the street. Tully pulled his Stetson low over his eyes and peered into the darkened interior. He could make out half a dozen figures moving around in the back. He and Pugh walked in and sat down at the bar. The bartender approached, eyeing them suspiciously.

"Two double shots of whiskey," Tully said.

Pugh gave Tully a look.

Tully winked at him. "Might as well enjoy this, Brian. Besides, I need something to settle my nerves."

The bartender brought their drinks. "Listen, fellas," he said in a low voice. "The guys here usually don't care for strangers dropping by. Be a good idea to finish your drinks and clear out."

Tully leaned across the bar and whispered, "We're actually pretty tough. Particularly my partner here. Sometimes I have to restrain him, keep him from going too far, you know what I mean?"

The bartender shrugged. "Just giving you some free advice."

Tully glanced at the group playing pool at the far end of the room. "It's Friday afternoon," he said. "Doesn't anyone in here have a regular job?"

"Yeah," the bartender said. "Me."

"Is Bev around?" Pugh asked.

"Yeah, she's sitting at the table over in the corner. She isn't feeling so good. A fella gave her a pretty rough time the other night and she's closed for business. Her, uh, boyfriend is that big guy shooting pool in the back with the guys. It's always a good idea to talk to him first, before you talk to Bev."

"Really," Tully said. "Well, we don't usually ask permission to talk to anybody, right, Bud?"

Pugh was studying the big guy.

"Bud!" Tully said, nudging Pugh in the ribs.

"Oh, yeah, right."

They picked up their drinks and walked over to Bev's table. She was holding an ice bag against the side of her head. As Pap might have said, she looked rode hard and put away wet.

She peered up at them with the eye that wasn't swollen shut. "I'm out of commission, guys."

Tully pulled out a chair and sat down. Pugh took the chair next to him. Tully said, "We need to talk to you, Bev, about the guy who smacked you with the pistol."

"You better talk fast, then," she said, "because here comes J.D."

A second later the huge man was looming over them. Tully and Pugh looked up at him.

The monster said, "I guess you guys don't know the rules, so I'll tell you. Clear out now, before I throw you out."

"I'm sorry, sir," Tully said, "but we were talking to the young lady."

"You ain't talking to nobody! Now out!"

Tully smiled at Pugh. "Your turn or my turn?"

"I think it's yours. I've had the last dozen. But I'll take it, boss. Hospital?"

"A couple days would be about right."

Pugh stood up. He stuck his head out around J.D. and yelled at the bartender. "You better call an ambulance. I think my friend here is having an attack of some kind."

The bartender stared at him. Then Tully heard two quick thumps. J.D. groaned and crumpled to the floor.

"Don't just stand there," Pugh yelled at the bartender. "This man is having an attack of some kind. Get an ambulance."

The bartender snatched up a phone and dialed.

Bev blinked her good eye. "Who are you guys, anyway?"

Tully wanted to say, I'm the masked man and this is my loyal sidekick, Tonto. Instead he said, "I'm Blight County sheriff Bo Tully, and this is my deputy Brian Pugh. I could arrest you if I wanted to, Bev, but instead I'm going to put you under protective custody. We need to know everything you can remember about that guy who hit you the other night."

She lifted the ice bag from the bruised side of her face. "It was one of the three guys come in here two, three times a week. I said something smart to the jerk and, wham, he hits me. Knocked me right out of my chair. I woke up on the floor. When I came to, they were gone. Joey said J.D. didn't lift a finger. I guess everybody was scared to death of them."

"And Joey is . . . ?" Pugh said.

She pointed with the ice bag. "He's the bartender. You can ask Joey about those guys, but he won't tell you nothing. He's as scared of them as everybody else."

Tully looked over at the bartender. "I think maybe he'll talk to me, Bev. Right now Brian here is going to take you to a hospital and have you checked out. Then he'll find you a place to stay. He'll get you everything you need. You don't have to worry. No one is going to hurt you anymore. I'll talk to you tomorrow."

The ambulance arrived so quickly Tully thought it must have been in the neighborhood. The medics wheeled in a stretcher, rolled J.D. onto it, and hauled him out. The big man was groaning and holding his side. Pugh helped Bev to his truck. Tully walked over to talk to the bartender. He showed him his badge.

"Joey, do you know if J.D. ever had an attack like that before?"

"I don't think so. Not that I know of, anyway."

"You might want to search your memory."

"Uh, yeah, now that you mention it, I think maybe."

"Good. Now, I want you to tell me everything you know about the guy who hit Bev."

"Gee, I don't know nothing about him. I'm the wrong person to ask."

Tully smiled. "It wasn't a request, Joey. I want you to tell me every last bit of information you have about that fellow and his two friends. If you're afraid of them, let me tell you, Joey, you're afraid of the wrong people."

"Okay, okay, I'll tell you what I know. It ain't that much. Him and his two friends have been hanging out here all summer. Actually, I think they first showed up sometime in the spring. They come in two, three times a week. The one hit Bev is the nice one of the three. The other two are stone cold. I can't even describe them."

"They been here today?"

"No, they haven't been back since the guy hit Bev. I hope they don't come back. The other two seemed pretty upset with the one that hit her. I don't think they like that kind of attention."

"You say they've been coming here since last spring?"

"Yeah. Maybe about the beginning of May. They never

caused no trouble before. They just sat and drank and talked to Bev. Even so, they scared people. I bet our business dropped by half after they started hanging out here."

Tully handed the bartender his card. "If any of them show up here again, Joey, give me a call."

Joey looked at the card. "Sure."

"Let me explain once again, Joey. I'm not making a request."

"Right, Sheriff. They show up, I'll give you a call."

For the first time, Tully noticed a strange silence in the bar. He looked toward the back. All the pool players were standing there, staring at him. "Go back to your game, boys," he called. "The entertainment is over."

12

TULLY DROPPED OFF his unmarked car in the Sheriff's Department's garage and went up to the office. Daisy had cleaned off her desk and was getting ready to leave.

"Any word from Pugh?" he asked.

"Yeah, he called from the hospital. He said the guy who had the attack at Slade's apparently had a kidney problem. They're going to run some tests."

"Good. I hope they're all painful. Anything else?"

"Yes, come to think of it. Your fortune-teller called and asked that you get in touch."

Tully grimaced. "First of all, Daisy, Etta Gorsich is not a fortune-teller. Second, she isn't mine."

"If you say so, boss."

Tully stood there and glared as Daisy picked up her purse

and strode out the door, her high heels clicking smartly on the marble-chip floor. Then he shrugged. By Monday he would be able to think up a good response. He would call Etta tomorrow.

He gulped down a hamburger and a beer in Crabbs Lounge and then drove over to the hospital. The cute red-headed nurse was working the admissions desk, but there was a line of people waiting for her attention. He sat down in the waiting room to give the line time to shorten. A drunk was at that moment pleading for her attention. She frowned sternly at him and pointed toward the waiting room. Tully grabbed up a magazine and pretended to read. He knew the drunk would head directly for him. He was a magnet for drunks. The guy sat down beside him. He looked and smelled as if he had been living in a Dumpster for the past month.

"I got beat up," he told Tully.

"That right?" Tully didn't look up from his magazine. He noticed he was staring at an ad on the latest weight-loss miracle.

"Yeah," the drunk said. "My brother did it."

"Oh."

"Yeah, my own brother. Can you believe that?"

Tully detected that the fellow hadn't been near bathwater in perhaps a year. He thought maybe his eyes were starting to water, because the weight-loss ad had blurred. He lowered the magazine and looked over at the nurse. A city cop was talking to her. The redhead pointed at the drunk. The cop turned and looked. He was a big guy, with a nose that had been broken too many times and multiple scars scattered about his face. His name was Tim Doyle and he worked the neighborhood that surrounded Slade's. He walked over and said hello to Tully. Then he spoke to the drunk. "You're coming with me, Willy."

"How come, Tim?" Willy said. "I didn't do nothing."

"You called in a complaint that Lyle assaulted you. Now I want you to come with me to hunt down Lyle. You make a complaint, we have to follow up on it."

"Okay." The drunk pushed himself up out of the chair.

Relieved, Tully lowered his magazine. "How's it going, Tim?"

"Same ol', same ol', Bo. Bet you're here to check out Scarlett."

"If by any chance you mean that lovely redheaded nurse over there, Tim, nothing could be further from my mind. What I really like is to stop by for conversations with people like Willy here."

"I bet. Well, Willy's all right. Come on, Willy."

Tully watched them. As the cop and Willy walked by the admissions desk, Scarlett called out, "Take care of yourself, Willy! You too, Tim!"

Willy beamed at her.

Tim shook his head. "He's going to be riding around with me the rest of the night, Scarlett."

The admittance line had disappeared for the moment. Tully got up and walked over. Odd, he thought. They're like some strange underground family here, cop, nurse, drunk, people who see one another almost every day. It's as if they look out for one another.

Scarlett glanced up. "You have to be Sheriff Bo Tully. I'm Scarlett O'Ryan. I've heard a lot about you."

"From whom, may I ask?"

"Your deputies, of course. They come in here to get patched up."

"I'm not surprised. They're a careless bunch. So you're the famous redhead. I can see now the boys haven't been exaggerating."

She laughed. "They're pretty nice boys, Sheriff."

"Call me Bo, please. Everybody does, even my criminals."

"I hear you're quite the fly fisherman, Bo."

Tully nodded. "Yeah, but I'm mostly a catch-and-eat kind of guy. Wet a fly now and then. That way I don't catch so many fish it becomes a distraction. I know some great fly-fishing streams, by the way, if you're interested in taking up the sport."

"Is that an invitation, Bo?"

"It definitely is. I'd be most happy to give you a few lessons."

She laughed. "Really? My father started me out with a fly rod when I was eight years old, if those are the kind of lessons you had in mind."

"They most certainly are. You probably can give me some lessons, Scarlett. Let's see, my mind seems to have gone blank for a second. Oh, yeah, I was going to say that right at the moment I'm tied up with some crimes and stuff like that. But I should be free in a couple of weeks. I'll, uh, be in touch. But back to business. You may have had a kid about twenty come in here to get a wound in his arm treated. Would have been the last few days."

"Sure, I remember him. I helped patch him up. He said he had fallen on a sharp stick but both the doctor and I thought it was a bullet wound. We cleaned it up, put in a couple stitches, and gave him a shot of penicillin."

"He give you a name and address?"

She shook her head. "He did but they were both obviously fake. He didn't have any ID on him. Called himself something like Bill Brown. I can look up the name and address for you if you want."

"Naw. They'd both be phony. Maybe if the wound gets infected he'll come in again. Give me a call, will you?"

"Sure."

"One other thing, Scarlett. My deputy Brian Pugh . . ."

"I know Brian."

"Of course you do. He was supposed to bring in a not-so-young lady earlier. Is he still here by any chance?"

"I haven't seen him leave. Hold on a sec, I'll check." She punched a couple of buttons and spoke into a speaker. "Is Brian still back there?"

Brian? Tully thought. So he's that well known around here.

"Yeah," a voice said. "Who wants him?"

"His boss. At emergency reception."

"He's on his way."

Brian came striding out. "So you tracked me down, Bo. What's up?"

"I was just checking on our two patients."

"They're going to keep Bev a couple of days for observation. She was hurt a lot worse than anybody at Slade's knew or let on. She'll be all right, though. J.D. apparently had a bruised kidney or something like that. Probably got it from a fall. But he should be out tomorrow."

"Good. J.D. will probably be politer to strangers in the future."

"I suspect so."

Brian nodded at the nurse. "I see you've met Scarlett."

"Bo and I may go fishing together in a couple of weeks," she said.

Pugh laughed. "I told you he works fast."

"Actually, Brian, I think I was the one who worked fast."

Scarlett was about to add something when her phone rang. She picked it up and said, "Blight City Emergency." She listened. "Yeah, Tim, he's still here."

She handed the phone to Tully. "Tim Doyle."

Tully took the phone. "Hi, Tim. What's up?"

"Bo, we just had a shooting outside the K-Bar convenience store on the north side. I think it's something you might be interested in. I'm on my way there. You want to swing by?"

"I'll be there in fifteen minutes, Tim. Thanks for the call."

Scarlet looked up at him. "Business, I bet."

"Afraid so."

"You need me, boss?" Pugh said.

"Naw, I'll handle it."

"Good," Pugh said. "I've invited Scarlett out for a late-night snack after her shift ends."

Tully gave the nurse a wink. "Watch out for this guy. He's got a bad rep."

She laughed. "Don't you all?"

"Well, sure, but Brian is one of the worst."

Tully pulled into the K-Bar lot and parked. The lot was crowded with police cars, an ambulance, and a fire-station emergency team. Several police officers were standing around a pickup truck. Tim was standing next to Willy, who was still drunk but an interested observer of the crime scene. Tim glanced in Tully's direction and then started to walk over. Tully could now see the side of the truck. He groaned. The driver's-side window was a spiderweb of glass, with portions completely missing. He could see bullet holes in the blue door on the red truck. He'd told Lennie, "You can't be dumb." But did he listen?

Tim walked up. "We checked for the guy's ID. He hasn't got any on him."

"His name is Lennie Frick, Tim. He lived at Four-oh-five East Sharp."

Tim took out his notebook and wrote the name and address down.

Tully said, "He did a bit of time a while back. He wasn't a bad guy, just a dumb one. He might have seen whoever did the killings up on Scotchman." He nodded toward the truck. "This pretty much proves it."

Tim looked up from his notebook. "So you think you know who did it?"

"Yeah, I'm pretty sure. I don't have any names, though. Not to mention proof."

"Things are pretty bad when a kid goes out for a six-pack of beer and gets blown away."

"Acme?"

"How did you know?"

"I'm psychic."

"Looks like the shooter used a .22," Tim said. "Very small bullet holes. I counted six. No casings anywhere. So it was probably a revolver. Strange thing is, nobody we've talked to heard any shots."

"I'm not surprised," Tully said. "I suspect the killer used a silencer."

"A silencer! Sounds like Blight City is getting into the big time."

Tully slept most of the day on Saturday. That night he called Pete Reynolds. "Pete, any chance you could take me for a spin in your airplane tomorrow?"

"Why, sure, Bo. For some reason I had the idea you hated flying."

"I do, Pete, but there's some stuff I need to check out from the air. Just a hunch I have."

13

SUNDAY MORNING, TULLY had no trouble containing his enthusiasm for the flight. He stopped at McDonald's and had his usual Egg McMuffin and coffee, then drove out to the airport. Pete was already there, tinkering with something on his plane.

"Doing some major repairs, I see."

"Naw, nothing major. A bolt here, a nut there, that sort of thing. Where we headed today, Bo?"

"I'm trying to solve a crime. People are getting killed for no reason I can figure out. I could understand if they were bankers or lawyers or people of that ilk, but they are just poor dumb kids scarcely twenty years old, if that. Anyway, I think Scotchman Creek may hold an answer."

Pete tossed a wrench back in his toolbox. "I haven't fished Scotchman in years but I can tell you the lower part of that crick is one unholy mess. The beavers run a series of dams crisscrossing each other all through there. It's impossible even to find your way to the crick anymore. Beavers helped turn it into one giant swamp. Some places the water comes up to your armpits, and that's if you ain't standing in quicksand. It was that way thirty years ago and probably a lot worse now. I imagine the beavers flooded hundreds of acres since then. Some mighty fine timber locked away in there but the beavers made getting it out more expensive than it's worth."

"I guess beavers aren't totally useless, then."

"Easy for you to say, Bo."

A few minutes later they were on the tarmac, sitting shoulder to shoulder in the plane's cockpit. As far as Tully could tell, the plane didn't bother to taxi but jumped into the air from a standstill, hurling him back into his seat.

"What kind of motor you got on this thing anyway, Pete?"

"The most powerful money can buy. No sense flying an underpowered aircraft, I always say. I tell you what, Bo, we'll circle around Scotchman Peak to warm up, and then cruise back down the crick away from the mountain. You see that clearing in those trees down there? Well, I had a chopper back then and had to put it down in that very spot a couple summers ago."

"Wow! That clearing doesn't look anywhere big enough to land a helicopter in."

"Shoot, until I landed, there wasn't any clearing there at all! Flipped over and mowed down trees like tall grass."

"I see."

The plane swept up and around Scotchman Peak. At some points, the vertical rock slabs of the peak looked close enough for Tully to reach out and touch.

Pete pointed to the base of a sheer granite wall. "You see that little lake down there, Bo? You ever fished it?"

"No. I didn't even know it existed."

"Hardly anybody does. It's haunted."

"Haunted? I've never even heard of a haunted lake."

"I hiked in there, oh, it must be twenty-five years ago now. Had my youngest son, Alan, with me. It was one heck of a hike and we planned to spend a couple of days in there, camping and relaxing. Alan was about fourteen. You see how the trees are thick as fur on a dog's back and how they come right up to the edge of the water? Oh, shoot, we've gone too far. I'll take us around again."

Tully shook his head. "It's okay, Pete, I saw the trees!"

The plane had already leaned over on its side as it made a sharp turn around the peak and back over the lake. Tully could now look straight down out his side window and see how close the trees came to the lake.

Pete tapped him on the shoulder. "You see, Bo? I can always take us around again."

"I see, Pete!"

Pete seemed to scratch an itch somewhere on his back while leveling off the plane. "Well, when Alan and I got to the lake, trout was rising all over it but the trees come down so close to the water we couldn't back-cast. There was a big snowbank at one end of the lake, almost like a glacier. So Alan fights his way through the trees and climbs out on the snow and then he's got plenty of room to cast, and right away he starts hauling in fish. I got a little frantic because I can't stand for one of my sons to outfish me. But then I found this narrow log stretching out into the water and I was able to walk out three-fourths of its length. The water was shallow under the log, maybe six inches deep, crystal clear, the stones on the bottom sharp as a picture. I make three or four casts and don't get a hit. Then I notice this little wake, like maybe a tiny, invisible shark fin traveling through the water. It starts out in the middle of the lake, makes a wide half circle, and comes right up under my feet. I'm looking straight down into that little wake, Bo, and you gotta believe there wasn't nothing in the middle of it, nothing making it that I could see. It was like an invisible finger had drawn it through the water. Well, I stood there a couple of seconds, trying to think what might make the thing, and I look out into the lake and another little wake has formed. And this one swings around in the opposite direction of the first one and comes right up under my feet! And Bo, I ain't makin' this up! There was nothing in the middle of that one either!"

"So what did you do?"

"I yelled at Alan, 'We going home, son! Grab your gear!' He yells back, 'How come, Pa?' and I yells, ''Cause this lake is haunted!'"

"You're telling me Alan didn't even question you about the lake's being haunted?"

"Nope, he never said a word about it, just packed up and started down the trail. Maybe it was mostly because he didn't want to be that far back in the mountains with a lunatic, I don't know. You're the only other person I've ever told about that lake being haunted. Alan's never mentioned it either."

I wish you hadn't told me, Tully thought.

"Later I heard the Indians wouldn't go within ten miles of that lake."

"I'm with the Indians," Tully said. "You don't suppose the haunt reaches this far up, do you, Pete?"

"Good point, Bo."

Pete leveled the plane and headed down Scotchman Creek, swooping in low over the trees. Because of the wings on the plane, Tully couldn't see much of the creek below. He pulled his camera out of his kit. "Can you tilt the plane so I can see below the wing, Pete?"

"Tell you what, Bo. I'll circle the peak again and then turn her up on her side. That way you can photograph the whole of Scotchman Creek. You snap pictures like crazy and then you can examine them in comfort when you get back to the office."

"Sounds like a deal."

Pete revved up the engine, circled the peak, and brought the plane back over the creek on its side. Tully snapped pictures for all he was worth.

"You want to do that again?" Pete asked, leveling out the plane.

"No!"

"Good! My old flight instructor used to tell me never to do that. Said planes can drop right out of the air when you do. It's never happened to me, though, except that one time."

"I don't want to hear about it!"

14

BY THE TIME Tully got to the office Monday morning, his pulse had almost returned to normal. He walked over to Lurch and handed him the memory card from the camera. "See what you can do with these photos, if there are any. I haven't been able to make myself look at them."

"I'll run them through Photoshop, boss, and get them sharpened up."

"Good. Call me when you've got them ready. If they don't turn out, we may have to do the shoot over. You like to fly, Lurch?"

The Unit gave an exaggerated shudder. "You know I hate it!"

"I don't care. If the photos don't turn out, you're going up!"

Lurch slid the memory card into his computer. "Take my word for it, boss, they'll turn out."

Lurch's fingers began to fly over the keyboard. "And now somebody whacks Lennie Frick. No way Lennie ever did anything to anybody to get taken out like that."

"You're right, Lurch. I don't know what's going on." Tully walked over to Daisy's desk. She was hunched over her computer, frowning in concentration. "You believe in water spirits, Daisy?"

"Hunh?" she said, glancing up.

"Never mind." He walked into his office.

He picked up his phone and dialed the Social Security office. A woman answered. "Social Security, Jennifer speaking."

"Jennifer, this is Sheriff Bo Tully."

"Hi, Sheriff. What can I do for you?"

"I've been thinking of switching sides and taking up crime. Now, suppose I stole my old father's Social Security check. How would I go about cashing it?"

Jennifer went into a brief description of how the crime might be pulled off. She explained that as soon as the legal recipient of the check notified Social Security he or she hadn't received the check, an investigation would take place to determine if and how the check had been stolen. "It would be very hard to cash the check without proper ID, Bo."

"Suppose I killed Pap. Then he couldn't complain. I now use his ID to cash the check at a bank drive-through. How about that?"

"In that case, you might get away with it for a while, as long as the victim couldn't complain and you had the proper ID, say Pap's driver's license, that you could send into the teller."

"Thanks, Jennifer. I'd appreciate you not mentioning this call to anybody, just in case I decide to kill Pap for reasons other than his piddling Social Security check."

"I won't tell a soul, Bo. So, when are you thinking of switching over to crime?"

"I'll see how this week goes, sweetheart."

He hung up, slid his chair back, and propped his feet on his desk. He sat there tugging on his mustache while he thought about Orville Poulson and Ray Crockett. Orville had supposedly gone off on his endless trip in January, leaving Crockett in charge of the ranch. If Crockett had killed him, he could have buried Orville anywhere on the ranch and there would be no way to find the body. The ground would be frozen in January, though—impossible to dig a grave. He supposed Crockett could have hidden the body under some hay in the barn and let it freeze. Then he could have waited for the ground to thaw in the spring. Tully thought he might follow Etta Gorsich's suggestion and look under the house. The ground there wouldn't have been frozen in January. It might be tough to get a search warrant for a body when you don't even know if there is one. Still, maybe he could get a search warrant from Judge Patterson. As Daisy liked to point out, Patterson was the best possible kind of judge: old and senile and one who would give Tully anything he asked for. And some people thought the justice system had gone to hell. What did they know?

Lurch opened his door. "I've got those photos up on the computer, boss. You want to come take a look?"

Tully got up and walked with Lurch back to his computer. The photo on the screen was surprisingly sharp, considering the circumstances in which it had been taken.

"What's that thing hanging down in front of the lens?" Lurch asked.

"Probably my tongue." Tully could make out a large patch of swamp below. He switched to another photo and then worked through the series. "Perfect! Just as I suspected."

"What did you suspect, Bo?"

Just then Daisy walked across the room and said in a low voice, "An Angela Phelps to see you, boss."

Tully glanced across the briefing room. A woman stood there, tapping her foot in a way that suggested impatience. He vaguely wondered why Daisy hadn't simply yelled across the room in her usual fashion. She apparently read his mind.

"FBI," she whispered.

"You're in for it now, boss," the Unit said.

"Nothing I can't handle, Lurch. The agent is a woman, after all."

Lurch smiled and shook his head as if in disbelief.

Daisy returned to her desk and showed the agent into Tully's office. He strolled slowly across the briefing room and stuck his head in the door.

"Be right with you, miss."

The look on the agent's face suggested she intended to truck no nonsense from this cracker sheriff. He walked back over to Daisy's desk.

"Maybe I should let you handle this, Daisy," he whispered. "The agent appears a bit piqued."

"That's a mild way of putting it. I would say she's totally—"

Tully walked into his office without hearing the rest of Daisy's assessment.

"Agent Phelps," he said. "Very nice of you to drop by. Please have a chair. You are by far the most attractive FBI agent I've encountered so far."

"I am impervious to flattery, Sheriff Tully. So it's useless to try it on me. Furthermore, your other wiles are equally useless. I have read through the rather thick file we have on you, and even a much larger one we have on your father. Both are devoid of any evidence of your having ever given the slightest assistance to the FBI."

He pulled up a chair and sat down next to her. Her black hair, neatly coiffed, had a bit of gray threaded through it. She wore a crisp white blouse under her black suit jacket, and there was no wedding ring on her finger. She was definitely a prospect.

"I find that hard to believe," he said.

"That we've never had an iota of cooperation from either of you?"

"No, that you have a thick file on me. So, what can I do for you, Agent Phelps?"

"It's our understanding that you have recently had three murders in a national forest and somehow neglected to inform us. As you probably know, the FBI likes to be notified whenever there's a crime on federal land, particularly if guns are involved."

"I was just getting to that. Yes, I kept telling myself, I must get word of the killings to the FBI. And here you are already, Agent Phelps, just as I was about to lift the phone and call."

"I bet. All right, tell me what happened, in case all the news accounts I've read are incorrect."

"I think the news accounts are surprisingly correct. Let me think. I have so many crimes going on I can hardly keep them straight. Okay, here goes. I had been working nights and days and weekends, so I decided to take Thursday of last week off and go huckleberry picking up on Scotchman Peak. That's when I discovered the three dead bodies in the huckleberry patch. All three had been shot in the back of the head. Young fellows, probably not even twenty yet. They appeared to have been farmworkers, guys who spent a lot of time working in the dirt. We have a few leads we're following up, but that's about it."

Agent Phelps scribbled furiously in her notepad. Tully could see she knew shorthand. "So, do you have any idea what the motive might have been?" she asked.

"Not a clue. It couldn't have been robbery. These guys probably hadn't seen a dime in the last six months. One of my associates claims it had to be money. My own guess is they knew something and were shot to shut them up."

"Anything else?"

Tully hesitated. He didn't want the FBI in town shaking things up and scaring off his criminals. "Listen, Angela, I'll tell you something but it's just a speculation of mine. Will you keep it under your hat until I get it checked out?"

"As you can see, Sheriff, I'm not wearing a hat. But if I were wearing one, I would keep your secret under it for a while. But you have to let me in on the investigation."

"I can do that. Can you stay in Blight City for a week or so?"

"I probably can, unless something or someone gets blown up somewhere else."

"Good. What I want to tell you is that I think there were four intended victims up at the huckleberry patch, but one of them got away. He was creased by a bullet and had the wound treated in emergency at the local hospital. I'm going out this afternoon to look for him. If we can find the fourth guy, if there is one, our case is solved, except for catching the killers. He'll at least know who the bad guys are. And let me say there is absolutely nothing to that other aspect of my fame with which you need concern yourself. I'm always a perfect gentleman." He watched her closely to see if the little grammatical flourish had made any impression. Apparently not. "If you would like to join me in my search, I would be most happy to have you along."

Agent Phelps smiled. She had perfect white teeth, a dimple in her left cheek, and deep blue eyes. She was surprisingly pretty when she smiled. "It's a deal, Sheriff."

15

A HALF HOUR later Tully and the FBI were cruising the neighborhood where Scotchman Peak Road crossed the railroad tracks into town. The street they drove on was unpaved and thick with dust. The houses were ancient and large, with numerous old vehicles parked out front. Several dried-up and weedy lawns were adorned with cars up on blocks. One yard contained an assortment of upscale motorcycles. Three men lounged on the porch steps, smoking and drinking beer.

"This looks like a good place to get some local information," Tully said, pulling over to the edge of the road.

"It looks more like a good place to get a serious beating," the agent said.

Tully got out. "It might be better if you stay in the car,

Agent Phelps." She didn't object. Tully strolled up the walk. He heard her window go down, so she must have reached over and turned on the ignition key. He suspected she had also drawn her gun.

The three men eyed him coldly.

"Howdy, boys," he said. "Nice day. I see you're out getting yourselves a little sun."

"And a little privacy," one of them said. He had a ponytail that flopped over his shoulder as he started to get up.

The apparent boss of the group, a large, tattooed, bearded, and beaded man, put his hand on Ponytail's arm. Ponytail sat back down.

"Relax, Lefty," the big man said. "No point getting yourself knocked senseless before we even know what the sheriff wants. So, how you doin' these days, Bo?"

"Fair to middling, Mitch. You been staying out of trouble?"

"What do you think?"

"I think not, but I've got other things on my mind today."

"Wouldn't be those killings up on Scotchman, would it?"

Tully put his foot up on the porch's first step and rested his hands on the back of his leg. "Yeah, it would. And also the killing of Lennie the other night."

The big biker shook his head. "Lennie never hurt nobody in his entire life. He was dumb as a rock but he was okay. And he knew how to keep his mouth shut."

"You and your friends here probably even helped him with his beer-can collection."

"We did what we could."

"The killers up on Scotchman probably didn't know Lennie possessed the talent for keeping mum about what he observed. It's likely he saw them up on the road and could have identified them."

Mitch leaned forward. "How come they wiped out those kids? You got any idea, Bo?"

"I've got nothing, Mitch. Pap says it had to be money, but I bet the kids didn't have a penny among them. I figure they knew something and were killed to shut them up. These are bad guys who did it—no offense."

Mitch snuffed out his cigarette on the step and flicked the butt into the yard. "Well, I'd like to help you, Bo, but we haven't seen any strangers hanging about all summer. We hear anything about who killed Lennie, I'll get in touch."

"Good. I knew you would. But what I'm looking for right now is maybe a house where a bunch of kids might be hanging out, a bunch of young guys, maybe some girls, probably runaway kids with nowhere to go but who may be getting by in a big old house around here."

Mitch turned and looked at the skinny one of the three, a mop of orange hair ballooning out from his head. "Tell him, Red. You may need a favor from the sheriff someday."

Red's jaw sagged open. He slowly shook his head.

"I said tell him."

"Uh, sure, Sheriff," Red said. "That big old house down there on the corner." He pointed. "The one with the broken picket fence around it. Must be a dozen hippie kids staying there at times."

"Thanks. I'll remember this, Red. What's your last name?"

"Smith."

"I'd already guessed that." He reached down and shook Mitch's hand. "I appreciate the help."

"I only do it for Lennie."

"I know, Mitch. Surely you didn't expect me to think you were getting soft in your old age."

As Tully got back in the car he noticed the FBI agent slipping her gun back into her shoulder bag.

"I see you were ready for action, Agent Phelps."

"You may call me Angie, Sheriff. And yes, I was. That's a mean-looking bunch."

"Those boys not only look mean, they are. I much prefer to deal with good guys, but good guys don't know anything."

"You're right about that. So, did you find out anything?" She kept her eyes on the bikers as Tully pulled out into the street.

"I found out what I was looking for, but I don't know if what I was looking for is what I need to be looking for."

"I can understand that."

Tully pointed to the house on the corner. "The bikers told me a bunch of hippie kids live there, probably mostly runaways or kids whose parents booted them out on the street. A boy with a bullet wound in his arm was picked up on the road down the mountain a ways from where the killings took place. The logging-truck driver who picked him up dropped him off in this neighborhood. So my hunch is he might at some point have lived at that house. Maybe he went back there after the shooting. Maybe he's still there."

He parked in front of the house with the broken picket fence. Agent Phelps got out with him.

"You don't have to bother with this," he told her.

"Yes, I do," she said. "I'm not along to observe Blight County law-enforcement methods."

He glanced at her as if surprised. "I thought you were."

"No."

"All right! Then I'll use my usual Blight County law-enforcement methods. I get results a lot quicker with them."

"That's my understanding, Sheriff."

"Call me Bo."

"Bo."

Tully knocked on the door. A girl's voice called from inside, "Who's there?"

"Sheriff Bo Tully."

"And FBI agent Angela Phelps!" Angie called out.

"There's nobody home!"

"I'll talk to you, then," Tully said, pushing open the screen door and stepping inside.

A teenage girl in tan shorts and a man's work shirt sat on a couch that looked as if it had spent several winters outdoors. "You can't just walk in here like you owned the place. Don't you need a warrant or something?"

"That's only on TV," Tully told her. "Besides, I'm not here to arrest anybody." He turned back to the door. "It's okay, Agent Phelps. This young lady invited us in."

Angie stepped in, shaking her head.

"I did not!" the girl said. She seemed to relax a little upon seeing a woman. "I really don't know anything about anything. And I'll be in big trouble if anybody finds out I talked to the police."

"How old are you?" Angie asked.

"Twenty-one."

Angie held out her FBI identification. The girl bent over and examined it. "I never talked to anybody from the FBI before."

"What's your name?" the agent asked.

"Jenny."

"Well, Jenny, you tell us what we need to know, we'll take care of you."

"Yeah, right, in juvie!" She rolled her eyes.

"No, not in juvie," Tully said. "We'll find you a place that's safe and where you're free to go as you please." He pulled up a ratty-looking armchair and sat down gingerly.

"Yeah, I bet. So what do you want to know?"

"A young man stopped by here a while back. He had injured his arm and went down to the emergency room to get the wound treated. Is he still living here?"

"No."

"Listen, Jenny, I'm not looking for him because he broke any laws. I think he may be in danger."

A nervous look came over Jenny's face. "Everybody seems to be looking for him."

"Who else?"

"Some bad guys. Really bad guys. They burst in and searched the whole house, but he had left already. They had guns."

Tully was silent for a moment. "Do you know where he went?"

"No."

The FBI agent spoke up. "Jenny, it's very important that we find him before the bad guys do. Can you tell us his name?"

The girl stared at the agent, searching her face for some kind of assurance. Then she said, "Craig."

"What's his last name?"

Jenny thought for a moment. "Wilson, I think."

"Do his parents live around here?"

"I don't think he has any parents. He sometimes talked about an uncle, a long-haul truck driver. Craig said he planned on becoming a truck driver like his uncle. He worked all summer hoping he would make enough for a down payment on a truck."

The agent jotted something in her notebook. "Do you know where the uncle lives?"

"Spokane."

"Do you know his name?"

"No."

"Where do your parents live?"

"Don't have any." She looked about uneasily.

"What's your last name?"

"Smith."

Tully handed her his card. "Jenny Smith, you have been a big help. If you need anything at all, you call me. We'll take care of you."

She looked at the card in her hand. "Okay."

"It might be a good idea not to mention to your friends that we were here. If the bad guys come back and you need help in a hurry, run to the house down the street where the biker gang hangs out. The leader is Mitch. Tell him you're a friend of mine and he'll take care of you."

"I know who he is," she said. "He's scary."

Tully smiled. "He's scary all right, Jenny. But I'm a whole lot scarier, and Mitch knows it. He'll keep you safe."

Back in the car, Angie said, "I thought that was nice, the way you told Jenny to run into the arms of a biker gang if she gets scared."

Tully sighed. "Mitch will protect her."

"You could have taken her to child services."

"Arrest her, you mean. For all you know, Jenny could be eighteen. She could be an adult."

They continued their argument all the way back to the courthouse. Tully introduced Angie to Daisy, Lurch, Herb, and a couple of deputies hanging out in the briefing room. He and Angie went into his office and he closed the door. She settled into the chair across the desk from him and he flopped into his chair.

"How tall are you?" he asked.

"Five eight. Why?"

"What's your shoe size?"

She eyed him skeptically. "None of your business."

Tully waved a hand as if to dismiss that idea. "Listen, I want you with me on the next phase of this investigation. That's a compliment, by the way. I've never before taken a woman with me on an investigation, particularly an FBI woman. Since you're the first, I want you to be properly outfitted."

"You're going to buy me an outfit?"

"Sure. Well, actually, the county is. So what's your shoe size?"

"Eight. I assure you, however, that the FBI is perfectly capable of buying me an outfit."

"Yeah, I know, but the Fed penny crunchers would demand a bunch of info and explanations and all that."

"Well, I suppose the county could loan me the outfit for a day."

"Now you're talking. So here's the plan. There's a swamp out north of town a ways. I have a feeling that swamp has something to do with the killings up on Scotchman."

"A swamp? A swamp was involved in the killings?"

Tully tapped a pencil on his desk. "Maybe. Years ago beavers built a dam across Scotchman Creek. The water backed up and flooded out the road, and the county had to raise the level of the road. Then the beavers built another dam and another dam, until they had dams stretching miles back through the woods. Other creeks fed into the whole mess. The area is impassable."

Angie leaned forward. "Let me see if I understand this. You think this swamp had something to do with killings that took place miles away, and now you and I are going to make our way into this impassable bog in search of something. Exactly what is this something?"

"I wish I knew. I flew over the area yesterday and shot a bunch of photos. I saw a few spots I want to check out and some things that looked like buildings. I don't know why someone would build anything out in the middle of a swamp."

"So what's the plan, Bo?"

"I'll pick you up at your hotel about eight tomorrow morning. You probably should wear work pants, if you have them."

"I always travel with a pair of jeans."

"Good. Do you have a hat with a brim on it?"

"How on earth could I forget an essential like that!"

Tully made himself a note. "I'll bring you a one-size-fits-all cap. My head lice have pretty much cleared up and I don't think you have to be concerned about them. The reason I mention a hat with a brim is that the mosquitoes may be fierce in the swamp. They'll lap up mosquito dope like it's good bourbon. The only way to keep them off you is to wear mosquito netting so it hangs down over the brim of the hat, but a cap will work. Wear a sweatshirt. It'll be hot but better than getting eaten alive. Otherwise, wear a shirt on top of a shirt. And wear gloves."

Angie shook her head and smiled. "This outing sounds like a lot of fun."

"Yeah, it's fairly typical of my workdays, imposing law and order on Blight County. You take care of your clothes and I'll bring everything else we need. Oh, and bring your hip boots."

"Let me see, I'm not sure where I left my hip boots. Now that I think of it, I don't own hip boots."

Tully laughed. "I can scarcely imagine an FBI agent without hip boots. I'll take care of the hip boots for you. Oh yeah, and come armed."

"I always come armed, Sheriff, particularly when I'm going to spend a day with a perfect gentleman." She flashed her smile again. "See you in the morning."

Agent Angela Phelps got up and left.

Tully stood in his doorway and watched Daisy watch her go.

Daisy turned and looked at him. "Nice tight skirt," she said. "And that FBI sure knows how to use it."

"Really?" Tully said. "I never noticed."

Daisy laughed. "That would be the first time in your life, boss."

"No, I missed you one day when you walked across the briefing room."

He went over to his desk and dialed Blight City General Hospital.

"Scarlett O'Ryan, please. Sheriff Bo Tully calling."

Scarlett came on the line. "Hi, Bo. What's up?"

"You're a fly-fisher, right?"

"Right."

"That means you have hip boots."

"Yeah. And waders too."

"Waders! They might be even better. I need to borrow them for an FBI agent who's about five eight with an eight shoe size."

"Sure, you can borrow them. Sounds like a pretty small FBI agent."

"This agent is a woman."

"I should have known. Anyway, sure, you can borrow the waders for her. They should fit. What's the big adventure?"

"Don't tell anyone, but we're going to investigate a swamp in the lower part of Scotchman Creek. On the other hand, if you don't hear from me by tomorrow night, you can tell someone. I suggest Brian Pugh. You know Brian. He's already saved my life a couple of times and should be good for one more."

"You got it, Bo. Swing by my place about eight tonight. I should be home by then and you can pick up the waders." She gave him her address.

Tully stopped at her apartment on his way home that evening.

She handed him the waders and invited him in for dinner.

"By all means. I could use a home-cooked meal. What are we having?"

"Hungry-Man turkey dinners."

"One of my favorites."

Tully got home a little after midnight.

16

TULLY PICKED UP Angie at her hotel the next morning. She was dressed as he recommended. He handed her the cap and she adjusted it to fit as they drove.

“This will be my first job off-pavement,” she told him. “I called my boss to report in, and he was thrilled to learn I was spending the day with you in a swamp. He wanted to know what we’re looking for. I told him I didn’t know and that I was simply following you. He said, ‘Oh, great!’ So the FBI is well aware of your activities and you can see the level of its appreciation.”

“That’s nice. I try my best to cooperate with the bureau every chance I get. You can’t imagine how pleased I am it has such a good opinion of me. By the way, how did you slip up?”

“What do you mean?”

Tully smiled as he turned off onto the Scotchman Peak Road. "FBI agents are usually sent to Montana or Idaho as punishment for having slipped up. So how did you slip up?"

"Perhaps getting born female."

"That would be my guess."

"Well, I'll have you know the FBI doesn't punish agents. Furthermore, I have had a very successful career. The bureau has long had a special interest in Blight County, and that's why they sent one of their top agents to investigate a crime here."

Tully glanced over and saw that she was blushing.

"I see. Sorry I asked."

"You should be." She turned and stared out her side window. "And I did something really stupid."

"Ah. Well, being the perfect gentleman I am, I won't attempt a guess."

"Thanks."

Tully backed his Explorer into a turnout next to the swamp. As soon as they got out he expected mosquitoes to swarm around them in black, hungry, vibrating clouds. Nothing. While Angie pulled on her gloves, Tully draped the mosquito netting over her cap. He tucked the bottom of the netting into her collar, leaving enough to billow out around her head. Then he handed her the waders.

"I thought you were bringing hip boots."

"I prefer hip boots on women because they're a lot cuter

than chest waders. The problem with hip boots, they're always one inch too short for the water." He handed her a strap with a buckle on one end. "Fasten this around your, uh, top, and it will keep most of the water out if you fall down."

Angie shook her head. "This is already so much fun I can hardly believe it. Aren't you going to put on some hip boots or waders?"

"Naw, I prefer to get by with as little as possible." He draped the mosquito netting over his hat and tucked the bottom into the sweatshirt he wore over his blue denim work shirt. "On the other hand, I can't stand mosquitoes. Why we're not being assaulted by them already, I don't know." He handed her a walking stick. "If you start to get sucked down by quicksand, hold the stick out to me. That way I can pull you out without getting too close."

"This gets better all the time."

"Doesn't it, though?"

Tully tried to take her by the hand but she shook him off. They went down a steep incline, sliding down on a carpet of pine needles and grabbing at tree branches to slow their momentum. The woods below were thick with trees and dark with shadows. Squirrels complained shrilly at their approach, and for several minutes birdsong died away as they thrashed their way through the trees. They came to an opening in the woods where towering ferns grew over mossy mounds that had once been logs, discarded in the distant past for some unknown reason. The moisture on the ferns soaked Tully sufficiently that he began to wish he too had worn waders.

Through a gap in the trees sunlight flashed on water. They were approaching the beaver dams and already he could smell the swamp.

The first dam wound off through trees long dead and whitened with age. The beavers had woven brush, logs, and driftwood into a dam that somehow held back an immense body of water. He and Angie approached the dam from the bottom, with water cascading and spouting through billions of small openings. The sound was almost musical. Standing beneath the front of the dam, Tully could barely see over the top of it. He wondered what kind of blueprint beavers had for creating such a structure—or did they simply start aimlessly weaving stuff together until they had a dam? Did they even think about creating a dam? Maybe dams were simply accidents that resulted from their fooling around, much like the Army Corps of Engineers' accomplishments.

Tully led Angie over to where the dam abutted the hill they had just descended. As they slowly worked their way out onto the dam, Tully explained the art of walking on beaver dams. Mid-lecture, one of his legs shot down, as far as his knee. As he tried to disentangle his foot from the network of willows, branches, and small dead trees, he told her, "Remember the words I used when my foot shot down this hole. They are very important when walking a beaver dam."

Angie laughed. "There were quite a few words, but I'll try to remember them. By the way, what is it we're supposed to be looking for?"

"A couple of islands." He ran his hands down his pant leg

and squeezed out as much water as he could. The water wasn't stained with blood, even though his leg felt as if it should be. He hated pain without blood. "I spotted the islands from the air. One of them contained something that looked like a building, a structure of some kind anyway. I asked myself why anyone would build something out here in the middle of a swamp. There were some large patches of bare ground, too. As you can tell, any ground we can see that sticks up above the water is covered with grass three feet high. And there are some massive crops of cattails everywhere you look. If we get stranded out here, we can survive on cattail roots. Ever eat any cattail roots, Angie?"

"No. Have you?"

"No! I read a book one time that said they were edible. Of course, there's a big difference between good and edible. Edible, I think, only means you won't die from it."

Angie stumbled and fell against him. "Sorry, this is my first time on a beaver dam." She steadied herself. "At least I now know the words to say if one of my legs breaks through."

Tully smiled. "Yes, remember those words. They are very important. But perhaps we shouldn't be creating such a high profile of ourselves." His eyes scanned the edge of the woods. "There could be someone who doesn't want us out here poking around."

"Now you tell me."

"Yes, well, you never know. Let's walk below the dam. It's pretty watery down there, but nothing you shouldn't be able to handle with your waders."

"Sounds good to me."

They worked their way down the face of the dam. Some openings spurted water through with considerable force. After working their way to the base of the dam, they moved out away from the gushing water. The shallower channels of water scarcely rose to Tully's knees. It had been an unusual stroke of brilliance that made him think of the chest waders for Angie. If he had remembered a life preserver, he could have floated her across several of the deeper pools. Occasionally, he detected signs of dissatisfaction on the face of the FBI agent. Then a string of words suddenly erupted from her as she stumbled again.

"No, no," he said. "Use those words only when you step through a hole in a beaver dam."

"Very funny! I'll tell you something, Bo! This is the last time I let some cracker sheriff talk me into slogging my way through a swamp!"

Tully smiled. "It requires a certain charm and talent."

"What, wading through a swamp?"

"No, persuading a pretty woman to do it."

He heard a sharp crack somewhere above them on the backwater of the dam, but close. He automatically ducked, then turned to check on Angie. She was crouched down, the water almost to the top of her waders. A revolver had magically appeared in her right hand. "Was that shot intended for us?"

"Probably," he said. "But I don't think we need worry. Beavers are notoriously poor shots."

"Are you trying to be funny?"

"Yeah. Sorry about that. That crack you heard wasn't a gunshot. It was a beaver slapping his tail on the water. That's a warning to other beavers that there's danger in the area. Namely us."

"A beaver?"

"It's a bit different from a gunshot but close enough to get your attention. I imagine by now all beavers in the area have lit out for their hiding places."

Angie slowly straightened up and tucked her pistol down somewhere inside her chest waders. "Whew! I thought somebody had us. It was so close."

"You're not the only one," Tully said. "I imagine the crack of a beaver tail raised the hair of more than one mountain man trudging through hostile beaver country. Not all beavers are hostile, but some are."

They at last came to where the beaver dam abutted against a higher piece of land. Tully thought it must be one of the islands he had spotted from the air. Water gushed through the dam and they had to fight their way up through it. Before pushing to the top of the dam, Tully stuck his head up and looked around. They had reached an island all right, and he could see no sign of life, wild or otherwise. He climbed to the top of the dam.

"I'm pretty sure we're alone out here," he said, "but it might be a good idea to watch for any kind of movement. I don't mean just bad guys. This is a great place for moose. A cow moose and her calf would be particularly bad news. Actually, any moose is bad news."

Angie looked around, her hands on her hips. "Now you tell me! And here I was only worried about bears."

"Oh, I forgot to tell you about bears. We have only black bears in Blight County but they get pretty cantankerous this time of year. Definitely, watch out for bears."

"No grizzlies?"

"Oh, occasionally someone claims to have seen a grizzly, usually in the high country over by Montana."

Suddenly she yelled his name, her voice tinged with panic. Great, he thought, now she sees a bear.

"I'm sinking, Bo! I can't get my feet loose!"

"Don't move!" he shouted. "It may be quicksand!" He had never heard of any quicksand in Blight County but if there was any, count on an FBI agent to find it. He plunged down off the dam. Circling around so as not to be caught by whatever had grabbed Angie, he came in behind her, wrapped his arms around her lower abdomen, grabbed his left wrist with his right hand, and wrenched back. She came loose, making a kind of *ooofff*ing sound as they both fell over backward in the water.

"Are you hurt?" he asked, holding her on top of him while she caught her breath.

"No, I'm okay. I thought for a second I was a goner. Scared me. You squeezed the dickens out of me with that lower Heimlich. I hope the lady you borrowed these waders from isn't too good a friend."

"Why?"

"Don't ask."

"Oh no! I'm sorry!"

"Only kidding. I'm okay. The waders are okay."

He stretched out, now lying nearly flat in the water, still holding Angie. The water was warm and cushy and smelled of decay. It occurred to him he liked holding her. He had never held an FBI agent before. The agent seemed to like it, too.

"Let's get out of here," he said. "This swamp may swallow us up before we find what we're looking for. I know a good guide we can get cheap. He knows this swamp like the back of his grubby hand."

17

ANGIE STRIPPED OFF her chest waders when they reached the Explorer. She opened the door to the cargo area and tossed them inside. Tully thought she had probably finished with waders forever. She was almost as wet as he was, no doubt because she hadn't tightened the chest strap sufficiently. Their clothes dried quickly in the heat of the car. He drove fast with all the windows open, the wind blasting them from all sides. He didn't want to explain that the air-conditioning on the Explorer hadn't worked in years. Who needs air-conditioning when you have windows? He turned north on US 95.

Angie stuck her hand out the open window and let it glide up and down in the wind as if it were a bird. "Where are we going now?"

"To see a fellow who probably knows that swamp better than anybody else."

"A friend of yours?"

"Sort of. I've locked him up a few times for poaching. He enjoyed the room service so much I could hardly keep him out of jail. I finally told the judge I'd had enough of Poke and we'd forget the bit of poaching he does to survive. I didn't get any complaint from the game warden either."

She pulled her hand inside. "Poke?"

"Yeah, Poke Wimsey. I think his actual first name is William, but Poke is all I've known him by. He told me one time he got the nickname when he was a young boy, because he was always late. Poke is never late anymore, because he never does anything he can be late for."

"He sounds like your kind of guy."

Tully ran up the windows. "He lives in a little log cabin back in the woods. I think it's on about a hundred acres of forest. He got the land by trading the old family homestead to the Forest Service. Most people around here are scared to death of him, the sensible ones anyway."

"He must be a real mountain man."

"Yeah, sort of. But he's a mountain man like you've never seen before. I doubt there's an ant or a spider or a wild plant in all hundred acres he doesn't know personally."

He turned off the highway onto a gravel road. There were farms on both sides. Presently, the forest started again and there were no more farms. The road turned into rutted dirt. Tully could see in the rearview mirror the dust curling up high behind them. After a couple of miles, he shifted into four-wheel drive.

The Explorer swerved in and out of the ruts. Then they came to a tree lying across the road. It was obvious the tree had been cut down so it would block off any stray traffic. Since nearly everyone in Blight County owned a chain saw, it was unusual that the tree had been allowed to remain where it was. Tully drove in and out of the ditch and into the woods, whipping the vehicle this way and that, and finally back to the road on the other side of the tree. Tracks indicated he was not the first to do so.

Angie turned and looked back at the tree. "Explain to me again, Bo, why the authorities allow someone to block a county road like that."

"It's simple enough. Beside the fact he doesn't mind in the least going to jail, Poke doesn't have any money, so it doesn't do any good to fine him. Furthermore, just about everybody in the county is afraid of him. No sensible person sees any reason to make an enemy of Poke. If you think about it, you realize people like him are about the only ones who achieve a complete state of freedom in modern society."

Angie shook her head. "I take it you're not afraid of this Poke."

Tully laughed. "You must think I'm stupid, Angie! Anybody with any sense is afraid of Poke!"

"I see. And exactly why is it we're going to visit him?"

"To see if he will guide us out into the swamp. The trick is not to give him any reason to kill us, pile some stones on our bodies and sink them somewhere out in a pool of quicksand, and let the water critters take care of any remains."

She gave a little shudder. "I'm so glad you eased my mind."

Tully turned off what remained of the road. The Explorer bumped and twisted through the woods until it came to a small clearing. Dozens of tree stumps dotted the clearing, in the middle of which sat a small log cabin. A man sat in a chair on the front porch. A rifle rested across his knees.

Tully stopped the Explorer and stared out the windshield at the man. "Sit here for a bit. I don't want to overwhelm him with company. I've left the motor running. If he kills me, whip the vehicle around and get out of here as fast as you can."

She heaved a sigh. "Great!"

"Oh, he isn't that bad. He used to be my high school biology teacher. It was the only class I ever got an A in. He told us he would kill any students who got less than a B, because they were too stupid to live and would eventually destroy the country. I'll give you a signal to come up to the porch."

"Wonderful. I can hardly wait."

He got out and walked toward the cabin. He could feel Poke watch him come, although Tully couldn't see the man's eyes under the brim of his faded and shapeless old felt hat. Poke had told Tully once he always liked to see a man's eyes. The old man stood up and grinned at him.

"Well, I'll be! Bo Tully! What brings you out this way?"

"A business proposition, Poke."

"Business? I ain't done a lick of business in fifty years. Who's that you got hiding in your rig? Tell him to show himself. I don't like folks hanging round I can't see."

Tully motioned for Angie to join him. She got slowly out of the vehicle, displaying no enthusiasm for the meeting.

"Gol-dang, Bo! You brought a woman! A mighty fine-looking one at that."

"You know me, Poke. That's the only kind of woman I hang out with. She's what you might call a gentlewoman. So watch your language."

Tully noticed Angie was carrying her shoulder bag, with the flap unsnapped and her right hand resting on top of the bag. She gave him and Poke a faint smile as she came up.

"Angie, I'd like you to meet an old friend of mine, Poke Wimsey. Poke and I have known each other all my life. He's taught me everything I know about the woods and a bunch of other stuff too."

Poke removed his hat and gave Angie a shy grin. "Pleased to meet you, m'am. Not often I get to meet a pretty lady like you."

Tully thought Poke had probably learned his manners from Gene Autry movies.

"Why, thank you, Mr. Wimsey," Angie said, obviously relieved.

Poke pointed to the chair. "Have a seat."

"Oh, I can't take your chair."

"I can't have a lady standing while Bo and I sit here jawing. He claims he's got me a business proposition."

Angie sat down in the chair, leaning slightly forward, her hands on her lap, looking unbelievably prim.

"I do indeed, Poke," Tully said. "I want you to guide us out into the swamp."

"Oh, I can't do that. The swamp is dangerous. Folks go out in it and are never seen again."

"Yeah, I've heard the stories, mostly from you and Pap." He turned to Angie. "Pap is my father. He isn't at all the gentleman Poke is."

"I know," she said. "I've read his file."

"File?" Poke said. "What file is that?"

"The newspaper file," Tully said. "So what I'm offering, Poke—the county will pay you a hundred dollars a day to guide us around in the swamp."

"A hundred dollars a day! That's a powerful lot of money, Bo."

"There's a reason it's a lot of money. It could be dangerous."

"That's what I just said. It's dangerous. I reckon you're looking for those men who have been messing around out there all summer. They're a nasty lot. Met up with two of them once when I was out fishing and thought they were gonna kill me for the fun of it. I got out of there fast. I think they left a week or so ago. So I'll take you up on that hundred dollars a day."

Tully smiled. "Actually, Poke, the hundred dollars is for day. We want to go out only during the night. It's fifty dollars a night."

"Fifty dollars! I lost fifty dollars just like that!" He snapped his fingers.

"Excuse me, Mr. Wimsey," Angie broke in. "Sheriff Tully is a little confused. Nights are twice as dangerous as days. So I believe the rate per night is two hundred dollars."

"Two hundred!" cried Poke. "That's more like it. I knew Bo was joking. There isn't any way I'd go out at night in a dangerous swamp for fifty dollars!"

Tully frowned at Angie. "Yes, I must have been confused. You see, Poke, Angie doesn't have to deal with a bunch of corrupt and vile and stingy county commissioners, so she can be much more generous with the county's money."

Angie ignored Tully and turned her whole attention to Poke. "Tell me more about the swamp's being dangerous, Mr. Wimsey."

Poke pulled over a block of firewood and sat down on it. "It started a long time ago. Some fellows were running a whiskey still out on one of the islands in the swamp. My popper was one of them. He was a young fellow back then, and his job was to sit out on the end of a dock and watch for revenuers. The head moonshiner gave him a shotgun and told him to shoot anybody he saw headed for the island. They worked only at night. So this night there was a moon out and it was pretty bright, but a fog was hanging low over the water. So Popper is sitting there, his legs dangling off the end of the dock, and he's bored to death because he never sees anything at all, let alone revenuers. All of a sudden he sees two boys gliding along on top the water. He knew right away they were ghosts, riding along on top of the water like that. He had never seen a ghost before and dropped his rifle right off the dock! Later, some of the moonshiners told him two boys had disappeared into the swamp and were never seen again, except for their ghosts that floated around the swamp from time to time. The current from Scotchman Crick flows right by the island, and that's what the ghosts were gliding along on."

"Good heavens!" Angie said. "Have you ever seen the ghosts yourself, Mr. Wimsey?"

"No, m'am, I haven't. And I don't want to either. But for two hundred dollars, I can chance it."

Tully was still scowling at Angie. "I bet you can, Poke. So when do we start?"

"Tonight's good for me."

"Can't do it tonight. I've got to drive into Spokane tomorrow, but I'll be back early in the afternoon. We could do it day after tomorrow. At night, I mean. That all right with you, Poke?"

"I'll have to clear my busy schedule, but sure."

"Great!" Angie said. "What should we wear, Mr. Wimsey, hip boots or chest waders?"

"Shucks no! You wade around in that swamp, you'll get sucked down by quicksand!"

Angie looked at Tully and returned his frown. "Quicksand. I never would have thought of that."

"No, m'am, we won't be doing any wading. I've got a log raft, a nice deck on it made of planks. We'll go in comfort. I pole around out there a bit, fishing for bass and perch and crappies and checking out the smaller wildlife. Fishing is good but I don't go out until the folks leave. Here's an odd thing. The mosquitoes have been gone all summer. Last spring I started chewing up and swallowing a clove of garlic every morning to keep the skeeters off me and it worked like a charm."

"I noticed that," Tully said.

"You wouldn't think that would clear all of the skeeters out of the swamp, too, would you, Bo?"

"Wouldn't surprise me one bit." Tully leaned back against the cabin wall. "You mention that the folks were gone from the swamp. What kind of folks?"

"Mean ones, at least the two I ran into last spring. After that I made a point of not running into them again."

"How many altogether, you guess?"

"Maybe a dozen. They seemed to be scattered about on the two islands. Some of them went back and forth to land with a big boat powered with a jet outboard the size of a hog. There's a short road into the swamp up where Scotchman runs in. They must haul the boat in and out with a trailer up there, but it's got to be one heck of a backing job. That road's as narrow and winding as the minds of our local politicians. No offense, Bo."

"None taken, Poke. A boat, hunh?"

"Yeah. Some of them stayed out on the island all summer."

Angie stood up and held out her hand for Poke to shake. "Thank you, Poke. Is it all right if I call you Poke?"

"Yes, m'am. A pretty lady like you can call me anything she likes, but Poke is fine."

"Good, Poke. And you call me Angie."

His grasp swallowed up her hand. "Mighty proud to know you, Angie. I hope you'll be coming along on our little adventure."

"I wouldn't miss it for anything. It'll make me feel just like Huck Finn, the log raft and all."

Tully got up and shook Poke's hand. "We definitely need to take Angie with us. She might turn out to be useful. We could throw her overboard if something leaps out of the swamp and attacks us. Anything you want us to bring?"

The old man screwed up his grizzled face in a thoughtful expression. "Just the money. Oh, some big flashlights would be good. And you might want to bring a rifle, Bo, if you've got one with iron sights. You can shoot a lot better and faster at night with iron sights than you can with a scope."

Tully frowned. "You think we might run into some bear or moose?"

"Oh, them, too. Just bring the rifle. A bottle of whiskey would be good too."

"Whiskey helps you see at night?"

"Not that I know of."

Driving back to town, Tully turned and grinned at Angie. "Well, what do you think of Poke?"

"I like him."

"You seemed to have fallen for his act."

She frowned at him. "What act is that?"

"That Poke is ignorant as a post."

"I didn't think any such thing."

"Well, it's all an act. He's written and published three books of poems. Besides that, he has hunted down and inventoried practically all the species of flora and fauna in the state. Recorded most of it on film."

"Actually, Bo, I did think he was wonderful, but I had no idea from talking to him that he was capable of such things. Never before in my whole life have I met anyone like Poke."

"He was some terrific high school teacher, I can tell you that."

"Is that why you're still afraid of him?"

"No! Didn't I tell you he's written three books of poems?"

They came to the log on the road and Tully bumped the Explorer out around it. "I've got a couple things I need to check out. One, I want to find the boy who escaped getting murdered up in the huckleberry patch. We find him, we've solved the murders. The other thing is I've got a missing person who also may have been murdered. His name is Orville Poulson. My only suspect in the case is his ranch caretaker, Ray Porter, aka Crockett. Tomorrow I want to check out the area in Spokane where Orville has his post office box."

"Check out the area where he has a post office box? That should be a big help."

"Yeah, well, you just wait and see, FBI person, what a cracker sheriff can come up with. And since you like odd characters so much, Angie, tomorrow I'll take you around to meet another really odd one. We may even take him along on our swamp excursion."

"Who, for heaven's sakes?"

"My father."

"The famous Pap Tully! I'd love to meet him!"

"If you like Poke Wimsey so much, you'll be absolutely delighted with Pap. I can't stand him myself but I suspect he's your kind of guy."

Angie laughed. "I can assure you I was much too young when the FBI went looking for Pap Tully. As I recall, all the bureau wanted Pap for was running houses of prostitution, illegal gambling, general corruption, and possibly murder."

Tully said, "I doubt if he ran anything, but he took a cut of everything. It made him rich. It's on record that he killed a number of people in his duties as sheriff of Blight County. Then there may be a number of off-record killings. As he will tell you and tell you and tell you, he was decorated by the governor for valor in the killing of three armed bank robbers. They hit him a number of times before he killed them with a pump shotgun. Maybe that's why the bureau didn't charge him with anything."

"No, it didn't," she said, rummaging around in her shoulder bag. "I'm not sure why. One thing was, he simply disappeared. I guess we figured at least he was gone and we had better things to do."

"He went to Mexico until the heat cooled off. Loved it

down there. Learned to speak a fair amount of Spanish. When you meet him, you may think he's an old-time hick sheriff, but he's actually very smart. With one exception, he's one of the smartest people I know."

Angie had turned down her visor and was using the mirror on the back to repair her lipstick. "So, did you get your intelligence from him, Bo?"

"Oh, no, he's not that smart. I got my intelligence from my mother, Rose. She's the real brains of the family. The only stupid thing she ever did was marry my old man twice. You ever been married, Angie? I notice you don't wear a ring."

She replaced the lipstick in her shoulder bag. "You noticed that, did you? No, I've never been married. I hate to tell you this, Bo, but the pickings are very thin out there when it comes to men. No offense."

"None taken."

"I've come close to getting married a couple of times, but the good one was killed in the line of duty, and the other one, a handsome devil, turned out to be one of the sorriest individuals I've ever laid eyes on. So now I've given up on men. You're perfectly safe with me, Bo."

He glanced at her. "Safe with you, Angie? That's a disappointment. I love a little danger when it comes to women. Here I've been giving you the full blast of my charm all day, apparently to no effect."

She laughed. "I wouldn't say that. When I was lying on top of you out there in the swamp, some old feelings came surging back. It really was quite nice. Then again, it might have been all that oozy stuff in the water."

After dropping Angie off at her hotel, Tully stopped by the office. The crew seemed glad to see him. The CSI Unit grabbed him by the arm and dragged him over to his corner. "Bo, you've got to do something about Daisy. She's been bossing us around like crazy. She'd have me sweeping the floor if I let her. After she wore us plumb out, she went down and laid into the prisoners. I think they're all scared to death of her, and we've got a couple of really dangerous guys locked up. What do you think's wrong with her?"

Tully scratched his chin. "Women are awfully hard to figure, Lurch."

"I know. That's why I asked you."

"Don't worry. I'll take care of it. The old Tully magic."

He strolled across the briefing room and into his office. Daisy followed him in.

"You look exhausted, Bo."

"I am. Worst day of my life." He slumped into his chair. "The FBI is driving me up the wall. No offense to womanhood in general, but this female agent is making me crazy. You know I'm not fond of the FBI in the first place, but a woman agent, if you can imagine such a thing! This is the worst day I've had in fifteen years of law enforcement."

Daisy brightened. "Really, Bo, she's that bad?"

"You wouldn't believe it. I can see now why her home office sent her out into the wilderness, as she calls us. She thinks I'm a cracker sheriff. Does nothing but grind me down. I tell you, Daisy, this agent What's-Her-Name has just about put me off women for the rest of my life. I can't stand another day with her."

Daisy's mood had improved so much he was afraid he might have overdone it. So he got down to business. "What's happening here?"

"Oh, we had a bit of excitement. Some residents over on the north side called in and said somebody was firing an automatic weapon in the neighborhood."

Tully tapped a pencil on his desk. "Anything new?"

"Yeah. A little bit later I got a call from your friend the lunatic, Mitch Morgan. He said a girl by the name of Jenny came flying into his house this morning. A great place for a young girl, the hangout of a motorcycle gang. He said a pretty rough-looking guy was after her, so one of Mitch's gang laid down a line of bullets from an AK-47 in front of him. I sent Brian over to pick up the girl. He came back with both the girl and the AK-47. He said the bikers raised quite a fuss about the gun, but he told them he knew they had all done time, so it was illegal for them to have any kind of firearm, let alone an AK-47."

"Good for Pugh. I take it neither Pugh nor the girl was harmed. What did he do with Jenny?"

"Dropped her off at Rose's." Daisy looked pleased with herself.

Tully was shocked. "Mom's! She'd be better off with the motorcycle gang."

"Bo, your mom is the sweetest person in the entire world."

"Daisy, you are such a poor judge of character, I don't know why I ever leave you in charge."

She smiled. "Because I'm the smartest person you've got on your staff."

"Sad, isn't it?"

"You're starting to make me mad, Sheriff."

He laughed. "Only kidding, Daisy. You do a great job. Anyway, you're going to be in charge all day tomorrow. I have to go into Spokane and check out this Orville Poulson thing, and there's a chance I might be able to run down the kid who escaped getting murdered up in the huckleberry patch."

"You taking the lady agent with you?"

"Why on earth would I do that? One of the reasons I'm leaving at five in the morning is to avoid her. Anything else happening?"

"Hold on a sec." She walked back to her desk and returned with her stenographer's pad. Reading from it, she said, "Your fortune-teller wants you to give her a call."

"Daisy, one last time, she is not my fortune-teller. She isn't anybody's fortune-teller. Etta Gorsich is an investment consultant. At least she was when she lived in New York. What else?"

Tully got up and walked around his desk. Taking a ring of keys from his pocket, he unlocked the metal gun safe and took out a rifle with iron sights.

"Uh-oh," Daisy said. "This doesn't look good."

He picked up a box of shells and dropped it in his pocket. "Just a precaution."

Daisy looked back at her pad. "Mrs. Poulson stopped by again. You have to do something about her, Bo. That woman is totally distraught over her husband. Ex-husband. Probably dead husband."

"Give her a call, Daisy, and tell her to come see me next week. We may have this mystery solved in a few days. It won't bring Orville back but we should know what happened to him. Get a warrant to search under Orville's house for a body. You can take all day, because I won't be in the office at all tomorrow. You'll have to babysit the FBI agent while I'm in Spokane. Take her out to lunch, go shopping, anything. Think of something."

"Noooo!"

"Daisy, I can't take her to Spokane. She'll turn me into a raving lunatic."

"I don't care. You take her."

"Oh, all right, I suppose I have to. Just remember it's your fault if I come back with my nerves in shreds. Now get out of here. I have to make a phone call." He walked her to the door.

Daisy went back to her desk, smiling. From across the room, Lurch watched her. He looked at Bo still standing in the doorway to his office. The sheriff mouthed the phrase "The old Tully magic." Lurch smiled, shook his head, and went back to work.

Tully pulled out his little dog-eared notebook and thumbed

through it until he found Mitch's number. He dialed.

Someone answered. "Yeah."

"Red, this is Sheriff Bo Tully. Mitch around?"

"Yeah. Hold on a sec, Bo."

Mitch came on. "Yo, Bo."

"Mitch, I appreciate your taking care of that little matter for me."

"No problem. The kid was terrified. Pugh came by and I turned her over to him. Hope that was okay."

"It was. Pugh is the best deputy I've got. Jenny's in good hands. Did you notice anything about the guy who was after her?"

"Not much. He drove a big ol' white pickup truck with dual tires. From behind, that truck looks like a fat old lady kicked in the butt. I hate those trucks."

"Me too. You get a license-plate number?"

"No. All I can tell you it was California. I doubt there's but one pickup like that in all Blight County, maybe in all of Idaho."

"California! Excellent, Mitch! By the way, I understand somebody laid down some suppressing fire from an AK-47. You know anything about that?"

"Nope. Must have been some guy passing through." Mitch turned away from the phone. "You know about anybody firing an AK-47, Red? Red says no, Bo. He don't know nothing about it."

"Tell Red whoever that fellow was, he probably saved Jenny."

"I'll tell him, Bo."

"I understand you lost an AK-47. I'll see if I can get it returned to you."

"No need, Bo. We've got a couple more."

Tully laughed. "Glad to hear it. I'll send Pugh around to pick them up."

"Yeah, well, you ever need another favor, Bo, just call."

"I'll do that, Mitch."

18

TULLY MET ANGIE at the hotel café shortly after five the next morning.

"You're a mighty early riser, Sheriff."

Tully pulled out a chair and sat down. "Yeah. And this is after I milked the cow, fed the chickens, and slopped the hogs. Did I mention my well is drying up and I have to dig a new one?"

Angie shook her head. "In one fell swoop, Bo, you wiped out any tiny bit of interest I might have had in you. The well finished it off."

He grabbed a menu from behind the napkin dispenser and perused it. "What, you don't like us farmers?"

"I was raised on a farm just like yours. Once I even helped my father dig a new well. It was ghastly! I get back there once a year to watch my folks work themselves to death. They claim to enjoy the life. Say it gives them a sense of independence." She nibbled a triangle of toast.

"That's the same with me. If I get fired from my job as sheriff, I know I won't starve to death. Maybe I'll start making cheese from my goats' milk."

"You never mentioned goats."

"Goats easily slip your mind. I do have a treat waiting for you in Spokane, though. We'll stop by the art galley that handles my paintings, Jean Runyan's."

"Don't you have any of your paintings at home?"

"Oh, yeah, I have four of my best watercolors up on a wall of my bedroom."

Angie laughed. "That sounds a lot like bait, Bo."

"You think so, Angie? I suppose it's your FBI training that makes you so suspicious. No, the reason I have the paintings in the bedroom is, when I wake up in the morning and look at them, I think to myself, Dang, Bo, you are good! If you ever get sick of sheriffing, you can become a full-time painter."

Angie smiled. "I think that would make an awfully nice life, being a full-time artist."

"You forget the fun I have dealing with criminals day in and day out."

"Well, sure, there's that."

Tully drove up US 95 to Coeur d'Alene and took I-90 into Spokane. He took the off-ramp at Main Street and drove north to the Meadow Park Shopping Center. A private post office with an outside entrance was housed in the mall. The First Miners Bank sat at the northern edge of the shopping center. Tully stopped in a parking area across from the post office.

He turned to Angie. "You really should come in with me. Pick up a few tips on crime investigation."

Angie opened her door. "Yeah, right. But it's a federal crime to mess with post offices. If you do anything illegal, I'll have to arrest you."

"Oh, in that case, maybe you should stay in the car."

"I'm going!"

An elderly clerk watched them enter. She seemed pleasant enough. A skinny young man with a shaved head messed with something in the back. Apparently, the business also did packaging, and he seemed to be wrapping up a small carton. Mailboxes covered one wall. Tully found the one with the number Ray Crockett had given him.

Walking over to the lady, he smiled at her as he took out his wallet and showed her his badge and identification. "Good morning, m'am. I'm Sheriff Bo Tully from Blight County, Idaho. This young lady is Agent Angela Phelps with the FBI. I wonder if you can tell us anything about a particular mailbox and the person who uses it."

"Good heavens, there are so many of them. People come and go all hours of the day and night."

"Your customers have access to their boxes at night?"

"Oh, yes. And on holidays. We close off this part of the

shop when we're not here, but customers can still get their mail."

"Can you tell me when this box was first rented?" He handed her a slip of paper with the number 281 on it.

"Oh, yes. I'll check the records." She called to the young man. "Viral, come and talk to these officers while I go check some records."

Sullen and bored, Viral slouched up to the counter. "Yeah?"

Tully smiled. "I take it your folks own this postal station."

"Yep. How'd you guess that?"

Tully shook his hand. "Just lucky. Can you tell us anything about Box Two-eighty-one?"

"Ha! Well, nooo. It just sits there like all the other ones."

Tully gave him a grim smile. "Viral? Did I hear your name right?"

"Yup."

"Well, Viral, have you ever thought of going into law enforcement?"

The kid's expression brightened. "I've thought about it. Why?"

"Because as a sheriff I'm always on the lookout for sharp young fellows to hire as deputies. It's dangerous work but you look like the kind of fellow who could handle it."

"Yeah! I really could, Sheriff!"

Tully nodded. "I bet you could, Viral. If you ever get the urge, you come see me over in Blight City and we'll talk about it. Now about Box Two-eighty-one. Can you tell me anything about it?"

"Yeah, an old guy rented it a year or two ago. Ma can get you his name. He don't stop by to check it very often. See, it fills up with junk mail and we have to empty it out and put all the overflow in one of those big boxes over there on the side. We stick a key to the big box inside the little box. When he takes the mail out of the big box, the key stays stuck in it. Ma's got a way of taking the key out so we can use the big box again. Sometimes he has a younger guy pick up his mail. Probably his son. We don't see them very often. They must come mostly at night."

His mother came back and handed Tully a piece of paper. "I wrote his name down there, Sheriff."

Viral said, "The sheriff says he could use me in law enforcement, Ma."

"That's nice, dear. As you can see, Officers, the old fellow who rented the box, his name is Poulson, Orville Poulson. For a couple of months, he would stop in and pick up his mail. I think he travels a lot. I don't recall seeing him in a long while now, but somebody empties out both the boxes about once a month. He probably comes in at night."

Tully folded the paper and slipped it into the inside pocket of his jacket. "Thank you very much, m'am. You've been a big help. By the way, would you mind looking to see if there's anything in either box?"

She walked around behind a partition and apparently checked the box. "Other than a couple of local ads, both boxes are empty."

"Thank you, m'am." Interesting, he thought. There

should have been at least one envelope for Crockett containing a Social Security check.

He and Angie walked out to the Explorer and got in.

Angie said, "You were kidding, weren't you, about hiring Viral as a deputy?"

"Not at all. There's always a place in law enforcement for dumb. Right now I'm pretty low on dumb. They tend to get killed, rushing into situations the smarter deputies avoid."

"I see. You're really a softhearted kind of guy, aren't you, Bo?"

Tully started the car. "Indeed I am, Angie. I'm pleased you noticed." He nodded at the other side of the parking lot. "Now I want to talk to somebody at the bank over there. I see they have a couple of drive-ins." He drove across the parking lot.

Angie stayed in the car while he went in the bank. Tully assumed she was bored with practical police work. A perky young woman at a round desk asked if she could help him.

"I hope so," he said. He showed her his badge.

Her mouth gaped. "Maybe I should get the manager, sir."

"That won't be necessary. My question is very simple. I see you have a young fellow working the drive-in window. Now if someone drove up in that farthest station, the teller wouldn't be able to see the customer all that well. Now, suppose that customer sent a check in through that brass vacuum tube over there. Would the teller cash it?"

"Oh, not without proper ID."

Tully put his badge and ID back in his jacket's inside

pocket. "Suppose the customer slid his driver's license into the carrier with the check."

"The teller would see if he had sufficient balance in the checking account to cover the check. If so, and the ID looked authentic, the teller would cash the check."

"Suppose it was a Social Security check."

"I think you had better talk to the manager about that."

"Oh, there's no need to bother him."

"It's a her."

"Sorry. You've been a great help, miss. Oh, I suppose the customer wouldn't have any problem depositing the Social Security check, if he had the proper deposit slip."

"I shouldn't think so. The teller would check the account, though, and ask the customer if he or she wanted a balance on the account. I know because I sometimes work the drive-in."

"I see. I bet you do a first-rate job, too."

She laughed. "Oh, you have to!"

"I hope you don't mind my saying, but you are an extremely attractive young lady."

She blushed. "Why, thank you. That's very nice."

"Oh, by the way, I don't suppose you could check your computer and see if a Mr. Orville Poulson has an account here."

"Oh, no. That would be strictly against our policy! I could be fired for that, I'm sure."

"In that case, I guess I will have to talk to the manager."

The girl punched a number on her phone. "Betty, there's a sheriff here at the front desk who would like to talk to you."

She listened briefly and hung up the phone. "She'll be right out, Sheriff."

The manager came striding out of her office. She wore a nice gray suit, a businesslike white blouse, and rimless spectacles. She was quite attractive for a professional type, as Tully had expected. She held out her hand and Tully grabbed it and held it lightly in his grasp. She gave his hand a tug, but nothing Tully took for a serious effort. After a moment, he released her hand, but not until a slight blush appeared on the manager's cheeks. "Yes?" she said. "I'm Betty McFarland, the manager of the bank. May I be of help, sir?"

"I'm sure you may. This nice young lady here has provided me with all the information she thought proper, and you should be very proud of her. She has refused to tell me if you have an account for a particular person, though. That is certainly sensible, but since I am law enforcement, I thought maybe you could provide me with that information."

She asked to see his ID. Tully showed it and his badge to her. "What is the name, Sheriff?"

"Orville Poulson."

She turned to the desk attendant. "Check for an account under that name, please, Janet." The manager looked over her shoulder at the computer screen. "Yes, we do have a checking account under that name."

"Excellent!" Tully said. "You've been a huge help."

They both beamed at him. Tully briefly thought maybe he should open an account there.

When he got out to the car, Angie was slipping her cell phone into her shoulder bag.

"How did that go?" she asked.

"Perfect. I'm beginning to see how Ray Porter, alias Crockett, has been pulling this off."

"Great," she said. "By the way, would you like to talk to Craig Wilson's uncle—one Ted Wilson?"

Tully stared at her. "How on earth . . ."

"I won't bother you with the details, but I do have my connections. Right at this moment he's crossing the Indiana border into Illinois, hauling a generator the size of a small house on the back of his truck."

"You're amazing, Angie!"

She smiled. "You don't think the bureau would send a rank amateur to deal with the famous Bo Tully, do you?" She handed him a slip of paper with a number written on it. "I've been on the phone with Ted while you were fooling around in the bank, Sheriff. I saw you working your magic on those two ladies. The one is much too young for you, though."

Tully shook his head and dialed. A gruff voice answered. "Yeah?"

"Mr. Wilson?"

"Yep. You're the young lady's associate, I take it."

"Associate? Yes, that sounds about right."

"She sounds pretty nice on the phone. Don't ask me how the devil she hunted me down, but I'd hold on to that one if I was you."

"I'll definitely try to, Mr. Wilson. What I need to talk to you about is your nephew Craig."

Wilson swore. "What's he done now, he's got a sheriff after him? That boy will drive me crazy."

Tully could hear honking and the sound of cars whizzing by.

"I don't know anything he's done, Mr. Wilson. The reason I'm looking for him, I think he can help me solve a serious crime. For that same reason, I think the people who committed the crime may be looking for him, too. His life is in danger."

Wilson was silent for a long moment. "Sheriff, I haven't laid eyes on him all summer. I let him stay at my house in Spokane but he's been working over in Idaho on a farm or something. If he's his usual industrious self, he's probably not making much money. I told him in case of emergency I'd stuffed two hundred dollars up in the toe of one of my shoes in a closet off a bedroom he sometimes uses. It's for him and he knows where it is. The next-door neighbors have a key to my house. Get it from them and go check the shoe. If the money's gone, he came back and took it. Usually it's the police after him for some fool thing he's done. He's not smart enough to be a criminal and I hope he's finally realized that."

"You have any idea where he might be?"

"Like you said, he's on the run from somebody. Go check the garage. There's a set of shelves on one side with camping gear on it. He loves backpacking. If the red backpack is gone, that's his."

"You got any idea where he might be?"

"What Idaho county you sheriff of?"

"Blight County."

"I'm sorry. Anyway, you familiar with Scotchman Peak?"

"You bet."

"Well, you drive up into the Hoodoo Mountains and there's a trailhead twenty miles north of Scotchman. It goes up to a little lake about straight down from the peak, the sheer side of the peak. You get an old Forest Service map, the trail should be marked on it. The trail is old. Used to go up to a lookout tower a few miles north of Scotchman. The tower's gone now, but you hit the top of that ridge, the going should be pretty easy until you drop down to the lake. There used to be a trail from the ridge down to the lake. There's half a dozen switchbacks leading down to the lake, with a lot of down timber across the trail. I don't think anybody ever goes into the lake anymore, but Craig and I fished it once. It would be a good place for Craig to hang out. I doubt anybody else would hike in there."

"I'm not surprised."

"That's my best guess, Sheriff. I think maybe Craig might have hit out for it and—wowee! Almost squished a hybrid. Bet I loosened up that fellow a bit. What was I saying? Oh, yeah, I've heard Craig talk about hiking in to the lake. If the money's run out of that job in Idaho and he's got the cops looking for him, I'd bet ten to one that's where he's gone. Nobody would think to find him in there."

"Thanks, Mr. Wilson. I'll check out the shoe and the garage. If I find Craig, I'll give you a call. Try not to squish any hybrids. Ford Explorers are okay, unless you come across one marked 'Sheriff.'"

Wilson gave Tully the address to his house and then beeped off.

Tully smiled at Angie. "Thanks to you and Mr. Wilson, we may have a lead. What do you think about a little backpacking, Angie?"

19

AS THEY APPROACHED Blight City, Tully pulled into the long paved driveway that led up to Pap's castle. Tully believed Pap had built the huge house on a hill so that he could look out his front windows and survey what he regarded as his domain, a broad expanse that stretched out over much of Blight County, bordered on one side by Lake Blight, on another by the Snowy Mountains, and on another by the Hoodoo Mountains.

"Good heavens!" gasped Angie. "This is gorgeous!"

"Yes, it is. You might want to keep in mind, if you ever start looking for real men again, that when Pap dies I inherit all of this. Just thought I'd mention it."

She smiled. "I'll definitely keep it in mind, Bo."

"On the other hand, the way Pap is going, smoking and

drinking and carousing all over the county, I suspect he'll never die, if for no other reason than just to torment me."

Angie laughed. "How old is he?"

"Just turned seventy-six. He stole a gorgeous young waitress from Dave's House of Fry about a year ago. Claims he hired her as his housekeeper. Turned out Deedee is now boss of the place and runs Pap around like he's a lowly servant. I love it."

"The House of Fry? I've heard it's the best restaurant in the county to eat."

They approached a wide parking area lit by several large lights on high poles. "It probably is. Claims to have the world's biggest and best chicken-fried steak. I've never found fault with the claim. The place is owned by a somewhat mysterious friend of mine, Dave Perkins. Dave pretends to be an Indian, but only because he wants to turn the House of Fry into a casino operated by his tribe of one."

Tully parked his battered old red Explorer next to Pap's most recent Mercedes, a small silver convertible that all by itself filled his son with unquenchable envy. And Tully didn't care that much about cars in the first place.

Angie dug a tube of lipstick out of her shoulder bag and, using the mirror on the back of the visor, refreshed her lips. The makeover completed, she examined it this way and that, shoved the visor back up, and said, "Your friend Dave sounds interesting. Why mysterious?"

"I'll give you one example. A while back we were eating in a little café up north, and a couple of young lumberjacks came in. They said we were eating at their table. Dave seems to be a mild-mannered guy, and he politely told them there were lots of other tables, choose one of them. The jacks told him they would move him to one of the other tables. One grabbed Dave around the neck and the other grabbed him around the waist and they started to lift. The next thing I knew, both men were lying on the floor behind Dave, both of them out cold and bleeding about the face. I was seated directly across from him and never saw him move. He was nibbling on a cracker. Now is that mysterious?"

"I would say it meets the definition. Do I get to meet him?"

"Before we get our recent murders taken care of, we'll no doubt bring him in as backup. I don't like to use him until a situation gets dangerous."

"You think this situation will get dangerous?"

"I'm sure of it." He jerked his thumb at the house. "Well, Angie, this is it. I might as well take you in and introduce you to Pap Tully. Don't expect too much."

"Oh, Bo, don't be silly. I'm sure meeting your father will be a treat."

Deedee answered Tully's knock on the door. "Oh, Bo! This is so great."

He introduced Angie. "She's an FBI agent."

"An FBI agent!" Deedee exclaimed. "My goodness, I've never met a real FBI agent before." She was shaking hands with Angie when Tully heard the rustle of paper, a piece of furniture knocked over, and the back door opening and slamming shut.

Tully rushed out the front door and around the side of the house. His father had already leaped into the convertible. Tully jerked open the passenger door. "Hold up, Pap. It's a woman agent. She's working with me. She's not after you. She just wants to meet you. You're her hero."

Pap turned off the convertible. "Really, Bo? You're not joshing me now, are you?"

"No. She's in town helping me on the killings up in the huckleberry patch."

"You say I'm her hero?" Pap looked skeptical but hopeful.

"She's read all about you. And she's very good-looking, particularly for an FBI agent. On the other hand, you should avoid committing any crimes while she's in town. I suspect she's the kind of agent who goes by the book."

Pap got out of the convertible. "If you say so, Bo, I'll check my list and eliminate any possible fed crimes. Good-looking, you say?"

"Yeah. Well, for a middle-aged lady. She's not one of those young hotties you're always checking out. Her name is Angela Phelps."

"Bo, any woman under sixty I consider a hottie. And quite a few over sixty."

They walked back into the house through the back door. Angie and Deedee were seated in the living room. Tully introduced Pap to Angie. She popped up from her seat and shook the old man's hand. "Mr. Tully, I have to tell you I've read everything ever written about you, and I have to say, you are a real-life legend."

Pap grinned. "A legend. Surely you exaggerate, Agent Phelps."

"Not a bit. And please call me Angie, sir. You son has been filling me in on even more of your extraordinary feats."

"Really? You sure it was Bo?"

"Yes indeed. Awarded a medal of valor by the governor. That's major, Mr. Tully. Major."

"They shot me three times," Pap said.

Tully shook his head. "Don't milk it, Pap. Which reminds me, Deedee, if you were thinking of serving tea, I take milk in mine."

"You are such a mind reader, Bo. Even though I hadn't mentioned it yet, I was very much thinking about offering you tea."

Pap said, "Would you like to see the medal of valor, Angie?"

Tully said, "Pap!"

"Indeed I would," Angie said. "And I don't know how a nice man like you, Pap, could raise such a grumpy son as Bo."

Tully rolled his eyes. Pap went off somewhere to retrieve his medal, and Deedee disappeared into the kitchen to make tea.

"You have quite the way with old men," Tully whispered to Angie.

She smiled. "It's my specialty. I'm surprised you didn't notice when we were in the swamp."

"Probably because I'm scarcely forty."

"Going on forty-three. Remember, I read your file, too."

Pap returned with the medal. Angie was impressed, perhaps

overly impressed as far as Bo was concerned. Presently Deedee came in with a tray bearing a silver teapot and china cups. Tully could tell that Deedee had been upgrading Pap's lifestyle.

After both Deedee and Angie appeared to be about finished making over Pap, Tully said to him, "Enough of this nonsense. I brought Angie over here only because I need some information from you about the swamp."

Pap chuckled. "I figured you was gettin' tired of these two beautiful women fussing over me." He grinned at the ladies. "Bo is about the most envious man you'll ever meet, when it comes to women."

"Yeah, yeah," Tully said. "Stop preening for a moment and tell me about the swamp."

"It's haunted." Pap settled back into his chair. "You know that, don't you, Bo?"

"So I've heard from Poke. In the past week I've heard about a haunted lake and now a haunted swamp."

"Poke's all right as far as he goes, but he don't go far. He's still too young."

"He was the first one to tell me it's haunted."

"Yep, and me and Eddie Muldoon was the fellas that haunted it. It's true, two young boys disappeared in the swamp, but that was long before Eddie and me came along. We was about ten, maybe even a little younger, when we heard that train robbers had buried their gold somewhere in the swamp shortly before they was killed by a posse. Now, you can check the old papers about the robbers, so you'll know that much is true."

Tully tugged on the droopy corner of his mustache. "I want to know all of it is true, Pap."

"It is, Bo, it is." Pap put his feet up on an ottoman, folded his hands on his belly, and prepared himself for storytelling. "Now shut up and let me get on with this. Where was I?"

"You and Crazy Eddie were ten," Deedee said.

"Right, we was about ten. I can't remember our exact ages. Anyway, Eddie found out about the robbers' treasure and came up with the idea we should build a raft and go look for it. We was in a powerful hurry to find the treasure because neither of us had a cent of money. The real Depression was going on at the time and any adults who had money, they didn't waste it on kids. Our raft wasn't much for show, because we built it out of cedar fence posts we borrowed from one of the Muldoon fences."

"Fully intending to replace them, no doubt," Tully said.

"You bet. Now are you going to let me tell this, or not?"

Angie and Deedee held fingers up to their lips, signaling Tully to be quiet. He expected Deedee at least to be familiar with Pap's fantastical yarns by now. But he held his hands up in surrender.

"So," Pap continued, "we slid the raft into Scotchman Crick and both of us got on, one at each end. That's when we discovered we were one or two fence posts short, because the raft floated along about an inch underwater. In no time at all, we had drifted into the swamp. We had made ourselves some paddles, but they wasn't much good for steering a raft. You might think a crick would know its way through a swamp, but Scotchman don't. It would go this way for a while, and then we'd find that was a dead end, and then we'd turn and go a different way. Pretty soon evening came on, and after a while it got dark and the air took on a chill. The moon came out and the raft continued to drift this way and that, mist rising from the water, owls hooting, and every so often a goose or a duck would take off squawking like mad from right next to the raft and scare us half to death."

Tully smiled at Angie. She didn't notice. "All at once," Pap continued, "we look up ahead and see a big fire burning on an island and men outlined against the fire, rushing around, doing some kind of work. I whispered to Eddie, 'We're saved! Those fellas will get us out of here.' And he hisses back, 'No way! They'll kill us for sure. They got to be some kind of pirates! Just stand real still and maybe they won't notice us when we float by.' That's when I see the lookout. He's sittin' on the end of the dock with his legs dangling over the water and he's got a rifle across his lap."

"Wait a minute!" Tully exclaimed.

Deedee and Angie both shushed him.

Pap gave Tully a little grin and went back to his story. "Well, that lookout sees us and jumps up and his rifle falls into the water. He turns around and rushes back to the men working around the fire and he's telling what he saw and is pointing right at us. All the men stop what they're doing and stare out at us. But just then we drift into a patch of fog. One of the men takes off his hat and whips the lookout across the head with it. An hour or so later—it seemed like at least a year—we got back in the main current and floated out of the swamp. I ain't never told anybody about our little adventure before, because I figured nobody would believe it. But that's the way it happened."

Tully looked at Angie. Her mouth was gaping. FBI agents are such pushovers. He turned to Pap. "Angie and I have hired Poke to take us into the swamp on his raft tomorrow night. I've got this feeling there may be something in there that holds a clue to the murders up in the huckleberry patch."

Pap scratched his chin. "In that case, we'd definitely want Dave along."

"Poke did suggest I bring along a rifle with open sights. I've got my old Marlin .32 Special in the Explorer right now, but don't expect I'll have to use it. If the fellows I'm after are hanging around out there in the middle of the night, they're stupider than I think."

Pap looked over at Angie. "Well, I'd better go along. I don't trust you one minute out in a swamp with a pretty lady, Bo."

Angie laughed. "Thank you for the compliment, Pap, but I think I'll be safe with Bo. I'd love for you to come along, though."

Deedee said, "Oh, please take him! He needs a little excitement. And I need some peace and quiet."

Tully stretched and yawned. "I guess that settles it, Pap. You're going whether you want to or not."

• • •

Driving Angie back to her hotel, Tully said, "Well, what did you think of the famous Pap Tully?"

"I thought he was wonderful, Bo! I about fell over when he told that story about rafting through the swamp. It fit right into what Poke told us."

"You believed it, then, did you, Angie?"

"Why, yes, I did. Why wouldn't I?"

"I take it the FBI doesn't let you interrogate suspects."

"Now that you mention it, I haven't had that particular experience. Why do you ask?"

"No reason."

20

TULLY WAS SURPRISED the next morning to get a full cup of coffee out of one of the five coffee pumps, the first four of which, as usual, only *fiss*ed at him. The last one squirted out a full stream of black coffee. There was even a little pitcher of cream next to it.

"What's going on?" he said, looking around the briefing room at his troops. "You left me some coffee for a change."

Several of the deputies chuckled. Ernie Thorpe said, "It was just an oversight, boss."

"Not really, boss," Brian Pugh said. "It was Flo's idea that we start being nice to you. From now on, you've got your own coffee pump, filled with French roast, I believe. Flo says anybody who sneaks a cup out of it will have to deal with her."

Tully stuck his head into the radio room. Flo smiled at him.

"Thanks, Flo. It's nice to have someone looking out for me."

"No problem, boss. I figured with you having to hang out all day with an FBI agent, you needed a little special care."

"Indeed I do." Tully guessed that she and Daisy had been discussing Angie. He glanced around the room. Daisy was at her desk. Lurch was in his corner. Undersheriff Herb Eliot was standing in front of the other deputies. "What's up, Herb?"

"I just finished my briefing, Bo. We've got some nut breaking into houses up on the north side. Because he doesn't seem to mind if folks are home, folks assume he's armed. So folks are going to shoot first and ask questions later."

"Yeah," Tully said, "and folks end up shooting one of their kids who gets up to go to the bathroom. Get over to the radio station, Herb, and be a guest on Jim Dinkum's morning show. Every idiot in town listens to it. Explain to our gun-happy populace that anyone firing a weapon inside the city limits for any reason will be in serious trouble."

"Got it, boss." Herb had settled into a chair and remained seated.

"One more thing," Tully said. "Everybody be on the lookout for a big white pickup truck with dual tires on the back and a California plate. If you spot it, don't do anything, but try to get the plate number. Not a good idea to stop the truck. The occupants would shoot you dead in a second. I'm not sure what they're up to."

Ernie Thorpe raised his hand. "You got some evidence against these guys, Bo?"

"No, I don't. What's your point, Ernie?"

The briefing room erupted with laughter.

Tully went on. "We had one possible witness but somebody killed him. Pugh, if you're out in an unmarked car and happen to spot the pickup, you might follow it at a distance, try to find where they're holed up, but don't get close. You understand?"

"Got it, boss."

Ernie Thorpe said, "You think there's a connection between the break-in guy and the pickup folks, Bo?"

"Naw, I don't think so, Ernie. The break-in guy is some nut who doesn't realize some of our Blight County folks will shoot him dead and bury his body in the backyard before they eat breakfast."

Herb was still relaxing in a chair. Tully glared at him. "So why are you still sitting here, Herb? Get over to the radio station."

"Right, boss." Herb shoved himself up out of the chair and shuffled out.

Tully pointed to three deputies one after the other. "Thorpe, Pugh, and Daisy, I want to see you three in my office. The rest of you guys hit the road and try not to get yourselves killed. Flesh wounds are okay, but nothing serious. Daisy will apply a Band-Aid. We can't afford more doctor bills."

The deputies shuffled off. Daisy, Brian, and Ernie went

into the office, pulling in a couple of extra chairs. Tully sipped his coffee and set the cup on his desk. He flopped down in his office chair and studied the three deputies. He started with Daisy. "You get that warrant from Judge Patterson?"

"Yes. It's in my desk drawer. He was more picky than usual. He wanted to limit the search for the body to the house."

"Body?" Ernie Thorpe said. "What body?"

"Orville Poulson's," Tully said. "I have some information the body may be buried under the house. The ranch-sitter may have killed him, but I don't think so. He's a sociopath but not a killer."

Pugh leaned forward in his chair. "You think there's some connection between Orville Poulson and whoever blasted Lennie Frick?"

Thorpe added, "And the huckleberry murders?"

"Could be, but I don't have a clue. I think the swamp has something to do with it, but I'm checking that out tonight."

"You taking the FBI lady?" Pugh asked.

Thanks a lot, Brian, Tully thought. He could feel Daisy's eyes boring into him. "The FBI lady is insisting on it. If we don't find anything tonight, maybe she'll head back to Boise tomorrow. Otherwise, I'm turning her over to you, Pugh. It's your turn to babysit her. I tried to get Daisy to do it but she refused."

"She's that bad, boss?" Ernie said.

"You wouldn't believe it, Ernie. Wait until you get a turn."

"Hey, I won't mind a bit! She's one good-looking woman!"

Pugh nudged Thorpe and rolled his eyes toward Daisy.

"I guess she's pretty pushy, though," Thorpe said. "I'm glad I don't have to babysit her."

"Anything else, boss?" Pugh said.

"Yeah," Tully said. "I just wanted to tell you, if I don't show up around here in the next day or so, go look in the swamp."

"Right, boss," Pugh said. "We'll drop everything and rush right out there." He and Thorpe got up and left.

Daisy said, "Mrs. Poulson is coming in this morning. Do you think we should tell her about the search warrant?"

"I don't know. What do you think, Daisy?"

"She's pretty tough. It can't be any worse than what she's been going through, not knowing what's happened to Orville."

"Suppose we don't find anything under the house?"

Daisy thought for a moment, tapping her pencil on her stenographer's pad. "Then we bring in some cadaver dogs and search the property, square foot by square foot. I don't want Orville's wife to go through any more torment."

"Ex-wife," Tully corrected. "Besides, Daisy, we only have a warrant for the house."

Daisy smiled. "I lied, boss. I got the warrant for the whole property. And I notified the cadaver-dog guy we may need his services."

Tully erupted in exasperation. "Sometimes I wonder if

I'm even needed around here! Daisy, that property is a thousand acres or more. It will cost the county a fortune to search the whole thing with cadaver dogs."

Daisy stood up and said calmly, "Well, if that's what we have to do, that's what we have to do." She turned and walked out.

Tully stared after her with a mixture of irritation and admiration. Who's running this outfit anyway? He shook his head. What would he do without Daisy? Might be nice to try, though. He picked up his phone and dialed Etta Gorsich's number.

21

TULLY WAS LOUNGING against the front of Crabbs when Etta drove into the parking lot. He thought it was too bad he didn't smoke cigarettes. That would give him a whole range of gestures. He could take the butt from his lips, snap it under a car with his fingers, exhale a stream of smoke, and squint at her through it. Now all he could do was stand up straight.

Walking up to him, Etta said, "You don't smoke, do you, Bo? That's one of the many things I like about you." She took his arm and led him toward the entrance. "Persons in your line of work usually inhale one cigarette after another. I don't blame them. The stress of the job must be awful."

"Nope, I don't smoke. Odd you should mention it. I guess the stress just comes and goes, Etta. Hey, it's good to see you.

As always, you look fantastic." Tully had been working on attentive. She was wearing a white dress with a bright red scarf around her neck. She actually did look great. Etta was dynamite, even if she sometimes did give him the creeps. Like bringing up cigarettes just now.

The manager, Lester Cline, showed them to a table himself.

Etta said, "Why, this is the same table we sat at last time."

"Yes," Tully said. "It's now our special table. Right, Lester?"

"Indeed it is, sir." He gave a little bow. "Would you like your regulars?"

Etta laughed. "Actually, Lester, I would prefer something that doesn't require a bib."

"Indeed, madam! Perhaps our honey-basted chicken breast, potatoes au gratin, and a salad. What kind of dressing, madam?"

"Blue cheese, please."

"And you, sir?"

Tully scowled at him. "Lester, if you don't drop the phony maître d' act, I'll have to stand up and knock you down."

"Jeez, you're such a peasant, Bo. How can I elevate the sophistication of Crabbs with patrons like you?"

"Maybe by elevating the taste of the food. I'll have the same as Etta."

"Thank you. I should go off in a huff, Bo, but I'm still working on my huff." Lester stomped toward the kitchen.

Tully said, "I liked him better when he was boosting cars."

Etta laughed and shook her head. "Blight seems such an unusual place. I guess that's why I like Idaho so much."

"You apparently haven't seen much of Idaho, Etta. Most of it is nothing like Blight."

"I suppose that's true. One of these day I'm going to get in my car and drive around the state for a whole month. Like to come along as a tour guide?"

"Sounds wonderful, Etta."

Lester returned with two glasses and a bottle of wine. "This is on the house, the best wine in Crabbs's cellar, I'm sorry to say." He nodded to Etta. "It's in honor of you, my dear, for having to put up with such a grouchy lunch guest."

Tully smiled. "Thank you, Lester. I'm sorry I was grouchy. Although I may try it again next time, if it gets us free wine."

Lester patted Tully on the shoulder. "Don't count on it, Sheriff."

"My goodness, Bo," Etta said. "A whole bottle of wine for just the two of us. You may have to drive me home."

Tully was pouring wine into one of the glasses and some spurted over the side, making a small red stain on the tablecloth. He poured the other glass and then set the bottle down so that it covered the stain.

Etta said, "Well, what did you think about my idea of exploring Idaho for a month?"

Tully smiled at her. "I'm still stuck on your suggestion that I drive you home."

Etta smiled back. "First things first, of course. This is actually very good wine, don't you think, Bo?"

"I think it may be the best I've ever had."

He felt Etta's foot slide up his leg. She must have slipped her shoe off. And here he had a ton of work to do this afternoon. But, as Etta said, first things first.

Lester came rushing back to the table. "Bo, you must have your cell phone shut off. Daisy's calling you. She says it's urgent."

It better be, thought Tully. He pulled his phone out of his jacket pocket and dialed the office. "What's up?"

"We just had a fatal accident on the Cow Creek bridge. A car crashed through the side rail and went into the creek." Daisy sounded out of breath.

"That's quite a drop."

"Yes it is. Brian is out there and he says it's very suspicious. He wants you out there as soon as you can make it."

Tully stood up. "Tell him I'm on my way. Has Brian identified the victim?"

"Marge Poulson!"

He winced. "Oh, no!" He beeped off.

Staring blankly at Etta, he said, "I'm so sorry, but I have to run. We have a fatality out by the Cow Creek bridge."

"Good heavens!" Etta seemed almost in a trance, as if she were watching a tiny horror movie projected on a screen he couldn't see. Her face had turned pale.

"Etta?"

She blinked her eyes and stared up at him, as if for a moment wondering who he was. "Oh, Bo, go! Quickly! Don't worry about me."

What a crappy job, he thought, rushing out the door.

Ambulances, wreckers, fire-station and law-enforcement vehicles lined the road on both sides of the bridge, a section of which had been taken out. The pavement showed where a car had skidded toward what was now a break in the railing. Tully pulled up in front of an ambulance and got out. He walked around to the rear of the vehicle. The doors were open. He climbed in, having to stoop as he did so. The body was on a stretcher, covered by a wet white sheet. Two feet protruded from under the sheet, one wearing a black high-heeled shoe, a style his mother would have referred to as "sensible." The other foot wore only a stocking. Water dripped from the feet to a puddle on the floor. The attendant stared at him. Tully said, "Pull the sheet down so I can see the face." The attendant did as he was told. It was Marge, all right. "Pull it back," he told the attendant. Climbing out of the ambulance, he almost bumped into the medical examiner. "Susan," he said. His voice was hoarse.

She was tucking her long blond hair up into a cap of some sort. "You knew her, Bo?"

"Yeah. She's Orville Poulson's ex-wife, Marge."

Susan said, "I talked to Brian and he said this was no accident. She was deliberately killed, according to the skid marks. Her car was forced off the bridge. Why would someone want to kill a little old lady? She couldn't do anybody any harm, and it doesn't look like she had much money or anything else."

Tully shook his head as if at a loss for any explanation. "Pap says people murder for two things, money and to shut someone up. In Marge's case, it had to be the latter. She has been hounding me for months to find her husband's murderer. So far we have no evidence he's been murdered or is even dead. We don't have a body."

Pugh had climbed up the embankment next to the bridge. He walked over to Susan and Tully. He was wet up to his waist.

Tully asked, "What do you think, Brian?"

The deputy wiped his brow. "Somebody killed her. The car was rammed from behind by a much larger vehicle. It hit her on the left rear corner and spun her around." He gestured toward the missing guardrail. "Then it pushed her car off the bridge backwards and it landed upside down in the creek. The car filled with water instantly but I think she probably was killed from the drop. I helped get her out of the vehicle and she felt like she was all broken up inside. Might even have been killed from the impact of the other vehicle hitting her."

Susan turned to Tully. "Any suspects, Bo? She's been talking to you about her missing husband, right?"

"Ex-husband. Yeah, I've got one suspect. He's someone she could cause a lot of trouble for. On the other hand, he doesn't seem the type to murder someone."

Susan frowned at him. "You think there's a type for murder?"

"I don't know. Given the right circumstances, I suppose just about anybody could kill somebody else. People are full of surprises. To kill a person like Marge, though, is pretty cold-blooded. My suspect is the only person I know who could profit from her death. He's not stupid, though. I'll bet you anything he's got an airtight alibi. If he does, you can be sure he had a hand in this. Knew it was going to happen. Maybe he even hired somebody to do it."

He turned to Pugh. "She was driving away from her home. You got any idea where she was headed?"

Pugh said, "I've got Ernie checking with her neighbors, to see if she had friends out this way or what. One of the neighbors said there was a big old farmhouse a few miles down that Marge rented out. She might have been headed there."

Tully tugged thoughtfully on the corner of his mustache. "I know who the renters are, Brian. Don't go near the place, except to drive by and see if a big white dual-tired pickup truck is parked there."

Pugh said, "You think . . . ?"

"It's possible, but don't do anything until I get back. I've got to go. I'm still pursuing the swamp thing. I'll meet you all back at the office in the morning."

22

TULLY DROVE TO his place. Bouncing down across the meadow toward his log house, he thought about how he and his wife, Ginger, had built it to become self-sufficient artists, he a painter and she a potter. After Ginger died, that dream evaporated, and he became one of a long line of Tullys to enter law enforcement. Eventually he became sheriff. He never locked the door on his house, even though his office often received reports of burglaries in the county. He opened the door and walked in. The huge painting he had made of Ginger hung on a wall by the door. It portrayed her coming through that very same door with a bouquet of wildflowers clutched in her hand, blond hair bobbing about her head as she smiled at him with the glee of a small child.

He went into his bedroom and changed into jeans, a

work shirt, and hiking boots. He took a small bottle of OFF! from the medicine cabinet and rubbed the repellent into all exposed parts. He slipped his shoulder holster on, shoved in his Colt Commander, and snapped the retaining strap across it. Finally, he took his khaki vest out of the closet and put it on, mostly to cover the gun and shoulder holster. As always, the pistol gave him a certain sense of security. Then he drove over to the hotel and picked up Angie, who was waiting for him out on the sidewalk. She was dressed pretty much as himself, including a vest.

Climbing into the Explorer, Angie said, "I heard on the radio about Marge Poulson. That's really sad. The newscaster said officials believe it's a homicide. Any suspects?"

"Several," he said. "One is the sociopath Ray Porter, alias Crockett. As far as I know, he's the only one to profit from Marge's death. Maybe he did it. I've known a lot of murderers, though, and for some reason he doesn't fit. On the other hand, she was drawing a lot of attention to him. You never can tell. So are you ready for our great adventure?"

"As ready as I'll ever be. I've soaked myself head to foot in mosquito dope, just in case. And I've stuffed the mosquito netting in my bag."

He laughed. "Maybe Poke's right about the mosquitoes, that they have simply disappeared."

"He should know. We certainly weren't bothered by them. But maybe they rest in the middle of the day."

"Mosquitoes never rest."

They picked up Pap. The old man climbed into the Explorer's backseat and laid his 30-30 rifle in the cargo section.

Tully said, "I see you brought some heavy artillery, Pap."

"Yep. I ain't shot that rifle in years but I nailed a paper plate to a tree out back of the house and put half a dozen rounds in the center of it. Made me think maybe I should go back to hunting with it. Killed my first deer with that rifle when I was eight years old."

Tully said, "Well, I hope you won't have need for it tonight. I've had enough killing for one day."

Pap tossed the seat belt to one side. "Yeah, I heard on the radio about the accident. Marge was a mighty nice woman, always helping somebody out."

"I don't think it was an accident, Pap."

"What! You think somebody deliberately killed her?"

"I'm sure of it."

"Well, if I ever found the—"

"Careful, Pap. We've got an FBI agent in the car. You don't want to give Angie the impression we have loose laws here in Blight County."

"Loose? We have a bunch of sissy laws around here anymore. You wouldn't believe the way it was in the old days, Angie."

"Oh, yes I do. Remember, Pap, I read the file on you."

He grinned. "You're so pretty, Angie, I keep forgetting you're an FBI agent."

Bo nudged her with his elbow. "Did his file say anything about his being a flagrant womanizer?"

"No way," Pap said. "The FBI doesn't invent a lot of nonsense like that, right, Angie?"

"That's right, Pap. We're only interested in the facts, nothing but the facts."

Poke was sitting on his front porch talking with Dave Perkins when they drove up.

Dave and Poke walked over and climbed into the backseat with Pap. Dave was dressed in his buckskin tracking clothes. They both laid rifles in the cargo area. Tully introduced Dave and Angie.

"We seem to be well armed for this expedition," Angie said. "Are we expecting trouble?"

"We always expect trouble when Bo invites us on an outing," Dave said.

Angie stuck out her hand toward the backseat. "You must be the famous tracker."

Dave took her hand and held it until she pulled away. He laughed. "Maybe the most famous tracker in Blight County. It's pretty easy to be famous here. I'm even famous for my chicken-fried steaks, which happen to be the best and largest in the world."

Tully said, "That's true. There's a big sign in front of his restaurant that says so."

"So, how much evidence could a person ask for?" Dave said.

"And the restaurant, if I recall," Angie said, "is Dave's

House of Fry. Does that mean everything served there is fried?"

Dave shook his head. "Not at all. We also serve water, coffee, and salads. Sometimes we're accused of frying the coffee but that's an outright fabrication."

"I see. Contrary to what I've heard, you have a well-rounded menu."

"Yes, indeed. It's not my fault if some folks choose to die on the premises."

Poke said, "Good to see you, Pap," reaching over to shake his hand. "I didn't realize you were coming too."

"You know how it is, Poke, us old guys has got to keep an eye on the whippersnappers and not let them go off prowlin' 'round swamps on their own. You look fit as a fiddle. So where you taking us?"

"I'll show you. Bo, go back the way you came in and turn north on 95. You know where the Old Culvert Road is?"

"I do, Poke."

"Turn off on that. It'll take us in on the north side of the swamp. That's where the raft is tied up. No need to hurry. The sun's about to go down. We don't want to head out into the swamp till it's dark."

Tully turned in his seat and glanced back at Poke. "You think we might run into some of those folks you were telling me about?"

"I don't expect to, Bo. But some of them could still be hanging around. Looks as if we got enough firepower along to take care of ourselves no matter what shows up. You packing, Angie?"

She nodded. "You bet, Poke. I'm always packing."

"You're my kind of woman, Angie."

Pap grinned. "They don't make 'em like her no more, Poke. That's another thing I hate about modern times."

Tully twisted around so he could see into the backseat. "Would you two quit trying to hustle this FBI agent?"

"Keep out of this, Bo," Angie said. "I like it!"

Tully turned off on the Old Culvert Road. Half a mile in, they drove under a power line. "When did they put that in, Poke?"

"About five years ago."

"I see they used cedar poles. I thought anymore they used nothing but steel towers."

"Well, they used cedar poles on this one. I hate the steel towers. They're ugly as sin, in my opinion. Now right up ahead, Bo, there's kind of an opening in the woods. It used to be a road and it's kind of grown up, but your rig should be able to manage it."

The road wasn't any rougher than the drive into Poke's, and Tully guessed the brush scratched hardly any of the remaining red paint off the Explorer. Oh, well, time for the shop boys to repaint it anyway. The vehicle was at least eight years old. Any speed over sixty miles per hour, the front end shook like a rag in a dog's mouth. It was time the commissioners got him a new one anyway. How can you chase down a criminal if you can't drive over sixty? Tully had no intent of chasing down a criminal over sixty miles an hour or at any other speed. That's what deputies were for. They loved that sort of stuff.

As they drove farther, the trees got larger and the woods darker. The setting sun sucked the last of the daylight up the tree trunks as if they were giant straws. Night closed in around them. Suddenly there was water directly in front of them. Tully hit the brakes. His passengers nearly slid off their seats. Pap erupted in profanity and then apologized to Angie, but the outburst was probably nothing Angie hadn't heard many times before. In fact, Tully recalled a recent occasion when she used some of the words herself. Meanwhile the Explorer had stopped with its front wheels in the water, and Tully could feel them begin to sink into the mud. He hit the four-wheel-drive button and slammed into reverse. With a little spitting and howling, the vehicle climbed back onto dry ground.

Poke said, "I was going to tell you, Bo, I thought the swamp was just a lick or two ahead, but you got there before I could think of the words."

Tully shut off the engine and opened his door. "Thanks a lot, Poke. You managed to get us to the swamp sooner than I expected and closer than I wanted, but you got us here. How far does the swamp stretch out this way?"

The old man pointed directly ahead. "Three or four miles across here at the bottom. Then it gets narrower as it stretches up toward Scotchman."

They got out and followed Poke along a game trail close to the water's edge. He stopped by a pile of brush.

"You fellows help me clean this off. I keep it hidden so youngsters don't come along and get hold of it."

"Good idea," Tully said. "They could take it out in the swamp and get lost or drowned."

"And leave my raft rotting away out there in the swamp!"

Once the brush was cleaned off, Tully gave a low whistle. "Poke, this is the finest raft I've ever seen."

Poke chuckled. "Isn't it, though? I put a lot of loving care into building it."

Tully said, "Those logs you've got under the deck, why, they're nearly as long and clean as those power-line poles we passed on our way in."

Poke smiled. "You think so, Bo? Why, that's mighty nice of you to say. Those power-company boys hauled a bunch of poles in one summer and left them lying on the ground for nearly a month. So when it came time to built my raft, I made some just like them. Oh, it was a powerful lot of work, Bo, but I got it done."

Tully nudged Angie. "Just look what a man can accomplish with nothing but a chain saw and an ax, if he puts his mind to it."

She didn't blink an eye. "It's the most beautiful raft I've ever seen, Poke."

"Thank you, Angie. Well, all aboard. The only downside of the raft, I haven't got a motor for it."

"A motor wouldn't do you any good anyway, Poke," Pap said. "Just make your raft go in circles. You know the only decent way to move a raft is to pole it."

"Danged if you're not right about that, Pap. I've got the poles leaning against a tree back in the woods. I'll go get 'em. They're long and slender and mighty fine to push with."

"Tamarack, I bet," Pap said. "The finest rafting poles there is."

"These have dried out for nearly three years. They're light as toothpicks and strong as iron. I'll go get them, if I can remember the tree I leaned them against."

Poke returned with two long, slender poles, one balanced over each shoulder. He gave them to Pap and Dave. "When you two get tired, Bo and I will take over."

Angie frowned at him. "Hey, where's my pole, Poke?"

"You're a lady, Angie! I can't have a lady poling my raft. It would be bad luck for sure."

Angie sat down in a pout on the front of the raft and crossed her arms and legs. "This is the worst case of male chauvinism I've ever come across, Poke, and I've come across a lot of it. This raft doesn't move until I get my own pole."

Poke appeared about to panic. "No, you've got to be the lookout, Angie! You sit right there on the front of the raft and keep us from running into trees and stumps and stuff. I wouldn't trust anyone else here with that kind of responsibility. Now here's how the rest of us will do the poling. Pap, you pole on that side." He pointed. "Dave, pole the other. Now both of you drag your poles in the water to the front of the raft and push them down till you hit bottom. Then you lean into the pole and push the raft ahead with your feet as you walk to the back of the raft. You got that?" Dave and Pap nodded. "If Angie yells 'Pap,' that means Pap stops poling but

Dave keeps on, and the raft will turn toward Pap's side. If she yells 'Dave,' he lets up and the raft turns his way."

Dave said, "Let me get this straight, Poke. We carry our poles back to the front of the raft each time we reach the back." He gave Tully a wink.

"No, no, no!" Poke yelled. "You drag the poles in the water. Otherwise you drip mud and swamp muck all over. We'd have a terrible mess in no time."

Pap said, "Been a long time since I rafted, Poke. Good thing you explained that to us."

Poke shook his head as if he couldn't believe the quality of crew he had brought aboard his raft. He walked over to Tully and tugged his sleeve. "You got a blanket in your rig? We need something to wrap the rifles in."

"You bet. I'll go get it." Tully walked back to the Explorer and returned with two blankets.

"You cold already, Poke?" Pap said. "I thought I could feel a bit of chill in the air myself."

"That's a mighty fine idea, Pap, and maybe I'll just take you up on it on our way back. For right now, though, I think we should roll the rifles up in the blankets so they don't slide all over the raft."

"I planned on being the lookout," Tully said. "Besides, Angie, if we get in a shoot-out, you won't be accustomed to my rifle."

"I qualified with one just like it at Quantico, Bo. It won't be a problem."

Pap and Dave began pushing the raft through the murky

water while Poke wrapped the rifles in the blanket. Angie sat up front with her legs crossed in the lotus position. "I know the front of a boat is called a bow," she said. "What do you call the front of a raft?"

"Technically it's called the front of the raft," Tully said.

"We could use 'fore' and 'aft,'" Pap said.

"Somebody hand me that extra blanket to sit on," Angie said. "My aft is getting sore already."

Tully laughed. "Good! That will help keep our lookout awake." He picked up the blanket and tossed it to Angie.

The technique of driving the raft along was soon mastered. Once they were under way it glided along with surprising ease. A murky darkness seemed to be rising out of the swamp itself.

"Anyone bring Maglites?" Pap asked.

"Yeah," Tully said. "I've got a couple of them in my vest. But I'd just as soon not use them until I'm sure we're alone out here."

Angie said, "I've got one in my shoulder bag."

The full moon began to rise and bathe them in light. They could now see large patches of greenish scum on the water.

"What we looking for, exactly?" Pap asked as he poled toward the aft of the raft.

"I don't know exactly," Tully said. "There are two big islands out in the middle of the swamp. I flew over them a few days ago. There were structures of some kind on one and what appeared to be a lot of bare ground on both of them. I didn't see any sign of life. Somehow, I think this swamp has a connection to the killings up in the huckleberry patch on Scotchman. The only thing I can think is the swamp provided a cover for some kind of illegal activity. It's not the kind of place you have people just dropping in for tea or that sort of thing, so you wouldn't likely be bothered by visitors. If you have workers that don't want to be there, they probably aren't going to take off wading through the swamp. Who knows, there could be quicksand out there someplace."

"Yeah," Angie said, turning around to shoot Tully a look. "Wading off through the swamp would be really stupid, don't you think, Bo?"

"Maybe not if you wanted to get rid of somebody, Angie." He was crouched down next to the rifles.

"Yeah, like the FBI," she said. "One thing we need to keep straight here, Bo, this is an FBI operation."

"It is?"

"If you think this swamp has something to do with the killings in a national forest, then those killings occurred in my domain. So I'm in charge of this little expedition. So far, I've been letting you wag me like the tail on a dog, but that's about to end."

"Well, let me say, a very attractive tail."

"No matter."

"Okay, Angie, you're in charge," he said. "What's our next step?"

Angie was apparently thinking of the next step when a Canada goose exploded out of the darkness right by her feet.

It went honking off into the dark. Everything was quiet for a few moments. Then Pap said, "Angie, do they teach you those words at the FBI?"

"Some of them," she gasped out. "The rest I picked up from hanging out with lowlifes like you guys. I can tell you this, boys, if I ever see a goose walking across the road, I'm going to run him down!"

Pap laughed. "Is it a crime in Blight County, Bo, murdering a goose with a car?"

"As you are aware, Pap, hardly anything is a crime in Blight County."

As Pap and Dave began to get the hang of poling, the raft picked up momentum. Now they only had to give an occasional push with their poles to maintain the speed. Dave said, "It just occurred to me, Poke—what do we use for brakes on this raft?"

"Beats the heck out of me, Dave. I never had it moving this fast before. I guess whatever we run into will be our brake."

"In that case, I hope our lookout is keeping a sharp eye on everything up ahead."

Angie said, "So far we have missed a number of dead trees and stumps by several inches, but there's a big mass of something coming up."

"Better just let it drift in, guys," Tully said. "It must be one of the islands I want to check out."

"Good," Pap said. "I need a rest and a cigarette." He dug out the makings for one of his hand-rolleds and deftly put them together. He snapped the head of a kitchen match with a thumbnail and held the flame to the tip of his cigarette. Something cracked loudly in the direction of the island. Pap dropped his cigarette in the water and crouched down. The cigarette sizzled into silence.

Angie laughed. "Don't worry, Pap. It's only a beaver."

"Well, that beaver's a pretty good shot, because he dang near hit me. That bullet whizzed by about half an inch from my ear."

Suddenly five shots were fired from the raft so fast they sounded as if they had come from an automatic weapon instead of a lever-action rifle. Tully spun around. He stared at Dave, who must have snatched his rifle from the blanket and fired. Tully had never heard a lever-action rifle fired so fast.

"I saw the muzzle flash near the top of the island," the tracker explained. "Probably didn't hit him but put enough lead in the air to scare him. We're not likely to hear from him again anytime soon."

Angie had her .38 out and pointed straight up. Any goose that surprises her now, Tully thought, is a dead goose.

23

THE RAFT BUMPED gently into the shore. Angie stepped off, her pistol still out and pointed straight up. Pap and Bo each grabbed rifles. Dave reloaded his with shells he dug out of his pants pockets.

"What do you want me to do, Bo?" Poke asked.

"Stay with the raft. If it drifts off, we're stuck here."

Angie jumped to shore and then turned around. "Dave, would you hand me my shoulder bag?"

He picked it up. "Holy cow! What do you carry in here, Angie?"

"Among other things, my entire arsenal." She took the bag. "Thanks, Dave."

Pap and Angie crouched low as they moved slowly up the higher ground of the island. It had once been a hill, before the swamp backed up around it. Large evergreens cloaked its crown. Angie was in the lead. Tully moved up alongside her and whispered, "Unless the shooter has backup, he's probably on the other side of the island by now. Must have come out by boat."

Angie stopped and crouched. Tully crouched next to her. Pap came up behind them. "What's the plan?" he whispered.

"Beats me," Angie said. "What do you think, Bo?"

"I don't know. Where's Dave?"

"He's over to the right."

Tully said, "There must be something on this island somebody doesn't want us to see."

Pap whispered, "Well, we sure can't see much with only moonlight. You figure we're gonna stay here till morning, Bo?"

"I'm not sure that's a good idea. What do you think, Angie?"

"Beats me. I think we should at least push on to the top. That seems to be where the shot came from, according to Dave."

"Okay," Tully said, "but I'm taking the lead."

"Be my guest."

"Mine, too," Pap said.

They moved slowly up the slope. The ground near the top opened up beneath the towering ponderosas. It was free of brush and covered with a thick carpet of pine needles.

"Whoever shot at us must have taken off," Tully said from a crouch. Slowly he stood up.

"If the shooter came by boat, he's probably in it right

now, headed back out of the swamp," Dave said. "Or maybe he's circling around to intercept us when we go back."

Pap peered off through the trees and clicked the safety on his rifle. "I don't think so." He pointed. A white object lay in the middle of a little clearing now bright in the moonlight. They moved toward it.

A large man wearing a white T-shirt lay on his back. Tully took out a Maglite and put the beam on him. The white shirt shimmered in the light. Blood oozed from two holes in his chest.

Tully bent to check his pulse, then straightened up. "You're some shot, Dave."

"Thanks. I've never cared much for killing, though."

Angie stared down at the body. "I've never killed anyone, but I've often wondered what it would be like."

"Like eating raw oysters," Pap said. "The first goes down pretty hard but the next ones are a lot easier. Pretty soon you start to like them."

Tully looked at him and shook his head. "I can't stand raw oysters. Cooked ones either." He reached down and closed the dead man's eyes. "Remind me when I last deputized you, Dave."

"You bet. I think the last one should still be in effect."

"We'll refresh it if it isn't."

"Good."

Angie took out a handkerchief and used it to pick up the dead man's rifle. She held it under Tully's Maglite to examine it.

Tully nodded at the scope. "What kind is it, anyway?"

"A good one," Angie said. "I figured it had to be infrared, but it's just top-of-the-line regular."

She asked, "You think he's the only one on the island?"

"That would be my guess," Dave said. "He was obviously a lookout, sent here or left here to kill or scare off anybody who came poking around. I suspect he was low man on the totem pole. The top guys don't usually stand guard."

Pap and Tully grabbed the dead man's feet and started dragging him down the hill. Angie and Dave followed, carrying all the rifles.

When they got back to the raft, Poke said, "I didn't hear any shots. Who killed him?"

"Dave," Tully said. "From the raft."

Poke's whispered expletive was one of amazement. "I've never seen shooting like that in my entire life."

Pap said, "You never will again, Poke."

Angie looked back up toward the top of the island. "So you think our dead guy was the only person on the island."

"Probably," Tully said.

They built a driftwood fire in front of a log near the water and sat in a row with the blankets pulled over their shoulders. Tully said, "We should have remembered to bring hot dogs and buns."

"And marshmallows," Angie added. "Actually, I could go for a s'more right now."

"What's a s'more?" Pap asked.

"A Hershey bar and roasted marshmallow sandwiched between pieces of graham cracker," she said.

Tully shuddered. "Sounds illegal to me. That could kill an old man like Pap."

Pap tossed a piece of driftwood on the fire. "I was thinking the same thing, Bo. This here campfire reminds me of the time I took a prime elk steak out on a camping trip with Pinto Jack. It was pitch dark when I started cooking it over our campfire with only a flashlight to see by. I could hardly make out when the steak was done on the top side. When I turned it over it was burnt to a crisp on the bottom—worse than that. It looked like a piece of cowhide tanned too long. But the top side was perfect—juicy and tender. So we cut it up in strips and ate it like watermelon slices, gnawing off the good side. It was the best steak I ever ate."

Poke said, "I've thrown away more than one piece of meat I thought was ruined, and I bet I could have sliced it up and eaten it like watermelon. You should write a cookbook, Pap."

"I keep thinking about it, Poke."

"Sounds illegal to me," Tully said, "Pap writing a cookbook."

Angie shook her head. "I hate all this talk about eating when we have a dead body lying behind us. On the other hand, is anyone interested in a turkey-and-bacon sandwich with cold curly fries?"

The three men stared at her. "You better not be just tormenting us, Angie," Dave said.

"Nope," she said. "I have five such sandwiches and fries, all prepared by the café at my hotel. They're for sale at a thousand dollars apiece. No checks, considering my present company."

"I want to believe it but I can't," Pap said.

Angie pulled a brown paper sack out of her shoulder bag and distributed the sandwiches. The men bit into them and groaned with pleasure.

Dave said, "No wonder that bag of yours was so heavy, Angie! I figured you planned to set up housekeeping out here."

"I'm afraid I forgot the glassware, Dave, but I did bring a bottle of bourbon." She took it from her bag and handed it to Pap. "So we'll all have to drink out of the bottle. I hope none of you have communicable diseases or are squeamish."

"Not me," Pap said. "But I may have to take up religion. This is a miracle!"

Later they relaxed around the campfire telling stories. Finally Tully said, "Dave's turn. Maybe he will enlighten us as to how he learned to shoot like that and all the martial-arts moves he obviously has."

Dave laughed. "I wouldn't call them martial arts, but I spent a year in Japan in the company of six Japanese gentlemen a good deal smaller than Angie. Every day for a year I paid them a lot of money to beat me senseless. They struck so fast you couldn't see them move. If you've ever seen a rattlesnake strike, that's how fast they were. By the end of the year, I was one massive ache but I could take out two of them in a match. I figured that was enough. From then on I worked on fleeing, just in case more than two bad guys showed up."

Pap laughed. "I myself have always favored fleeing right up front, so nobody gets confused about my intentions."

One by one they dozed off, curling up on the sand next to the campfire.

The following morning they explored the island. On the far side they found an aluminum canoe turned upside down on the bank, with one paddle under it, the transportation the sniper had apparently used to get through the swamp.

As Tully had noticed in his flight with Pete, a large portion of the island was barren of trees and the ground appeared to be tilled. There were watering cans scattered about near endless rows of stalks cut close to the ground. They found a pole shelter, the front of which was open. There were four cots inside containing a few rumpled blankets. In the back of the structure were half a dozen bags of commercial fertilizer and a pile of empty bags. The fire pit out front contained partially burned pizza boxes and wrappers for other fast foods.

"I guess we know what was going on here," Tully said. "They were growing marijuana. The murdered guys were the ones who took care of it, watering the plants and hoeing the weeds and so on. I figured them for farm laborers of some kind, and I guess that's what they were."

"Looks as if they weren't treated too badly," Angie said. "But there was no way off this island. They were essentially prisoners here."

"You don't feed prisoners pizza," Tully said.

"Yeah," Pap said. "And they could have got away if they wanted to. Something kept them here. My guess is they were promised a cut of the profits. So in the end the guys running the operation decided it would be cheaper to kill the help than pay them. It would also keep them from blabbing to the cops, if they got ripped off. It's like I always say, murder is done for money or to keep someone quiet. Hey, Angie, how about killing someone because you don't want to pay them?"

"It might seem the reasonable thing to do, if you don't mind murdering people."

Tully squatted down to get a closer look at some of the stubble. "If you're so smart, Pap, what happened to the marijuana?"

"Why, they harvested it! What do you think, Bo?"

"I think a couple tons of the stuff is pretty hard to market and distribute all at once."

"Yeah," Dave said, "but where are you going to store a couple tons of it? Haul it to a commercial warehouse? I don't think so."

Angie put her hands on her hips. "Okay, Bo, I'll say it. How about a barn?"

Tully stood up, wiping his hands on his jeans. "That's an A for Miss FBI. And who do we know has a barn? The Poulsons! And Mr. Poulson, the owner, happens to be missing and presumed dead, and his wife has been murdered. The ranch has a very large barn out behind his house. It is watched over by an extremely smooth sociopath by the name of Ray Porter, alias Ray Crockett, and Mr. Porter has a criminal record. Furthermore, who has been urging me to search the Poulson place for the body of Mr. Poulson? The ex–Mrs. Poulson! And what happened to her?"

"She was pushed off a bridge and killed," Pap said. "No doubt to take heat off the ranch. I hate to admit it, Bo, but you might be on your way to making a pretty decent sheriff."

Tully smiled. "Thanks, Pap. Maybe we'll get this whole business wrapped up in a couple of days."

Angie said, "And this ties into the huckleberry murders exactly how? Some evidence would be nice."

Tully tugged on the corner of his mustache. "Well, Angie, since the FBI probably isn't going to let us do this the Blight way, we'll have to tie the dead huckleberry pickers to the island. Maybe we can do that with fingerprints on the watering cans and whatnot. But to really pin the murders on the guys who ran the marijuana operation, we have to track down the fourth man, the kid who escaped the murder plot, Craig Wilson."

Angie said, "I don't think we'll solve anything standing around here."

"That's right," Poke said. "Besides, that fellow you killed, Dave, is going to spoil pretty fast in this heat."

"Not to mention I'm starving to death," Angie said. "Crabbs is actually starting to sound pretty good to me."

Tully laughed. "I hadn't realized we were undergoing such extreme hardship, Angie. Guys, we better get back to civilization before Angie goes even more wacko on us. Anyone who thinks Crabbs isn't so bad is right on the brink." He stepped backward and almost fell over something. "Hey, what's this?"

Pap bent over and looked at the little contraption. "It's a fogger!"

Dave scratched his head. "A fogger? What's a fogger?"

Pap said, "It explains why there aren't any mosquitoes in the swamp! They put the fogger in their boat when the wind is just right and drive across one side of the swamp. It puts up a big cloud of insecticide that drifts across the swamp and kills all the mosquitoes and any innocent bug who happens to be passing through. Now that we've got the missing-mosquito mystery solved, shouldn't one of us paddle the canoe back?"

"Leave it for now," Tully said. "I want all of us to stick together."

They trooped back to the raft. They wrapped the body in one of the blankets and leaned the rifles against it. Angie and Poke took up their positions fore and aft, and Dave and Pap manned the poles. "Point the way, Poke," Tully said.

"What you mean, 'point the way,' Bo? Weren't you paying attention when you poled us in here?"

"No, I had you as a guide."

"Hunh. Well, it was dark. Let's see. I reckon if we head this way, it will take us back the way we came in."

"That way!" Pap shouted. "That ain't the way we come in."

"Well, what way you think it was, Pap, you're so dang smart?"

"I wasn't paying that much attention either. I figured you were the one knew the swamp."

"Shucks," Poke said. "I've never been in this far on a dark night with some fellow shooting at me."

Angie put her hands on her hips. "If all you mountain men will just shut up for a moment, I'll tell you how to get out of here. See that line of dead trees over there? Well, follow along them until we see green woods. Then we'll know we're moving along the north edge of the swamp. We keep the green trees off to our right until we see Bo's red Explorer."

"That's right," Tully said. "I was checking to see if Angie had been paying attention, and by golly, she was."

Angie rolled her eyes.

Two hours later they were in the Explorer and headed back to Poke's. Tully paid him three hundred dollars in cash and they were on their way into town.

"What we going to do with the stiff?" Pap asked.

"Drop him off at the medical examiner's."

"You think that's a good idea? In the old days we would have taken him out in the woods and buried him. Or we could have got some stones and sunk him in the swamp."

Tully turned and looked back at him. "Have you forgotten we have an FBI agent in the car?"

"That's right," Angie said. "And I haven't quite acclimated myself to the Blight way."

"That's a pity," Pap said. "It complicates matters no end. Susan will want to know why we didn't leave the body where it was until she did her examination."

Tully said, "And I'll tell her we would have had to pole the raft back out of the swamp, drive into town, notify her and her crew, then lead them back to the swamp, load them all on the raft, pole them out to the island, and—"

"Stop!" Angie cried. "I get your point!"

"So the way we're going to work this," Tully said, "we're going to drop Angie off at her hotel, then we'll haul the body to the medical examiner, ask her to get some prints off it so maybe we can get an ID."

"Sounds good to me," Pap said.

"I don't think it sounds that great," Angie said. "I have to file a report."

"We'll give you everything you need for your report," Tully said. "You might have to write in a few gaps. You do know how to write gaps, don't you?"

"Actually, no."

"Well, I'll teach you. Here's your hotel."

Angie said, "I have to take a nap, to get my mind working again. Just remember, everything in my report has to be the truth."

"It'll be the truth."

"It better be. Otherwise I may find myself permanently assigned to Blight."

Tully and Pap stopped at the medical examiner's office. Tully went in and got Susan and two attendants with a stretcher on wheels.

"Jeez," one of the attendants said. "He's all bent."

Tully said, "Yeah, well, you'd be bent too if you had to ride in the cargo space of an Explorer for fifty miles. Strap him down and he'll flatten out nicely when he warms up. We just spent a night out in a swamp with him, so you can't expect everything."

"What happened?" Susan asked.

Tully told her his version and afterward said, "You understand that's our story, sweetheart, and we're sticking to it."

"The usual, in other words. So what do you want me to do?"

"I can give you the exact time of death, so you don't have to bother with that ugly stuff. You can do whatever you do, as long as you wait until I'm out of here. The main thing I want are the prints off the guy. Then get them over to Lurch so he can try to get an ID. I checked the guy's pockets but he didn't have a billfold. He paddled out to the island in a canoe, so there should be a vehicle somewhere near the swamp, unless he was dropped off by someone. In any case, this guy was involved in a large-scale marijuana operation. His pals are still out there running around and they're very dangerous."

"So you think you know who they are?"

Susan's attendants were strapping the corpse to an examination table behind them. The sounds were ugly. Tully shuddered. "Yeah. They're the same guys that killed the three kids up in the huckleberry patch. One down and two to go. The problem is, I just don't have proof of anything yet. There are some watering cans and various tools out on the island. I may get Lurch out there to see if he can pick up some prints.

It hasn't rained since the murders, so the prints should be okay. That way we can tie the murdered guys to the island."

Susan laughed. "You're looking for proof, Bo? Whatever happened to the Blight way?"

"That's my fallback position."

He dropped Pap off at his house, then drove over to the courthouse and went to the department office. The crew didn't even bother to look up. He tried his special coffee pump. It filled his cup with dark black coffee that smelled wonderful. He smiled in surprise. He stuck his head into the radio room. "This is great, Flo. I like having a pump all to myself."

She favored him with one of her blazing smiles. "Anybody else tries to use it, boss, I break his wrist."

Daisy looked up. "Well, it's about time, Sheriff. Do you ever think to turn on your phone, so we don't have to worry ourselves sick about you?"

"No way you need worry about me. Old Tully knows how to take care of himself. We did have to kill a fellow who took a shot at us. Pap was lighting one of his hand-rolleds in the dark, and I guess the assailant took offense and tried to gun the old man down. I can't say I blame him. Maybe he hated those hand-rolleds as much as I do. One of our party—not me—drilled the sniper through the chest. We've got some prints coming in from the dead guy, Lurch. You may be able to get an ID on him."

"Great," the Unit said. "I'll check with Susan."

Daisy said, "We should know better than to let you out unsupervised."

Pugh asked, "You say you didn't shoot him, Bo?"

Tully shook his head. "No, Brian, Dave did. The guy was apparently aiming for my father and barely missed him. Anyway, we ended up spending the night in the swamp. Now, Brian, I want you to put together a raiding party for seven o'clock tonight. Get Ernie and six other deputies. Make sure they're well armed and wearing their vests. I'll be back at four and will fill you in then."

Daisy asked, "Can I go, Bo?"

"You bet, sweetheart. You're a deputy, after all. But wear your vest. There could be serious shooting."

She said, "You really think these guys are dumb enough to shoot, Bo?"

"I hope so. We'll have Dave along. Give him a call at the restaurant, just to remind him, Daisy. He's probably already sacked out, so give him a couple of hours. Oh, and be sure to inform the FBI. She'll be at her hotel. What's her name again?"

"Agent Angela Phelps."

"Right. Tell everybody we'll meet here at seven."

He walked into his office and shut the door. After staring at his painted window for a moment, he dug out his tattered pocket notebook. Putting his finger on a number in the book, he sat down and dialed the phone.

"Yeah?"

"Mitch?"

"No, I'll get him."

Mitch answered. "Yeah?"

"You guys need to hire a receptionist, Mitch. The phone manners there are terrible."

"I'd do that, if I was a rich sheriff. How you doin', Bo?"

"Fair to middling. I spent the night camping out and every bone and muscle I've got is aching. But enough about that. I've got a stiff down at the medical examiner's, and I was wondering if one of you sterling citizens might be able to identify him."

"We don't have any fresh kills, Bo, if that's what you're thinking."

"Remember the guy who chased the little girl into your house and one of your guys laid down a line in front of him from an AK-47? I'd like someone who saw the guy to come down and see if the stiff is the same fellow."

"One second, Bo."

Tully could tell Mitch had his hand over the mouthpiece but he could still hear him giving an order. Someone shouted, "What! No way! I ain't!"

Mitch said, "Red will be right down, Bo. He may be a little worse for wear but he'll be right there."

"Thanks, Mitch. I appreciate it." He hung up.

Tully sighed and sipped his coffee. When he had drained the last drop of it, he wondered if Flo had got over her divorce from her loser husband. If so, she'd be a good prospect for a live-in housekeeper. On the other hand, he didn't think he could stand listening to a woman constantly gripe about her ex-husband. You need to let divorcées cool for about a year. He put both hands flat on his desk and slowly pushed himself up. He walked out into the briefing room and caught Pugh just as the deputy was leaving.

"Do we have Bev out of the hospital yet?"

"Yeah. She seems to be okay. I put her up at the Pine Creek Motel, on the county, of course."

"I hope you explained to her that it is not a good idea to start turning tricks out of there."

"That slipped my mind. But she talked about taking up a new trade."

"Good. In any case, I want you to pick her up and bring her down to the M.E.'s lab. I want to see if she can identify our dead body as one of the guys that used to sit at her table in Slade's."

"You got it, boss."

"See the two of you there in an hour."

As he walked by Daisy's desk she spun around on her little swivel chair and said, "Bo, you better go home and get some sleep. You look terrible."

"Maybe. First, though, I have to stop by the medical examiner's. One of the guys from Mitch's gang is coming down to see if he can identify the body. Brian's bringing our prostitute. It's a party. Then I'm headed home."

"Oh. Well, say hi to Susan for me."

"You bet," Tully said. "I suppose you know she hates me."

"Maybe. But single desperate women can get over hate for a man pretty fast."

He grinned at her. "I'll keep that in mind, Daisy."

Pleased to see her blush, he worried all the way out the door he might be hit in the back with a blunt object.

He was waiting in the reception room at the medical examiner's office when Red showed up outside on his motorcycle, the machine apparently unencumbered by a muffler. He walked out to meet the rider. "Hey, Red, I expected you might bring along those AK-47s."

"What AK-47s you talking about, Sheriff? Pugh picked up the only one we had. Mitch said for me to tell you we didn't know what it was, so we used it for a wall hanging."

"I see. Well, I appreciate your stepping in and protecting Jenny."

"Anytime, Sheriff. She seemed like a real nice little girl. If one of the guys laid a finger on her, Mitch would have shot him dead on the spot. Well, I guess he would have taken him out behind the house and shot him there. He wouldn't want Jenny to see any more violence. Not that Mitch, being a convicted offender, has a gun. I don't want you to think that."

"I'm sure you don't, Red. Let's go in and have a look at the body."

Red raised his shoulders in a quivering shudder. "All right, but I really hate this, Sheriff. It gives me the creeps, having to look at a dead body. Still, it's better than being one, I suppose. Otherwise I wouldn't be here."

"Really. I'd guess you'd made a few of them in your day, Red."

"You got that wrong. I got no stomach for dead people."

They walked into the lab and Tully introduced Susan to Red. Then she whipped the sheet back off of the dead man's head. Red sucked in his breath and swayed back and forth. Tully grabbed his arm and steadied him.

Red gasped. "Cover it up!"

Susan pulled the sheet back over the body's head. Red turned and lunged back out into the reception room.

Tully thanked Susan and followed him out. The man was pale and shaky. "You okay, Red?"

"I hate this kind of stuff!"

"Maybe you should take up another line of work."

Red shuddered. "Don't think I ain't thought about it. I might even start at the junior college."

Tully sat down in a chair next to him. "Good idea, Red. What do you think you might major in?"

"Arithmetic."

"Arithmetic used to be a good major but now everybody's got a computer that does the adding and subtracting. You might want to look into something computers don't do, whatever that might be. So, did you recognize the corpse?"

"Yeah. He's the same guy chased the little girl."

Brian walked in with Bev. She gave Tully a big smile. The discoloration was almost gone from around her eye and she was much prettier than he remembered. She blurted out, "Oh, Sheriff! I'm so glad to see you. I can't begin to tell you how wonderful Brian's been to me. Why, he even—"

Pugh gave her a sharp look. "Enough about me, Bev! I think the sheriff has a little job for you."

"I do," Tully said. He took her by the hand, led her back into the lab, and introduced her to Susan. The M.E. pulled back the sheet.

Bev gasped and put her hand to her mouth. "That's the guy who hit me! His name is Stark. I think it's his last name. One of the other two called him that several times. He was a mean one, but I could tell he was scared of the other two."

Susan pulled the sheet back over the man's face. "Cause of death was two gunshot wounds to the chest. One bullet went clear through but we saved the other one. You want it, Bo?"

"Naw. Oh, on second thought, give it to me." She put the bullet in a tiny plastic envelope, sealed it shut, and handed it to him. He dropped it in his shirt pocket. He turned to Bev. "You getting along all right financially?"

"Brian's been providing me with money but I need to get out and find a real job."

"No hurry, Bev. Take it easy for a few more days and get on your feet." He almost said, "instead of off them," but caught himself in time.

The room suddenly erupted in a thunderous roar. Both Tully and Pugh reached for their guns. Then Tully said, "Just Red, leaving on his motorcycle."

Pugh left with Bev. Tully turned his attention to Susan. "You happy these days?"

She smiled. "Do you really care, or are you just trying to be attentive?"

He laughed. "No, I really care, Susan. I want you to be happy. Anything new in your social life?"

"I've been out with another flyboy a couple of times. So far he hasn't set off any chimes. How about you?"

"Nope. Oh, there's one lady shows some interest in me. She's very nice but kind of sophisticated. A little weird, too."

"Etta Gorsich," Susan said.

"You must be psychic!"

"No, I just eat at Crabbs too. Lester has a thing for me and keeps me abreast of all your comings and goings."

"Lester!"

"You leave Lester alone, Bo! You give him any trouble, you'll have trouble with me. Like with the bullet you just slipped into your shirt pocket."

"Oh, don't worry about Lester. I'll leave him alone."

"So, what's it like, dating a fortune-teller?"

"As I get tired of repeating, Etta is not a fortune-teller. She's an investment consultant. She's a very nice lady and doesn't discuss cutting up dead people while we're having dinner. I've scarcely been able to eat a bite since my last dinner with you, and that was weeks ago."

"Well, you needed to lose a few pounds. And even if you don't believe it, I'm glad you found somebody."

"Thank you. And I'm glad you found yourself a new pilot. The free airfare will be nice. See if you can get tickets for Etta and me."

"What, there's not enough room for two on her broom?"

Tully thought it quite inappropriate for an attractive woman like Susan to laugh so hard while standing next to a dead person.

He went home and slept for two hours. Then he stopped by Angie's hotel to check on her. It was after two o'clock and she was seated in the café eating breakfast. He pulled up a chair across from her and sat down. "You recovered from our little adventure?"

"I just woke up! You, by the way, look terrible, Bo."

"Thanks." He picked a piece of bacon off her plate and munched it. A waiter came over.

"Would you like to order, sir?"

"Yeah, I would. I'll have what she's having."

"Good," Angie said. "Then I can consider that piece of bacon out on loan. So what's happening?"

Tully lowered his voice. "I'm putting together a raid. We're going to hit Orville Poulson's farm tonight."

"Tonight! What's the big hurry? Give us a chance to recover."

Tully eyed another piece of Angie's bacon but she snatched it up and started nibbling it. "Well, when Stark doesn't return—Stark, that's what we think the name of the dead guy is—then the other two are going to get concerned. They'll pull out as soon as they think the jig is up and they'll take their hemp with them."

"So what are you arresting them for?"

"Possession with intent to sell. A couple tons of the stuff, maybe more, that we should find at the barn tonight. And after we've picked up a bit more evidence, murder. Daisy has cadaver dogs on order for tonight. I have a pretty solid hunch we'll find Orville's body under the house. As for the huckleberry murders, we might be able to hunt down Craig Wilson to identify the guys who killed his friends and shot him. I hope you're going to stay and help me with that."

She took a large bite of hash browns and spoke around it. "You're pretty sure the marijuana is stashed at Poulson's?"

"Yeah. Pretty sure, anyway. What better place than a barn?"

"So your sociopathic friend Crockett may be involved in this?"

"Yeah. In fact I suspect he's the brains. And he was sitting there on a ranch with a huge empty barn."

"So what's the plan?"

"As I told you, Daisy has arranged for cadaver dogs to accompany the troops. A judge has given her a warrant to search the whole ranch, but the main place I want them to check out is the crawl space under the house. Poulson disappeared in the winter, supposedly on a trip to Mexico, and the ground around the ranch would have been frozen solid. I don't think these are the kind of guys who would hack a grave out of frozen ground."

Tully's order arrived. Angie called in her bacon loan and nibbled it thoughtfully. Tully tasted the hash browns. Not perfect but not bad.

Angie said, "They could have stashed the body under some hay in the barn and waited for the ground to thaw in the spring. Then they could have dug an eight-foot-deep hole with a backhoe, and dumped the body in. I don't think cadaver dogs would detect him that deep down."

"Quit trying to confuse me, Angie."

"Why don't you just go up and use my room?"

Tully stared at her. "But I need sleep."

She laughed. "I promise I won't bother you. I'll go shopping. I have a very strong urge to go shopping."

Tully thought for a moment. "Okay, I'll take you up on your offer. Wake me at six?"

"You got it, Sheriff. What time's the raid?"

"We meet at my office at seven sharp."

"Good. Are you bringing Dave in on it?"

"Yeah. Dave would never forgive me if I didn't. He was pretty upset over the killings in the huckleberry patch."

Angie gave him her key and he went up to the room and used her phone to call Daisy.

"Boss! I thought you went home. I just tried to call you."

"No, I'm sleeping in town in the FBI's hotel room. It's not what you think, Daisy. It's perfectly innocent. She's gone! If you have any problems, call me here." He gave her the room number.

"Innocent? This would be a first, then?"

He groaned. "Daisy, get real. We've got some serious work going down tonight. Have the deputies ready to move at six forty-five, all of them armed to the teeth and wearing their vests. You, too. I know the vest conceals your nice little figure, but we all have to sacrifice. The cadaver dogs ready to go?"

"Straining at the leash, boss. So is their handler, Gordy something."

He yawned. "Good. I'm stopping in for a little visit with Ray Crockett about six-thirty. I'll be there when our guys come in to bust the joint. Oh, and the FBI wants in on this. If we nab the guys responsible for the huckleberry murders, they'll fall under Angie's province, if they're still alive. She can have them however they are. Have Ernie pick her up at her hotel."

"Got it, boss."

"Just remember, you're the best I've got, Daisy."

"How about the best you've ever had?"

"Let me mull that over." He hung up.

24

AFTER TELLING THE plan to his assembled deputies, Tully drove out to the ranch. As he turned into the gravel road he could see the large white boat parked in an open-sided shed out back. The barn loomed darkly behind it. He went up the walk and knocked on the door. Ray Crockett opened it. For a fraction of a second, his face registered shock. Then the old Ray took over. "My goodness, Sheriff, what brings you out at this hour?"

"Business, Ray, business."

"I hope you haven't come to haul me in for the murder of Orville Poulson."

"We'll have to talk about that, Ray." He glanced into the living room. A tall, slender, white-haired man was refreshing his drink at the small bar.

Ray Crockett said, "Sheriff Tully, I guess you and Orville Poulson already know each other."

The man turned around. "No need for an introduction, Ray," the man said, smiling. "Bo and I have known each other for twenty years or more."

Poulson strode across the living room and grabbed Tully by the hand. "Wonderful to see you, Bo! Can I fix you a drink?"

Tully couldn't find his voice for a moment, then croaked, "As a matter of fact, you can, Orville. Make it a large one. And while you're at it, I need to call my office. May I use your phone, Orville?"

"Help yourself, Sheriff. It's in the hallway."

Tully dialed the department number. Fortunately, Daisy was still there.

"Hi, boss. We're ready to move out."

"Cancel the cadaver dogs, Daisy."

"How come, Bo?"

"Don't ask questions. I'll tell you all about it tomorrow."

"Is the raid still on?"

"Yes. No point in canceling now."

He hung up.

Back in the living room, Orville was seated in a rocking chair, sipping his drink, and Crockett was on a sofa across from him.

"I can see you're as busy as always, Bo," Orville said. "Your drink's on the bar. Scotch straight up, as I recall."

Tully picked up the drink and took a gulp. "Perfect, Orville. Just what I needed. Yeah, I've got more than enough crime to keep me going. What brings you back?"

"A sad situation that you're familiar with. A friend got word to me about Marge's accident. True, we haven't been on the friendliest of terms since our divorce, but we were married almost forty years. Happily married for about thirty. Those years become a part of you. I was shaken to the core by the news. Now Ray tells me the paper says there's suspicion she was murdered. Is that right, Bo?"

"That's right. And we have evidence, too."

"Evidence! I can't for the life of me think of anything Marge might have done that someone would want to murder her."

Tully sipped his drink. "I can't either, Orville. But these days it takes very little to get someone murdered, even someone as sweet and innocent as Marge. I think there are people who viewed her as a nuisance and were concerned she might draw attention to their little scheme. Because she hadn't heard from you in a long while, she was sure you had been murdered and she was dead set on my arresting the person she thought had done it."

"For heaven's sakes, who did she think that might be, Bo?"

Tully glanced at Ray, who was smiling at him.

Tully sighed. "Well, to be blunt about it, Orville, she thought it was Ray here. She thought he had killed you and buried you under the house. She was after me constantly to arrest Ray for your murder, but of course, your body was hard to find since you were wearing it."

Ray continued to smile and Orville shook his head. "She must have been teched, Bo. Maybe the divorce was harder on her than I thought. I know she didn't like the idea of me trusting the whole ranch to Ray here, but shoot, I even trust my Social Security checks to him. He must have a dozen of them stashed away for me."

Tully glanced at Ray. He had stopped smiling. "Sounds to me as if you've put a lot of trust in Ray."

"Why not, Bo? He's one of the nicest people I've ever come across."

A low rumbling came from behind the house. Ray got up, walked into the kitchen, and looked out a window. "Oh, it's just some fellows who came to pick up their boat. They said they didn't have any place to park it and wanted to know if they could leave it in your shed, Orville. I said, 'Sure.' Hope that was okay."

"Okay with me," Orville said. "There's no walls on the shed so their boat's not very secure. Used to be a kid around here who stole anything not nailed down, so I hope they didn't leave any valuables in the boat."

Ray said, "Orville, the guy who owns the boat is headed for the back door. I'd better step out and talk to him. Uh, Sheriff, is something wrong?"

"If you're referring to the gun I have trained on your head, Ray, yes, indeed, something is wrong."

Orville gasped out, "Wha—?"

Then came a rasping blast from a bullhorn: "Gentlemen, stand right where you are! Raise your hands, put them behind your heads, lace your fingers together, and drop to your knees! Nobody move!"

"What on earth!" Orville said.

"No problem," Tully said. "Just remain seated, Orville, and we'll get this all straightened out. Find yourself a chair, Ray. This may take a while."

Tully walked into the kitchen and looked out the back window. A large moving van had pulled in behind a white pickup. A deputy with a shotgun was standing over two men on their knees in the beams of the pickup's headlights. Tiny moths flitted about them. Pugh was handcuffing another man, apparently the driver of the van. The man shouted something at Pugh. Not a good idea. Pugh said something to him. The man sat down on the ground. Ernie Thorpe came running from the barn. Dave Perkins was just getting out of his car. Angie emerged from the passenger side. Dave walked over to Pugh. Thorpe was waving his hands and telling them something. Dave shook his head. Pugh turned and looked toward the house. He wasn't happy. He pointed to the back door. Thorpe came running over. Tully let him in.

"I hate to tell you this, boss, but there's not so much as a toke of marijuana anywhere in the barn!"

"What!"

They both turned.

Orville was standing there. "Marijuana in my barn? What on earth are you saying, young man?"

Thorpe looked at Tully. The sheriff shrugged helplessly and nodded for his deputy to reply.

Thorpe's voice was shaky. "Uh, we had a suspicion that marijuana was being stored in your barn, sir. But . . . but we couldn't find any."

"I should think not!" Orville said.

Thorpe shook his head and went out to talk to Pugh.

Tully heard the front door open and close. Then it opened again. He walked into the front room. Ray was backing in through the door followed by Daisy, who held the muzzle of her revolver practically on his forehead.

Daisy said, "I caught this fellow sneaking out, boss. I thought maybe you wanted him to stick around."

"Good idea, Daisy. Where were you going, Ray?"

"With all the excitement, I needed a breath of fresh air. I was only stepping out to the porch."

"Stay seated until we get this mess straightened out. Daisy, shoot him if he moves. Ray, what's that moving van doing out there?"

"Beats me, Sheriff. I don't need it. Everything I own will fit in my car. Maybe they got the wrong address."

Orville said, "Bo, I hope you can explain all of this."

"I hope so, too, Orville. What we know is that there was a large marijuana harvest near here and it had to be stored somewhere. For a number of reasons, we thought it had to be in your barn."

Orville stared at him. "In my barn? Bo, I've got *three* barns on the ranch. The one right here, another out in the meadow, and one down by the river."

Tully felt his jaw start to sag. "Three barns!" he said. "Just one moment, Orville. I have to speak to one of my deputies."

He stepped to the back door and yelled, "Thorpe!"

The deputy came running over. "There are three barns," Tully said.

"Two more barns!" Thorpe blurted out.

"Yes, one in a meadow and one down by the river. Check them out. Fast! I don't know how long I can go without my heart beating."

Thorpe signaled two deputies to follow him. The three of them climbed into a department Explorer and roared off toward the river.

Ray shouted at him from the living room. "I think you're supposed to have a search warrant, Sheriff!"

Orville, who had followed Tully, said, "Surely you have a search warrant, Bo."

"Of course I have a search warrant." He pulled a warrant from his inside jacket pocket and started to hand it to Orville. "Oh, wrong one. This one's for your body."

"For my body?"

"Never mind. Here's the one to search for marijuana."

Angie walked in the back door, showing her FBI identification. "Looks as if you have everything under control, Bo."

"I hope," he said weakly. He introduced her to Orville.

"The FBI!" cried the old man.

"Orville!" Angie cried. She shook her head and said to Tully, "Pugh got the names of the guys in the pickup, Stanley Kruger and Rupert Quince, both from Los Angeles."

Tully said, "Orville, it's a long story, and I can't tell you the whole thing now. But as soon as we have time, we'll be able to explain everything to you, right, Angie?"

"I hope so."

Pugh stepped in behind Angie. "I'm loading up our two murder suspects, Bo. What do you say I swing by the motel and see if Bev can identify Stanley Kruger and Rupert Quince as the guys at Slade's? That will tie them to Stark and the swamp."

Angie said, "Those two are mine, Deputy. Take them to jail. I'll interview them tomorrow."

Pugh looked at Tully for confirmation.

"Yeah, take them to jail, but let Bev look at them first. Don't let them see her, though. Right at the moment I'm not sure if we can hold them."

"Maybe they'll make a break for it," Pugh said.

"We're not that lucky, Brian. Lock them up in separate cells, far apart so they can't communicate."

"Jeez, boss, all the cells are already full."

"Well, stack some of the regulars and put each of these guys in a cell by himself."

Angie said, "And Sheriff, I don't want you talking to either of them unless I'm there."

"Perish the thought, Angie. Since the huckleberry murders were in your domain, why don't you ride in with Pugh, just to make sure they arrive at the jail safely?"

"Actually, I think it would be a better idea if Dave followed Pugh in. I'll ride shotgun with him."

I guess you have to be a tracker, Tully thought. "Fine. Just remember, I want them to arrive at the jail alive. Tell Dave that."

Tully and Orville walked back into the living room. Ray was sitting on the couch with his head in his hands. He looked up. "Sheriff, I didn't have anything to do with the killings up on Scotchman."

"Killings?" Orville said. "What killings?"

Tully said, "Three young guys were murdered up in a huckleberry patch. We think they were used all summer to cultivate a marijuana crop out on islands in the swamp. When their bosses didn't need them anymore, they executed them."

"Executed them! Why on earth . . ."

"I'm not sure, Orville. Maybe only because they didn't need them anymore. Pap thinks it was because of either money or silence or maybe both. I do have a question for you, Orville."

"What's that?"

"How did you get around down in Mexico? You drive, or what?"

"Drive! In Mexico? No way! Even if my eyesight and nerves were that good, I don't think I could manage it. No, I fly down and take cabs and buses and trains. It's a lot safer for the Mexicans."

"So you didn't need your driver's license?"

"No, I've got my passport. That's all the identification I need."

"So your driver's license is here someplace."

"Right. I left it in a drawer in my bedroom. Why all the interest in my driver's license?"

Tully looked over at Ray, who seemed to be shrinking into the cushions of the sofa. "I'll tell you later, Orville."

Tully heard a vehicle roar into the backyard and stop. He glanced out a window. Ernie Thorpe got out of a department Explorer and ran in through the back door.

"We got them, boss! The barn in the meadow is chock-full of weed. I left two deputies to guard it with their lives. Dave Perkins checked out the boat and found some marijuana seed there. I had two deputies search the boat before him, and they came up with nothing. Dave is something else. We've got them!"

Tully wondered for a moment if Dave's boat search involved something of the Blight way. Naw.

Dave came in. He was dressed in jeans, a gray suede jacket, and a black turtleneck. He looked terrific. Tully thought maybe that was his secret, high fashion. Dave said, "Bo, we're about to head in. Angie and I will follow Pugh, just to make sure the bad guys don't escape. Or try to escape. Pugh is still upset about the huckleberry murders."

"Yeah, it won't hurt to keep an extra eye on Pugh."

Tully turned to Ernie. "Good work, Thorpe! We're back in business. Round up the van driver and anybody else you find in the neighborhood and have some deputies haul them to jail."

He walked back into the living room. "Daisy, put your cuffs on Crockett and take him in. You need a backup?"

"What do you think, boss?"

Tully looked at Crockett. "Naw."

She cuffed Crockett behind his back and herded him out to her patrol car.

Tully went out in the backyard and found Thorpe. "Ernie, I'm leaving you in charge here. You and some of the deputies will have to spend the night. I'm headed home to bed. I'm wiped out."

"Looks like we got them nailed, boss."

"For the weed, at least. I'm not sure about the murders. But those are Angie's problem, come to think of it."

Dave walked up. "Looks like your case is coming together, Bo."

"Yeah, we can charge them with possession and intent to sell a couple tons of weed. But mostly I want them for the three murders up on Scotchman."

"Me too," said a voice behind him.

Tully turned. Angie was standing there. "I have to tell you, Bo, Dave is a terrific shot but I don't think he's an Indian."

Dave laughed. "And Angie, you don't look like any FBI agent I ever imagined."

Tully said, "While you two are chatting, I'm headed off to bed."

Dave said, "You sure you won't join Angie and me for a celebratory drink, Bo?"

"Too tired."

"What celebratory drink is that?" Angie asked.

Dave smiled. "The one you and I are having."

"And what are we celebrating?"

"Remains to be seen."

Tully stumbled off toward his Explorer.

25

TULLY SLEPT UNTIL noon the next day. Still lying in bed, peering up at his paintings, he thought about his next move. For one thing, he would send Lurch out to the island in the swamp to collect the watering cans and any tools he could find that might contain fingerprints. Next, he needed to find the guns used in the killings at the huckleberry patch. He would check with Pugh to see if he found any guns in the rigs at the ranch. Some silencers wouldn't be bad either. He needed to grill the driver of the moving van, who no doubt was connected to the buyer of the weed. He obviously intended to haul it somewhere. The big white pickup needed to be hauled into the shop and have the front bumper tested for paint matching that on Marge Poulson's car. His head whirled. He turned over and went back to sleep.

An hour later, he got up, showered and dressed, and drove down to McDonald's for his Egg McMuffin and coffee but had to settle for a Big Mac. Then he drove over to Etta's. She beamed at him. "Oh, Bo, I'm so glad you stopped by. You've been so busy lately I didn't know if I'd get to see you before I left."

He looked around the living room. Several suitcases were scattered about in various stages of being packed.

"You're leaving?"

"Yes, but I'll come back sometime. Moody, Simms and Cline has offered me a nice sum to do a little job for them. It's such a terrific offer I couldn't turn it down."

Tully shook his head. "I can't say I'm happy about it, Etta. We've been getting along so well. But I understand. When a big chance comes, you have to go for it."

"Oh, I'll be back in Idaho before the snow flies. Maybe we'll still have time for that trip up through Idaho. At least we'll be able to do our lunches at Crabbs."

Tully said, "What I came to tell you, Etta—the guy we thought was buried in the crawl space under the ranch house, well, he turned up alive."

"Wonderful! I told you I wasn't a fortune-teller, Bo."

She stood on her tiptoes and kissed Tully on the mouth. He felt it all the way to his toes. A few years older and he would have died from it. "Good-bye, Bo."

Tully stumbled out the door and, grasping both handrails, made his way slowly down the steps.

He drove the Explorer over to the hotel to pick up Angie.

She appeared exhausted. She pointed at the sun. "Doesn't that bright orb up there realize it's September? This heat is killing me."

"Something's gone wrong, all right. I blame it on the Weather Channel. If those weather people would stop fooling around with their satellites and stuff, we probably could get back to normal."

Angie smiled at him. "I didn't realize you were such a science buff."

Tully nodded his head. "Oh, yes. Except for algebra in high school, I probably would have been a scientist instead of an artist. I also had a problem with fractions. Every time I divided one half by one half, I ended up with one. It was crazy!"

Angie smiled. "What did your teacher say?"

"Miss Busbee? She said it beat the heck out of her too. She was also the volleyball coach. I was dynamite at volleyball so she gave me good grades in math."

Angie slid over closer to him and rested her hand on his leg. He noticed she wasn't wearing her seat belt but decided to ignore the infraction. "I guess it all works out in the end," she said. "Sometimes, though, I wish I'd become a teacher. Of all the worthwhile professions, I think teaching is best."

"Better than catching criminals?"

"Sure. Maybe a good teacher prevents a lot of criminals, if she teaches them the right stuff. I bet half the guys in prison can't read. You ever notice how few smart criminals there are?"

Tully nodded. "I've told a lot of them, 'You can't be

dumb,' but they never listen. Then they turn up dead or in prison."

Angie said, "So you think you can choose not to be dumb?"

"Hey, look at me. I tell myself all the time not to be dumb. How else do you think I got to be this smart?"

"I've wondered about that."

Tully came to an intersection, checked for traffic, and then drove through a red light.

"Do you realize you just drove through a red light?"

"Yeah, but I'm sheriff, remember."

Angie shook her head.

"So what's the plan here, FBI?" Tully asked.

"You're the smart one. You tell me."

Tully tugged thoughtfully on the droopy corner of his mustache. "I'm absolutely certain we have the bad guys locked up."

"By 'the bad guys' you mean the genteel chaps we picked up last night."

"Yes, beginning with Ray Porter, alias Crockett."

"You think Crockett is the mastermind?"

"Yeah, I think he's running the whole show. He probably ordered the huckleberry murders, not that his partners needed any encouragement. Whatever the reason for the killing of those three young guys, I don't think he had the stomach for doing the thing himself."

Angie nodded. "I was thinking about what Pap said, that there are only two reasons for murder—silence and money.

It's pretty obvious the young guys didn't have any money. So what kept them working like slaves on those islands? They could have figured out some way to get out of there."

Tully thought about this. "You're right. Their bosses couldn't have had a gun on them twenty-four hours a day. They had to be there voluntarily."

"Right. And it wasn't their silence the killers were worried about, at least not entirely. The victims had to be complicit in the marijuana project."

Tully glanced at her. "And why would that be?"

"Because they were supposed to get a cut of the profits. They worked like slaves for nothing all summer, because there was going to be a big payoff for them come the harvest."

Tully turned this over in his mind. "You think so?"

"It's a theory. In the end, it's cheaper to kill them than pay them. They couldn't very well not pay them and let them go. They would have tipped us off, maybe just spilled the beans over the phone and then beat it."

Tully gave his mustache another tug. "You wouldn't think they'd fall for a scam like going out to pick huckleberries."

"Nobody said they were smart."

"At least one of them was smart enough to hit the ground running. That's Craig Wilson. He's still out there someplace."

"Without Wilson, we really don't have all that much," Angie said. "It would be tough even tying them to the marijuana."

"How about the moving van?"

"The driver could claim he pulled into the ranch to ask directions to somewhere."

Tully sighed. "Maybe Lurch will be able to match some of the bullets to their guns."

"Did you find any guns?"

"No! Why do you keep harping on details!"

Angie said, "Crockett would be the easiest to break, don't you think?"

Tully shook his head. "I doubt it. That would be a death sentence for him in prison, and he knows it. The other guys seem scarcely smart enough to tie their own shoelaces."

Tully pulled into his parking space behind the courthouse, and he and Angie went down to the jail. He introduced Angie to Lulu and then asked the matron to bring Ray Porter, alias Crockett, into the interrogation room. "You need any help with him, Lulu?"

She laughed. "He'll be right in, boss."

Angie said, "How do you want to handle this, Bo?"

"I suggest we start with the rubber hose and then go to the electric wires and battery."

"I'm serious!"

"I suggest we try to scare him."

"I'll let you lead," Angie said.

"No, you!"

Lulu brought Porter into the interrogation room. He was dressed in the standard orange jumpsuit. True to his sociopathic character, he was still quite amiable.

"Have a seat, Ray," Tully said, pointing to a chair across from him and Angie.

"Thanks, Sheriff."

"You're welcome."

Angie said, "You know, Mr. Porter, you're involved in five murders here."

Ray went white. "Murders! I never hurt anyone in my life! I need my lawyer!"

Angie went on. "Listen, Ray, you can have a lawyer anytime you want. You don't have to say one word to us. It might be helpful to your case if you do talk to us right now, but I'm not promising anything. It does seem at this point that you were involved in a plot that resulted in the murders of five individuals."

Ray looked as if he was about to pass out.

Tully said, "You see, Ray, you started a sequence of events that ultimately led to the deaths of six individuals, counting Marge Poulson and a guy named Stark. It really doesn't make much difference you weren't holding a gun. We know we can nail your associates, and once we do that, they'll give you up in a split second."

Ray put his face in both hands. "I have a splitting headache. Do we have to do this right now, Sheriff?"

Angie said, "We can wait until you're feeling better, Mr. Porter. But any help you give us will be helpful to you at your trial, which, by the way, won't take place here in Blight but in a federal courthouse."

"A federal courthouse!"

"Yes, the murders up on Scotchman occurred in a national forest, so the FBI has jurisdiction. You are involved in a federal crime."

Ray groaned.

"I know how you feel, Ray," Tully said. "Blight laws are fairly flexible. They might give you a little wiggle room. And if every defense fails, there's always graft. Alas, I'm afraid you will be at the mercy of hard-nosed Feds like Agent Phelps here. Play-by-the-book types."

Ray jumped up. "I feel sick!"

Tully nodded to Lulu and she took him back to his cell.

Tully sighed and leaned his chair back against the wall and asked, "Which of the other guys do you think runs the operation?"

Angie thought for a moment. "Well, we know it wasn't Stark. Bosses don't stand guard at night in a swamp. Of the other two, I'd say the bigger one, Kruger, Stanley Kruger. I suppose it could be the other one, Rupert Quince."

Tully shook his head. "No, not Quince. Nobody named Quince ever gets to be boss, to say nothing of Rupert."

"You're probably right, Bo. I say let's grill Rupert first."

They had Lulu bring in Quince. Tully thought the orange jumpsuit looked like natural attire for him.

Quince sat down in the chair across from Angie. She said, "Mr. Quince, this is Sheriff Bo Tully. He has some questions for you."

Tully said, "Actually, Rupert, I get you because I'm not all that smart. The lady here gets to question the leader of the bunch."

Quince sneered. "What makes you think I'm not the leader?"

"Well, it's pretty obvious, isn't it?"

"You think I'm dumb, hunh! You should have left the cuffs on me, because for two cents I could grab you by the neck and squeeze the life out of you!"

"I know. That's why I've instructed our jail matron here to shoot you dead if you make the slightest move toward me."

Quince turned and looked at Lulu. She had her hands behind her back. One of the nice things about Lulu, she looked as if she wouldn't hesitate to shoot a person dead.

"So what do you want to know?" Quince asked.

"For starters, did you shoot the kid with the blue door on the red pickup?"

"What is this? A trick question? I was home watching TV when that dope was killed. Who drives a red pickup with a blue door anyway? That's enough to get anybody killed. Maybe you should ask Stark."

"Can't."

"Why not?"

"Stark is dead."

Quince was quiet while he mulled this over. "How did he get dead?"

Tully wanted to say, "He refused to answer our questions," but he thought Angie would raise a fuss.

Angie said, "He was standing guard out in the swamp and made the mistake of shooting at law enforcement. What was he guarding, Mr. Quince?"

Quince sighed. "I don't know anything about that. Since Stark is dead, I can tell you he's the one gunned down the kid in the pickup. I didn't have nothin' to do with that. But I ain't saying anything more."

"In that case, Lulu," Angie said, "you can return Mr. Quince to his cell and bring in Mr. Kruger."

Lulu took Quince out.

Angie switched off the tape recorder. "What do you think, Bo?"

"That we got zip. What do you think?"

She shook her head. "Zip is a bit excessive. He did indicate Stark gunned down Lennie Frick. Why kill Lennie if he didn't see them up on Scotchman right before the murders?"

Tully sighed. "How can we prove Lennie was even up on Scotchman? He told me he was and we have a fingerprint on a beer bottle. What more could you ask? They shot him because they recognized his vehicle, the blue door on the red truck."

"How do you know that?"

"Angie, you can be a real pain."

"Hush! Here comes Kruger."

Quince was big but Kruger would tower over him, big chest, big belly, big everything. He pulled out a chair, spun it around, and sat down astraddle it, his big arms resting on the back.

"It doesn't look like my lawyer is here yet," he said. "So I suppose the reason for this meeting is to tell me I'm about to be released."

"Not quite yet, Mr. Kruger," Tully said. "We just had a very interesting talk with Mr. Quince."

Kruger laughed. "Quince is an idiot. He blabs all day long. Nothing he says makes sense, which you must know by now." He looked relaxed but wary.

"Actually, he was quite informative," Tully said.

"You've got nothing on us, Sheriff, and you know it. Nothing! Nada! We happened to stop by a place where some jerk stored marijuana. And you try to pin it on us!"

"Suppose I tell you we have an eyewitness?"

Kruger's eyes turned into hard, mean slits. "You don't have any eyewitness because there wasn't anything to eyewitness."

Tully laughed. "You forget. One of your intended victims got away."

Kruger appeared about to leap over the table. "There were no intended victims! Nobody got away!"

Tully nodded at Lulu, who instantly stepped forward and tapped Kruger on the back. "C'mon, big guy," she said. "Back to your cell."

"I'll settle with you later!" Kruger growled, pointing a finger at Tully.

"Take a ticket. There's a long line."

After Lulu had returned Kruger to his cell, Tully shut his eyes, leaned back in his chair, and rested his head on the wall behind him.

"What now, Bo?"

"How do you feel about camping, Angie?"

26

THE TIME TULLY liked best in the mountains was early morning, with the sun rising through the trees. It had taken them two days just to find the trail to Scotchman Lake. The trail hadn't been touched by the Forest Service in years. Trees had grown up in the middle of it. Other trees had blown down and crisscrossed it from every direction. Scotchman Lake obviously hadn't been a popular destination for many decades. The scars of blazes that originally marked the route for Civilian Conservation Corps crews back in the thirties could still be seen on a few trees.

Tully had fired up his tiny backpacking stove before Angie had even opened her eyes. She poked her head out of the small green mountain tent. "Breakfast ready?"

"Almost. I've got the bacon nice and crisp and the potatoes and onions sizzling."

"Great. Let's see, for the past two days we've had bacon, potatoes, and onions for every meal."

Tully grinned at her. "I'm also cooking pancakes this morning. I'll spread peanut butter and jelly on them and roll them up for our lunch. Doesn't that sound good?"

"It sounds delicious! And you better not be lying, Bo!"

"Would I lie to you?"

Angie laughed and then groaned. "I'm a single great ache from one end to the other. And I haven't been out of these clothes for three days!"

"I know."

Angie pulled her shirt up to her nose and sniffed. "Do I really smell that bad?"

"I wasn't thinking of smell."

"I'll tell you this, Bo. When we finally get to that lake, I'm going skinny-dipping and you better keep your back turned. The only thing I'll be wearing is a gun."

"Ha! From the sound of it, you'd think I'd waited my whole life to catch a glimpse of a naked FBI agent."

Angie stepped over behind Tully. "Hey, someone's coming down the trail."

He stood up and squinted against the sun. He could just make out a figure stopped on the trail. Twice the man looked back over his shoulder, as if trying to decide whether to run back up the trail or continue down.

Angie stepped out on the trail and gestured for him to come down. "Come on, Craig! It's okay! You're safe now. Nobody is going to hurt you!"

The hiker stared at Angie for a long moment. Perhaps because she was a woman, he plodded on down.

Tully flipped the skillet. The pancake rose a good three feet in the air, gradually turned over, and landed back in the skillet. Perhaps this artful maneuver also had a calming effect on the hiker. Nobody flips a pancake and then tries to kill you.

"That's the first time I've seen anyone do that," Craig said, walking into their camp.

"First time it's ever worked for me," Tully said. "So you're Craig Wilson."

"Yeah, and you must be Sheriff Bo Tully. I suppose you've come to arrest me."

"No, as a matter of fact we came because we need your help to keep three bad guys in jail."

"You have them all locked up—Kruger, Quince, and Stark?"

"Stark is dead."

"Wow!" Craig said. "That's a surprise. Not that I mind."

"We have Kruger and Quince in jail, along with another fellow by the name of Ray Porter, aka Crockett, who may be the brains behind the operation. We need you to testify about what you know, in order to keep them there."

Craig slipped off his backpack and squatted down alongside Tully. "I saw Porter only once but I heard them talk about him sometimes. They'd kill me if they could. They already tried it once. I told the guys on the way up to pick huckleberries this was a setup but they didn't believe me. So when we started down toward the patch I was ready to take off. I was on the right-hand end of the line of us pickers. The instant I heard the shots I hunched over and ran like crazy. As I rounded the brush, something stung my arm but I hardly felt it. I ran until I couldn't run anymore. There was a thick grove of evergreens down a couple hundred yards and I hid there. They sent Stark down to find me but after a while he gave up and went back. Then I worked my way down farther and hid by the road until I saw the white pickup go by. I must have hid for another hour until I stepped out and waved down a logging truck."

Tully said, "That's about the way we thought it went down. I don't understand why all you guys didn't take off earlier. You could have built a raft and paddled off the island."

"Yeah, we could have, but they had promised us each ten thousand in cash at the end of the summer. All we had to do was cultivate the weed. We knew it was illegal, but I figured for ten thousand dollars I could take the chance. They were nice enough to us, except for Stark. Once Kruger slapped Stark senseless for punching one of the guys. They brought in great food—pizzas, tacos, burgers, milk shakes, anything we asked for. Used a big white boat to haul the stuff in and the grass out."

"Porter ever come out to the island?" Tully asked.

"Yeah, he came out just the one time. He was pretty slick. You could tell he was the boss of the operation, that he was the one with all the connections."

Tully smeared raspberry jam on a pancake, rolled it up,

and handed it to Craig. The kid ate it as if it was the best food he had ever tasted.

Angie said, "Make me one of those, Bo!"

Tully picked up another pancake, smeared it with raspberry jam, and handed it to her. Apparently it was also the best food *she* had ever tasted. "So, Craig, why did you get suspicious about the trip to pick huckleberries?"

Craig licked some jam off his fingers. "For one thing, it was the day we were supposed to get paid our ten thousand apiece. It was something about their attitude. Suddenly they had all turned stone cold. I'm pretty sure they'd been discussing why they should pay these four guys forty thousand dollars and then have them running around bragging about it. It was probably Stark who came up with the solution."

So Pap was right, Tully thought. This time it was both the money and the silence.

It suddenly occurred to Tully to introduce Angie.

"Craig, this is Angela Phelps, with the FBI."

"Hi, Craig," Angie said. "I've talked to your uncle. He's the one who told us how to find you. You can't believe how happy I am to see you."

"The FBI!" Craig choked out.

Tully said, "Yeah, the FBI, Craig. The FBI will be looking after you from now on. The murders were committed on federal land. As far as your part in growing the marijuana, that occurred in Blight County, so we get a piece of you for that. If Angie and her FBI bosses agree, I think we can work out some community service right there in the sheriff's office."

Angie said, "You help us convict the bad guys, Craig, and we'll look out for you."

"As a matter of fact, Craig," Tully said, "I just thought of a community service project for you. I need a new well dug."

Angie rolled her eyes. "So the Blight way kicks in!"

"Yes, indeed."

Craig looked back up the trail. "Just about anywhere is better than that lake. No wonder nobody goes there anymore. It's one scary place."

"So I've been told."

27

THREE WEEKS AFTER Etta Gorsich left town, human remains were found buried in the crawl space of a house being demolished two blocks away from hers to make way for yet another strip mall. So Tully had a new mystery to solve and a culprit to find. He thought he should phone Etta and tell her. Her vision or whatever it was had proven correct after all. Daisy found the number for Moody, Simms & Cline in New York.

When the receptionist learned he was a sheriff calling from Idaho, she put him through to a vice president.

"Etta Gorsich!" the man said. "Why, she's just down the hall. You don't happen to be the Sheriff Bo Tully Etta's been telling us about?"

"Depends on what she's been telling."

"All good, sir, all good. It's a pleasure to talk to you! We could use some of your Blight ways here in New York. I'll get Etta for you."

She came on. "Bo! What a pleasant surprise!"

"Etta, I just had to tell you—we found human remains in the crawl space of a house two blocks away from yours!"

"Oh, Bo, that's terrible but wonderful! Maybe I am a psychic! You don't mind hanging out with a psychic, do you?"

"Not at all, if that psychic is you."

"Are we still on for that trip up through Idaho next summer?"

"You bet, Etta. Just the thought of it will keep me warm all winter. See you then." He could hear her laughing when he hung up.

Brian Pugh walked in carrying a cup of coffee. "You were right, Bo. The Slade gang was staying at the old farmhouse on the other side of Cow Creek. Marge Poulson had rented it to them. She was probably headed out there to collect the rent when they killed her. Just down from the bridge we found tracks on a little side road where they waited for her. The tracks match those on the pickup. You think they killed her to keep from paying the rent?"

Pugh sat down, brushed some papers aside on Tully's desk, and set his coffee cup down.

Tully leaned back in his chair and clasped his hands behind his neck. "I doubt they were concerned about the rent, Brian. It was meant to get her off Ray Porter's back. She was calling too much attention to Ray and the ranch, and they were afraid the whole operation would fall apart if we started poking around looking for Poulson's body. We would have found the marijuana instead."

Brian said, "So Craig will testify the three of them murdered his friends and wounded him. Kruger and Quince are goners, don't you think, boss?"

Tully smiled. "That's exactly what I think, Pugh. And we can make a pretty good case Ray Porter was the brains behind the whole operation, including the murders. Angie will be ramrodding the murder case, of course."

"What about Porter?" Pugh asked.

"Angie may get Ray, too, if Kruger and Quince turn on him and claim he was the mastermind behind the murders. We've already got him for cashing Orville Poulson's Social Security checks. As soon as I found out Orville had left his driver's license at the ranch, I knew we had Ray for the checks. That was the money he was living on. I have no doubt Orville's hours, if not his minutes, were numbered when he showed up back at the ranch. We've already got Ray for storing the marijuana at the ranch he was managing. So I think we can say good-bye to Ray Crockett alias Porter for a long, long time."

"Oh, I almost forgot something," Pugh said. He took a sip of his coffee.

"What's that?"

"We found three .22-caliber revolvers at the farmhouse and three silencers. I just gave them to Lurch to check for prints."

Tully stared at him. "Gee, thanks for telling me, Pugh!"

• • •

The following week, the weather cooled and Tully took nurse Scarlett O'Ryan fishing and camping on the Saint Joe River. The camping produced the first rain of the season and finally reduced the threat of forest fires. Scarlett turned out to be a terrific fly caster and taught Tully a whole lot of things he had never tried before. Not only was she beautiful, she was a nurse, and all nurses know CPR. When you're a forty-three-year-old man out fly-fishing the Joe for a week with a beautiful young woman, it's reassuring to know that if CPR should suddenly be required, you're with someone who can perform it.

BROKEN VESSELS

A Story About How God Uses Broken People

Joey Candillo

Critical Mass Books
Davenport, Florida
www.criticalmasspublishing.com

Cover Design	Eowyn Riggins
Interior Layout	Rachel Greene

ISBN: 978-1-947153-27-1

1

NOT QUITE A STORY-BOOK CHILDHOOD

I LOVE SHARING my story. Whenever I have the opportunity to go out and speak to a different congregation from my own at Grace Church, I am able to give my testimony. The home crowd has heard it all before.

There's a lot to the story.

I don't share it to glorify myself. You will quickly see that I am no hero. Far from it. The hero of my story is...

Jesus Christ.

I'm going to share the long version of my journey in this book. No holds barred. I will not gloss over things that aren't very pretty. In fact, they're downright ugly.

Ugly as sin.

Though my story will take us back years—to when I was four years old—I like to start off years later, when I lived at 1216 East Morgan Street in Boonville, Missouri. The place was old. It had been built about twenty years after the Civil War. Way back then, it was the *Missouri Training School for Boys*. But by the time I moved there—or *was moved* there—it had a new name.

The Boonville Correctional Center.

You guessed it. I was in prison.

How did I get there?

★

As I mentioned, my story goes back to when I was four years old. I grew up in California. My Mom and Dad met in Independence, Missouri, but Mom had family in California. So, I was born out there, in Long Beach. We lived there until I was about seven years old. We moved around a lot. It was my Mom and Dad, and my older sister and brother and me. My Dad was an over-the-road truck driver, so he was gone a lot. He was also an alcoholic. A bad one.

My brother was my best friend. I remember this one time the whole family was at the beach. Two boys came over and they threw sand in my eyes. I went back to the blanket where my Mom and Dad and my brother, Jeff, were sitting. I was crying. Jeff asked me, "What happened?" I could just barely see out of one of my eyes because of all the sand, but I pointed at the two guys. He went over there and beat the crap out of both of them.

I remember thinking, *this is going to be good, having an older brother around to take care of you.*

But my most vivid memory from back then was, as I mentioned, when I was four years old. My dad was out of town. We had this old wood-paneled station wagon. Mom loaded us up and we went for ice cream. We got it to go, and on the drive home we made a bit of a mess eating in the back seat.

I don't know when we got back to the house, it was kind of a mad scramble, but my brother had eaten all of his ice cream and had crawled all the way in the back of the station wagon and fell asleep. Everyone else went inside the house.

The details about what happened next are a bit fuzzy—after all, this was more than four *decades* ago. But I remember the pertinent things. I went back out to the car and climbed inside. I started playing with a cigarette lighter that was in the front seat. Both of my parents smoked, and so there were lighters everywhere. I don't know why I was fascinated with fire growing up. I know there was at least one time when I burned down our house. I remember another time burning a field.

I caught a piece of paper on fire.

Then it got out of hand. I threw the paper down and jumped out of the car. It happened so quick. I ran a few yards, and by the time I turned around the car was engulfed in flames. I freaked out, realizing at that point that my brother was all the way in the back of the station wagon. I never heard him scream. I like to think he never even woke up. I just backed up. The car was parked out on the street, and I ended up in between our house and the neighbor's house. I just watched that car burn and didn't know what to do. I remember seeing my Mom race out of the house, screaming hysterically. I watched the firetruck pull up and try to quench the flames.

But it was too late.

The whole car burned up, and my brother was dead. The police asked me if I saw anything. I was scared. I told them, "No, I didn't see anything." I didn't know if they were going to throw me in jail, or what. I was responsible. I watched it happen. So, it was a secret I had to carry around with me.

Needless to say, this whole episode really messed me up. As I stood there between those houses, I froze in place, but looking back, I also remember being frozen in time. It was almost like I was watching a movie. And down through the years, that movie looped over and over again in my brain. In fact, I didn't really get past it until long after I had actually been in the ministry for several years. It took an intense counseling session with some dear friends—Don and Sheryl Rooks—to find real relief from that pain.

I remember that a few days later they had the funeral for my brother, but I wasn't allowed to go. And that tore me up, too. They said I was too young.

*

My Dad had been out of town when my brother died. I can't imagine what it was like to get a call because your son was dead. Dad was a mean person, someone who never seemed to enjoy life—just bitter about everything. Of course, the whole episode made it worse. He drank all the time. And he was a *mean* drunk. He would curse at me, Mom, and my sister. Sometimes when he came home drunk, he would use us as punching bags.

Then, not long after my brother died, my Dad's father died, which just made his drinking and abusive behavior worse. We moved around a bit after this, back to Missouri for a year or so, then Louisiana for another year, then back to Missouri. It wasn't a very stable situation. When we moved back to Missouri the last time, Dad and I went first, with Mom and my sisters scheduled to follow us a week or so later.

I was about seven-years-old and we stayed at a relative's house while we waited for Mom and my sisters. I remember Dad getting all dressed up one day and heading out to hit the bars. I was left by myself. I watched cartoons for a while, then I got curious and started roaming the house. I opened a closet in one of the rooms, and I remember seeing weeds hanging from the ceiling—a bunch of them.

When that relative got home, I went to the closet and asked, "What is this?" My relative smiled and said, "Oh, you don't know what that is? It's marijuana." Then my relative pulled a little leaf from the closet ceiling, crumpled it up, and rolled a joint, handing it to me and saying, "Here, smoke this." So, I sat there watching *Scooby-Doo*, while smoking a joint at the age of seven. I didn't know any better.

And I know I didn't like the way it made me feel.

After my Mom got back to Missouri, I told her about our relative getting me high. Needless to say, she was very angry. They got into a huge fight. I felt a little bad about being a snitch, but then again, I really didn't know any better.

It was all part of my storybook childhood.

2

"I CAN'T BELIEVE YOU SAID THAT TO ME."

BY THIS POINT in my life, I was very confused. I was seven years old and felt all jacked-up inside. I started hanging out with the wrong kids and getting into trouble. Even before I got to middle school, I had already been to jail four times—a couple of times for breaking out windows, and another time for shoplifting at *Kmart*. Clearly, I had no direction in life—except downward.

But the deck was stacked against me. I remember watching my Dad steal. One time I saw him go into a gas station and rip the tag off some sunglasses. He put them on and just walked out. He was such a wonderful example, which, of course, just compounded my confusion.

When it came to religion, my parents were nominal Catholics. Mom would talk to me about God sometimes, but nothing that I would now consider to be biblical. However, I did have an innate sense about God. I think everybody does. I remember being seven or eight years old, when I would sort of talk to God. In these conversations with God, if things were going bad, I would blame myself and say, *"Well it's your fault because you killed your brother. You're just being punished for this,"* or *"If you hadn't done that your brother could be here to fix things."*

Then, there would be other times where I would talk to God and blame *Him* and just say, "*God, I was only four years old. Why would you do that to me? Why did you let that happen?*"

★

Then something happened that became a turning point for me. I've mentioned my father's anger. He always seemed to be angry. He was self-employed, doing odd jobs—pretty much anything for a buck. He ran an advertisement in the local paper that said: "ANYTHING HAULED." He hauled trash, brush, or anything people needed to have carted off. He also did construction work here and there. But he never made much money at any of it. We were quite poor. We lived in a very small house, one that was run down with junk in the yard—old cars, washing machines. It was the dump of the block. I was so embarrassed—I didn't want anyone to know I lived in *that* house, so I'd have friends drop me off way down the street.

Sometimes my dad would take me to work with him as a helper. But he would inevitably get mad and throw things at me, whatever was close at hand—a hammer, a shovel, pretty much anything. One day he escalated to adding insult to injury.

Literally.

Big time.

He looked at me with rage in his eyes and said: "Why couldn't you have died instead of your brother?"

I was devastated. It crushed me. I thought to myself, *I can't believe you said that to me.* And he didn't just say this once to me, but several times, when he would get angry with me. Of course, any love, respect, or admiration I may have had for him vanished with those incredibly hurtful words.

In fact, I hated him.

I honestly just started living on the streets when I was 12 or 13 years old. I moved from house to house, staying with friends of mine. I also would go stay with my cousin and his dad a lot. His dad always had bags of weed, and he would let us smoke pot all day long. I would come home for clothes every few days. Then I'd be off and running again. I don't know why my mom allowed that. I just think she realized how chaotic it was at our house. My dad was always cursing at people, throwing things, breaking stuff, and hitting with a closed fist. He would punch me in the back.

And he also would punch my mom.

I saw my dad beat my mom on numerous occasions. One time, he threw one of those large candles in glass at her. She ducked, but it hit her in the back of the head, nearly knocking her out cold. Another time, he knocked down her large china cabinet, breaking everything in it. He pretty much destroyed the house that day. In fact, that was the day she walked out, taking us to live at Hope House, a shelter for battered women.

But he found us.

It's sort of weird, because I felt sorry for him and actually came back home with him while my mother stayed at HOPE HOUSE. Looking back, I now see him as a "Jekyll and Hyde" kind of personality. He could be a great person to be around sometimes. But then, he would turn into a monster.

*

By the time I got to high school, I had been hanging out with the wrong crowd for quite a while and I was partying all the time—drinking and smoking pot. The harder stuff would come later. I really don't know how I managed to get through those years, but I did eventually graduate.

Then I started working as a roofer. I would make a little money and then spend it on booze and drugs. Eventually, one thing led to another and I started selling weed. I made better money doing that than nailing shingles to a roof, but I was on a slippery slope to disaster.

When I was 21, I sold an eight-ball of cocaine to an undercover cop. I only did this once. She wanted to meet me again, but I refused. For about six months I was totally unaware of what was coming my way. Then one night I was out partying with some friends, and we got into a shootout with some other guys at a party. When the police arrived, they hauled me off to jail for being in possession of a firearm while intoxicated. It was then that

I learned I had a Class B felony warrant for selling to the undercover officer six months earlier.

Now, I had been to the local Independence police station on many occasions, but this time they took me to the Jackson County Jail. That really rocked me. I was thrown in with killers and big-time dealers—serious criminals. Needless to say, I was scared. It was a wake-up call—at least a little. I remember thinking, *I don't want to keep doing this. I don't want to live like this.*

When I went to court, they were about to only give me probation, but it was revealed that I had neglected to tell my attorney that I was already on probation for an earlier possession charge. He was less-than-happy and said, "My hands are tied, man. I can't do anything. You're going to spend at least four months in prison."

It was a few weeks before Thanksgiving.

For whatever reason—maybe the spirit of the season—the judge said: "I'm going to let you spend the holidays with your family, and on February 9, I want you to turn yourself in." Maybe he wanted to give me some time for soul-searching. If so, it worked. But the night before I was supposed to report to prison, two of my buddies came by to pick me up. My plan was to stay in and crash the last night of my freedom, but they wanted to go out partying.

So, we did.

We went to the casino, and the next morning I showed up at the jail drunk and high on meth to begin serving my sentence.

★

The next day they took me down to the *Fulton Reception and Diagnostic Center*—not far from the state capitol. I would be there for about a month.

The facility exists to process new inmates and evaluate their mental and physical health, as well their particular security needs. These assessments are the basis for a prisoner's housing for the duration of the sentence.

The place really freaked me out. I was scared about being beaten, or even raped. Fortunately, nothing like that happened to me, but it was the most humiliating ordeal I've ever been through. I went into a small room with about 50 other guys, all shoulder-to-shoulder. The room was very small. We stripped and stood there naked as the day we were born. We were treated like cattle. I guess that's par for the course. Then they put me in a gym where there were about 60 bunk beds.

I was really scared. That first night I actually cried myself to sleep. I remember feeling like such a sissy. But the next day I saw a big African-American guy do the same thing. In fact, I came to find out that most guys cry their first few days in jail. I guess the seriousness of the situation really hits home. After all, prison is not supposed to be *Disney World*.

The whole time in there I was thinking, *I can't believe I'm here!* From that room, they took us to another room where they threw lye soap and powder at us and then showered us with what was surely a fire hose. Again, humiliating and degrading, and *exactly* what I needed to humble me.

At that time, I had just a little knowledge of God. Certainly nothing all that Biblical, but I remember praying God, "God if you'll get me out of here, I'll go to Africa as a missionary. I'll do anything." I'm sure the Lord regularly hears such prayers from jail—and foxholes. I did feel that God was saying, *You're still not serious yet. You still don't understand what it is, what it means to be a follower.*

Eventually, they transferred me to the Boone Correctional Center. It was a very regimented facility. I had to wear a button-up shirt and slacks every day. There were drug rehab classes six days a week. Sunday was the only day I could sleep in—all other days wake-up was at 5:00 a.m. Then it was "up and at 'em, make the bed, clean the room"—stuff like that. It was all about discipline.

That had never been my thing.

3

"BUT THIS GUY DOESN'T KNOW WHAT I'VE DONE."

WHILE IN PRISON, I had a lot of time to think, and many things were weighing on my mind. As I look back, I'm sure the Holy Spirit was bringing these thoughts as part of His convicting work. There was one thing that really kept coming back to me again and again. It happened a couple of months before my arrest. I was in my apartment getting wasted and some of my friends came over. One of them asked me, "Joey, do you want to see a dead body?" I thought it was a joke. But they were serious—dead serious, if you'll pardon the pun. They said that they had been to a nearby cemetery and saw an actual dead body—actually a skeleton that was about a hundred years old.

So, I went with them.

It was late at night and very dark (of course, it was). There were seven of us, five guys and two girls. We climbed a fence and then went over to a small stone structure—it was, in fact, a crypt. It had a large steel door. There was also a window with huge steel bars. Somehow the two middle bars had been pried open wide enough for a small person to crawl through. I looked into the crypt and saw a space of about ten feet as well as a wall with nine slots for caskets. One of the guys was small enough to fit through the bars, and he climbed in and pulled one of the caskets out from the crypt. I remember it had a woman's name on it and it was more than one hundred years old.

I said, "See if you can open it."

He tried, but it wouldn't open. So, he started jumping on it. It started to break, splintering into little pieces. And there inside was a woman. Her skull still had hair. She was wearing a blue dress. I remember thinking, *that reminds me of a prom dress.*

"See if she has any jewelry," I said. But there wasn't any.

Then he threw the skull at me, hitting me in the chest, after which it dropped to me feet. Another friend started kicking at it and saying, "Hey, let's play soccer." Just then, I saw a flashlight in the distance. I was pretty sure it was a security guard heading toward us. We ran as fast as we could back to the fence, jumping over it and getting away.

When we slowed down and caught our breath, I said, "Man, that was messed up! We should not have done that. God will get us for it." Of course, I wasn't really thinking in Biblical terms. I was simply afraid and had a vague notion of the fear of God. But you know what? Bad things started happening after that. The skinny guy who climbed into the crypt got shot and spent six months in the hospital.

And of course, I wound up in prison.

As I lay there night after night, I had a hard time getting to sleep, and when I did doze off, I had recurring images of that lady in the blue dress chasing me around. I had no peace at all.

*

One Sunday morning, I was lying in bed and thinking once more about that nocturnal trip to the graveyard. We were in a dormitory-like room on the third floor of the facility. I woke up to the sound of music. It was coming from the basement. As it happened, there was a church service going on down there. For whatever reason, I felt strongly drawn to it. I now know that it was the Holy Spirit calling me. So, I got up and dressed. I asked a couple of guys who were in the room, "Do you want to go to that church service with me?"

They said, "Sure."

We all went downstairs. When I entered the room, I had a weird feeling wash over me. It was something I'd never experienced before. In fact, I began to cry as I walked through the door.

There was a man at the front of the room. He was preaching. I found out later that he was the prison chaplain. We sat down in the chairs at the back of the room. As I listened to the message, I started crying uncontrollably. Just bawling. The guys who came with me looked at me like I was crazy.

I looked over at them and said, "I don't know what's going on!" I was simply overcome with emotion—all of sin and shame and all the crazy things I had done. The preacher said, "No matter what you've done in your life, God is ready and willing to forgive you!" I thought, *But this guy doesn't know what I've done.* I had robbed people, beaten people up, stolen cars, burglarized homes, and caused so much mayhem. Damaging or stealing property is bad enough, but it was the thought of the people I had hurt that really got to me. I sat there, thinking, *I don't think God would forgive this. I don't think he would forgive me. Maybe other people, but not me.*

But the preacher just kept saying it. "No matter what you've done, God will forgive you."

As I cried my eyes out on that back row, I decided, *Okay. If God's willing to do that, I'm willing to take a chance, to risk it.* Just then, the preacher gave an invitation for people to come forward if they wanted to change.

I practically sprinted to the front of the room.

I was the first one there and I took him by the hand. There were three other guys right behind me. The chaplain asked all of us to pray something he repeated. I was still sobbing. I got down on one knee and asked Jesus to forgive me and forgive all of my sins.

Now, I know that not everybody has an emotional experience when they get saved, but I did. I literally felt God reach down and take a giant weight off of my shoulders, like a backpack full of bricks had been lifted.

That's what I felt.

I felt a profound sense of *release*. I stood up and wiped the tears out from my eyes. I had a smile on my face. I was changed. I was a brand new person. The chaplain gave me a Bible, and he highlighted 2 Corinthians 5:17:

> *"Therefore if any man be in Christ, he is a new creature: old things are passed away; behold, all things are become new."*

This verse has been precious to me ever since, because it is my very own true story. Christ came into my heart, but I also have been placed in Him. The day I was saved I became a totally new creature. My old life passed away—that implies a progressive passing, a process. And from that great day on, all things have been becoming new. A new life. A new hope. A new destiny. A new character.

As I began reading the Bible, I was reminded that the preacher came to Booneville every Tuesday night to lead a Bible study. So, I, along with a few friends, attended the following Tuesday. What I remember the most about those first days in the faith was a sense of accelerated growth. I was soaking up the things of the Lord like a sponge. I was reading the Bible every night before bed.

That first Bible I had was the *King James Version*. Then someone told me that if I wrote to a church they knew about, that church would send me a *New International Version*. I didn't even know what that was, so I wrote to them. They sent me a paperback NIV Bible. It said, "free," on the inside.

I still have it.

I started reading it. It was much easier to understand. I read and read and asked questions. Every morning I would wake up with a smile on my face, one that would stay in place all day long, because I was so happy. One day, one of the female counselors called me into her office. She said, "We think you're on some drugs or something. You're just so happy all the time. Do you have a stash somewhere?"

I laughed and said, "No. All I can tell you is that God has given me a second chance at life." I added, "I can't wait to get out of here and see what the rest of my life looks like." At that point I had no clue that I was going to be a pastor. I just wanted to follow God.

*

Though I was scheduled to serve 120 days, my actual full sentence was five years. This is done, I think, as a kind of scare tactic or rehabilitation program. If you can do the 120 days without getting into to trouble, you don't have to do the rest. This is largely due to overpopulation in the prison system.

After I had been incarcerated for three months, the judge in my case inquired about how I was doing. He wanted to know if was I keeping my nose clean, or if I was getting into trouble. Based on the prison's response, I'd either be released at the end of the 120 days, or I would have to do much more time.

As it happened, some of the guys used religion as a way to gain favor with the judge. They would keep a New Testament in their front pocket, go to Bible study, and talk about how they got "saved." Then they would get a letter from the judge: "Congratulations! You're going home tomorrow." I watched as they took out that New Testament and threw it on the table and said, "I don't need *that* anymore." To them, it was just a good luck charm. I remember thinking even back then, *that's not real.* They didn't want or have a genuine relationship with God. I didn't want my faith to be like that. I wanted the opposite. I wanted my relationship with God to be real.

And it was.

A while later, I got my letter from the judge. I was going home. The thing was, I didn't have any clothes to take. I just had a box they gave me. They said, "You're going home today, but the clothes you're wearing need to stay here. Here's a box from *Goodwill.* You can look through it and find something to wear." The only things in the box were some clothes that were, shall we say, vintage 1970s. So, when I got out of prison, I had on a butterfly collar button-up shirt with bell-bottom pants. When my girlfriend picked me up, she must have been quite impressed.

I guess I need to tell you about her.

I'm probably burying the lede, but when I was 21 years old, I had a girlfriend. We had a baby girl about eight months before I went to prison. She had her first birthday while I was inside. My girlfriend and I had been talking about getting married, but I was constantly cheating on her. Not great husband, or dad, material. I hadn't been a good man.

But that was all changing...

4

"YEAH, THIS IS WHERE I NEED TO BE."

WHEN I GOT home, the first thing I saw was a stack of bills on the table. I had been gone for four months and they had piled up. My first thought was, *Man, I want to go back to prison. It's easy in there. No stress. As long as you don't drop the soap.* I never had a worry in prison. I knew I would be fed. I had a place to sleep, a schedule to follow, and a relatively stress-free environment. I think this is why there are some people who, in prison, decide to follow God, only to fail when tested by real life when they get out. That's when and where the rubber meets the road and decisions have to be made about how you're really going to live or what you're going to do. Are you going to go back and hang out with your old friends at your old stomping grounds? Are you going to just fall back into the same routine that got you into trouble? Or are you going to do something different? There is a saying in the recovery world that goes like this: "Nothing changes if nothing changes." Indeed.

Just before I was released, a prison counselor met with me for my "exit interview." She told me that the recidivism rate in Missouri is approximately 85%.

I replied, "*Recidi-what?* I can't even pronounce it. What do you mean?"

"The recidivism rates is the rate at which people end up coming back to prison. More than eight out of every ten convicts released will eventually be back. Only 15% manage to stay free," she said. Then she added, "I suggest you do something different than what everyone else is doing."

Well, there's another old saying—this one from a pretty smart guy named Albert Einstein—which goes like this: "Insanity is doing the same thing over and over and expecting different results." Now, I'm no Einstein, but I am smart enough to know truth when I see it. I was convinced that I needed to make some real changes in me and in my life.

And that's where my faith comes in.

★

About an hour after I got home from prison, I decided to find a church. But which one? As I thought about it, I remembered something from a few years earlier.

When I was younger, and was spending as much time away from my chaotic home as possible, I often stayed at a particular friend name Jeremy's house. He had a 12-year-old sister who was tragically killed in a car accident. I went to her funeral at a Baptist church in Independence, which was pastored by a man named Otis Nixdorf. Pastor Otis officiated the service and shortly thereafter Jeremy's family started attending that church.

Soon Jeremy invited me to go with him. A cute girl that I was interested in also went to that church, so, when he invited me, I said, "Sure. I want to go." I attended a few times and even got baptized, which was because I wanted to do what Jeremy did, not because I was committing to follow Jesus. I went to that church a few more times, but my attendance soon trickled off and I stopped going altogether.

So now, years later, I was ready to go to church. I thought about my mom's Catholic church, but I remembered it being very boring. *Nope. Not going there.* I knew that there was a large Mormon population in Independence, but I didn't think I wanted to be a Mormon.

Then I remembered Pastor Otis.

I drove over to the church and as I pulled up I remember feeling intimidated. I didn't know if the pastor would remember me. I knocked on the door. It was around noon on a Wednesday, and the pastor came to the door. He looked at me and said, "Hey Joey, how are you doing?"

I was blown away by the fact that he remembered who I was and even remembered my name. That really impressed me and made me feel valued.

The man had the gift of encouragement. He's one of those people that people want to be around. I went with him into his office.

"What have you been up to?" he asked.

I took a deep breath, then said, "Well, I'm going to be honest with you. I just got out of prison about an hour ago. But I gave my life to Christ a month ago while in prison. I know God wants me to be in church and I don't really know any churches. Can I come to yours?" In the years since, I've thought about why I felt I needed to ask permission to attend his church. I suppose it's because I was an ex-con and really didn't know the rules. I didn't know what it meant to join a church. Were there secret rituals? Was there a special club I had to join? I had no clue.

He immediately put my fears at ease and smiled at me and said, "Absolutely! You don't have to ask to come to our church. You are very welcome." He then pulled out a piece of paper and wrote down his phone number. He gave it to me and said, "Joey, you can call me anytime, day or night. Matter of fact, we have a Bible study tonight. Why don't you come back for that?"

I said, "Okay." I remember thinking, *Yeah, this is where I need to be. I need to be around people like Pastor Otis.* I got back to the church at 6:00 p.m., and when I walked through the door, the Pastor grabbed me by the arm and began introducing me to everyone in the lobby.

"This is Joey," he said several times to different people. "He just got out of prison. I want you to meet him and make him feel welcome."

I thought, *Wow!* I felt a little embarrassed, but at the same time I liked it. *Hey, I got no secrets. People need to know that I have a past and if they're going to judge me for that, then that's on them.*

Nobody did.

In fact, I was blown away by how friendly and welcoming they were. Whenever I share my testimony, I tell people that if it wasn't for Pastor

Otis Nixdorf and his church, I wouldn't be where I am today. I likely would have eventually found myself back in prison. I would have fallen right back into my old lifestyle. I fell in love with the church and I wanted to be there every time the doors were opened.

I started making new friends there.

*

Of course, there was a period of adjustment. At times, I thought church people were a little bit weird. And they were. Still are. Some church people are socially awkward, but I knew that almost all of them had grown up in church. But I needed to be around people like that because I was so ragged and raw. I didn't know anything about God, I didn't know anything about the Bible. I didn't know much about church.

So, they began to disciple me.

I was growing in my faith like crazy. I was there every time they opened the doors. I was there for Sunday School and then the main church service. I came back Sunday night and then again Wednesday night. I even joined the church choir, even though I can't sing a lick. I just wanted a reason to go to church another night. I was relieved that I didn't have to audition for the choir, because my singing strongly resembles the sound of feral cats fighting.

On Tuesday nights they taught me how to tell others about Jesus. The church used a program called *Operation Go.* We went into the community door to door inviting people to church and telling them about Christ.

I loved all of it.

I used to get to church on Sundays before anyone else—even Pastor Otis. I wanted to be there all the time. In fact, one day I asked him, "Can I just live here? I just want to live here at church!"

He just laughed and said, "No, you can't live here."

I said, "Well, I just feel like whenever I'm here, the devil can't get to me." I don't think that's necessarily Biblical or doctrinally accurate, but at the time that's how I felt. I felt safe when I was at church.

And when I walked out the doors, I felt like I was being attacked all the time.

5

"YOU'RE GONNA HAVE TO MAKE A DECISION."

OF COURSE, I had some addictive patterns in my life to deal with. I had struggled with alcohol and crystal meth, but didn't really need to detox, because four months in prison had cycled the stuff out of my system. But old friends from the old life tried their best to pull me back into their swamp. They started calling me up and asking, "Hey, do you want to go hang out?"

I told them, "Nope. I'm going to church today. Do you want to come hang out with me?"

I can't imagine what they must have thought, but they said, "No way. We don't want to do that."

Finally, I just stopped taking their calls. I just couldn't hang out with them. It was summertime and parties were everywhere—barbecues and drinking. I remember thinking, *Man, I really want a drink.* But I knew I couldn't take even one drink because I have an addictive personality. I don't do anything halfway, and there is a good chance that one drink would've led back to prison. I couldn't. Never in my life have I ever had just *one* beer. I have no clue what that's even like—just one drink? If I couldn't have six, then I wouldn't drink, because when I drank, I always wanted to get drunk.

I remember one day, after I had been out of prison for a couple months, some of my old buddies called me up and said, "We know you said you're not going to hang out with us, but we're just going to go to the park to play basketball. It's nice out."

I thought, *Well, that sounds good. I can do that.* They came and picked me up. There were six of them in the car. I climbed into the back seat. I remember driving down the road and one of them fired up a joint and quickly they were all smoking it in the car. I said, "Hey, can you pull over?" I had to get away. The driver pulled over and stopped the car. I got out said, "I have to go. I don't want to go back to prison. Not for you; not for anyone. It's clear you guys don't care about me because if we got pulled over, I'd be the one going back to jail—not you guys."

I walked home.

And I really didn't have much to do with them after that day.

*

As I began to grow in the faith, things changed between me and my girlfriend. My daughter had her first birthday while I was incarcerated. That was really hard on me. I felt like the worst sort of human being. But when Christ came into my life, changing everything, I was so filled with joy, that I just had to call my girlfriend from prison. I told her, "I just got saved!"

"What does that mean?" she asked.

"I don't really know. But I am a new person. And when I get out of here, I'm going to start going to church. Will you go with me?"

She hesitated for a few seconds, then said, "I don't know. Maybe...I guess."

In retrospect, it wasn't a solid commitment.

When I got out of prison that Wednesday, I asked her to go to church, but she said no. I asked her again on Sunday—morning and evening. She said no. It started to make things tense between us. Now, our relationship had always been somewhat toxic. She had caught me cheating more times than I can remember, but she always took me back. I think she was in love with the "bad boy" image. I was a drug dealer and got into trouble—she seemed to be attracted to that. But now things had changed. I wasn't a bad boy anymore. In fact, I was trying my best, by God's grace, to be a good man—a godly man.

And it was becoming clear that her feelings toward me were changing.

I remember one night a couple of months after I got out of jail, I pulled my truck up to a pay phone (remember them?). By the way, I used to love pay phones, because when you were angry at someone on the other end of the line, you could really slam the phone down. Sometimes it would even break. For some reason, that made me feel better. You can't do that with an Iphone. Those were the good old days. Anyway, my girlfriend and I got into a big fight over the phone. She hung up on me, and—yes—I slammed that phone down! Almost like a scene from a movie, I looked up and saw a bar where I used to hang out. It was just a couple of hundred yards away. The lights were glowing and seemed to be calling me. It was called *Fat Chance*.

Appropriate.

I vividly remember thinking, *You know what? Screw it. I'm gonna get drunk tonight.* I was so frustrated and stressed out, and I was defaulting to how I used to deal with things before I got saved.

Then something hit me.

I'm pretty sure it was the Holy Spirit, because I had this thought: *Before you go down there and get drunk why don't you call Pastor Otis?* I remembered that I had his number in my pocket. So, I pulled it out started to dial the numbers. Then I thought, *Man, he's not going to want to take my call. It's 10:30 at night. He's in bed with his family. I don't want to bother him...*

.

There is a great saying in recovery programs. "When you're in your own mind, you're behind enemy lines." And that was very true of me in that moment. But I pushed through and made the call. It was a key moment in my story. Pastor Otis answered and I said, "Man, I'm struggling right now! My girlfriend and I just got into a fight over the phone, and a bar I used to hang out is right in front of me. I have a strong urge to go in and get drunk."

He talked me down from the ledge. I don't remember any of the specific words he said, but, whatever they were, they fixed things in that moment. After talking with him, I went straight home and went to bed. When I woke up the next morning, everything was good. I was fine. I was no longer tempted to throw my sobriety away.

A few days later, it was Sunday and I was getting ready for church. My girlfriend said, sarcastically, "You're going to church again?"

"Yes, I am," I replied.

She countered, "Joey, this is getting out of hand. You're gonna have to make a decision."

"What decision?"

"You're going to have to choose between me and God," she said.

I just laughed and said, "Are you serious? That's not even a hard decision. God has done way too much for me to turn my back on Him now. No way." And I walked out of the room.

We broke up on the Lord's Day, and I have never looked back.

I couldn't believe that she gave me that ultimatum, but it turned out to be a great thing. It helped me put everything into the right perspective. I *did* need to choose between her and Him. The Lord is the only one who was always there for me.

Though we had split up, I still had a daughter with her. I was able to take her to church on Sundays, and when she got old enough, I took her to *AWANA* on Wednesday nights. That went on until she was about 12-years-old. Then my ex-girlfriend started keeping her from going to church with me.

It was a struggle.

That's what sin does. It complicates things. God's plan is for a man and a woman to get married, stay married and have children. When we don't follow His plan, pain comes our way. We suffer. The kids suffer. Society suffers. But I had created that mess, so I had to live with it.

By the way, my little girl just turned 25.

6

"...SOMEONE HAD BEEN PRAYING FOR ME ALL MY LIFE."

PASTOR OTIS WAS big on reaching people, or as church people refer to it, soul winning—AKA, evangelism. Early in my spiritual journey he not only taught me how to share my faith, but he also told me that I had, what he called, "the gift of evangelism." I learned the most basic ways to approach people, as well as a basic "ice-breaker" question, which was very effective: "If you died right now, do you know for sure that you would go to heaven?" Otis told me, "You just need to fan those flames in your heart and keep sharing the gospel."

So, I did.

Of course, this meant trying to reach those closest to me in my life. And on the top of that list was my mom. One day, I went over to her house and said, "Mom, can I ask you a question?"

She looked at me and said, "All right."

So, I gave her my best shot, "If you died right now are you certain you would go to heaven?"

She snapped back, "No. I know I wouldn't go to heaven! I know enough about God and the Bible to know that I am not right with Him. My heart is filled with hatred and bitterness. And I know that's not right."

I was stunned by her apparently well thought out response. "Why don't you make it right with God? Why not get saved?" I asked.

She said, "I'm not ready."

"Okay," I said. Then I asked her the same question a few more times. It was all I had. And soon she broke down and began to sob. She told me that she wanted to be saved. I led her to Christ and prayed with my mom right there in her kitchen. It was amazing! She was baptized shortly thereafter, and she started going to church and growing in her faith. In fact, to this day, my mother is a faithful member of the church where I serve as pastor. She is a great worker, serving as a helper in our children's ministry.

After I prayed with my mom that day in the kitchen, I walked through the house to the back room where my father was.

But I need to give you a little "back story" about him.

*

My dad was a big burly Mexican guy—think George Lopez, the comedian. He was about six feet tall. He worked in construction. When I was in prison he called me one day, and said, "Hey, I've got some news." "I went to the doctor this week. I've been feeling a little weird and they tell me that I have cirrhosis of the liver." At the time, I didn't know what that was. So, he explained, "It's from drinking my whole life. The doctor said my liver is shot, and if I don't get a new one—a transplant—I'm gonna die."

He was only 47-years-old.

I was stunned. Looking back, I believe with all my heart that God allowed me to go to prison to get my attention. I don't think I would have ever changed had I not hit that part of rock bottom. And I also think that my dad's diagnosis was his rock bottom.

So, that day, after my mom opened her heart to the Lord, I went to that back room and said, "Dad, Mom just gave her life to Christ."

"Oh yeah?" he asked. "You know, your cousin Rocky came over here one day about 13 years ago and I prayed that prayer with him."

"Really?" I asked. "That doesn't make much sense to me because, well, look at how you live. I don't see anything that looks Christian."

"Well, I prayed it. I'm good," he replied, blowing me off.

To say the least, I was perplexed. First, at his response to me. But also, because I didn't really think there were any real Christians in my family, on either side. But I did have this vague feeling that someone had been praying for me all my life. I found out that my father's cousin had been a youth pastor at a large Assemblies of God church in our area. I also found out that my great-grandfather (dad's grandfather) had been a pastor. Actually, he was a church planter. He came to America from Mexico to start churches.

So, God had been working on us for generations.

I was very burdened for my dad. His health was fairly dramatic. He could try to assure me all he wanted, but I did not think he was truly saved. So, I kept on his case.

Then one Tuesday night...

*

I went to church that night and we were involved in something called "Operation Go." Basically, this meant that we would go out, two-by-two, for the purpose of evangelism, or as we called it "soul winning." My partner was guy named Ralph. He was a long-time church member and had memorized the "Roman Road," select verses used to lead someone to Christ. I remember thinking, "I wish I could memorize verses like that."

The way it usually worked was we'd have a short training session that we'd leave with some contact cards—names and addresses of people who had visited the previous Sunday. But on this particular night, as we were walking out to the parking lot, Ralph said, "I think we're going to visit your dad tonight."

My first response was, "But we have these cards. Let's do these."

He said, "No, let's visit your dad."

I said, "He's not ready. I've talked to him several times."

He just kind of looked at me and said, "Trust me. We're going to talk to your dad."

Turns out that Ralph knew something I didn't know—he had a kind of discernment. We got to the house and knocked on the door. My mom invited us in. I saw my dad. By this time, his health had started to fail. He was laid up on a recliner in the living room watching television, which is what he did most of the time at this point. His skin was very pale and yellowish because his liver was shot.

My parents both asked us what was up—curious as to why we were there. Ralph said, "Well, I wanted to come over and talk with Terry." I asked my mom to go with me into the kitchen, but I could overhear the conversation in the living room. Mom and I just stood there and listened.

Ralph got right to the point with my dad. He asked, "Terry, if you were to die today, do you know for sure you'd go to heaven?" I listened closely, expecting him to reply with something about how he had prayed with my cousin Rocky, but Dad didn't do that. I heard him sigh. Then he told Ralph that he didn't really know if he would go to heaven. Then he added, "but, I'd like to."

I heard Ralph open his Bible and share those verses from the Book of Romans. And as Mom and I listened, right then and there my Dad accepted Christ as his Lord and Savior!

I cried—I was really emotional because I never really thought he'd do that. He came to church the next Sunday, and a few weeks later he and Mom were baptized. We immediately went from being a dysfunctional family to a church-going family. It was an amazing transformation.

It was also a little weird for me—something I can't explain. I mean, it was such a dramatic change. I remember one time even suggesting to Dad that he might go to another church, but he kept coming. And it really was one of the coolest things ever. But of course, his health kept failing.

God worked in my Dad's life. Not just in saving him, but it *changing* him. I mentioned his temper earlier. He used to be mean and bitter. But now, he was cheerful and jovial. Even though the guy was dying. He had a whole different manner about him.

One day I came over to visit him. He was, by this time, almost completely bed-ridden. He said, "Sit down on the bed, I want to talk to you about something." So I sat down and watched him pull out a notebook. "I've studying the Bible all day, and I have a list of questions." We sat there and talked through his list. I didn't have all the answers, but it was so cool to be able to have time like this with him.

Another time when I visited, he found the strength to get out of bed and took me out to the garage. "I want to give you something," he said. He grabbed an old brown paper grocery bag that was rolled up at the top. Then he said, "Here, I want you to throw this away for me." I looked inside and the bag was filled with pornography—magazines and video tapes. His secret stash.

But it wasn't so secret to me when I was a kid. That's the stuff that I discovered back in elementary school. He used to keep it in a drawer by the side of his bed. I found it and got addicted—in the fourth grade. I remember that I would skip school and sneak back home to watch his porno tapes. So, it was amazing to me how things had come full circle.

He said, "I know God doesn't want me to be looking at this kind of crap." Of course, I gladly got rid of all of it for him. And I remember thinking and rejoiced about the amazing way God was working in his life.

Sometime later, after I got accepted into Bible college, I went over to his house to share the news. Well, my mom kind of ridiculed me a little. "So, *you're* gonna be a pastor?" I told her I didn't know for sure, maybe I'd be an evangelist or something. She laughed, adding, "You don't have what it takes." She always had the "gift" of negativity.

Right about then, my dad—who was across the room in his recliner––piped up and said, "Leave the boy alone. If God wants him to be a pastor, then he can be a pastor!" It was the first time he ever gave me any encouragement about anything. I planned to head off to Baptist Bible College in Springfield the end of that summer.

That June my mom called to tell me that they had found a liver for Dad and moved him to the front of the list—transplant surgery was scheduled for the next day. He checked into the University of Kansas Medical Center in Kansas City. I headed there to pray with him.

As I walked into his room, it hit me that it was June 29th—20 years to the day since my brother Jeff died. I had never come clean with anyone about how he died. It was still on my conscience, still bothering me. There was my dad lying in bed and possibly close to death. In the moment, I decided I needed to tell him how Jeff died. I felt compelled to do so.

So I walked over to his bed. Mom was there, too. I said, "Mom, Dad, today's the day that Jeff died 20 years ago. I need to tell you something." Now, his death was not something we ever talked about. It was just off limits. So, Mom said, "No. I don't want to talk about it."

"Well, I need to," I said. "I need to tell you what happened so I can get this off my chest." I took them through the whole story. How I caught the car on fire and all of it. I'm sure mom felt guilt over the years about how he fell asleep in the car. When I told the story it was like a large weight was lifted off my chest.

It's hard for me to find the words to describe what happened next. My dad puts his arms out and drew my mom and me close to him. He hugged us and said, "It was a long time ago, and we can't change the past. Let's just move on." His words healed my heart. For the first time in my life, he became the father that I needed when I was growing up. He became a spiritual leader in that moment.

Early the next morning, they came and took him back to surgery for the transplant. Everything went very well. A few days later, he started getting stronger and they said everything was good. But three weeks later, he took a turn for the worse. His body was rejecting the liver, and he was dying.

A week or so before I was supposed to head to Bible college for orientation, I walked into his room. Several nurses and doctors were there. He was excited to see me and said, "Hey everyone, I want to gather around here. I want you to meet my son. This is Joey and he's getting ready to go to Bible college next week. He's gonna be a pastor. I'm so proud of him." Then he looked directly at me and said, "I love you, son."

Now, I never heard him say those words to me during my whole childhood. He never came to one of my football games. Never showed up at a practice. I would look up in the stands and see my mom, but never my dad. He was disinterested, I just think he was all about doing his own thing. So, when he told me he loved me it was beyond special.

It turns out, that was the last conversation I ever had with him.

The next day, he was hooked up to a ventilator and couldn't talk. But he had joy written all over his face. Even though he knew he was dying, he would point to his chest and pointed to heaven with a wink, then he gave me a thumbs up sign. He was right with God—which is right were you need to be when you are ready to meet God.

Dad met his heavenly father a few days later.

Hearing those words from dad on his death bed brought me so much closure. I didn't know it at the time, but I really needed to hear him say he was proud of me and loved me. I honestly questioned whether he loved me because of all the times he told me that he hated me when I was growing up. It brought a lot of healing to my heart. Before that I felt incomplete. I'm grateful that God let me have that closure. It didn't not erase all the damage done by the way he raised me, but it did begin the healing process.

7

"I HAD TO LOOK IN A MIRROR..."

I LOVE THE book *Wild at Heart*, by John Eldredge. I strongly recommend it to anyone who has faced hurt in their past. It had a profound impact on my life. I've read it several times, and it truly opened my eyes to a lot of things.

I mentioned earlier that my father told me that he wished that I had died, instead of my brother. When he said that, it really compounded the hurt that I was already feeling about my brother. It also contributed to the mess I made of my life.

One of the things that Eldredge talks about in the book is how everyone has a wound from their past. Usually from their childhood. He talks a lot about the father's influence, suggesting that our past hurts are often tied directly to something the father said or did. That really resonated with me. Eldredge also laid out the differences between boys and girls and how they are different as they grow up. For example, most girls like to play with dolls and dream about their wedding day, while most boys want to play with guns.

His approach was very insightful.

I didn't realize until months after I had read the book that the wounds my father inflicted on me were actually affecting me in a big way. And honestly, it impacts my life to this day, showing up sometimes in subtle ways. I think of it as a "pre-existing condition" in my heart.

After my mom and dad got saved, there was a time when we were all going to church together, which was amazing. Everything seemed to be going really well in our family. But deep inside me, there was that "pre-conditioned" sense that things weren't really that great. The deep wounds from my father, to be honest, couldn't just be fixed by an apology.

I've heard it said that you can't un-ring a bell. Or you can't put toothpaste back in a tube once it's been squeezed out. It was like that with my dad's words, when he said those hurtful things to me. It crushed my spirit. It caused me to act out in many unhealthy ways. Since I read Eldredge's book, I have become painfully aware of how much it still affects me.

I've also seen how others act out as a response to past hurts. I see girls who grow up without the love and affection from their father. They try to get the attention from older men that they never received from their dad. Though it may be a subconscious thing on their part, it is really sad to watch.

I'm currently raising two daughters—one is 11 and the other is 12. I see in their life where they still crave affection. I love to hug them. Every morning, the first thing I do is go in and give them a great big hug. Grace, the 12-year-old, sometimes goes through phases where she will push me away and act like she doesn't want it. But later, on her terms, she will come over and give me a great big hug. And I know that she needs that. Probably even more so at this age. And in the next couple of years, as she grows into a young woman, she needs healthy affection from her father so that she won't need to run to another man for a warped version of that affection. It is very powerful thing when painful wounds come from a father. These wounds remain for years.

When I was in my mid-thirties I went to a conference hosted by ministry friends, Don and Sheryl Rooks. While there, I had to work through my situation. I had to look in a mirror and deal with the fact that I continued to blame myself for my brother's death. But I needed their help working through some issues I had with my dad. I was still harboring bitterness towards him.

I know that the Bible says that harboring bitterness is unhealthy. It was not good for me to carry that ugliness inside of me, no matter how wrong my dad was. So, I had to actually forgive my dad. I had to be *intentional* about it. And even though my dad had been gone for many years, and could not specifically apologize for the wrongs that he had done in his life, I know that he was sorry for the things he said to me. But I still had to get past it, because if I didn't forgive him, I was never going to be fully healthy myself. For example, I still struggle with anger issues, like my father did. I learned this behavior by watching my dad. I still catch myself becoming very angry at times for very small reasons. That is what I always saw in my dad. He was an angry person, always yelling and cussing and throwing things at people. I vowed that I didn't want to become like him. But I catch myself starting to feel that way. So, I have to stay aware and keep myself in check. I know I'm not the only one who has unresolved issues in life.

That is why I strongly recommend Eldredge's book.

*

I heard a statistic on sexual abuse. I was never sexually abused while growing up, but when I talk about this subject, it resonates with many. It is, sadly, a pervasive problem in our culture. It's a powerful and traumatic occurrence in many people's lives. Years ago, another ministry friend, Ron Sears, shared a statistic at a "Stress in Ministry" conference (also hosted by Don and Cheryl Rooks). Ron talked about how one out of every three girls has been sexually abused while growing up. And one out of four boys has been sexually abused. This is staggering. He went on to say, "It's probably much higher than that because those are just the cases that are reported."

So, I had started thinking about how that affected those around me, today. If it was true, that meant that many people in my congregation had been abused sexually. It also meant that there was probably an abuser sitting in the congregation—maybe an uncle or a father. This insanity is one of the reasons that our society is so messed up. We have all of this pain and trauma happening behind closed doors and few seem to be dealing with it. Child molesters only get a slap on the wrist too often.

Years ago, I spoke at a church in the small town of Hale, Michigan. I shared my story, and I talked a bit about people being molested and abused. After I was done speaking, a woman in her mid 60s asked if she could speak to me. She was crying uncontrollably. She told me that she was molested by her dad when she was a little girl. He was dead and gone by that point. She went on to say that her entire life had been messed up because of that, and that she needed to work through it and forgive him. For nearly 60 years this woman had been dealing with the hurt and trauma from what had happened at the hands of her father. Just like so many others, she went through life with unresolved inner conflict and deep-seated childhood wounds that continued to traumatized her.

As a society, it seems like we do not know how to deal with things in a healthy manner. Instead, we choose the unhealthy way. We pick up poor coping mechanisms that not only don't fix the problem, but actually compound it. When you go through a divorce, or lose a loved one, you may get angry with God and start drinking to cover up the pain. But soon the drinking causes more problems. We need to start teaching people healthy ways to work through the pains of life. Bad things happen to everybody. Some people have it worse than others.

But our reaction to the trouble may make everything worse.

8

"JUST A BUNCH OF INNER-CITY KIDS"

IT WAS THE Spring of 1998, and I was on fire, filled with passion for the Lord. I was leading a good number of people to faith in Christ. This, I guess, impressed Pastor Otis, who, as I said, was big on evangelism. People seemed to respond to me and he interpreted that as evidence that I had "the gift of evangelism." I asked him to explain what he meant. He talked about how every believer is endowed with certain spiritual gifts from God. These gifts are to be used for the building up of the Body of Christ and the advancement of the Kingdom of God. During that conversation he also dropped a bomb on me. He said, "You know, Joey, it might be that God is calling you to preach."

"I don't know about that," I replied, with a great deal of skepticism.

He said, "Well, you should pray about it."

So, I did. I prayed. And I prayed some more. The next time I talked to him about it, I said, "Well, I don't know about God calling me to preach, but I do know that I want to do this the rest of my life. So ,if that's the 'call' then I guess you're right."

Then he said, "Joey, if you are called to preached, then you probably ought to go to Bible college."

"Bible college? I've never heard of that. I don't know of any around here."

"Well, the one I went to is pretty good. It's over in Springfield."

"I've never been to Springfield, Missouri."

"Okay, well, just pray about it. It's called Baptist Bible College. You should look it up, sometime," he added.

That conversation took place on a Sunday. At the time, the job I had involved some travel. I installed telephone lines and computer cable. I would report to work on Monday mornings and would be sent to little towns in Missouri where they had contracts. Most weeks, I was on the road from Monday to Friday. Well, on this particular Monday, my boss told me, "Hey, you're going to Springfield for the whole week."

Coincidence? I think not.

One day that week I got up the nerve to visit the BBC campus after work. The very idea of college kind of freaked me out. I was 24 years old at the time, and I had never liked school. Not even a little bit. I still don't know how I made it through high school. I only graduated by the skin of my teeth. Yet, there I was walking into the administration building on a college campus and telling someone, "Hey my name is Joey. I don't know, but I kind of feel like God is calling me into the ministry. My pastor suggested I check this place out."

"Why don't you fill out an application?" he said.

Of course, I was filled with self-doubt. Almost consumed by it. I remember saying something to the effect that the college probably wouldn't accept me.

The man said, "Well, just fill it out anyway."

So, I did. And to my everlasting surprise, they called me on my cell phone a couple of days later—I was actually still in town—and told me that I had been accepted as a student in the incoming freshman class that August. To say I was blown away would be an understatement. Over the next few months, I made preparations to move to Springfield and started studying for the ministry. God had opened a great door for me.

*

One of the things I felt strongly about when I left Independence for Springfield was that I needed to be a good father to my young daughter. I didn't want her to feel abandoned by me. So, I made a commitment to return home every single weekend to spend time with her. It was tough, and it made my time in college more of a challenge, but I knew it was the right thing to do. I also spent the summers between semesters back in Independence.

During my second summer in college—between my sophomore and junior year—I got a call from my cousin. He was a youth pastor at the time, serving in a small Southern Baptist Church in the inner-city of Kansas City. He told me that the church was looking for a new pastor and also looking for people to fill their pulpit in the interim. He said, "We want you to come over and share your testimony."

It was the first time I ever really preached.

I was, of course, apprehensive about the opportunity, but I accepted. When I got to the church, I met the man who was serving as the church's interim pastor. His name was Mike Bobbitt. There were about 30 people in the service. I shared my story and gave an awkward invitation.

Two people were saved.

I was completely blown away by that. After the service, Interim Pastor Bobbitt walked up to me and said, "I've got a youth ministry here in Kansas City. I'd like you to come and share your story with the kids sometime." I told him that I would love to do that.

A few days later, I went over to the youth center. It was called The Milestone. Pastor Bobbitt ministered to more than a hundred teenagers in the course of an average week. They played basketball and other games, then they'd go to the upstairs room for a Bible study. I shared my testimony in that "upper room." Several young people gave their hearts to the Lord. I can still remember the powerful connection as I spoke.

Just a bunch of inner-city kids.

After the meeting I talked more with Mike Bobbitt. "What's the deal with these kids?"

"To be honest," he replied, "we have kids like this coming all the time. We get them saved and teach them some Bible. But the problem is, there are no churches around here that want them."

"Why?" I asked, with a tone of unbelief.

"Because they're just kids. Kids who are sometimes troubled. And most churches in the area think of them as 'undesirable,'" he replied.

This hit me like a ton of bricks. And I remember being instantly burdened—so deeply burdened—for these kids. I went back to school that fall and prayed constantly for them. I also became increasingly convinced that God was leading me to start a church for those inner-city young people.

A little time went by, but finally I summoned the courage to call Mike Bobbitt to tell him what was on my heart—the idea of an inner-city church plant. When he answered, I said, "Hey Mike, this is Joey Candillo."

There was a brief pause and then he said, "It's interesting that you just called."

"Why?"

"We just got done with our staff meeting here and as we were praying God was laying you on our hearts for some reason. We've been talking here about planting a church and God keeps putting your name on our hearts every time the idea is brought up."

"Well, that's why I'm calling, actually. I feel like God is telling us to plant a church there in the inner city, maybe even at The Milestone."

It was a real God moment.

*

The Milestone was located in a rough part of downtown Kansas City. The population was diverse—a blend African-American, White, and Hispanic people, all living in close proximity. There were many "gang-bangers" and prostitutes, and it was a pretty violent section of town. Young people living there didn't have a lot of options, and I felt a tremendous burden for them. I felt connected to them, especially when I had the chance to talk with them.

Though I had called him about the idea of a church plant there, I wasn't ready to plunge right into it. I told Mike Bobbitt, "I don't feel like I am prepared to start a church yet. After all, I have about two years of college left."

He said, "Let's just keep praying about it." And I agreed. But the idea was never far from my thoughts. It became a preoccupation. Call it a magnificent obsession. And so, it should come as no surprise that a few months after my graduation in May 2002, we launched the long-prayed for church.

On Saturday, September 14, 2002 we had our first service. Two hundred and fifty people showed up, many more than we had anticipated. It was, to say the least, pretty chaotic. We decided to meet on Saturday nights at first, because that was the best time to get young people to come. We quickly settled into an average attendance of 70 or 80 teenagers. A few young adults from churches in the suburbs came to help us here and there, but it was basically a rough and rugged work.

And sometimes crazy things happened.

*

As we went on week after week, trying to reach kids with the gospel, we did our best to engage the young people with some "out there" things, like one we called "Fear Factor." It was just a fun way to loosen up the kids, by daring some to do some pretty rough things. Kids love that stuff. The grosser the better. And sometimes the kids would come up with things that we'd let happen, occasionally to our dismay.

I remember one night, four of the kids from the neighborhood—they were 10 or 11 years old—came up and told me that they had written a "rap about God," and asked if they could share it in the service. I thought, *how cool is that?* So, I said, "That's awesome. Sure, you can do it." Suffice it to say that it wasn't one of my more "thoughtful" ministry moments. I learned a great lesson that day about screening something beforehand.

I was pretty green.

The boys got up on the stage and announced the title of their rap: "God is Better than a Pimp." And it was all downhill from there. I cringed. My pastoral ministry was almost over before it began! After the ordeal was over, and I somehow managed to get through the rest of the service (including my sermon), I asked them what they were thinking. Their response floored me. Basically, in their world, a pimp or a drug dealer was the king of the hill, the most successful and prosperous people they knew. So, they decided to talk about how God was better than that. True, of course. It made sense, on some level.

But I told them that there may be better metaphors.

9

"HOW DO I TELL HER?"

ONE BENEFIT OF holding our church services on Saturday nights was that I could speak at different churches on Sunday mornings. And invariably, after I got done sharing my guest sermon on Sunday, some little old lady would always come up to talk to me. There must have been a network of them all around town. And what she had to say usually went something like this: "Oh, my granddaughter would be perfect for you. You should meet her." But I'd say, "I'm fine." I really wasn't looking for a wife.

But a single pastor brings out the best (or worst) in would-be matchmakers.

Despite all my protestations, however, there was one Saturday night after I preached at our church, when a girl came up to talk with me. She was very attractive and just about my age. We had hung out together a few times, but never dated—nor had I been interested in dating. Anyway, on this particularly Saturday, she said to me, "God spoke to me last night and said that you and I are supposed to get married."

I laughed, probably a bit awkwardly, and said, "Well, He didn't tell me. I feel like He would have let me in on that if it was His will." Then we both laughed a bit. And that was that. Not long after this, she left the church. I guess she was looking for a connection with me and that didn't happen. A few months later, I was preaching a sermon on the subject: "How to Know the Will of God for Your Life," and I told the story about how this girl had approached me. I turned it into a humorous illustration.

It became sort of a standing joke around our church.

*

Fast forward a couple of years. By now, I had been a single pastor for about three years. But I was beginning to think that I was ready to get married. I had moved into my 30s, and, at times, I was a little discouraged that I didn't see that certain someone on the horizon. I remember particularly praying about it one Thanksgiving night. Now, you need to understand. I wanted to do this right. My background before I was saved included promiscuity. So, the prospect of dating scared me. I didn't fully trust myself not to fall into old patterns. I told the Lord, "So God, you're just going to have to show me who you want me to marry because I am not going to be dating."

How's that for a prayer ultimatum?

Well, guess what? He put Megan on my heart. Oh, yes, He did. I remember praying, "Megan? Are you sure, Lord?" She was an attractive girl, about my age, who worked at the youth center when I got there. I had looked at her as just a friend. Then, all of a sudden, on Thanksgiving, God told me that I'm supposed to marry her.

The problem was, how should I tell *her*?

It took me three months to break the ice. It was February 14—Valentine's Day. I got up the nerve to call her. Oh, did I mention that she lived just six doors down from me? When she answered the phone, I asked her, "Megan, could you come up to my house for a second? I need to talk to you."

"Okay," she said. "Be right there."

When she got to my house, I said, "I don't know how to tell you this. In fact, it's the strangest thing. But I've been praying for a while about who God wants me to marry. And I feel like you're the one." Talk about a pick-up line.

She began to tear up and she acted uncomfortable. So, I asked, "Is everything okay?"

"Yeah," she said, brushing a tear from her cheek. "God told me the same thing, but I wasn't going to say anything because of that story you tell about that other girl. I was never going to bring it up unless you did."

Megan was scared to become just another sermon illustration.

I didn't know what to do next, but two weeks later I went out and bought a ring and proposed to her. Two and a half months later, on May 21, 2005, we were married.

After more than 16 years, we're still doing great. I certainly don't recommend such short engagements for everyone, but I believe that God wanted that for us.

*

Of course, some people told us it was a mistake to do what we did. I believe they were well-intentioned when they said it would never last. It certainly flies in the face of conventional wisdom. But it worked out for us because God guided us.

So, we got married, having never even dated before. We got to do all the dating stuff after we got married. My wife had never been with a man before we got married. Of course, that wasn't my story. Things were a bit awkward, at first.

I speak at a lot of youth camps, and one of my messages is about sex and God's plan for abstinence before marriage. But our current culture is so crazy, because when I talk about these things, the kids look at me as if I have three eyes, like I'm from another planet. They have never heard that before. I can relate, because I didn't know that either until after I was saved.

I remember when I was first saved and I had been coming to church for a few months. I was sitting in the service and my pastor was sharing a message about sex. He made this statement: "God expects you to wait until you get married to have sex. Sex is reserved for marriage."

I leaned over to the person sitting next to me and said, "Did he just say what I think he said?" It was actually the worship pastor's wife, and she laughed a little, and said, "Yeah."

"Is that true?" I asked. "Are we supposed to wait to have sex until we get married?"

She just laughed, and replied, "That's in the Bible."

I was blown away. It was the first time I'd ever heard that. I went home and started studying all the scriptures about sex. I was quickly convinced and made the decision to stop having sex.

I was a little upset, honestly, because I was 22 years old. No one in my life had ever told me that I was supposed to wait to get married before having sex. I was ticked off that the world was the way that it was and how I'd done so much damage to and with my life. So, then and there, I vowed I was going to do my best to teach everybody God's plan for sex and marriage.

★

I was reading the Bible for the first time. Someone gave me a *MacArthur Study Bible*, and I was determined to read it from cover to cover. I started with the Book of Genesis. And I thought, *"Man, this is some good stuff."* Then I got into Exodus and read about Moses. Again, I thought, *"This is amazing stuff."* It helped that I love history. I was blown away by the Bible.

Then I got to Leviticus, and I thought, *"What the heck is happening now? I don't know what's going on here."* Then Numbers and Deuteronomy. I didn't know what to make of it all, but I kept going. I was determined that I was going to do whatever I found in God's Word.

When I read Leviticus, I came to the part where it talked about unclean animals and food. It said not to eat an animal with a "split hoof," or that "chews the cud." And I was confused.

Then it dawned on me. *"A split hoofed animal?"* That's deer. I've been a deer hunter my whole life. In fact, as I read that passage, I had a whole freezer full of deer meat.

But I decided to follow it literally. The Bible says I'm not allowed to eat any animal with a split hoof. And no pork. I knew it was going to be tough, but I quit bacon—cold turkey. Ham, too. And, yes, I gave up venison.

A few months went by, and I was at church and made a passing comment to my pastor, saying, "Man, this being a Christian is pretty tough."

"What are you talking about?" he asked.

"It's hard not eating pork," I replied. "Probably the hardest thing for me is not eating pork."

"What are you talking about?"

"I read in the Bible where we're not supposed to eat pork, so I stopped eating it."

He laughed out loud. He took the Bible and showed me in the New Testament where all foods were declared clean. "You're allowed to eat whatever you want," he said.

"Oh my gosh. Thank you so much!" It was an awesome revelation.

On the way home from church that day, I stopped at a grocery store for some bacon. Amen!

10

"STARTING GRACE CHURCH"

I PASTORED AT Bales Baptist Church in the inner city, for 12 years, the first three years as a single man. Then Megan and I got married. She lived six houses down from me, so we decided that I should move into her house. It was in a terrible neighborhood, one of the worst in Kansas City. Lykins Park was directly across the street from us. There were frequent shootings. Police helicopters flew over the house almost daily as police looked for suspects and criminals.

This was our environment, but in a strange way, I found it somewhat exciting.

When I heard gunshots, I would run outside to see if I could see anything. There was always something to see. Just down the street it was common to see prostitutes working. A car would pull up and drive down the street, often parking right in front of our house. I would try to get them to move, and ask them not to park in front of my house to have sex.

When I was single, I didn't mind the chaos and danger. I could deal with it. But after I got married, and especially after we had our first child–—a son—it began to bother me more. Eventually, we had four kids, all fairly close in age. And I began to see the neighborhood in a different light. I feared for my family. I was suddenly acutely aware that something bad could happen to the people I cared about most about. It was at this point that I started losing my love for the inner city.

A move to the suburbs started to sound appealing.

*

In the summer of 2013, I was fervently praying that God would tell me what He wanted me to do. I felt restless, like I was coming to the end of my time at Bales Baptist Church. I felt like I was ready to leave. God gave me peace about leaving Bales. I made plans to resign, and a couple months later I told the church I was leaving. I honestly had no clue what my next move would be. It was the first time in my life that I had ever found myself in that situation—waiting for the Lord's direction.

One day I decided to take a drive.

I went back to Independence, where I grew up. My home church was there. The city of Independence has about 120,000 residents, roughly the size of Springfield, Missouri. And like Springfield, there are many churches in town. Good churches. But that day I felt that God was saying to me, "Go plant a church in Independence." I was conflicted about it. After all, my sending church was there. I did not want to hurt them or betray them. I wrestled with God for a week or two about this. And I finally was able to discern that God was saying that, yes, there are a lot of good churches. But He wanted me to plant a *different kind* of church. He wanted me to use my life experience to help people just like me. Like I used to be.

So, I said yes.

Once I was determined to move forward in God's plan for me, I got on *Facebook* and went through my whole list of friends. I let everyone know that I was going to start a church. I reached out to people who went to church and people who were unchurched. I told them that if they didn't have a church family, that I was inviting them to be a part of ours.

I had resigned in August, 2013. By that October, I already had a core group of people from Independence who were ready to help me start the church. So, we started meeting together to discuss the launching. God worked everything out for us in an amazing way. We found a beautiful building on the square, and we were able to rent it. It was so beautiful, that it looked like an art museum. The owner was asking for $6,500 per month for rent. I told him we hadn't started our services yet, so we didn't have any money.

I told the owner that we simply could not afford $6,500. He asked me how much I thought we could afford. I talked with our team and told him that we could maybe scrape together $2500 per month. The building had sat empty for so long the owner was just happy to have it rented and said yes to $2500. It was exciting. But he also wanted $5000 up front for first and last month's rent. This tempered that excitement.

Like cold water on a fire.

The next day, I received a phone call from my sister who had just gotten a settlement after injuring herself in a fall at *Walmart*. She said that she was going to give me a check for $10,000, as her tithe. So just like that, we had the money to rent the building.

It was one of those "God moments."

Beginning on November 15, we began six weeks of *preview* services. We met on Sunday mornings and practiced what we would do when we officially launched—a dress rehearsal of sorts. Eighty people showed up for the first run through, and in the weeks following that number grew to 100. We set January 5, 2014 as our official launch date. The plan was to have two worship services. We had a team of people ready to serve, including a worship pastor, and a children's pastor. I was so excited. We passed out tons of flyers in the community.

My prayer was that 500 people would show up at our launch service. Based on the feedback we received, I really believed that we were going to make that goal. The whole team was excited and filled with anticipation.

Then on Saturday, January 4, it began to snow.

I tried to pray it away—"Please, Lord, don't let it snow!" But it snowed all night, and by the next morning there were six inches of beautiful, white snow covering the ground. Honestly, I was disappointed and angry. I was mad at God. I thought, "Why did You tell me to do this?"

As soon as the snow started falling, people started calling asking if we were still having church. I told them that church was still happening. I decided we would still move forward with both services. I was so stubborn. Even though every other church in the town of Independence closed down because of dangerous road conditions, I did not care. I got on *Facebook* and said that we would open, no matter what. We were definitely having church. So, on January 5th, with six inches of snow on the ground, we showed up and had a great morning. We had 159 people show up at our first service, which was amazing, considering the circumstances.

Even with the success of our first day, I was still disappointed because I had wanted 500 people. So, I got back on *Facebook* that week and put it out there that we were going to do a "launch 2.0" the following week. That service drew between 200 and 300 people. From that day on we were growing and reaching people. There was an excitement surrounding everything we did—a buzz in the air.

*

After the first year, we were averaging more than 300 in attendance. We added a third Sunday service. We also had a Saturday night service. After two years, we had outgrown our space and began looking for a new venue. The only place we could find was the local high school. We held our Easter Service that year at the high school and approximately 1,000 people showed up. So, in September of 2015, after only 21 months in existence, I announced that in January we would be going portable and having church in the high school, setting up and tearing down every week. We raised money and put everything that we owned on wheels.

Over the next three months, 100 people left us.

Attendance went down to around 200 people. I was struggling with disappointment. I did not understand. After all, I had prayed about it and believed that it was what God had asked me to do. Did I misread the situation? I don't think so. It is just one of those things that I have come to understand. Whenever a pastor makes changes in a church, people are going to leave. But even though you lose some people, you also gain new people. And you usually trade "up." Looking back, the people who left were not really that committed to the church. They were just on the periphery.

Going mobile was simply an excuse for them to jump ship. But at the time, I took it *very* hard. We had made all the plans, expecting that everyone was going to stay with us, and that we would continue to grow. But we stayed stuck at around the 200 mark for a long time.

When we started at the high school it was pretty exciting. For a while. And then we grew weary of setting up and tearing down every weekend. So, after about nine or ten months of that, we found a permanent space in a storefront building.

*

When I started the church, it was with a burden to help people in recovery. But we are not a church just for people in recovery. Before we launched, when I invited people to attend, I made it known that I hoped it would be a church where people recovering from addiction would feel at home. I have had to work hard to erase the stigma that we are solely a recovery church. People would say, "Well, I'm not in recovery, so I don't need to go to your church."

I am happy to say that about half of the people in our church are in some type of addiction recovery. We are reaching the people in our community. The town of Independence has a reputation for being riddled with drugs. Substances like crystal meth and heroin run rampant. When I was growing up, our town used to make the national newspapers because we were known for being the "Meth Capital of the World."

How's that for a claim to fame?

When I was in high school I fell into that world. There were meth labs everywhere. I knew of several of them. Thankfully, God delivered me out of my addiction and that world. And now he wants me to go back in and reach others for Him.

It is one of the greatest joys I have, to see people struggling with addiction walk through the doors of our church. Many of them are homeless. Some of them come in high on meth or heroin. Just last year, I conducted six funerals for people who had overdosed on heroin. The overdoses on heroin and fentanyl are killing people. It is a huge epidemic. And we are trying to help eradicate that. One person at a time.

Our church is filled with people who remind me of the demon possessed man in the Bible. He was living in a cemetery. He was breaking chains. He was naked. He would cut himself with rocks. The people couldn't contain him or his madness. He was wild. And then he met Jesus, and Jesus freed him from all of those bonds.

As I look out on the congregation every Sunday, there are people that, when they first came, were absolutely demon possessed. Addicted to heroin or meth. They are covered with tattoos. They look like they have lived a hard life and have been put through the wringer. But they are there. They are searching for a different life. They are clothed. They are in their right mind. Just like the demonized man in Gadara.

One day my old drug dealer walked through the doors of our church. I used to get my drugs from him, when I was a dealer. He was a big-time dealer. He got saved and now comes to church with his family. We often talk about some of the crazy stuff we did when we were out in that world.

And it is only by the grace of God that we are even still breathing, let alone going to church together and making a difference in other people's lives.

Our mess became our message.

That's pretty cool.

11

"ADDICTION"

I WANT TO talk about addiction, more specifically about how to help people in addiction. Although I don't want it to be too extensive, because I have been jotting a lot of notes down for the next book. It will be about how to help people in addiction, as well as what role churches can play in addiction recovery. Because a lot of people don't know how to help people in addiction. Unless a person has been in addiction himself, most people do not know how to help addicts, and in trying to help, simply enable the person. But that's another book. Back to this one.

A few months after we started Grace Church, things were going really well. We were growing in attendance. I really wanted to start some type of recovery program, so we could help meet the needs in the community. We had many addicts and recovering addicts attending church every week. So, we started brainstorming about what we could do as a church to support them.

Our first endeavor began with a conversation with a church member. He was in his mid-fifties and was a secular psychologist, with a doctorate in psychology. I met with him a few times, because he had run recovery programs in the past. I was a little bit apprehensive about his input, because he was a secular psychologist. I believe that there is a biblical approach to counseling and addiction, and I wasn't sure if his secular approach would line up. But I asked him, "What would it look like for us to start a recovery program in our church?" I had a dream, but had no idea what it would look like, even though I had a history of going to A.A. meetings. So, I just knew that I wanted to start something like that, but from a Christian perspective.

I knew there were programs out there such as Celebrate Recovery. So, I did some research and looked into it. I also visited churches that had the Celebrate Recovery program. But I just didn't see it working for us. First, although it is a great program, it is very expensive. You are required to use their material. In a larger church with the resources, this may not be a problem. But in a small church like ours, it just wasn't possible. Second, it takes a lot of volunteers to start the program and to keep it running. I knew of a church that started a Celebrate Recovery program. I went to their first night and they had a great turnout. Around 100 people showed up. The program started with a 30 minute worship service, and then they broke up into groups. There was a group for alcoholism. There was a group for drug addicts. There was a group for sex addiction. There was a codependency group. There were a lot of groups. But each week the numbers went down. After a few months they were struggling to keep it open. When I asked the man in charge what the reason for the decline was, he said, "Well each group has to have its own leader. The problem is those leaders sometimes relapse."

And I've heard in other places that this is a common problem in Celebrate Recovery. Because people struggling with addiction do relapse. So, it makes running a big program like this complicated for a smaller church. We would have been setting ourselves up for failure if we had chosen to go this route.

So, as I met with this psychologist who attended my church, he shared with me that he had been wanting to start a program in a church for some time. In fact, he was ready. He already had the material ready. He said, "Let me run with this." So, I put out a message to the church saying that if you have a problem with addiction, or if you are in addiction recovery, come this Monday night.

So that Monday night we met at the church. We had a great crowd. I was excited about the possibilities. But then my doctor friend got up and droned on for about two hours. He just got up there and lectured. It was one of the most boring things I had ever heard. He passed out three ring binders to everyone. He had all of this material, but it was too clinical. It was like a semester's worth of material. He tried to go through it and gave us a lot of information about addiction and recovery, but it seemed too complicated. And worse than that, it wasn't from a Biblical perspective. It was all secular-based. He kept talking about how we have a reptilian brain and we need to retrain it.

It was confusing to everyone there, and there were too many red flags. After two hours of lecture, we were finally done. I gathered our core group together after the meeting and said, "Hey, this sucked. We are not going to do this." They all agreed that they wouldn't have come back if that was what it would be like. I wouldn't have either. We decided that we would meet again the following Monday, but we would just wing it. I had to have a hard conversation with the doctor. I simply told him that I appreciated his help and his input but that we were going to go in a different direction. He was kind of devastated. It was hard. That is one of the things that I have learned in ministry and leadership is that you have to have hard conversations with people.

I didn't let his disappointment derail what was happening at our church. I really believed that God wanted us to help addicts and that great things were going to happen. So, on that next Monday night, we met at 7:00. I told the group that came that we were going to go for an hour and a half. And we did. I simply started with a devotion, and took about 10-15 minutes to share my thoughts and my heart. And then we went around the room and talked about our struggles. We shared where we were at on our addiction/recovery journey. It was really powerful. We saw some really great things in there. So, this became our normal format that we still use today.

At first, I always led the meeting. But over time, other people have been trained and equipped to lead. So now we have a regular rotation of leaders. I serve once per quarter. However, I do attend the Monday night group every week. Each week we start with prayer. Then we open the Bible and the leader shares a devotion that is relevant to addiction. For example, he may choose a passage that talks about dealing with temptation. Once he's done with the devotion he will say, "Tonight's topic is temptation. How are you guys doing with temptation?" This works for us, because no matter where on their journey an addict is, temptation affects everyone. So, everyone shares their own experience.

We even have family members and friends of people in addiction attend the group. They are there because they need help in helping the sick loved one. So, our group is all encompassing. We have alcoholics, drug addicts, porn addicts, loved ones of addicts, etc. It is such a powerful group because we all have a chance to discuss and talk about what we are struggling with at our level. It creates empathy and understanding, no matter what you are experiencing. We learn from each other. We support one another. There is a great deal of wisdom that is shared. We pray for one another. And we do it all through the lens of scripture, cross-referencing different passages as we feel led.

12

"THINGS I WANT IN MY FAMILY…"

MOST OF US experienced something traumatic in our childhood, something we didn't know how to process. As a result, in adulthood we have been hindered in our ability to have normal, healthy relationships with people. We struggle *now* because we never took care of it *then*. But when we were children, no one told us how to deal with trauma.

My grandpa died when I was six or seven years old. I had never been to a funeral before. I remember being there and seeing his lifeless body in the casket. It freaked me out. I was terrified. I didn't understand why he didn't wake up. The adults were trying to explain his death to me, but I just didn't understand it. I didn't know how to process what I was feeling.

That traumatic memory has stuck with me.

I don't believe that God created us to go through traumatic experiences as small children. We are supposed to grow up in healthy, happy, and safe families, while learning healthy boundaries. That was God's perfect plan. But due to the brokenness of this world, that's not the experience of most people. Many people face trauma in their childhood. Maybe a pet died. For many, a pet dying is like the passing of a loved one. I've never been a big pet guy, so that kind of thing never bothered me. But my daughters are very attached to our cats, so they may be traumatized when those cats die.

Hopefully, I will help them through it.

Maybe you witnessed a traumatic event when you were growing up. Maybe you saw someone die. I knew a kid whose father hung himself, and my friend was the one who found him.

One of the biggest causes of childhood trauma is the physical or sexual abuse of a child, especially at the hands of a trusted loved one. The statistics on the number of kids who have been abused are staggering. Other people had childhood trauma caused by neglect. Some children were bullied. Some children had parents who divorced, and they blamed themselves.

The list can go on and on.

But the bottom line is that our children deserve to grow up in healthy families where they are not exposed to traumatic things. Now, as parents, we can't always shelter our kids from everything, but we can do everything we can to protect and support them. It blows my mind how often adults turn a blind eye to what is happening to their children, not to mention how lenient the justice system can be on these criminals who hurt kids. Personally, am a huge proponent of the death penalty for people who hurt children, because the threat of that kind of punishment will be a deterrent to such people.

I recently saw a letter from a little girl who is in the foster care system. It is a wish list letter, things that she hopes for one day when she has a family. It is titled, "Things I want in my family," and it reads:

> *I want food and water. Don't hit on me. I want a house with running water and lights. I want love. Mom and dad don't fight. I want no drugs in the house. Don't kill my pets. I want help with school. Nice clean clothes, no lice, no bugs in the house. Clean house, clean bed with covers. Don't sell my toys. Treated fair. Don't get drunk. TV in the house. Let me keep my games. School stuff. Nice shoes. My own comb. Soap. Nice house and safe. AC and heater. And a toothbrush.*

This blew me away. She listed these things because people have neglected to give her the basic courtesies of life—things most of us take for granted. I get emotional just thinking about it. And it's not an isolated example. There are many kids in our society who have similar experiences growing up. When children grow up in circumstances like that, they will have long term effects in their life. They will have a hard time adjusting well in society.

I like to hope that these children will be adopted by good Christian families that take care of them and teach them right from wrong and protect and provide for them. But even if the most loving people in the world adopt them, they are starting with such a disadvantage. They've been traumatized. They are behind the eight ball, as far as life goes, facing an uphill battle. And this scenario is all too common.

We have to figure out how to work through our hurts so that we can live healthy adult lives.

*

Sean Sears is a good friend of mind. He pastors a church in Boston. His dad is Pastor Ron Sears. Ron and I are also good friends, and he has been a mentor to me through the years. In 2003, Ron wrote a book called *Diamonds are Forever.* It is about his wife. Ron was a pastor for his entire adult life. He married Marilyn when they were still in their teens. They were really young and have a great relationship.

In the book he tells us that everything wasn't always that great. He recounted that, through the years, she felt closed off to him. She struggled with intimacy. Not just sexual intimacy, but the simple intimacy of letting someone be a part of your life. They finally sought counseling and, as they went through therapy, she was finally able to admit that she had been sexually abused by her father throughout her childhood.

Her father was a deacon in the church. She did not know who she could tell. Who would believe her? So, she just kept it to herself and ended up really messed up emotionally. When they wrote the book, she was in her mid 50s. One would think that, with counseling, the trauma and its effects would be diminished by then. But she still suffers today, even in her 60s. The horrible memories of what her dad did to her continue to haunt her.

It is said that "time heals all wounds," but that is not true. Time may heal your physical wounds. But if emotional scars are not addressed and dealt with, or if they are suppressed, they will eventually come out. We have to learn to deal with hurts in a healthy way.

So how do we deal with these things? How do we deal with our "junk?"

*

The way most of us deal with painful things is by *masking* them. We put on a mask and pretend that everything is fine. It's like using an *Instagram* filter. We post photos that don't actually look like us because we try to make everything look perfect. I have *Facebook* and *Instagram* friends that I'm not even sure what they look like, because I've never seen a real picture of them. They look 20 years younger than they are. That's convenient on social media, but it doesn't help in real life. Our lives are falling apart, but we put our *Instagram* filter up and make everything look good when it's really not.

When we have hurtful things in our lives, our default mode is to deal with emotional pain from our past in a negative way. And there are different ways that different people do this.

First, there is the *stuffer*. These people stuff things down. They suppress things. Whether something happened to him as a child, or if he has gone through a recent divorce, he simply doesn't know how to process his feelings and thoughts. So, he stuffs his feelings down. But do you know what happens when you stuff feelings down? They tend to explode on people. Maybe you are arguing with your spouse, or your coworker is driving you nuts, and all of a sudden you are lashing out in anger. And then you think, "I don't know where that came from." But that's not true. It actually came from inside you. It's always been there.

You just had been stuffing it down.

Next, there is the *eater*. The eater tends to eat his feelings. He eats over his problems. Whenever emotions get out of whack, he goes to the freezer and gets the half gallon of ice cream and eats the whole thing.

Then there is the *drinker*, or the *user*. These people get drunk or high. When they start to feel the emotional pain, and they don't know how to handle it, they self-medicate. But all that does is numb the pain. The pain is still there. When they wake up the next day, the pain is still there, and they're hungover. Or if someone is getting high, he may wake up five days later, not knowing where he is or how he got there, or worse, he could wake up in jail. The problems are still there, and new problems have been added on top of them.

Then there's the *self-loather*. The self-loather blames himself for everything.

There are people who are *bitter*. Toward people. Toward God. They ask, "Why did this happen to me?" They never take any fault. It's other people's fault. It's God's fault. God could have prevented it. They live life mad at the world.

There are people who want *revenge*. They are angry and vindictive. These are dangerous people.

There are people who deal with hurt by hurting others. Hurting people hurt people. When someone lashes out at me for seemingly no reason, I usually pause before reacting, because I know that I am not their actual problem. They are actually upset about something that someone else did and they are taking it out on me. Mad at your boss? Go home and kick your dog. People react this way all the time. We hurt others when we are hurting.

And finally, there is the *isolationist*. This is one of the worst ways a person can react. Instead of putting on a "mask" and coming to church and saying, "I'm fine," they just don't show up. They disappear for a while and isolate themselves, avoiding everyone and everything.

But this only makes things worse.

13

"EXTRA GRACE REQUIRED"

GOD DID NOT create any of us to go through life on our own. He created us for community. We have to be able to be honest with one another. I have a couple of Biblical examples of this.

The first example comes from the Book of Job. Job was probably the wealthiest and most successful man of his day. He had everything. He had money. He had material possessions. He had ten children. And the Bible says that one day Satan wanted to test him. So, he took everything from him—in one sad and devastating day. Job lost his livestock. He lost all of his money. His house burned down. And he lost all of his children.

That was indeed a bad day.

Job and his wife were, of course, devastated. But he handled it well. He declared that God was the one who gave them everything, and therefore, He could take it all away. He said they came into the world naked and they were going to leave the world the same way. He would give God the glory no matter what happened.

That was the right response. He could have handled it differently. He could have gotten drunk. He could have been angry. But he chose to accept the situation as it was and trust God.

His wife, however, did not take this news quite as well. She was heartbroken and angry. She asked Job, "Why don't you just curse God and die?" She was talking about a form of suicide, similar to death by suicide by cops. They want to end their lives but don't have the courage to do it themselves, so they give the cops a reason to do it for them. That was Job's wife's plan. She thought if they just cursed God, then maybe God would kill them and end all the pain.

When I think about it, I kind of understand where she was coming from. I feel like we have all been there, at times. We know we are going to heaven when we die. If today was my last day, if I dropped dead of a heart attack right now, the best is yet to come. It's going to be really great. The world we live in is messed up. It's hard to keep trying to do the right thing. Life is hard. We long for heaven. But, while I can't wait for that day, I have never considered suicide. That's not part of my DNA.

But I have had passing thoughts. "Come on, God, let's just get it over with." Or I start thinking about how much I miss my dad and my grandpa and I can't wait to see them again. I think about stuff like that. But I always remember God has me here on earth for a reason. Heaven is waiting for me. And if you are a Christian, heaven is waiting for you, too. But we shouldn't try to take a shortcut through God's plan for our lives. Even if we are going to go through messy and painful things. We're going to have to deal with plenty of EGR people—*Extra Grace Required*. Thankfully, God gives us the grace to get through it. If we walk with God, we can go through this life with grace.

Job and his wife handled their trauma in different ways. In the end, it all worked out for them.

*

Another example is found in The Gospel of John, chapter 11. This is the story of Lazarus, a friend of Jesus. He had two sisters, Mary and Martha. They all lived in a small town called Bethany. Whenever Jesus was in that area, He would stay at their house. They put Him up in their guest bedroom. They were all very close friends.

One day, Jesus was ministering a couple of towns over, and someone sent word to Him that Lazarus was very sick, and if Jesus didn't come right then, he would die. Jesus decided to wait for two more days, and then He got word that Lazarus had died. His disciples wondered why they hadn't gone sooner. But Jesus had a plan and told them they were going to go now. This confused the disciples because Lazarus was already dead. And Jesus responded by saying that Lazarus was merely asleep.

So, as Jesus was getting close to the home of Mary, Martha, and Lazarus, Martha met Jesus outside and grabbed on to him, saying, "If you had been here, my brother wouldn't have died!" She was very upset. She wasn't necessarily accusing Jesus of anything, but rather acknowledging that she believed Jesus could have saved her brother from death. She was in pain. She was hurt. But she trusted Him. That was a proper response.

In John 11:32-35, it says, *"When Mary arrived and saw Jesus, she fell at his feet and said, 'Lord, if you had only been here, my brother would not have died.' When Jesus saw her weeping and saw the other people wailing with her, a deep anger welled up within Him, and He was deeply troubled. 'Where have you put him?' He asked them. They told Him, 'Lord, come and see.' Then Jesus wept."* (New Living Translation) In other translations, verse 35, has only two words, "Jesus wept."

The shortest verse in the Bible.

Jesus went to their home and He healed Lazarus. He raised him from the dead. Lazarus had been dead for four days, and he stunk, but Jesus brought him back to life.

If you don't know a lot about Mary and Martha, let me give you some context. Mary is the one who broke open an alabaster box filled with expensive perfume at Jesus' feet. Traditionally a father would give this box––worth about one year's wages—to his young daughter, and she would save it for her wedding night. When that night came, she was supposed to be a virgin. The alabaster box was a signification of that. She would break it open on her husband's feet, as a symbol that she had saved herself for him and remained pure.

It was beautiful and symbolic.

According to tradition, Mary had been demon possessed. Jesus cast seven demons out of her. She was also “a lady of the evening”—trading sex for money. But when Jesus healed her, and cast the demons out, she was completely set free. But like many of us, she had a past. She had some “junk” that she had to work through. She had baggage—even cargo. She had trauma.

And now her brother was dead.

I have had trauma in my life, and when I experience the death of a close friend or relative, I don’t always handle it well. We don’t always know how to handle things in healthy ways. That’s why people get drunk, use drugs, or do any number of things to numb the pain.

Mary had a lot of baggage from her past, and was hit hard when her brother died. So, when Jesus finally got there, she poured out her heart to Him. And Jesus ministered to her in her sorrow.

Then He brought Lazarus back from the dead.

Mary is a great case study on someone who has had a lot of trauma in her life, but has a relationship with God.

14

"WE MUST BE INTENTIONAL."

I SAW A meme recently that said, "If you don't heal from what hurt you, you'll bleed on people who didn't cut you." That's profound. It describes what is happening all over the world today. There are so many people who struggle to have healthy relationships with the people they love because they haven't dealt with the "junk" that has been suppressed deep down. We have poor relationships with friends and coworkers because we haven't healed from past hurts.

God created the church to help. The purpose of the church is to glorify God and to build up, encourage, and support one another. Yet, I am blown away by the number of churches who don't even try to do this. I have been blessed to be a part of a church that takes this calling seriously. But even in my church, we still have people who are wearing masks. People who have had the worst week in their lives, but when asked how they're doing will answer, "Just fine." You're falling apart at the seams. Your marriage is failing.

But you said you are fine.

When we do this, we will never find healing. Churches have got to find a way to help with that. We need to encourage people to be honest. I came across a video about this:

> *What is church? It's a group of people with the same belief. It's a community after God's own heart. All of these people giving love, showing love to one another. But too often, in church, we said the word fake. Too often, we see people hiding, hiding their hurt, hiding their questions, hiding their struggles. Too often, we come to church, put on a mask, and then go back home with our same pain and uncertainties. Why aren't we allowed to be honest? Why can't we be true with one another? Why can't we have questions about faith? Everyone has questions. If everyone does, that means the person next to you right*

now has doubts. That means pastors have doubts, but we don't ask these questions. We go on living with our mask, hiding our questions, even to ourselves. Why don't we question?

Let's recreate the word church. Let's make it a place where people can come broken down, sad, hurting, and questioning. Let's be honest, truthful, ask questions. God desires us to seek after Him. God wants to be pursued, so beg for His attention and His truth. It's time for a change, but it takes each and every one to open up. Be honest and be loved. As community, as a family, reach out to each other and ask for support as you grow in your relationship with Christ. Become a community where doubts are welcomed and pain is received. It's time to change. Change from a church where we see fake to a church that is all about honesty and desperately seeking the truth.

That kind of church doesn't just happen. We must be intentional about loving and knowing each other. It doesn't just happen by coming to church on Sunday mornings and listening to the preacher. There must be community outside of what happens on Sunday. That's why small groups are so important. Something happens when we gather together in an intimate group and open up the scriptures and process things together. That is when real healing happens. It happens in those small circles.

I've been sober—off drugs and alcohol—for more than 24 years. I don't have to white knuckle it today. I'm thankful that the desire to drink does not control me anymore. There is always a fleeting chance, so I must never be over confident. Today, I choose sobriety and I have things in place in my life to keep me accountable. Because life hits hard sometimes. I have stress. I'm a sinner. I still struggle. But I can face life on life's terms today without using alcohol or drugs to get me through the day.

The highlight of my week is when I get to my recovery group on Monday nights. Even 24 years later, I look forward to going into that room and sitting around with a group of people who have the same struggles and simply talking about how our week was. I need that. I need to be able to talk to people honestly about what I'm feeling. If I'm having a great week, I want to share it. The Bible tells us to rejoice with those who rejoice and weep with those who weep. Almost every week someone in that group breaks down and says, "I've had the worst week I've ever had." And then they receive encouragement and support. We come together and rally around them. We pray with them and build them up.

Healing happens.

We all need a circle of friends we can talk to about what we are going through. Everyone needs that kind of support. You don't have to struggle with addiction to need that type of recovery. Everyone is recovering from *something*. And healing can begin when we find a group of people and simply talk about how our week has been.

Honestly.

We need a place where we can be vulnerable and open enough to tell our closest friends that we are struggling, barely hanging by a thread. When we hold it all in and don't get it out in a healthy way, we tend to do foolish things that we may regret. When we share about our struggles, we can be talked off the ledge.

We need to talk to one another.

A person can't fix you. I can't fix you. A spouse or parent can't fix you. Only God can fix you. But He won't unless you ask Him to—and you cooperate with Him. He won't force Himself on you. Healing usually doesn't just happen. You can't just ask someone to lay hands on you and the trauma of your childhood vanishes. No, prayer is just the beginning of working together with God to heal our hearts.

I think of the little girl in that letter I mentioned earlier. I think of her wish list. If I just prayed for her, it would not make her problems go away. That's not how it usually works, because if we don't deal with things properly, even though there may be relief from the struggles for a time, the problems remain to pop up at the most inopportune time. And we have to go back and deal with it all over again. We just don't pray and all of our emotional issues are gone. Salvation happens in an instant, but everything else is a process of growing in Christ and dealing with life, with Him by our side helping us. Lasting change is a slow process of being willing to look at ourselves and submit to God, allowing His love to change us from the inside out.

*

Ezekiel gives us a good example of this. The children of Israel had forsaken God. They were worshiping idols. They had basically given God the middle finger. They didn't want to follow God's ways and thought there were better ways to live. But God never gave up on them. That is the amazing thing about God. He tells them that there would come a day when the nation of Israel would return to Him, and He would welcome them back. And when that happened, He would do something for them.

Ezekiel 36:25 says, *"Then I will sprinkle clean water on you and you will be clean. Your filth will be washed away, and you will no longer worship idols, and I will give you a new heart and I will put a new spirit in you. And I will take out your stony, stubborn heart and give you a tender, responsive heart. And I will put my spirit in you so that you will follow my decrees and be careful to obey my regulations."*

That is what God does for us, as well.

He did it for the children of Israel, and we can trust in His faithfulness to do it for us. Many of us have stony hearts. We have stubborn hearts. We are rebellious by nature. We fight against God. And God simply wants us to stop fighting and surrender, allowing Him to take over. He wants to heal us. He wants to take out our stony, stubborn hearts and replace them with tender and responsive hearts. We need a heart transplant. We don't need to try harder. We don't need self-help books. We need the love and power of God in our lives.

Here are some practical tips to help if you are dealing with pain or trauma in your life.

First, *make it a priority to spend some time with God.* Carve out intentional time for prayer and reading His Word. Put it on the calendar. Spend 30-60 minutes each day. Set aside a place, and communicate with God. If your heart is broken, and if you are struggling through pain and trauma, whether big or small, tell Him all about it. If you are mad at God, tell Him. He already knows our thoughts. And He wants us to tell Him about it. He wants an honest conversation.

Second, it helps to *write out your feelings.* Write a letter. Keep a journal. Write out what you are feeling and thinking. There is great power in just putting pen to paper.

Third, *find someone to talk to* about how you are doing. It only needs to be one person. Someone you trust and who will keep your conversation private. Someone who can keep it confidential. Someone who loves you and cares about you. Sit down with them, or take them out for coffee and just pour it all out. If they love and care about you, they're not going to judge you. They will hug you and pray with you. We need that in our lives.

Finally, seriously consider Biblically-based counseling. Sit down with someone who has been trained to help people.

Ask God for help. Reach out to Him and to others who love Him. Be courageous and go after change. Have faith and hope in the promises of God. One definition of insanity is "doing the same thing over and over, expecting different results." You won't get better on your own. Quit the fight. Surrender to His love.

And be healed.

15

"WE ALL HAVE ISSUES."

EVEN IF YOU don't have a problem with alcohol or drugs, the principles of recovery can apply to you. You may hear the very word "recovery" and think that because you don't struggle with addiction, the lessons don't apply. That couldn't be further from the truth. I've been clean and sober for more than 24 years, and I'm here to tell you that the principles can apply to you, because we all have a *sin* problem.

Often, sin presents as addiction. If you begin drinking alcohol too often, and for the wrong reasons, you may become chemically addicted to it. If you start to take drugs, your life may become unmanageable. You can even become addicted to some more benign things, like ice cream or cookies.

Anything that brings us pleasure can become addictive.

Nobody starts out wanting to get addicted. When you see a person whose life is unmanageable due to drugs or alcohol, it's likely because they are masking their pain—self-medicating. Something deep inside them is wrong and they don't know how to deal with it. They just mask it. They have problems they can't face, so they say, "Screw it, I'll just get drunk (or high)." The next day they wake up, hungover, with the same problems as the day before, and possibly more problems due to poor decisions made while under the influence. And it becomes a vicious cycle of escaping, then turning to drugs and alcohol for a solution, that in turn only causes more pain and problems.

No matter your struggle, God wants you to figure out what's *really* going on. We all struggle with sin. It is easy to look at an obvious addict and point your finger at them, thinking, "Yeah, they're messed up." But I believe God wants us to look in the mirror and say, "Well, what about you?"

We all have issues. People who don't have the obvious problem of addiction often know they are messed up, but they don't know how get better. Or maybe, because of pride they are not willing to deal with it. Some people conceal their problems better than others. But the internal struggle is just as real and dangerous as drugs and alcohol are to the addict. Maybe nobody knows what your sin problem is, but if you don't deal with it, you will struggle with it for the rest of your life.

And there is a good chance people will find out.

What we don't realize is that if we were to shout out loud about our struggle, we would find there are other people who share the same issue. Too often we aren't willing to bring such things to light. But if we don't bring them to light, 15 years from now we'll be dealing with the very same problems—because we never faced them.

Christians have access to freedom in Christ. So, if 15 years from now we don't have victory over our struggles, it's because we haven't truly given them to Christ. The more reliant we are on Him, the greater our victory over bondage.

The *Oxford Dictionary* defines the word "recovery," first, as a return to a normal state of health, or mind, or strength. The second definition is the action or process of regaining possession or control of something stolen or lost. I like the second definition better, because every single human being has an active enemy—Satan. He's a real being, and he works overtime in our lives. That's why you have issues in your relationships, in your marriage, and at your job. It's why you struggle with sin. Satan knows exactly what your particular sin problem is. He knows the one thing that you struggle with more than anything else, and he loves to tempt you. He loves to bait you. And when you take that bait, he's the first to accuse you. He's been stealing your life, your joy, and your freedom.

The good news is that, whether you are an addict or simply an average person who struggles with sin, God is in the business of restoring what Satan has stolen. In fact, there's a verse in the Old Testament (Joel 2:25) that says that God will give you back what the locust has eaten.

Another definition of recovery is restoring sanity. In A.A .or N.A., there's a lot of talk about this. There's a level of insanity in active addiction that can't be denied. And the effects of drugs and alcohol over long periods of time can be brutal, with lingering effects on the mind and body. There can be permanent damage. But, as a pastor and someone who does a lot of work in the recovery field, I'm blown away by the miracles that can happen in recovery. It's like when the Bible talks about the demon possessed man who, after an encounter with Jesus, was seen clothed and in his right mind again (Mark 5:14-20). I've seen people who have given up drugs and alcohol and now have a job, a family, and a clearly sound mind.

That kind of miracle is due to the grace of God.

★

In chapter four of the Book of Daniel, we find the story of King Nebuchadnezzar. I like to call him King Neb, for short. He was King of Babylon, a very prideful ruler. At this time the Jews were exiled to Babylon as slaves. Daniel was one of King Neb's court advisors.

To make a long story short, King Neb went out on his terrace and looked over his kingdom, and said, "Look at this great Babylon that I have built by my own hand." As soon as he said that, he became insane. This had been prophesied by God. He was basically a lunatic for the next seven years. He was driven from society. He lived in the wilderness with the wild animals, and he ate grass.

Daniel 4:34 tells us, *"After the time had passed, I Nebuchadnezzar looked up to heaven. My sanity returned and I praised and worshipped the God, the most high and honored the one who lives forever."* That is encouraging to us, because it shows that even when people make poor choices and mess up their lives, when they dedicate themselves to God, God starts putting the broken pieces of their lives back together. It's amazing how that works.

16

"NO HALF MEASURES"

I HAVE SEVERAL thoughts about recovery in our lives. First, the goal is to be free from addiction through dependence on Christ. That's right, our freedom flows from dependence. Now you may ask, "how can I be free if I am dependent on someone else?" Because we will never be free from God's rule. We are either a slave to the devil or a slave to God. It's like Bob Dylan said in one of his songs:

You may be a preacher with your spiritual pride
You may be a city councilman taking bribes on the side
You may be workin' in a barbershop, you may know how to cut hair
You may be somebody's mistress, may be somebody's heir
But you're gonna have to serve somebody, yes
You're gonna have to serve somebody
Well, it may be the devil or it may be the Lord
But you're gonna have to serve somebody

God wants us to be a slave to Him. Jesus said, "Take my yoke upon you because it is light." That's the goal. To be free from dependence on substances through dependence on Christ.

But that's just the beginning. You can't go on a journey until you take that first step. If you are a basketball player, you will miss one hundred percent of the shots not taken. If you never shoot the basketball because of fear, you are never going to make anything. If you are a baseball player, and you are up to bat but you never swing, then you will never hit a home run. Many people may not swing because of fear of striking out. Yes, you may strike out, but you also may hit the ball over the fence.

In baseball, if you have 300 batting average over the course of your career, you will make the Hall of Fame. Do you know what it means to bat 300? It means that seven out of 10 times you're making an out. Strike out, ground out, fly out—o-u-t—out. But you are considered among the best in the game. It's pretty much about failing your way to success.

Do you understand how much failure is in you? It simply boils down to fear versus faith. Are you fearful? Do you avoid taking the first step because you don't want anyone knowing your business? You don't want to be exposed or found out as a failure?

You will never start the journey of victory over sin and addiction unless you take that first step.

In John chapter five, we learn about a man who had been crippled for 38 years. The Bible says, *"Afterward Jesus returned to Jerusalem for one of the Jewish holy days. Inside the city near the sheep gate was the pool of Bethesda with five covered porches. Crowds of sick people, blind, lame and paralyzed, lay on the porches. They were waiting for a certain movement of the water. For an Angel of the Lord came from time to time and stirred the water. The first person to step in after the water was stirred was healed of whatever disease that person had.*

"One of the men lying there had been sick for 38 years."

We don't know how old he was. We don't know if he was born sick, or if he had gotten sick later in life. We find out a little bit later that the sickness had something to do with his legs. He had a deformity that made him unable to walk. He spent his life on a mat. And every day he laid by the pool. All day long. Waiting for the stirring of the water and the opportunity to be healed.

Most theologians believe that this was just superstition because they found out later that there were actually underground springs that were feeding the pool. So, sometimes the water would come from underneath and cause a bubbling. The people believed that it was the Spirit stirring the waters.

"When Jesus saw him and knew he had been ill for a long time, He asked him, 'Would you like to get well?'"

Now, when we read that verse, it seems like a dumb question. Of course, the man wanted to get well. He'd been in that condition for 38 years. He couldn't walk, and he sat by the waters every single day. He obviously wanted to be healed, or he would have been somewhere else.

But then I start to think—maybe he didn't necessarily want to be healed.

I have the privilege of pastoring a church that has a reputation for helping people in recovery. Every week or two, someone I don't even know will reach out to me and tell me that they need help, because they are struggling with drug or alcohol addiction.

As I offer help, the first question I ask them is, "Are you willing to do whatever it takes?" Because, what I have found, over the years, is that, while many people want help, very few are actually willing to go to any length to stay clean and sober. It's like they think that I have some supernatural powers and that I can just somehow lay hands on them and pray for them and they will automatically get better. All of a sudden, they will get their kids back. They will be saved from having to go to jail. They won't have to go to court. Everything will just miraculously be fixed.

People really do think that. Now, don't get me wrong. I believe that God heals and can take away the bondage of addiction. He delivered me 24 years ago when I got out of prison. I wanted to get off drugs. And after a few months of doing the right thing, God took away the desire for any drugs and alcohol. To this day I have no desire. But I also make wise choices. I'm not at the clubs every Saturday night. I don't hang out with people who are smoking crystal meth and shooting heroin. I've removed the temptations from my life.

I have to put in the work.

If you have an issue in your life, God is not just going to zap you and take it away. He absolutely will heal you, but it may be a process. You don't usually recover overnight. You didn't ruin your life in one day, and your whole life is not going to be fixed in one day. You still have to show up at court. You still have to go through the steps to get your kids back.

I know many people in recovery who lost their kids during active addiction, and there was a system and a process that had to occur to get them back. I've walked through that process with people and it seems slow and tedious, taking months and even years to regain custody. It's frustrating. There are setbacks. It feels like one step forward and three steps back. But you just keep pressing forward. One step at a time.

I believe that is how God most often chooses to work.

The paralyzed man was lying by the pool every day for 38 years. Why would he not want to get well? It seems like an obvious answer. But Jesus asked the question because He knew the man had a choice. You see, sometimes people do not want to get well. Sometimes, even if they are struggling with a stronghold in their lives and their lives are unmanageable, they just aren't ready to give it up. Or they don't really want to change, but they just want to get out of trouble. That is why I ask people if they are willing to do whatever it takes.

No half measures.

During active addiction, addicts and alcoholics are all in. They give their life to it. They spend all their money. They steal from those they love to get what they need. They are willing to go to any length to get high or drunk. So, when they decide that they have had enough and want to stop, I ask them if they are going to put as much work into their recovery and following Christ as they did on feeding their addiction.

Because that is what it takes.

17

"ROCK BOTTOM"

SO WHY WOULDN'T someone be ready for real change when their life is such a complete mess? I think the first reason is that people become accustomed to their situation—maybe even comfortable with it. Life is messed up, but they have become used to it. You can get used to being broken. You can get used to being homeless.

I was recently talking to a man from *Community Services League*, a local charity founded in 1916 by a group of women including the future First Lady Bess Truman. He said they have opportunities for everyone who is in need. He said there is no real reason for people to be on the streets. If they need a place to stay, there's a spot for them. But some people are not ready to get off the streets yet. They would rather live on the streets as addicts than get clean. And there is nothing that can force them to take that first vital step.

Have you ever tried to change someone? If you're married, have you tried to change your spouse? It doesn't work. If anything, you just became more frustrated. We cannot change people. Sometimes, when trying to change people, we actually make things worse. Sometimes in trying to help them, we end up *enabling* them, and we actually become part of the problem and not the solution.

Second, some people are not willing to get better because they haven't yet hit their rock bottom. Until people hit rock bottom, they will not change. I recently saw a meme that said, "Once you hit rock bottom and you find out that Christ is the rock at the bottom, then you find freedom."

That'll preach.

Some people don't hit rock bottom because their loved ones don't allow them to. Mom keeps stepping in and rescuing them from consequences. I tell people that going to prison was the best thing that ever happened to me. I would never have found Christ if I hadn't gone so low. Now prison wasn't exactly a party to me, but I know now that I had to go to prison so I would hit my rock bottom, and so I would find Christ as the Rock at the bottom waiting for me.

Maybe you have people in your life that you are always trying to rescue. They get in trouble and you pay their debts. Or maybe you bail them out of jail. But jail may actually be the best thing for them. So, when you rescue them, you are, in effect, playing God. You see, God has orchestrated some circumstances in their life so that they will fall flat on their face and hit bottom. But it pains you to see them suffer, because you love them. Maybe it's a spouse or a child. But get out of God's way and let God work.

I have a friend, Jeff Danforth, who has been sober for eight years. Before that he had been on crystal meth for his entire adult life. He had never gone to rehab, but every so often he would just come home and tell his mother, "I'm sorry, this time I really do want to get help." And she would always take him back in and help him. But it never lasted. Finally, she got to the point where she told him that he was not welcome at her house anymore. She told him that not only was he messing up his own life, but he was messing up her life. And she couldn't allow it anymore. So, she cut him off.

He had to find his rock bottom.

It was a tough lesson, but he now says that if she hadn't have done that, he never would have hit his bottom and become desperate enough to find help. After he started on his road of recovery, then he was able to go back to his mom, and she, seeing he was willing to do whatever it took to stay clean, allowed him back into her life.

So, we need to stop trying to protect people from their consequences.

The third reason people don't change is because drugs and alcohol actually affect their decision-making abilities. They are erratic. They lack the capacity to make sound choices. They drive while drunk. They don't see the danger when they are under the influence. They don't see the necessity to get sober when they are drunk. Their minds are not operating in a sound manner. Their decision-making process is, in effect, blocked.

Finally, some people do not recover because they have given up hope. I see this all the time. People go in and out of rehab. It is just an endless cycle of trying to get sober. Trying to get clean. And they keep failing. Some people struggle with addiction because they have been called a loser their whole life. Maybe their parents were on drugs and everyone just expected them to follow in their footsteps.

But there is always hope.

I've seen people who have faced hardship after hardship, and they have become free. They have thrown off their shackles of addiction and said, "I don't care what anyone says about me. You can call me a failure. You can call me a loser. You can call me an addict. But I'm going to follow Jesus. That is my new identity. I am free in Christ."

*

So, back to the story. Jesus asked the paralyzed man, *"Do you want to get well?"*

> *"'I can't sir,' the sick man said, 'for I have no one to put me into the pool when the water bubbles up. Someone else always gets there ahead of me.'"*

Two things come to mind when I read that verse. First, he doesn't seem to have any good friends. This is also true with alcoholics and addicts. When they are out there partying, it seems like they have a lot of friends. But when they want to clean up their life? Those so-called friends disappear. Remember the story of the prodigal son? He was out spending money. Blowing money. Buying drinks for everyone. But when he ran out of money, he ran out of friends.

So, this man didn't have any friends to help him. That is why it is so important that we offer help and support when someone is serious about getting better.

Second, his response was an excuse. Instead of saying, "Yes! I want to get well!" He blamed his situation on the fact that he didn't have friends to help him. Sometimes people don't want to take responsibility for their own problems and their own recovery. They have excuses for everything. It's always someone else's fault. It was their parents' fault. It was because of how they were raised. It was genetics. It's never their fault.

Every single person can come up with an excuse for anything if they want to justify it. But this does not lead to healing, life-change, and recovery. Excuses keep us sick. Excuses keep us stuck. Until you start taking ownership of the sin you are struggling with, and start taking responsibility for it, you will never have freedom. But you can have freedom if you are willing to say, "You know what? I did have a bad upbringing. Maybe my parents did feed into that. Or maybe I do have a genetic predisposition. But it doesn't matter. I still chose to do what I did. And I'm ready to own up to that and take the steps to change." You have to get rid of the excuses.

In verse eight it says, *"Jesus told him, 'Stand up, pick up your mat, and walk!' Instantly the man was healed. He rolled up his sleeping mat and began walking! But this miracle happened on the Sabbath."*

What an amazing miracle! He did what Jesus told him to do and he was healed. He stood up, rolled up his mat, and started walking.

And then something crazy happened. Now, you would think that his family and friends would be ecstatic. And I'm sure some of them were. But some people weren't happy for this man. That just blows my mind. But I've seen it happen in our day, too. Sometimes when someone starts to do better in life, some people do not like it. Not everyone celebrates positive life-change. There are haters. Relationship dynamics change, and people don't like it.

That's when you find out who your actual friends are. Anyone not happy that you are doing better, is someone who you may need to cut out of your life. If they are not happy for you, if they don't rejoice at your new success, then you don't need them to be a part of your life. You don't need them if all they do is criticize you. Some people seem to think that criticism is a spiritual gift. It's not. There are some people who can find fault in anything.

Verse nine says, *"But the miracle happened on the Sabbath."* The Jewish leaders objected because it happened on Saturday, and according to Jewish law, you weren't supposed to work on the Sabbath.

In verse 10 it says, *"So the Jewish leaders objected. They said to the man who was cured, 'You can't work on the Sabbath! The law doesn't allow you to carry that sleeping mat!'"*

Now, if I were him, I would have taken that mat and slapped someone with it. Or kicked someone. After all, he could now use his legs. That's what I would have done. Because I would have been so mad that, after 38 years of begging, they couldn't be happy that I had been healed, simply because of the day of the week? How could they let a miracle go like that? How could they nitpick the details when something so miraculous happened.

People criticize. They look for fault. Rare is the person that can look past all your faults and say, "You know what? In spite of that, I see God working in your life. You're not perfect, but look at how much progress you have made. You've come so far. I see God working in your life." Find these kinds of friends. Surround yourself with people who don't criticize your shortcomings, but rather, who recognize your progress.

Starting in verse 11, we read, *"But he replied, 'The man who healed me told me, "Pick up your mat and walk."' Who said such a thing as that?" they demanded. The man didn't know, for Jesus had disappeared into the crowd. But afterward Jesus found him in the Temple and told him, 'Now you are well; so stop sinning, or something even worse may happen to you.'"*

After the man was healed, he went straight to church. And Jesus found him there and called him to repentance. You see, if you have had an encounter with the God of the universe, the One who created everything, and if you've met Jesus as your personal Lord and Savior, and your life is not in some way different, then I would say that you are mistaken. You didn't meet Jesus. Or you are believing a lie. Because when you have an encounter with the God of the universe, your life cannot stay the same. Because God gives us the gift of the Holy Spirit. We may still struggle, but He helps us through it.

I gave my life to Christ more than 24 years ago. But I wasn't struck perfect overnight. Some of the things that I used to do, I still did. But after I was saved, I wasn't happy about it. I couldn't enjoy the sin that I used to enjoy because the Holy Spirit convicted me. And He gave me the desire to change.

It's called repentance.

Jesus told a man to stop sinning or something worse could happen to him. And no matter where we are on our journey we should be constantly repenting of our sin, changing as we go.

And in verse 15 it says, *"Then the man went and told the Jewish leaders that it was Jesus who had healed him."*

18

"EVERYONE STRUGGLES WITH SOMETHING."

THE FIRST STEP in recovery is admitting that you have a problem. If you have an issue in your life, it is a sin issue. But sin can become an addiction. If it becomes an addiction, you have to admit that it has led to unmanageability in your life. You will never find healing and freedom from the problem until you, first, identify the problem.

Admitting you have a problem requires honesty and humility. It takes humility to look in the mirror and know that you have stuff that needs to be cleaned up and changed. It takes honesty to go to another person and admit your faults. Now, this doesn't mean that we have to air our dirty laundry on *Facebook*, for all the world to see. No. Simply find one person who loves Jesus, and confess your sins to him.

It leads to freedom.

If you have ever carried a secret, if you've ever done something wrong and nobody knew about it, it has a way of eating you up inside. There is something liberating about going to someone and confessing your wrongs. Afterward, you may be waiting for the hammer to drop, but oftentimes you find out that you are not alone. You fear judgment, but you find compassion and understanding.

Everyone struggles with something. And God's way out of that struggle is to free yourself through confessing your sins. It is cathartic to be able to go to another person and share with them that you have issues. It is freeing to be vulnerable and transparent with them, and find them showing you love and empathy in return.

People who conceal their sins never find freedom.

Second, refusing to admit you have a problem is called *denial*. We've all met someone who is in denial about something. I frequently see people who are in denial about their addiction. I can see through them, because it takes one to know one. I used to be on drugs. If you come into my presence and you're on drugs, it's almost like I have a sixth sense. I can just tell. Drug addicts think they are fooling everyone. But people know.

We can be in denial, not just about addiction, but about many other things. Kids are notorious for this. I saw a video recently, and it went like this:

"John, what are you eating?"

"Nothing."

"You didn't eat anything?"

"Yeah. Nothing."

"John, look at mommy?"

"Anything."

"Are you telling me the truth?"

"Yeah."

"You didn't have any snacks?"

"Nope."

"Let me see. You don't have any snacks? Open wide, let me see. Really? You didn't have any snacks?"

"Yeah."

"John, come here. John, can you explain to me why the sprinkles are empty?"

"Well, they're not empty."

"John, look at me."

"They are empty."

"Did you eat those sprinkles?"

"No. I did not."

"You know it's not nice to tell stories and to lie, right? Look at mommy. You're not supposed to lie. Tell me now, did you eat those sprinkles?"

"No. I did not eat those sprinkles."

"John?"

"Mm-hmm (affirmative)."

"You have sprinkles on your face."

"Oh, no. No. I did not eat sprinkles."

*

I find this hilarious. I had almost the same conversation about sprinkles with my daughter a few years ago. She had sprinkles all over her face and when I asked her if she had eaten them, she said, "Nope. I didn't have anything."

That's how we are with God sometimes. And that's how we are with people that we care about. We try to cover up our sin. We convince ourselves that no one can see, but everyone can see. We can cover our sins for a while, but Numbers 32:23 says, *"be sure your sin will find you out."* That is a powerful verse and I have found it to be true in my life and in the lives of those around me.

This is the way God set it up. It is a God thing. God wants us to own up to our sins and confess our sins to one another. That means that you need an accountability partner. You need somebody that you are able to trust and share things with. You don't necessarily have to have a recovery group, but just one person who really knows you. If you refuse to do that, God will see to it that it comes to light somehow, and you will be embarrassed and humiliated.

I have found that if I am proactive about a problem and share what is going on in my life, it leads to freedom. There are no secrets. But if you try to conceal it and hide it, then you are in denial about your sin, and God will bring it to light.

A good acronym for denial is "**D**on't **E**ven **N**otice **I** **A**m **L**ying."

When people are in denial, they say many different things. They may say, "I can quit anytime." "I don't have a problem." They can't admit the truth. And without honestly looking at yourself and facing the truth, you will never have healing.

*

One of my best friends in high school came to me five years ago. This friend had struggled with crystal meth, on and off, for most of his adult life. He had just lost his house, his business, and just about everything. He came to me and wanted to talk. I told him that I could help him, but that I was not God. I told him that he needed to get off drugs and do whatever it took to make that happen.

So, we called a recovery house to ask for help. My friend then proceeded to get into an argument with the person on the phone. He didn't want to do what the man was telling him. He was in so much denial. He kept insisting that he didn't really have a problem. I asked him if he was high right then and he said that he was but that he could quit anytime. I asked him why he didn't quit. And he told me because it's not a problem. And we just talked in circles. The conversation was going nowhere. He left the office that day and to this day has not found freedom. He's in rough shape and it astounds me that he is still in denial.

But that denial is strong in so many of us.

Another excuse that people in denial will use is, "Well, I'm not hurting anybody else, right?" What they don't see is how much they are hurting the people who care about them. Children are often involved and are victims of the addict's wreckage. You see, your sin never affects just you. It always has a ripple effect. Collateral damage.

Another excuse for not getting help is that they insist that, even if their addiction is unmanageable, they can still function. They can still hold down a job. They are still married. They still have their kids. This is the hardest type of person to convince that they have a problem. They have not hit the same type of bottom as other addicts and alcoholics. When you have lost everything, it is easier to accept that you need help. But these people haven't lost anything. So, they stay in denial. Because it's just not that bad.

There is a woman at my church named Cindy. I was best friends with her son. Her first husband owned a body shop. He was very successful and made a lot of money. He had it all. A family. A business. A beautiful house. They were living the American dream. But Roy would get off work every day at five o'clock, and on the way home he would buy a 12-pack of *Michelob* in the bottles. He would go home and sit on the couch and just slam them back. I was over there a lot, and my mom would ask me if he was an alcoholic. And I would say that he wasn't. He was just a person who drank every day.

You see, to me, an alcoholic was my dad. He would drink a case of beer and then disappear for three days, come home drunk, and then start swinging on me and my mom. To me, that was the definition of an alcoholic. Someone who was verbally, and physically, abusive and mean.

Roy wasn't like that. He would simply sit on the couch and drink a 12-pack in a night. I never saw him drunk. I never saw him stumbling around, so I didn't think he had a problem.

Now, I believe Roy was an alcoholic. He was probably drunk, but was just accustomed to it. And, after years and years of alcohol abuse, it did ruin his marriage and took his business from him. Sin has a way of catching up with us. A person who is a "functioning" alcoholic or addict may be the worst kind, because they don't know that their life is out of control yet. Generally, the addict is the last to know.

Thomas Jefferson said, "Honesty is the first chapter in the book of wisdom." We need to be honest about where we are in life. Have you ever met a person who was totally self-unaware? I'm the worst singer in most rooms that I walk into. If we were to have a contest, I could win worst singer. I could have been on *American Idol* and I would have become famous like the other people who couldn't sing. I always felt bad for them, because someone told them that they could sing, and encouraged them to go on the show. But they can't sing and were the last ones to know. And the whole country was laughing at them.

We need to be aware of our situation. Aware of our shortcomings. In John, chapter eight, Jesus said, *"If the Son sets you free you will be free indeed."* And the people who were listening to him said, "Free? We're Jews! We've never been slaves to anybody." I think Jesus must have thought, "What?" Because Jewish history was filled with slavery and exile.

A brief history lesson of the Old Testament tells us that the Jewish people were slaves in Egypt for 400 years. Then they became slaves of the Philistines and the Moabites. And then they were slaves to the Babylonians for 70 years. And during the time of Jesus, the Jews were oppressed by the Roman government. And yet, the man was telling Jesus that they had never been slaves before. He was completely self-*unaware.*

We have to step into awareness. We have to get honest with ourselves, with God, and with others. We need to let people know where we are, what we are struggling with and ask for help. We need to start working on ourselves and work toward freedom.

Everyone has sin that they struggle with. Do you believe that God can help you? Are you willing to ask for help? That's the first step. Being honest and humble enough to ask for help. Are you willing to do whatever it takes to get better? Because that is where the rubber meets the road. It does you no good to know what you need to do and be unwilling to do what's necessary to change. It talks about that in the Book of James. It's like a person who looks in the mirror and then walks away.

A semicolon is often used when a sentence could have ended, but didn't. Many people now get a semicolon as a tattoo, because it represents a life story, and it says that God is not finished writing my story. The best is yet to come.

If you could have seen the first half of my life, it looked very different than it does today. It was messed up. It was defined by drugs and alcohol abuse and all of the insanity that comes with it. But the second half of my life includes God.

And the best is yet to come.

19

"DO YOU WANT TO GET BETTER?"

EVERYONE KNOWS SOMEONE who has a messed up life because of drugs and alcohol. We all sin, so we're all in the same boat. I find what Paul wrote the Galatian Christians to be helpful. In chapter six of his letter to them he wrote in verse one, "Dear brothers and sisters, if another believer is overcome by some sin, you who are godly should gently and humbly help that person back onto the right path." He says, "And be careful not to fall into the same temptation yourself." In verse two he says, "Share each other's burdens and in this way obey the law of Christ. If you think you're too important to help someone, you're only fooling yourself. You are not that important." I like how he just insults all of us right there. He says, *You ain't that big of a deal. You're not that importan*t. And so that's what we're talking about today. We're talking about people who have strayed off of the path, and how we can help them get back onto the right path.

How do we do that, because everyone has somebody they care for that's wrecking their own lives and we are helplessly standing by, watching it happen. It's breaking our hearts. We try to help and oftentimes we actually hurt the situation. We don't know how to help without hurting. And we do it out of love and compassion. We try to step in and help them from ruining their lives, but just end up furthering the situation along because of that.

The first thing I want you to understand is that you cannot change another person. How many of you know that you cannot change people? You can't. If you're married, say amen. You already know that. You thought when you were going to get married, *this person has some issues and we're going to fix it by saying, I do*. But that didn't fix it. All it did was make you more frustrated because now you're married to a person that won't change. I can't change my wife. I've tried. I've tried to send her to obedience school, it didn't work. No, just kidding. I can't get my dog to stop peeing on the carpet. I can't get anybody to do anything that I want. I barely keep my own head above water. I can't get my kids to pick up after themselves. I can't get you to stop doing what you're doing.

The frustration we have in wanting to change people is exactly the way God feels with you and with me sometimes. God wants us to change, but he won't force it on us. Remember the story from John, chapter five, with the man who had been in a situation for 38 years. He couldn't walk and Jesus walked up and he didn't heal the him right away. Remember, He asked him a question. "Do you want to get better?" You see, Jesus knew that not everybody wants to get better. The interesting thing is that Jesus always asks for permission before he heals people. He never went up and laid hands on somebody and restored their sight and they said, "Get your hands off me." No one ever did that. No one was ever mad or upset that Jesus healed them because He never forced it on them. God has never forced you to do anything. Everyone has free will and God wants the best for you. He wants you to choose right every day, and often He's in the same boat we are. He's frustrated.

He's frustrated with you sometimes because you won't do what He wants you to do, because you think you're smarter than He is and you think your will is better than His will. He just takes his hands off the situation sometimes. He lets us see that following our own will doesn't go well. I've found that to be true for me, so I have learned that we just need to stick with His will.

So how do we help other people with an addiction? People who are on drugs, pain pills, alcohol, or any number of things that people struggle with? And everyone in here struggles with something. First, we have to remember that we struggle too. We never want to be so high and mighty trying to help others that we forget that we need help with our struggles too. The steps that it takes to overcome addiction should also be used in our own lives, even if we don't have an addiction problem. The solution to addiction applies to all of us. Because every one of us has a sin problem. We must first look inward before we look to help others.

When I was growing up, Independence was the meth capital of the world. We made national news for being the meth capital of the world. I don't think we still hold that title, just because all the meth that's in Independence now comes from Mexico, instead of being manufactured here. I recently heard that Tennessee is considered the meth capital of the world (now Independence is just famous for Harry S. Truman, which is a much better claim to fame). I grew up with all of that, just knowing that our town was full of drugs. It really is sad. And the only reason that Independence is not the meth capital anymore is because it spread, and the whole state and the whole country is dealing with this. It really is an epidemic. As I mentioned earlier, I did six funerals last year for people who overdosed on heroin, and it's to the point where I'm not sure I can do them anymore.

I'm a minister and people will call me all the time to help them through the effects of addiction and it's so heartbreaking. I sit there with the families, grieving with them, and so sad the suffering is completely preventable. This is not like cancer or some other disease that took a person's life because there was no cure or treatment. This is something we can do something about. We can change. If you have an addiction, whatever it is, it's preventable. You don't have to ruin your life. You can change and God can heal you. And it just tears me up inside to see people suffering. I want to help people, but I can't do it for them and I can't do it for you. Because I am the pastor of a church, people that I barely know reach out to me all the time on Facebook messenger or email, wanting me to talk to a loved one about their addiction.

I'm always happy to reach out to someone who is suffering, but I'm not God. And even if I was God, God doesn't usually heal someone against their will. And I often tell them that it will never happen if the loved one doesn't want it for himself. The addict or the alcoholic should be the one reaching out to me, not the parent. I understand that the families just want to help, but what they are doing is hurting more than helping. They're enabling, and are actually contributing to the problem because if a person wants to get help, that person needs to take the responsibility to do it. They need to put in the work to reap the reward.

So when parents call me about their son or daughter, I tell them to have the son or daughter call me back—not to simply hand the phone to them. The person struggling must call me himself, because it shows some initiative. We have to let people do this themselves. We will not let them walk through the process by themselves, but they have to show some initiative and make that first step.

I have come up with a list of do's and don'ts to help guide you in helping a loved one who struggles with addiction.

Number one. If someone you care about is ruining their life because of an addiction, DO confront them. Now, if you're like me, you may hate confrontation. I hate to have to go to someone and have a hard conversation. Seriously, I'd rather watch the Packers win a game. My wife is a Packer's fan. I've tried to convert her and it's too late. I just don't want her corrupting my children. That's all I'm aiming for now.

But, when it comes to addiction, you're going to have to confront them. That's always the first step. Bring to light the fact that you know what they are doing. Whether they've got an alcohol problem, or you find out they are on meth, or even looking at pornography, you have to confront them. The problem just doesn't go away by you wishing it would. You've got to sit down with them and have a hard conversation.

When you confront somebody about something, it's going to go one of three ways. Your concern may be met with denial, deflection, or a readiness to change.

Have you ever talked to somebody and they just deny that they have a problem? In our recovery group, we've encountered people like this. People only show up because someone is making them go. And we respond with the facts. For example, we won't tell them they have a problem with alcohol, but the facts show two DUIs in the last six months. So we suggest that maybe they have a problem. Maybe their addiction has caused them to lose jobs, or their marriage, or their children. We suggest that the facts show that they may have a problem. We say that we understand that the person doesn't think it's a problem, but we point out that they've got all the consequences from being an addict. Sometimes it works, and sometimes it doesn't. Denial is a powerful thing. Here are some Do's & Don't's:

- DO confront them
- DO educate yourself about their addiction
- DON'T blame yourself
- DON'T enable them
- DON'T rescue them from the consequences of their actions
- DON'T financially support the addict
- DON'T prevent them from hitting rock bottom
- DO let God work
- DO pray for them
- DON'T ever give up

20

"RELAPSE"

AS WE DEAL with issues related to recovery, it is important to talk about *Relapse*. If you know anything about addiction recovery, then you know that relapse is a very real part of it. It's an all too common factor. Not many people I know who are on drugs or have an alcohol problem stop and then never have a relapse. That's not a realistic expectation. Relapse is just part of it. It's not a good thing, but an addict can learn from it.

If you're a Christian, we don't usually use the term *relapse* for our sins––we call these things *setbacks*. Everyone in the church has had setbacks in your life. You're going along, trying to grow in your faith, and sometimes you have setbacks. You fail, and sometimes you get discouraged. When you have a setback, or a relapse, you have two choices. You can give up or you can get up and keep going.

John Maxwell is a leadership guru, who has written many books. One of my favorites is a book titled, *Failing Forward*. The whole premise of the book is that everybody fails, but if you're going to fail, fail forward. He gave an illustration. If you're going to fall, while you're down there you might as well make the best use of your time. So, pick something up while you're down there.

If you're a person who struggles with a setback and you keep messing up, learn from it. I always say this: it's okay to make mistakes, but it's not okay to keep making the same mistakes over and over again. Eventually, we are supposed to learn some things. I look at the failures in my life as growth opportunities, because they really are. It's not the end of the world when you mess up and relapse or have a setback in your Christian journey. It *is* the end of the world if you just stop growing—if you give up and stop pursuing Christ and make a decision to go back to your old way of living.

That's never good.

I love Romans chapter seven because there is a passage that I identify with so much. Maybe you do, too. "We know that the law is spiritual; but

I am unspiritual, sold as a slave to sin."* Let me give you some context. The person who wrote this, the apostle Paul, used to be known by his Hebrew name Saul before he became an apostle. He was the chief persecutor of Christians, making a name for himself as a member of the Jewish ruling council, the Sanhedrin. His job was to round up Christians and even oversee their execution.

Then one day, as he approached the city of Damascus, he saw Jesus. He had an encounter, and it transformed him. He became a follower of Jesus. From that point on, instead of going around rounding up Christians, he went around preaching the gospel and setting up churches. In my opinion, he's one of the most spiritual people in the history of Christianity. He might be the godliest man who has ever lived. Based on everything I know about him, he might be the greatest Christian who ever lived, yet he writes to the Roman Christians and says, "I'm a slave to sin."

Do you know what it means to be a slave? You're a slave to anything that controls you. Anything that has control over you is your master. For some people, it's drugs. For some people, it's alcohol. For some people, it's prescription painkillers. By the way, painkillers are subtle things. Just like alcohol. Because alcohol is legal, sometimes people think, "Well, it's legal, so drink, drink," and then they find out they've become addicted to it. It's the same with painkillers. I've seen many people have a knee surgery or a shoulder surgery, and go to the doctor for pain. The doctor prescribes some opioids, and they're supposed to take them. Then they get to the end of the bottle and find out, "I don't want to stop taking them," so they go get it refilled—again and again and again—and then they realize they have are hooked. I've never been addicted to painkillers, but I've talked to a lot of people about this, and they've told me that getting off of them has been the most difficult thing they have ever done.

So, we have to be careful.

There are all kinds of things that can control your life and become your master. It could be food for you. You might have a food addiction. Maybe you just can't stop eating cake or doughnuts or other sweets. It might be video games. I know people who are so addicted to video games that they stay up all night and lose their jobs because they were gaming. For some people, it is the smartphone. Or *Facebook*. You just can't stop looking at social media. For some people, it's pornography and sex.

If something has control over you, that is your master. That's what Paul was talking about. Verse 15 says, *"I do not understand what I do. For what I want to do I do not do, but what I hate I do."* This could have been written by Dr. Seuss. It is like a tongue twister. Every time I read this whole passage, I have to think hard about what he is saying. *"I do not understand what I do. For what I want to do I do not do, but what I hate I do."* Then, in the next verse, he says, *"And if I do what I do not want to do, I agree that the law is good. As it is, it is no longer I myself who do it, but it is sin living in me."* In other words, he is acknowledging that there is something working inside of him. Really good things that he wants to do, but he can't seem to bring himself to do it. And conversely, all of the bad things that he doesn't want to do anymore? He constantly finds himself doing it. It's almost like on autopilot. He concludes that he doesn't understand himself.

Have you ever felt like that?

Have you ever looked at somebody before and said, "What is wrong with you?" Have you ever looked in the mirror and thought, "What is wrong with you?" I've said it many times. My wife often says it to me too.

Let me tell you what is wrong with me. Let me tell you what is wrong with *you*. The apostle Paul is teaching us in this passage and in other passages that we have dual natures. You have an old you and a new you. The moment I accepted Christ as my Lord and Savior, I was converted. My favorite passage in the Bible is 2 Corinthians 5:17: *"Therefore, if any man be in Christ, he is a new creation. Old things have passed away; behold, all things have become new."*

I'm a new person, yet I still find myself dealing with the thought processes and the actions of the old me. Let me describe it like this: the old you is the person you were before you met Jesus, then, when you got saved, you became a new person, and you're supposed to put on Christ. But the old you is just crouched down nearby, and he or she is available anytime you beckon that person.

---

[1] Romans 7:14

21

"THERE IS A CONSTANT BATTLE..."

THE NEW YOU may be doing well. You're going to church. You're reading your Bible. Positive things are happening in your life. Then, as if out of nowhere, you begin to have thoughts, or you say something, or you find yourself on sin autopilot. You drive past a bar where you used to hang out and the old you seems to say, "I'm here. Did you call for me?" Anytime you need it, the old you is available for whatever you want or crave. I wish that old me would go away forever. That was the apostle Paul's frustration, as well. The old me keeps rearing its ugly head at the worst possible time.

Paul taught us in Galatians chapter two and verse twenty: *"I am crucified with Christ. Nevertheless I live, yet not I but Christ that lives within me."* He teaches in other places how we are supposed to, on a daily basis, *crucify* the old person. The person who you used to be is still very much there. He never really goes away. It's like riding a bike. If you jump on a bike right now, even if you haven't ridden for years, you still know how to ride a bike. And no matter how long you have been following Christ, you still know how to sin.

That's just the way it is.

So, on a daily basis, we must make a conscious decision that we are not going to serve that old, sinful person, but, instead, put on Christ and choose to put on our new nature, walk in that freedom. But it has to be a daily thing. Today, you might have a great day. You might feel energized and ready to go charge hell with a water pistol. You're floating on cloud nine. However, tomorrow, you might wake up and feel completely different. And the old you is right there, waiting to tempt you. That's why we have to take it one day at a time, choosing Christ every day.

This is what Paul is saying. We have dual natures. There's the flesh (the old you) and the spirit (the new you.) That explains the war that goes on inside us. In Romans 7:18, Paul says, *"For I know that good itself does not dwell in me, that is, in my sinful nature. For I have the desire to do what is good, but I cannot carry it out. For I do not do the good I want to do, but the evil I do not want to do—this I keep on doing."* He is frustrated that he keeps sinning and doing what he knows is wrong. It is because he's a sinner. And *you're* a sinner.

We all are.

There was nothing good about the old me. But when I became a new creation, Christ is always pulling for me. He is on my side. He wants the best for me, and he tells me this is the person I *can* be if I walk in the Spirit and follow Him. The old me is sinful. The only good God sees in us is His own reflection in us. So, the more I can reflect Christ, the more He sees the good. Let me say it this way: the only good that's in you is that of God that is in you. That's it, because we are sinful to the core. That's what the Bible teaches.

In Romans 7:20 it says, *"Now if I do what I do not want to do, it is no longer I who do it, but it is sin living in me that does it. So I find this law at work: Although I want to do good, evil is right there with me. For in my inner being I delight in God's law; but I see another law at work in me, waging war against the law of my mind and making me a prisoner of the law of sin at work within me."* Now, that may seem like it was written by Dr. Seuss.. But I can relate to it so much.

There is a constant battle going on inside us. I have to constantly train my mind to think, *"That's not me anymore. I'm a new person in Christ."* Look at what he says in Romans 7:24: *"What a wretched man I am!"* I don't know if you can relate to that or not. I don't really use the term *wretched often*, but I often say, "*What is wrong with me? I'm an idiot."* The old me is an idiot. The old me is a failure. The old me is worthless. But the new me is what I must focus on, because the new me is righteous because of Christ.

I've said this before. You're only a failure if you stop trying, because God is taking you places. It's a process. Proverbs 24:16 says: *"The godly fall seven times, but they keep getting up again."* You're only a failure if you don't get up.

I came across a meme that says, "You may have to fight a battle more than once to win it." Think about that. There are battles I have fought that I thought were completely won. There's a story in Matthew chapter four about the temptation of Jesus. The Bible says Jesus, right after His baptism, was led into the wilderness where He fasted for 40 days. He hadn't eaten for 40 days, and in His physical weakness, the Devil was constantly tempting him. We know about the three temptations, where the Devil would try to twist scripture to tempt Jesus. To counter that, Jesus always quoted scripture back at him—correctly and in context. He always put the devil in his place. I think the most interesting thing about that was that at the end of the 40 days, the Devil left Jesus after He passed the test. But it says he left Him until the *next* opportune time. What that tells me is what I already knew. The Devil doesn't give up tempting me, and he doesn't give up tempting you.

He'll be back.

You might have a good day today, and you might win its battles. But, he's coming back tomorrow. He doesn't give up on you. He doesn't just go completely away. No. He's just looking for other means by which he can come at you.

*

In his frustration, Paul said, *"What a wretched man I am! Who will rescue me from this body that is subject to death?"* Then he answered his own question in Romans 7:25, *"Thanks be to God, who delivers me through Jesus Christ our Lord!"* That's the good news. He says, "You know what? Jesus Christ is Lord." You can overcome, but it's not because of the willpower inside of you; it's the power of God. Whatever you're battling right now, it's probably going to be a battle until the day you die.

A really good friend of mine, Ron Davis, passed away a couple of years ago. I conduct his funeral. I was very hard because we were so close. In fact, he was probably the closest person to me to die since my father went home to be with the Lord. Ron was an amazing guy. I knew him for about a dozen years. He started coming to church when we were down in the city. He came in and got saved right away. His wife, Shirley, was already a believer. I baptized him, and he just started growing in his faith. I love that. To me, that's the greatest thing—to see new believers make great progress.

He used to call me and ask a lot of questions. He called me one time because he had an evil thought about somebody. He said, "Pastor Joey, is God going to send me to hell? Because I had this thought today." I told him, "No, that's not how it works. It's good that you're convicted about it. That shows God is working in your life that you're sorry about it, but it's not the end of the world." We used to have some of the best conversations.

I saw God do amazing things in his life. The reason I brought his name up is because he has now arrived. He's there. He doesn't have to battle this old sin nature anymore. He's right now in the presence of Jesus. He's walking on streets of gold. He lived a couple of years longer than doctors expected. He had dialysis every other day—all kinds of health problems—but he was a fighter.

His last few years were rough. He was in and out of the hospital. That's what sucks about life on earth. We have these bodies and they get old and break down. But my hope is not in this body. My hope is not in this world. My hope is in Jesus Christ. And Ron's hope was in Jesus Christ, and he's with Him today. He's not struggling anymore. He's not calling me anymore saying, "I had a bad thought." He'll never do that again.

I can't wait to see him again.

22

"IT'S NOT THAT COMPLICATED"

I WANT YOU to understand that you're going to have setbacks until the day you die. But thank God, because of Christ Jesus, we get to go to heaven for all of eternity where we won't have to struggle anymore. But until that day, we will struggle, and so I want to give you a few thoughts about relapse.

1. You have to remember that recovery is a process.

Think about it. Your entire Christian life is a process. You're not going to come to Christ and get saved and then suddenly your old baggage disappears, because it is all washed in the blood the lamb. Don't get me wrong. All of your sins, past, present, and future, are cleansed. God has forgiven you of everything, but you still smoke, and you still cuss, and you still do all sorts of these things.

You're going to battle that for a long time. Don't get down on yourself. This is how I want to encourage you. I see so many people get frustrated. *I* get frustrated. You're going along, and God is working in your life, and you're taking two steps forward, and then, every once in a while, you have one step back. Then you make some more progress, a few steps forward, and then you have one step back. Some of you have come an incredibly long way, so don't beat yourself up too much. Just acknowledge your setback, and keep going, because every time you fail, it's a learning experience. Do you know how many learning experiences I've had? I know a lot of pitfalls. Sometimes I still fall in the hole, but I'm learning and I'm growing.

So are you.

I love memes. They can be powerful. "Slow progress is better than no progress," or, "A little progress each day adds up to big results," or, "Recovery: It's work. It's a process. It's worth it. It's possible,." I really like this one: "You can change the plan, but never change your goal." I'm probably on Plan Z. I've been doing this for twenty-something years. I've had a lot of setbacks. But, according to another great meme, "Recovery is about progression, not perfection." Just think about that. Your Christian life, walking with God, is not about perfection; it's about *progression*. It's about learning and getting better each and every day.

2. You need to understand how temptation works.

I think most of you probably do. What is your temptation? For some, a donut can be a major temptation. Donuts were a huge struggle for me, and now I'm on a diet. I would like to have one, but I don't like the results. Donuts represent temptation to me. James chapter one teaches us about temptation. It says, *"Temptation comes from our own evil desires, which entice us and drag us away. These desires give birth to sinful actions."* You have a desire. You entertain that in your mind. It gives birth to sinful actions. *"And when sin is allowed to grow, it gives birth to death."*

It *always* ends in destruction.

I shared a sermon series a few years ago about fishing. If you look in the original language, the verse from the Book of James is a fishing analogy. Two thousand years ago, they wanted them to understand what temptation is like. So he wrote that temptation comes from our own desires, which entice us and drag us away.

In fishing, we know a big catfish will live underneath a rock, and it will come up at night to feed. If you want to catch a catfish you must get lures or bait and drop it down in front of the fish and get him to bite. Now, the method of fishing that you use depends on what you're trying to catch. The methods can differ.

Satan does this with us. He knows exactly what your color is. He knows exactly what you love because he has been watching you your whole life. He has been studying you, so he knows what you like and what you don't like. So, at the worst possible time, he's going to drop a lure right in front of your face, and you're going to want to bite the bait.

Afterward, you may think, *"I can't believe I did that again. I can't believe I said that again. I can't believe I ate the whole box."* These are things that will puzzle us. *"I can't believe I did that. Why did I fall for that stupid lure again? Every time I go for it, I get pulled out of the water and end up on somebody's trophy case."* That's what Satan does. He wants you in his trophy case.

He knows exactly what to use to lure you.

1 Corinthians 10:13 teaches us about temptation. It says, *"The temptations in your life are no different from what others experience."* What that tells me is the things I struggle with... I'm not the only one. I've struggled with things before and thought, *"I'm the only one who struggles with this,"* only to find out that I'm not. When I share my struggles with another person, I find I'm not alone, and it's really healthy and cathartic to share. That's why the Bible says to confess our sins one to another.

I don't need to confess my sins to you so you'll forgive me. I just need to have at least one person with whom I can be open, honest, and transparent. You see, whatever it is that you're going through is common to people around the world, as well. And I promise that what he said remains true: *"God will not allow the temptation to be more than you can stand. When you are tempted, he will show you a way out so that you can endure."*

I believe the Bible from cover to cover. I believe this is true. But I'm not sure I've always put it into practice and believed it in the moment of trial. Whatever your temptation is, God has an escape route available for you. I used to go to the Worlds of Fun amusement park in Kansas City. There was a cool ride called the Orient Express. They had what was called a "Chicken Exit" for someone to use if they were too scared to ride.

I confess, I used it.

Well, in a very real sense, there's a chicken exit for every temptation. You're sitting there with a doughnut. God has made a way out for you. If you don't want to eat the whole box of doughnuts, you should probably stop putting them in front of your face. That's how temptation works. It's possible to get rid of the temptation altogether. In fact, in the model prayer Jesus gave us in the Sermon on the Mount, it says, "Lead us not into temptation."

Stop putting yourself in the same situation. I know people who are trying to quit drinking alcohol. They're alcoholics, and they declare, "I want to quit drinking," but they keep going back to the same bar. They're just white knuckling it. They say, "I'm going to hang out with these people, but I'm not going to drink with them anymore."

There's a thing in addiction recovery and A.A. that we talk about. If you go to a barbershop long enough, you're going to get a haircut. That's true. So, if you don't want your hair cut, don't go to the barbershop, and if you don't want to drink, stay out of the bar. "But what if all my friends drink?"

Well, get some new friends.

You may say, "Well, the only places I hang out is with other alcoholics in bars and other places." Well, you know what? The local church is a pretty cool place to hang out, too. The people in the bar are not the only people you can hang out with. You have to stop going to those places, and you have to stop doing that. This leads me into my next point. In fact, the principle of "fellowship" with people who can help you is a major part of all 12-step programs.

3. You need to change your playgrounds and playmates.

It's not that complicated. If you're in recovery and trying to quit drinking or doing drugs, you have to stop hanging out with those people and going to those places. The same is true for every person who struggles with sin. Whatever your sin is, you have to stop feeding it. You have to stop putting yourself in those temptation-laden situations.

23

"SELF-SABOTAGE"

4. You need to learn what your triggers are.

FOR A LOT of people, stress is a trigger. They get stressed out, and it drives them back to their vice of choice. Satan knows this, and Satan is pretty smart, so he comes at you. Maybe you used to do crystal meth, and so he says, "Hey, how about some crystal meth?" And you say, "No. I've had a long week, and I'm just tired. I don't want to go back to crystal meth." So, he suggests, "Well, how about this? Do you want *this* color? Why don't you just drink a beer?" So you say, "Okay. One beer is not that bad…" And then two beers and three beers. Then, before you know it, you're smoking weed, and it's just a matter of time before you're back at crystal meth. That's how Satan works.

All of it goes back to that. It all ends in death. It all ends in destruction. He's trying to ruin your life. He doesn't care what color he uses. He just wants to get there one way or another. So, you have to learn what your triggers are. Like I said, for a lot of people it's stress. You can't live life on life's terms, so your coping mechanism has been smoking weed and drinking alcohol.

My suggestion is for you to turn to the one who created life. Turn to God every day, and He can help you get through life. I recently saw a meme that shows an acronym of *HALT*: *hungry*, *angry*, *lonely*, *tired*. These are very real triggers for people. There are a lot of people who get triggered because they're hungry. Maybe you stayed up too late because you wanted to binge watch the latest show on Netflix. So you didn't go to bed until 4:00 in the morning, and then had to go into work at 6:30. You're tired, and you haven't been eating right. You're hungry and tired, and that causes you to get angry. They call it being "*hangry*."

It's all related.

5. You need to remind yourself of your true identity in Christ.

Have you ever met someone who is sabotaging their own life? I used to do that before I was a Christian. I would start doing well, get a good job, and then just wreck everything. Sometimes it's a person who comes to church. They want to get their life right, so they get saved and baptized, and things start going well for them. God gives them a really good job, and then they do something to screw it all up. Have you ever met somebody like that? Maybe it was you?

That type of self-sabotage comes from the old nature. A person who self-sabotages is a person doesn't know who they are in Christ, and therefore doesn't believe they deserve a better life. I know a lot of women who allow their spouses to verbally assault them and physically abuse them. That would never be allowed if they knew who they were in Christ. If you're a woman who knows who you are in Christ, you will never let a man talk to you that way.

This is what I tell my daughters. They are never going to let a man talk to them that way. And if anyone tries, they will be calling me on the phone, and a couple of us will be paying this man a visit. I know who I am in Christ now, so I'm not going to sabotage my life. But, so many people do that.

In the movie, *Talladega Nights*, Ricky Bobby is the main character. He has a dad that he hasn't seen in decades. Now that he's an adult, his dad comes back into his life, and, at first, things went great. They were sitting in a restaurant together and Ricky Bobby's mom was even there. She said, "You know, we should go ballroom dancing." She started talking to him about all kinds of things that normal families do, and it starts eating him up inside. As he was sitting there, he was thinking, "I've got to get out of this."

He caused a big scene in the restaurant, so they threw him out on the street. His son followed him outside and said, "Dad, everything was going so great. What is wrong with you?" And his dad made this statement: "I don't know what organ or bone people are born with that makes them act right, but I was born without it. I'm no good."

He was partly right.

The old me is like that "bone," but that's not who I am anymore.

Go to the Bible and look at what God says about us. When God looks at me, he knows I have this old selfish and sinful nature, but that's not who he speaks to. He looks at me, and he tells me about the person I *can* be—about the person he *wants* me to be. He's not condemning me for all the bad stuff I've done. He's just drawing me to my new nature in Christ.

6. God is the God of second chances.

Aren't you glad about that? Maybe you're not on your second chance with God. Maybe you are on chance number 4,329. So am I. I'm so glad God doesn't ever look at me and say, "Nope. That's enough. I've given you enough chances." He never does that. He just says, "Come on. Let's do it again." He's not mad at you. He's not upset. He just wants you to get up and keep going.

Another one of my favorite verses in the Bible is Philippians 1:6, *"And I am certain that God, who began the good work within you, will continue his work until it is finally finished on the day when Christ Jesus returns."* He's going to keep working in your life until you're done with this life.

Be patient.

24

"ONLY YOU CAN DO THAT."

ALCOHOLICS ANONYMOUS (A.A.) IS well-known self-help program, but in a real way it is also spiritual program. The steps are largely Biblically-based. The twelfth step says: *"Having had a spiritual awakening as the result of these steps, we tried to carry the message to alcoholics..."*

They understand, just like we should understand, that whenever God does something for us, we need to share that with another person. God is not interested in doing miracles in your life just so you can keep it to yourself. God loves you, and if you're His child, He loves to bless you. He loves to work in your life. But if you just keep that blessing, and if you don't broadcast message that to everyone—or at least to somebody—you've missed the point. God didn't do that just for you. He loves you and He wants to bless you, but He also wants to use you to help others in the same way you have been helped.

There are so many people who have lost hope. There are people who are struggling with addiction. There are people in our community who have been to church before, and they've been burned and don't want to go back. They're looking at you, and they just want to know, "Is this God thing real?" And you can tell them, "I may not be perfect. I don't have it all together, but I'm just sharing with you what God has done in my life."

This is a little bold, I know, but this is the whole point right here—you are *obligated* (that's a strong statement) to share your story. I can prove it from beginning to end, especially in the New Testament. Whenever God did something for somebody, he expected them to share that with others.

I've lost a lot of weight, recently. I try not to push that on people. But when I'm out and about and I see people who are really overweight, I want to go grab them and say, "I can help you." But I can't do it for them. They have to go to the gym. At the end of the day, it's about diet and exercise. No one is breaking any new ground. No one is coming up with a new thing.

There are no magic pills.

If I could take a pill and lose weight, I would do that. But the reality is, if you want to lose weight, you have to put in the work. You just do. If you're overweight, I can't lay hands on you, pray over you, and take all the fat away. That would be great. Maybe Jesus could—but not me. Maybe the apostle Paul had that kind of power, but I don't. You *can* lose weight. It just takes a lot of work.

When God shows up and does something in someone's life, God wants them to turn around and share that with people. Here's what some people do. In our addiction recovery program, we often see people come in and get right with God and they stay sober for a while. They might have several months of sobriety.

Then then they stop coming.

I've heard people say, "I think I've got this now." To me, hearing that is like fingernails on a chalkboard. If you say, or even think to yourself, "I've got this," you might as well just put a bull's-eye on your back. Satan is coming after you. That's just how it works. That's a level of pride that you don't want to have.

Sometimes, God will begin to put the broken pieces of someone's life together, and things are going well. Then they stop coming to church, which is usually a symptom of a deeper problem. And it's just a matter of time before things start to unravel. My point is God didn't save you just for you. God didn't do all of those miracles in your life just so you could keep them as your little secret. He expects you to share that with the world.

It's not just about you.

---

[1] https://www.thepitchkc.com/independences-rap-as-meth-city-usa-needs-tweaking/

25

"CONTACT WITHOUT CONTAMINATION"

SEVERAL STORIES IN the New Testament illustrate what I'm talking about. The first one is in Mark, chapter five. It's about a demonized man. We don't know exactly how many demons he had, but they called him a *maniac*, a demon-possessed maniac. This guy was living in a cemetery. He was an outcast from society—a cultural pariah. The whole town couldn't control him. They even tried to put chains and shackles on him, and he broke them. It kind of sounds like someone on PCP (a.k.a. "Angel Dust"). Sometimes people manifest almost superhuman strength. That's often the stuff of the demonic world. This guy was filled with thousands of demons. We know it was thousands because when Jesus met him, he asked, "What's your name?" and the tormented man replied, "My name is Legion, for we are many."

A legion was the largest military unit in the Roman army in those days, made up of roughly 5,200 soldiers. So, there's a clue right there. Jesus talked directly to the demons and cast them out of the man. He sent them into a nearby group of 2,000 pigs. The pigs then ran off the cliff and drowned. There is a connection between demonism and self-destructive behavior.

Now that the man was delivered from his bondage to the devil, the scripture says that he "was in his right mind." When the people from the town came to the scene, they saw this man. He was there clothed and in his right mind. Isn't that a great story? This was a guy they couldn't control. He was living in a cemetery. Dark stuff. Horror story stuff. He would take rocks and cut himself. He wouldn't wear clothes. He was just a lunatic of a person without God.

Then he met Jesus, and found "his right mind."

It reminds me of so many people—and myself, as well. There was a time when you were a lunatic—doing crazy and self-destructive things. There was a time when society didn't know what to do with you, so they locked you up, or you were just an outcast. But you were one of the people

God specializes in helping. He says, " Watch what I can do with this person if they would just humbly submit to my will." The people of the city came out to the cemetery and they saw the lunatic in his right mind.

But they were not happy.

What?

They were upset because of the pigs. Remember the pigs that ran off the cliff and drowned in the sea? They were mad because, even though Jesus did an amazing miracle, they were more concerned about what happened to the pigs. Which is ironic, because they weren't even supposed to have pigs. They were likely Jewish people, although many Greeks lived in the area. Jews weren't allowed law to have pigs as a matter of law. That's probably why He killed them. But the people so upset about the loss of their "deviled ham" that they couldn't celebrate the fact that the troubled man had been set free.

So, what happened?

I don't know what you would have done after you had thousands of demons inside of you and Jesus had miraculously healed you. Here's what this man did. It says in Mark 5:18: *"As Jesus was getting into the boat the man who had been demon-possessed begged to go with him. But Jesus said, 'No, go home to your family, and tell them everything the Lord has done for you and how merciful he has been.'"*

The man was saying, "I want to go with you, Jesus."

Let me caution you. I know a lot of people who struggle with this. They get saved, and they only want to spend all of their time with other believers. There are some people who just sit around in "holy huddles." They look at people who don't go to church and people who are lost, and they seem to say, "I don't even want to rub shoulders with you. I don't want to get your stuff on me, or your stink on me."

That's not good.

You should go to church and you should be part of a small group and you should read your Bible every day and you should love spending time with other believers, but don't be so holy that you distance yourself and can't relate with people who are lost. The Lord would remind us that He doesn't want us to follow Him if we aren't going to share Him with others. He heals us so that we can tell other our story and help others find life in Him.

That's the takeaway.

There are some people who forget where they come from. If all of your friends think like you and act like you, if all of your friends are Christians, then that can be a problem. You need to have at least a few friends who don't know Jesus, so you can introduce Him to them and influence them. On the other hand, make sure they don't influence you. Don't start hanging out only with those who don't know Jesus, and start doing what they're doing. Make sure you're not going to their places and drinking what they're drinking and smoking what they're smoking. You have to make sure not to fall victim to that. Don't ever forget where you come from.

We must have contact without contamination.

Jesus told the man, *"Go back and tell them."* And the next verse says, *"So the man started off to visit the Ten Towns of that region and began to proclaim the great things Jesus had done for him; and everyone was amazed at what he told them."* Do you think this guy was a theologian? He wasn't. He didn't know all of the answers. I'm sure people would ask him questions. And he would have had to reply, "I don't know. I just know that I was lost and now I'm found." It's as simple as that. This guy would just go around and preach and say, "I met a guy named Jesus, and he changed my life, and he can do it for you too."

That's the story right there.

The next story that relates to this idea of spreading the good news is in John, chapter four. It's about a Samaritan woman. Jesus was there. His disciples had gone to get food, and He was there at a well, and a Samaritan woman came to draw some water. She was there in the middle of the afternoon, the hottest part of the day, because she was an outcast in her village. People who were outcasts didn't get water in the morning and the evening when the sun was down, like the rest of the women. No. She had to go in the middle of the day.

Jesus asked her, "Can I have a drink of water?" She was blown away that He would even talk to her, because she was a Samaritan and He was a Jew. There was a racial conflict. The Jews considered Samaritans to be "half-breeds" through intermarriage, and therefore inferior. She couldn't believe that Jesus was speaking to her. But Jesus began a dialogue with her, and they went back and forth. Then they starting talking about church things, "Where do you worship?" But then Jesus cut right to the point, when he told her to go get her husband.

Maybe she was thinking, "This guy is a religious man. He might be the Messiah, because of some of the things he knows." She told him, "I don't have a husband." He replied, "You're right you don't have a husband. You've had five husbands, and the man you are living with now you're not even married to." She was stunned, "Has this guy has been reading my mail? Is he a psychic or something? How does He know these things?"

She realizes He is the Messiah.

Do you know what Jesus was doing? He wasn't bashing her because she'd been married so many times. As she was trying to argue religion with Him, He was pointing out that her problem was not that she couldn't keep a relationship. No, her problem was that she was broken on the inside.

Jesus would likely have told her that He knows of the heartache that she has faced in all of these failed marriages, and she was the only common denominator in all of these destructive relationships. He passed all the religious debate, and He said, in effect, "Let's deal with this." Through all of that, she was converted. She believed in Jesus as her Savior, and then she went back to her village, and told them what had happened to her. This is where we pick up the story, in John 4:39: *"Many Samaritans from the village believed in Jesus because the woman had said, 'He told me everything I ever did! When they came out to see Him, they begged him to stay in their village. So he stayed for two days, long enough for many more to hear his message and believe. Then, they said to the woman, "Now we believe, not just because of what you told us, but because we have heard him ourselves. Now we know that he is indeed the Savior of the world.'"*

So, this woman, who was an outcast, went back to her village and said, "I met a man. I think He's the Messiah, and He changed my life." Because of her testimony, the whole village was changed. She wasn't a preacher. She was not a theologian. What did she know? She just knew Jesus changed her life.

And that was her testimony.

26

"WE'RE NOT IRREDEEMABLE"

ANOTHER STORY IS found in John chapter one. John the Baptist had disciples. His purpose was to prepare the way for Jesus. He was the Messiah's advance man. John the Baptist was really secure in who he was. He had to be, because some of his disciples would become Jesus' disciples. Maybe people asked him, "Are you okay with that?" and he might have replied, "No, that's the point. I'm not the Messiah. *He* is. So, when you see Him, follow Him."

So, many of his disciples went and followed Jesus. One of them was Andrew, brother of Simon Peter. Andrew found Jesus first. In John 1:40, it says, *"Andrew, Simon Peter's brother, was one of these men who heard what John said and then followed Jesus. Andrew went to find his brother, Simon, and told him, 'We have found the Messiah' (which means 'Christ').*

Then Andrew brought Simon to meet Jesus. Looking intently at Simon, Jesus said, 'Your name is Simon, son of John—but you will be called Cephas' (which means 'Peter'). The next day Jesus decided to go to Galilee. He found Philip and said to him, 'Come, follow me.'" Philip was from Bethsaida, Andrew and Peter's hometown.

Philip went to look for Nathanael and told him, 'We have found the very person Moses and the prophets wrote about! His name is Jesus, the son of Joseph from Nazareth.' 'Nazareth!' exclaimed Nathanael. 'Can anything good come from Nazareth?' 'Come and see for yourself,' Philip replied.'"

I always like to put my hometown, "Independence," in there. "Independence? Can anything good come from Independence, Missouri?"

We're not irredeemable.

That's the point of all of this. You don't have to be a theologian. You don't have to have the whole Bible memorized. You just have to be able to say, "You know what? I may not have the answers to all of your questions. I just know God can change your life, because He did it for me, and He has done it for so many other people. If you'll let Him, He can do it for you."

I wrote earlier about King Nebuchadnezzar. He built Babylon, the great empire. He looked out one day and thought, "I'm so awesome," and God replied, "We're going to see how awesome you are."

The King became a lunatic and lived for seven years in the woods. The Bible says his hair grew like eagle's wings. You know how back in the 80s we used to feather our hair on the side? It says his hair was like eagle's wings and his fingernails grew so long they were like eagle's claws. After seven years, God brought him back and put him back in his right mind. He was a lunatic, and then he was restored to sanity.

Do you know the first thing he wanted to do?

He wanted to proclaim something: "I have to tell everyone in my kingdom that God is awesome." That should always be our reaction when God does something. We should never think, "Hey, thanks, Lord. I'm about my business now." No. You should say, "Who can I tell? Who can I find to share this with? I've got to share this with somebody."

There's yet another story in the New Testament about Matthew, the writer of the book that bears his name. He was a tax collector, and when he met Jesus, he threw a party for all of his tax collector friends. He probably said, "Hey, I want you guys to meet Jesus. He changed my life." He didn't have all of the answers. His friends probably had questions that Matthew couldn't answer. But he just wanted his friends to come meet him and know for themselves.

That's how it works.

A man named Lazarus did the same thing. It's recorded in John chapter eleven. He had been dead for four days. He was one of Jesus' close friends. Jesus would stay at his house whenever he came through Bethany. Jesus was a couple of towns over when Lazarus died, and He just stayed away. When he got to his friend's home, Lazarus' sister Martha was upset. She was scolded Jesus, "If you really loved us, you would have come and prevented him from dying. Here you are healing all of these other people, but you didn't heal my brother."

Then, Jesus brought him back from the dead.

One question I've been asked is, "Where was Lazarus for four days while he was dead?" I don't know. He was dead. You can ask him when you get to heaven. It really doesn't matter. But after four days, he was brought back. The Bible says in another place that after that after Jesus rose him from the dead, he went around telling everybody. If you were dead for four days and you were literally raised from the grave, wouldn't you be testifying to everyone too?

The Bible says the Pharisees tried to shut him up, threatening him with death. I think he laughed in their faces. "You want to kill me? Go ahead. I've already been dead once. That's not a threat." We should live our lives like that, saying, "I don't care if you want to shut me up! I want to tell you what the Lord has done for me!" Everyone talks about what's important to them. Everyone wants to cuss at you. Everyone wants to share their worldview with you. Why are you not allowed to share yours? You should tell people what God has done for you. Don't ever be fearful of that, because God is in control.

The last story I want to share with you is about Mary Magdalene. She was an amazing woman. There are things we know about her and things we don't know. One of the things we know about Mary Magdalene is that she was a prostitute, and while she was a prostitute, she was possessed by seven demons. When she met Jesus, He cast out the seven demons from her. Some theologians believe she was the woman caught in adultery. We can't prove that, but many Biblical scholars believe that.

She's also the woman who came and broke the expensive bottle of perfume and poured it out on Jesus' feet. Why would she do that? Because this man changed her life. She had been a raving lunatic with seven demons in her, sleeping with anyone who would have her. Then she met Jesus, and her life was drastically changed. Wherever she went, she shared that with people.

How could you not share what God has done for you? If you're a person who used to be in the grip of addiction and God has delivered you, it is really selfish of you to keep that from other people. That thought might make you mad, but it's true. It's selfish of you to deprive everyone of that kind of blessing, because they've lost hope and they want to know that God can do it for them too.

Let's take it a step further. If you are a person who has been saved, that means that, at one time, you would have spent eternity in hell separated from God. God snatched you from that and set you on a solid rock, and now you are saved. If you drop dead right now, you're going to heaven. You don't have to worry about that. How could you not share that with somebody? How could you live your whole life and keep that to yourself? To me, that's the most selfish thing we can do.

27

"THAT'S HOW YOU DO IT."

I KNOW MANY people, particularly from my church, who love to share their stories. One such person is Trina. She has been coming to our church for a couple of years. I remember the first time she walked in. It was on Monday night at recovery group. We were about to start, and she came in. She looked like she was running from the cops or something. She came in and sat down. She had only been sober for a couple of days, and she couldn't sit still, but she just had this smile on her face. Even then, she had an amazing personality. I've watched God do a miracle in her life over last couple of years, and I've asked her to share her story with our church. Here's what she said:

> *Good morning. Before I knew Christ, I was completely inundated with addiction. My whole life revolved around drugs. Drugs are what I ran to for comfort. They're what kept me going. They what kept me sane. They kept me grounded. That was the only thing I knew. I wasn't only addicted to drugs and the substances. I was addicted to the entire life drugs offered...the chaos and the pain (self-inflicted, and others who inflicted pain), the unhealthy relationships, the mental and physical abuse, the revolving door of crime that I had to keep myself in to feed my habit. Whatever that entailed. Everything I thought, the way I thought, the way I was wired from a small child was totally wrong, was demented and twisted, from how I was supposed to be treated to how I treated other. My inner thoughts and my self-worth, what family meant, what loyalty meant. It wasn't just drugs that gave me a sickness. I was completely sick from within. My heart was sick. I was broken in every sense of the word.*
>
> *How I received Christ... I always knew God was real, and now I can clearly see the evidence of when and whereHe protected me and who he put in my life to orchestrate the plan to bring me to Christ, even*

though that took 10 years to come full circle. But with people's prayers and, of course, God, it finally happened.

God gave me a revelation of the second death. Up to that point, I couldn't care less what happened to me or where I went. I knew I wasn't going to go to heaven, but I didn't care. But this revelation God gave me literally knocked the wind out of my chest. That was the first time I accepted the truth in Christ.

But I didn't surrender my whole self to God. I wasn't involved in church. I wasn't baptized. I wasn't going to meetings. I was sober for a while but was doing it on my own. That "I've got this," but I didn't have this. So, God let me go for a while on my own with my own will, and then I fell really, really hard. April 9, 2018, is when I surrendered my entire self to Christ, gave my entire self to Christ. I had literally lost everything, but it was all by the doing of God himself. God did this.

He loved me so much He created this plan to where I had nowhere else to turn. I had no other avenues to go down. I literally had to turn to Him, and I did, with conviction and raw emotion. I was ready. I was tired of the pain, and I begged Him to take this addiction away, because this is what was destroying my life and what kept the pain in my life. So, I begged Him, and I prayed to Him. "I want to follow you, Jesus."

I remember going to sleep that night and just feeling at peace. It was literally a miracle. When I woke up the next morning, I was completely sober-minded. Now, I had been running hard for a while. When you come off of drugs, you need detox time. You need time to sober up. You need that time, but I didn't. It was a spiritual awakening. I was sober and clear-minded, a changed heart. That's not to say I didn't have things to work on, because of years of pain and addiction...

It was amazing. I can't say anything else but God did an amazing thing in my life, and he continues to do amazing things in my life. I'm not just recovering from addiction. I'm recovering from my past, but my past doesn't define me anymore. I am a child of God. God defines me. I am redeemed, and I am saved, and God did that. I'm not going to hell. I'm not going to die the second death, and I am still sober to this day. I was baptized, and I stay in groups, and I'm here in church with my family. I have healthy relationships, and that's all because of God, because of Jesus. That's it, guys.

*

I love what God is doing in Trina's life. She married Mason recently. She used to have a big gap between her teeth. I'm not making fun of her, and I'm not telling you anything no one knew, but she recently got *Invisalign*. She even said, "I was really self-conscious about this. I really wanted to fix my teeth." Now, there's no gap.

The reason I bring that up is because some of us watched the whole thing happen, and that's how her spiritual life has been too. We watched her from the day she walked in to that meeting. It's amazing what God can do with people, but it doesn't happen overnight. It's a process. If you will let God work in your life, he will do amazing things, and it's visible.

Let me share five things about sharing your story about God's work in your life:

1. Do it naturally.

Don't force it. Don't browbeat anybody. If they don't want to hear it, then that's fine. But just let it be in a normal conversation. I look for natural opportunities. Sometimes people will say, "You've been sober for a while. How did you do that?" And that's the perfect icebreaker.

You don't have to know the whole Bible inside and out. Don't accost somebody. And if someone says, "Oh, I don't want anything to do with God," you don't have to beat them over the head with your Bible. You just say, "Okay. But I'm just telling you God is the one who changed my life."

That's how you do it.

2. Don't bore people.

If you're sharing your story with them, don't bore them with too many details. You don't have to tell them your whole life story. They don't want to hear it. You ought to be able to share your testimony relatively quickly. When I asked Trina to share her testimony, I messaged her and said, "What I'm looking for is I just want you to share your testimony about three, four, five minutes, something like that." She said, "I would love to share my testimony in only three minutes." If you've ever had to get up and speak in front of people, it can be terrifying. They say public speaking is the number one fear people have in America. Number two is death. That joke I've always said is at a funeral, people would rather be in the casket than the one giving the eulogy.

Just let the conversation be a normal one-on-one talk, not a speech about your life. Whether it's with a coworker, over lunch, or a neighbor who asked to borrow your rake, if there's an opening, you just share. You don't have to tell them your whole story for 25 minutes. Just say, "You know what? Let me tell you, this is the person I used to be before Jesus, and this is the person I am now."

It's not that complicated.

3. Don't glorify your past.

I've tried to work on this, because I have a huge past, and I want to make sure that when I tell my story I'm not glorifying it. Someone may respond to your story by saying, "You did some crazy stuff. Sounds pretty good. Sounds like you had a lot of fun." I'm going to be the first one to admit to you sin *is* a lot of fun. It just is. I wouldn't lie to my kids and say it wasn't fun. It's just that it has consequences. All of the sin we entangle ourselves in can be enjoyable in the moment. It just bites in the end, so God wants us to steer clear of those things. Be careful not to glorify your past.

4. Just explain what God has done in your life.

We don't have to over complicate it. Just say, "Here's what God did." It can be a quick testimony." I was struggling with this, and God came through and miraculously did this for me." That's a testimony.

5. Give them an invite.

I would love for you to be able to share your faith and say, "God did it for me. Would you like for Him to do it for you?" But that may not be a reality. At the very least, give them an invite to church. Just like some of these other stories with Philip and Nathanael. They might pepper you with questions. You might be trying to talk to someone about God, and they might say, "Well, what about this, or what about that?"

I don't ever engage in all of those. If they're not believers, I'm not going to try to convince them of that. I just say, "Hey, come and see if you want. If you're not ready, that's fine. I'm not going to force that on you." But if they're ready, if someone is really interested in spiritual things, you can simply ask them to come to church to learn more.

Or help them find a church in their area.

Find one person. There's at least one person you can share your story with. Share with someone what God has done in your life.

FINAL WORD

There are three groups of people reading this book. There are those who have never surrendered their life to Jesus Christ, those who have but are backslidden, and those who have been born again.

If you have already been saved then you need to be sharing that Good News with others. If you are backslidden you need to recommit your life to God.

If you have never accepted Christ as your Lord and Savior I want to encourage you to do what I did.

I didn't understand it all when I was saved.

I took a step of faith.

Until you have a relationship with God you always feel as though something is missing in your life, because there is. It is a real relationship with the creator of the universe. He loves you and has a plan for your life. He wants you to experience real life. Stop chasing after the things that this world says will make you happy and apply that same energy to following Jesus.

If you would like to give your life to Jesus Christ then pray this prayer:

Dear Lord Jesus, I know that I am a sinner, and I ask for Your forgiveness. I believe You died for my sins and rose from the dead. I turn from my sins and invite You to come into my heart and life. I want to trust and follow You as my Lord and Savior.

That was literally the best decision you have ever made. I suggest you let another Christian know of your decision. You should contact a good Bible believing church and tell the pastor of your decisions. He will help you take your next step.

You can also email me at jcandillo21@yahoo.com and I will pray for you and help get you some resources.

ABOUT THE AUTHOR

Joey Candillo is a husband, father and pastor. Most important, he is a child of God. He has been married to Megan since 2005. They have five children.

God has allowed him to plant two churches. He planted the Milestone Church, in inner-city Kansas City, in 2002 and he served there for 12 years. In 2014, he planted Grace Church in his hometown of Independence, Missouri and he currently still serves as lead pastor.

He graduated from William Chrisman High School in 1992. He earned his bachelor's degree from Baptist Bible College in 2002.

He is an avid outdoorsman. He loves to hunt and fish. He also serves as the chaplain for the William Chrisman Football Team.

When he was growing up Independence was known as the "Meth Capital of the World." He went to prison in 1997 for selling drugs, but became a Christian while locked up. His church is just down the street from the apartment where he used to sell drugs.

He went from pushing dope to pushing hope in his hometown.

He lives by the motto "THE BEST IS YET TO COME!"

THE BEST
IS YET
TO COME!

Made in the USA
Monee, IL
28 June 2021

72016504R00105